Fudge Berries and Frogs' Knickers

A romantic comedy by

Lynda Renham

About the Author

Lynda Renham writes romantic comedy novels. Lynda's novels are popular, refreshingly witty, fast paced and with a strong romantic theme. She lives in Oxford UK and when not writing Lynda can usually be found wasting her time on Facebook.

'Lynda Renham is right up there with chick-lit royalty! I'm not talking princess either, for me, the Queen of Chick-lit.' – Booketta Book Blog.

Lynda is author of the best-selling romantic comedy novels including *Croissants and Jam*, *Coconuts and Wonderbras*, *Confessions of a Chocoholic*, *Pink Wellies and Flat Caps*, *It Had To be You*, *Rory's Proposal* and *The Dog's Bollocks*.

Lynda Renham

ISBN 978-0-9927874-6-2

first edition

Cover Illustration by Gracie Klumpp
www.gracieklumpp.com

Thanks to Emma Freemantle for her insight into life on a narrow boat and added thanks to Tim Cook for advice on the walk of shame.

Printed for Raucous Publishing in Great Britain by
SRP (Exeter)

www.raucouspublishing.co.uk

Chapter One

Don't you just hate surprises? Maybe you don't and generally I don't either but when the surprise is your darling daddy appearing on the tele surrounded by policemen, trust me it's the kind of surprise you don't need. I'm used to seeing my father on the tele. I'm just not used to seeing him wearing handcuffs. Armani yes, but handcuffs no. I stare bleary eyed at the silent television screen.

'That's your father isn't it?' mumbles Chelsea while trying not to crack her face mask. 'Are those handcuffs?'

I wipe the cucumber juice from my eyes and blink. Yes that's Daddy all right. That's his side parting, and his Gucci tie. That's my daddy, my knight in shining Armani. The handcuffs aren't his of course, at least he wasn't wearing them the last time I saw him. And they don't look designer. Daddy wouldn't be seen dead wearing anything but designer, at least not by choice.

'Can you turn the sound up Bonita?' I ask, trying to ignore the churning in my stomach and the pounding of my heart. After all, it isn't every day you see your father in handcuffs is it? Well maybe you do but I certainly don't. Even the moaning whales in the background are doing nothing to calm my nerves, whale music that is, not real whales. I know this is an exclusive health club but whale singing while you have your toenails done is pushing it a bit isn't it? Bonita turns from my Dior Vernis toenails and presses the remote. The voice of the newsreader reaches me and I feel my blood turn cold.

'This is a shocking blow for the government. Minister for Family, Sir Rupert Wellesley, is seen leaving Westminster police station a few minutes ago and what a shock to his constituency. Sir Rupert Wellesley charged with fraud ...'

Fraud? Never mind the shock to his constituency what about the shock to his bloody daughter?

'Fudge berries,' Chelsea squeals.

Chelsea, my best friend, who says *fudge berries* an awful lot and spends a great deal of time stating the bloody obvious.

I try to stand but the toe separators make it almost impossible. I waddle to the tinsel-decorated TV screen like a penguin. My numbed brain thinks that if I get a closer look I may find the Armani belongs to someone else, but no, that's Daddy all right. My phone starts to flash and bleep, and Bonita looks at it fearfully as if it will blow up at any moment. I grab it and silence the ringing.

'It's me,' cries my hysterical mother. 'Will this affect my allowance?'

Never mind her allowance what about *my* allowance?

'I'm not surprised,' she continues without waiting for me to reply. '*Minister for Family,* that's a laugh. When was he ever interested in the family? If he'd spent more time with his family and less time helping those on death road we would still be together.'

'Death row,' I correct, feeling like I'm on it myself right now.

'He wouldn't change your nappy. Do you remember that?'

Considering I was only three months old I'd be amazed if I could.

'I remember like it was yesterday. He was too busy saving those on the row,' she continues. 'He's always been big on human rights. What about *our* human rights I used to say. It comes to something when you can't change your daughter's nappy.'

Why we're talking about nappies at a time like this I have no idea. I'm thirty-two years old and I can assure you I don't wear them now.

'I had a nanny?' I say.

'I said to him once, let them all die.'

'The nannies?'

'Death road inmates, of course.'

Bonita switches channels and there's Daddy, again, again and again. I swear his side parting moves more to the left with each channel change. He's looking more like Hitler by the minute. His Fabergé watch twinkles under the light of the flashing cameras. Three words come from the broadcaster and I feel sure my heart stops.

'*Bank account frozen.*'

Bonita looks as shell-shocked as me. I expect she's afraid I won't be able to pay her. *I'm* afraid I won't be able to pay her. How long does it take a bank account to freeze over? Quicker than hell I imagine. I pop a Lindt chocolate truffle and relax as the flavour explodes in my mouth. Thank God for truffles. They really do make everything easier to bear.

'I have to go,' I tell my mother. 'I'm at the salon getting everything gelled.'

'Enjoy it. It may well be your last gelling. Good God Poppy, just think. You may actually have to get a job,' she says, and I can almost see her satisfied smug face.

Is she insane? I've never had a job in my life.

'Don't be ridiculous,' I scoff. 'I'm getting married in six weeks. Roddy has pots of money.'

'Ha,' she laughs mirthlessly. 'He won't want you now. He only wants your money darling. He may have pots but the way he spends it he'll be lucky if he has one left to piss in.'

She sighs.

'We won't get any sympathy you know that don't you? I'll tell you where you'll find sympathy, right between *shit* and *syphilis* in the dictionary. God knows what I'll do. I'm fifty-six for goodness' sake.'

'You're fifty-seven,' I correct.

'Are you sure?'

'Absolutely.'

'That makes it even worse then. Trust your father to get found out four weeks before the holidays. He'll be happy to know he's ruined my Christmas. I need a large G and T.'

You and me both but I don't think Bonita serves booze. Mother begins to cry and now it's my turn to sigh.

'I have to go. I'm sure it's all a big mistake,' I say.

Please God, let it all be a big mistake.

'Yes, of course,' scoffs Mummy. 'People are always mistakenly arrested for fraud aren't they? You'll be saying it's a case of mistaken identity next.'

If only it was. I hang up and watch my phone vibrate across the table as text after text is received.

'Fudge berries,' says a stunned Chelsea for the second time. 'This is mind-blowingly awful isn't it Truffles?'

Ah yes, I should mention my nickname is *Truffles*, the chocolate variety that is, not the mushroom, and if you saw the number of them that I eat, chocolate truffles that is, not mushrooms then you'd understand how I got that name. I'm the truffle queen. I know every single truffle in existence and I also know the best truffle to buy. Right now I could do with a truck load of them. I pick up my ringing phone.

'Poppy Wellesley speaking,' I say, wishing for the first time in my life that I wasn't.

'Martha Clegg here,' says a clipped voice.

'Mrs Clegg, I haven't forgotten our meeting tomorrow for Help the War Victims.'

'I'm not one to judge Miss Wellesley, as you know.'

Not much.

'But there are some that do. I'm sure you'll agree that until this situation is resolved it would be better if you stepped down from the committee.'

'But ...'

'We wouldn't want those poor disabled lads to think they were getting illegal money, would we?'

'The money has been donated it didn't come from my father,' I argue.

Oh God, was that admitting my father's money is illegal?

'Yes but it would be tainted, wouldn't it? I'll announce your decision to the board this afternoon.'

But I haven't made a decision.

'Yes but ...'

The phone goes dead. She's cut me off along with Daddy. I fish my American Express from my Hermes handbag. Bonita tries to behave nonchalantly and reaches for it in slow motion, but her fingers are twitching. She pretends to admire my handbag.

'I would so love a herpes one day,' she says passionately.

I somehow think she is alone in that one.

'There's always someone willing, I'm sure,' I say wincing.

'Hermes,' corrects Chelsea through tight lips. 'It's Hermes, not herpes.'

'Take the usual tip,' I say. I cross my newly painted fingernails in the hope that the card isn't declined. I've never had a declined card. I'm not sure I'd know what to do. There is a tense moment as Bonita pushes the card into the machine and a small bead of perspiration forms on my forehead. I scratch at my neck nervously and I hear Chelsea utter *fudge berries* for the umpteenth time.

'Your skin is erupting,' she says with a grimace taking two steps back as if I've suddenly become radioactive. I throw myself at a mirror and gasp. I've got tiny red spots all over my neck. The ghastly rash is rapidly spreading down my arm.

'I used the same products,' stammers Bonita, frantically punching buttons on the card machine.

'It must be the stress. God knows I'm amazed you didn't have a heart attack. That was quite a shock,' says Chelsea, stepping further away from me.

Bugger, I'm dining with Roddy's family this evening. I can't have him seeing me like this. Okay, don't panic. Just breathe. I take three gasping breaths and give up.

'I think you're hyperventilating,' says Chelsea. 'You're looking a bit blue now.'

'Do you need a brown paper bag,' offers Bonita.

If this rash gets much worse I may well do. But right now I just need that buggery transaction to go through.

'It's travelling up your neck and into your face,' Chelsea announces. She's like Alastair Stewart on breaking news.

'I need antihistamines,' I say anxiously, feeling sure my tongue is now swelling. Oh God, I'm going to have anaphylactic shock. I'll elbow Daddy off the telly with news of my own. *Socialite daughter of disgraced MP dies after swallowing tongue.* I really had hoped for a more glamourous death. I rub ferociously at my arm.

'Surely that only happens if you have an allergic reaction to something,' says a wise Chelsea.

'I'm allergic to being poor,' I say miserably. 'I need a chemist.'

I head for the door grabbing my truffles as I go.

'Card went through,' says a relieved Bonita.

'I'm coming,' says Chelsea, grabbing her fur coat.

I stare at her. She looks like a furry cucumber.

'You're still wearing your mask.'

'Oh cripes,' she groans and rushes back to Bonita.

I scratch my neck and nervously peer in the mirror again. Oh no. It's spreading up my neck and little red spots are now sprouting on my chin. I look like a strawberry. Losing my money is turning me into Frankenstein's daughter. Oh God, this is disastrous. How could Daddy do such a thing? We burst out of the beauty salon and onto the cold streets of Belgravia, swinging our Hermes and Chanel handbags. We pass bustling Christmas shoppers trundling along with their packages. I'd forgotten it was Christmas. The awful realisation that I may be spectacularly poor after being spectacularly rich somehow pushed Christmas onto the back burner. Chelsea peeks at my face and makes a huge effort not to look horrified.

'Is it spreading?' I ask.

'No, not really,' she lies, pulling up the collar on her fake fur. 'At least you're not blue any more.'

That's comforting. I feel sure I am getting strange looks. Chelsea phones her driver after deciding it might not be a bad idea to see a doctor, which clearly means it is spreading. I dive into Chelsea's Rolls and we hurry to Harley Street.

'It's a nervous reaction,' says the doctor.

'I've had a shock,' I say.

'A terrible shock,' echoes Chelsea. Specks of avocado champagne face mask evident on her chin.

Well I have haven't I? Daddy's been arrested and my allowance will be frozen along with his bank account. I'm Poppy Wellesley, I can't possibly be frozen. I'm rich, in fact I am very rich, that is I was very rich. I've no idea how not to be rich. I have only rich friends, why would I want anything other than rich friends? I live in a penthouse in Belgravia. We have a country estate in Oxfordshire. We're the privileged. I am the daughter of Sir Rupert Wellesley, multimillionaire and MP for Belgravia and now a crook if you believe the news. My fiancé is one of the richest men in the country; at least his family are which amounts to the same thing. I'm to be married in a few weeks. Royals will be attending. It will be the socialite wedding of the year. I do my grocery shop at Harrods. Oh buggery. Please let this be a bad dream.

'I need it to be gone by six,' I say.

He looks at the clock on his consulting room wall.

'Can't be done,' he says casually.

'What?' I cry. 'But you have to. I can't let my fiancé see me like this. What if I pay you double?'

What am I saying? I don't even know if I have enough to pay him single.

'She has a Valentino wedding dress,' says Chelsea.

Is she suggesting I use that as part payment? We both look at her. You'd never think she went to a Swiss finishing school would you?

'What's my wedding dress got to do with it?' I ask.

'Just saying,' she mumbles.

'I'm afraid even a Valentino dress cannot work miracles,' says the heartless doctor.

'Can't you give me an injection or something?'

'Yes, of course, what kind of injection would you like?'

This is ridiculous.

'This is Harley Street,' I huff. 'Give me an injection that will shift the rash by six.'

'Unfortunately even Harley Street can't turn water into wine.'

'She doesn't want you to perform miracles, we just want some cream to get rid of it by six,' grumbles Chelsea.

'That would be a miracle,' he says.

'I'm seeing my fiancé.'

The doctor shakes his head.

'I'm sorry. I can only suggest you calm down. Try meditation and deep breathing.'

Meditation? Deep breathing? Is the man off his trolley? I haven't got time for josh sticks and chanting. I'm barely shallow breathing at the moment, forget the deep breathing.

'Let's get a second opinion,' says Chelsea, flinging her faux fur around her shoulders, scattering speculums and specimen bottles in her wake. We sweep out of the consulting room in disgust and visit three more doctors who also tell me there is nothing they can do in time for my dinner with Roddy. I leave the last doctor doped up on Valium, me that is, not the doctor.

'If you're calm then it's bound to disappear,' says Chelsea comfortingly.

I nod in agreement. I'm already feeling calmer by virtue of the Valium. Then my phone rings and the familiar ringtone sends a chill through my bones. It's Jeremy, Daddy's financial adviser.

'We're up the creek without a paddle I'm afraid. Are you free for a spot of lunch?' he asks.

'Ooh,' I mumble in my drug-induced stupor.

'I've booked a table at The Ivy.'

Can I afford The Ivy?

'Can you be there for two? That gives you an hour.'

'I'm meeting Roddy at six,' I say.

'Ah yes, Roddy.'

What does that mean?

'It won't take long,' he says.

That's not a good sign. I pop another Valium and tell myself things can only get better.

Chapter Two

'Is he guilty?' shout the paparazzi.

I don my Alain Mikli sunglasses, pull up the collar of my coat to hide my neck, and wait for my driver, Eddie, to open the door for me.

'I'll be back in an hour,' Eddie says in his Essex accent.

'I'll phone if I need you earlier.'

My stomach churns as I climb from the Bentley. There are flashes all around me and security staff from The Ivy rush forward to shelter me from the cameras.

'Have you seen your father? Did you know he was on the fiddle?' shouts a photographer, flashing at me for all he's worth, with his camera obviously, although if he had flashed anything else I doubt I'd have noticed. I'm so doped up. I trip entering the restaurant and picture tomorrow's headlines: *Socialite daughter of disgraced MP arrives stoned at celeb's favourite restaurant.*

I allow the maître d'hôtel to take my coat and then check my reflection in the mirror. God, I look stoned too. The rash, thank heavens, has stopped at my chin and I'd managed to cover it with Touche Éclat. My newly highlighted blonde hair is shiny and I'm wearing it loose to cover my neck. My blue eyes are sparkling, if just a little vacant, and I'd applied the minimum amount of make-up as I didn't want to aggravate the rash. I look rather good for someone who's been frozen. Jeremy jumps from his seat knocking over a glass in his nervousness. He pecks me on the cheek and sits back down.

'Frightful business,' he mumbles.

A waiter rushes forward and pulls out a chair for me.

'Good afternoon Miss Wellesley,' he says with a smile. 'How are you today?'

As poor as a church mouse it seems.

'I'm fine thank you,' I lie.

'I've ordered your favourite. I hope that's okay,' says Jeremy, fiddling with his cutlery.

I struggle to recall my favourite.

'Roasted Devonshire Chicken,' he reminds me and gestures to the waiter.

'A bottle of Quincy, Sauvignon Blanc,' he orders.

'Just water for me,' I say, feeling certain my head will flop onto the table any second. If I have the wine on top of the Valium there is a good chance the whole of me will flop to the floor in a heap. Jeremy peers at my neck and frowns.

'What's going on there?' he says pointing.

I push his hand down.

'Don't point,' I hiss. 'I've erupted. I think it's the stress.'

'Nasty business,' he says, studying my neck.

'I know. It's spreading everywhere.'

'I was talking about your father.'

Oh yes, that's a nasty business too. I nod miserably.

'Up the creek without a paddle,' he repeats.

'Yes quite,' I say, taking a gulp from his wine glass.

'Up the creek without a paddle and facing a pack of sharks,' he continues.

Never mind the paddle, what about my money?

The waiter places the chicken in front of us and I feel myself gag.

'Frightful business indeed,' Jeremy repeats. 'They've frozen the bank accounts I'm afraid. I'm not going to sugar coat it Poppy. There's no money. I won't be making any transfers to your account for the foreseeable future.'

He knows how to break the news gently does Jeremy. I swallow and scratch my thigh. God, don't tell me the rash has gone to my legs. I throw back the rest of his wine and glance at the chicken.

'Don't worry; it's on your father's account, the last of the expenses. Think of it as your last supper so to speak,' he laughs.

I'm glad someone's laughing.

'You'll have to make some cutbacks,' he says, slicing through his broccoli.

'Cutbacks?' I repeat dumbly.

He leans towards me across the table.

'Sir Rupert's pleading not guilty. It could drag on for months.'

I stare at him.

'Of course,' I say. 'It's clearly a mistake.'

The waiter tops up his glass and I take another gulp.

'Of course,' he agrees.

I push the chicken around my plate. We are silent for a time and all that can be heard is the chatter of other diners and the irritating sound of Christmas music playing in the background.

'What am I going to do?' I say finally. 'I've got to pay my driver and there are the staff salaries ...'

He holds his hand up.

'I don't know Poppy. I only know that there'll be nothing going into your account. Your American Express will be stopped. As for the apartment, well ...'

He gestures to the wine waiter to top up his glass.

'Are you sure you don't want one?' he asks.

I shake my head.

'I'm taking Valium,' I mumble.

'I thought you looked a bit out of it.'

He points at my chicken.

'Aren't you going to eat that?'

I shake my head and push the plate towards him.

'The flat belongs to your father. He has it down as a second home, on expenses. You will have to get out as soon as you can Poppy.'

I fight back the urge to cry. He looks at me uncomfortably and takes my hand.

'They're some shares I can trade. That should tide you over for a bit and maybe ...' he hesitates. 'Maybe you can sell some things?'

I stare at him appalled.

'You expect me to go to a pawn shop?' I say.

'Of course not, obviously I'll get someone to go for you.'

Obviously. I'm not handing over my jewels to just anyone if that's what he's thinking. I wouldn't even trust them with my mother. Anyway, many of them were given to me by Roddy. Remembering Roddy and I feel calmer. I pick at a piece of bread.

'I'm getting married in a few weeks, so everything will be okay. Daddy's already paid for the dress and ...'

'What does Roddy say about all this?' he asks, beckoning for the dessert menu. God, he can certainly eat. It's good to know that my calamity hasn't affected his appetite.

'I haven't spoken to him,' I say. 'But I know he'll be supportive.'

He nods and I look down at my sapphire and diamond engagement ring and feel a warmth of security.

'Nice piece you did for that glossy,' says Jeremy.

I smile. Roddy and I have been together for nine months. We are *the* socialite couple. Only last month we did a special spread for *HELLO!* magazine on our forthcoming wedding. I've known Roddy since I was a child; I always knew I'd marry him. We have the same circle of friends and share the same interests. Fortunately for me Roddy has pots of money so he won't care if I don't have any for a while. After all, I can't be poor forever. Let's face it I don't know how to be poor. I fiddle with my napkin and ask the inevitable question.

'Did he do it?'

Jeremy orders a caramel chocolate pot and raises his eyebrows.

'Don't you want dessert?' he asks.

I shake my head. I can't eat a thing, I really can't.

'Truffles?' he asks.

'No, I couldn't.'

'Blimey you are taking it badly. Well, the claims are outrageous, clearly ridiculous. That's the line we're taking and if you're asked that's all you need to say,' he grabs his wine glass before I can reach it.

I debate whether to take another Valium and decide my veins have enough drugs and alcohol pumping through them. This is the rich life all right, drugs booze and fraud, not forgetting *HELLO!* magazine. Hell's bells, I hope they still cover the wedding. I'd really look the poor relation if I don't have my wedding photos in *HELLO!* magazine.

'Your father is at his Oxfordshire estate, but I wouldn't recommend going there. The press are having a heyday.'

'He's not in prison?' I say relieved.

Jeremy looks at me and laughs.

'Good Lord no. Sir Rupert in prison, don't be silly. He's on remand. Do you want a coffee? You look like you need one.'

I shake my head.

'I need to go home. I'm seeing Roddy at six.'

I go to stand up and a waiter rushes to pull my chair back.

'Right,' says Jeremy. 'Lovely lunch, ghastly subject but good to see you and I'm sure all will be fine. You'll keep your glad rags and all that.'

He forces a laugh which doesn't fill me with any confidence. The maître d'hôtel checks the front of the restaurant and beckons to the doorman.

'Good day Miss Wellesley. We look forward to seeing you again soon.'

I glance back into The Ivy. An awful premonition that I will not step over the threshold again washes over me. How stupid is that? I'm marrying Roddy aren't I? Everything will be all right.

Chapter Three

'I thought you could use a large Pimm's,' says Camilla, handing me a glass with a sprig of mint floating on the top.

Crikey, if I drink any more I'll be comatose before I get to see Roddy.

'Thanks Camilla,' I say gratefully, tucking my Burberry clutch under my arm.

'*Awful* business, *awful*,' she says, stressing the awful and patting my hand each time she says it.

I nod, although what's more awful are all these people at Roddy's family home. His mother would have to have one of her cocktail parties now wouldn't she?

'Isn't it just *awful* Sophie?' she repeats.

'Abslootly,' declares Sophie, wafting towards me on a cloud of Chanel. She looks at me as if I've grown scales. Mind you if they could see my rash they'd probably think I have.

'Did you know?' she asks.

I open my mouth to answer and spot Roddy enter the drawing room. Thank goodness. He is wearing one of his monogrammed shirts and I cringe. Isn't it enough his name is Rodney Arthur Tarleton, without advertising the fact on his shirts? Somehow RAT doesn't do it for me. I can cope with most things, I am not afraid of spiders or snakes but I do have a bit of a thing about rats, and there is nothing more off-putting than having your fiancé stroll sexily towards you in his RAT towelling robe. It most certainly dries up the juices if you know what I mean. His dark hair flops over one eye and he strokes it back with his hand, the diamond from his signet ring glittering under the lights of the chandelier. He strolls towards me, stopping to pat someone on the shoulder or kiss a woman on the cheek. He's gorgeous and I feel so grateful that he is mine, all mine. A man of Roddy's means is very sought after and I know my friends envy me. He finally reaches me and pulls me into an embrace, and I feel the tension leave my body. After the wedding I will get rid of all his RAT clothes. He smells of Creed's Angelique

Encens cologne and it reminds me of Daddy and that of course reminds me of the fraud which in turn reminds me that I have been frozen, and I shiver.

'M'ma decided to have a little thing,' he whispers in my ear. 'Not great timing I'm afraid.'

I sigh.

'The thing is Roddy, I need to talk to you about ...'

'Yes ... Yes, I know about that, don't treat me like a bloody fool. Put me down for three grand and ...'

'What? That's nice of you Roddy, but we'll be married soon and ...'

'I don't give a damn. I've always been as good as my word haven't I?'

I don't know why he's shouting.

'Well, yes ...' I stammer.

Oh dear, things are going from bad to worse. Now I've offended my fiancé. He turns his back on me.

'I'll get the money, I always do don't I?'

'Yes, I know but ...'

I then see he is talking into his Bluetooth earpiece. He looks like the chief communications officer of the starship Enterprise. He's not been talking to me at all. I sip at the Pimm's and try to ignore the pitiful looks the other party guests are giving me. Roddy's mother makes a beeline for me and I look for an escape route.

'Roddy, your mother's coming over,' I say nervously.

'She's a good mare,' says Roddy.

I wish he'd come off the phone.

'Hello, Lady Tarleton,' I say, air-kissing her cheeks.

'Poppy, you're looking very pretty,' she smiles.

'Looks like she should be put down,' bellows Roddy.

'He's on the phone,' I explain to Lady Tarleton, at least I hope he is.

'So darling, how are you holding up,' she asks much too loudly.

'She's probably wearing a bra,' laughs Sir Henry Tarleton. 'Are you on that damn phone again, Roddy?' he snaps.

I flick my hair nervously. All this attention is making me anxious and I'm sure it is playing havoc with the rash.

'Oh, I'm fine. It's nothing,' I say flapping a hand.

Nothing, that's an understatement if ever I heard one, I'm more frozen than a Findus fish finger and up the creek without a paddle and surrounded by sharks, well paparazzi, which is one and the same thing really. People jump off buildings for less don't they?

'Pretty ghastly though. Henry said it's splashed all over the evening news. There's going to be a big piece in *The Guardian* tomorrow apparently.'

Jeremy never mentioned that. Too busy stuffing his face with my chicken I suppose.

'Frightfully embarrassing for you and your mother, talking of which, how is Lady Wellesley coping?'

I knock back the Pimm's and feel my head spin.

'Taking it in her stride,' I say.

The truth is she is most likely now in her car with a G and T, and the exhaust for company. She never was good at coping. I suppose that will be the next headline for the Wellesley family.

'Well, it must be very difficult. I really don't expect you to stay for dinner. Not with this scandal looming over you.'

She looks around before leaning close to me.

'Obviously we love having you but don't you think it would be better for everyone if you left before dinner? Less embarrassment all round. Everyone would understand if you made your excuses.'

'Well ...' I begin.

'Splendid. I must say hello to the guests.'

She floats off wearing a forced smile and I feel myself wobble on my Guccis. Is she really telling me to leave? I'm Roddy's fiancée for goodness' sake.

'A word in your shell-like, darling,' says Roddy taking me by the arm and leading me to the roof garden. The cold December air cuts through me.

'We're going down to the country tomorrow. P'pa thinks it best, just for the weekend.'

What a relief. At least I'll get away from London and the press, not to mention the horrendous news headlines. Perhaps Mummy can come. I'll dose her up on G and T. By the time we get back this stupid business will all be over. Roddy twirls his ring around his finger nervously. He bites his lip and I wait for him to speak.

'God, this shirt,' he mumbles running his finger under the collar. 'Too much damn starch, bollocking housekeeper.'

I find myself staring at his neck.

'It's the damnedest thing Poppy but you know that Paloma Picasso cuff I bought you from Tiffany's for ...'

A gust of wind almost knocks me off my feet.

'Can we go inside Roddy, it's freezing?'

He sighs.

'This is a bit awkward Pop. The thing is I'm in over my head. I'll get it from old pater in time. He's just being damn stubborn at the moment. I lost quite heavily on the gee-gees and well ...'

I so wish he wouldn't call me Pop. It makes me sound like someone's grandparent. He rubs his finger around his neck and I feel my rash itch in sympathy. I shiver and pull my pashmina around my shoulders. At this rate I won't have to worry about dying from starvation. It'll be the hypothermia that gets me.

'Of course,' I say. Roddy is going to be my husband in a few weeks so I can't really say no can I?

'Thanks Poppy, you're a trouper, you really are. It's just this chappie is a bit ... well that's grand. Thanks for that. Can I send my man round to you this evening?'

My teeth chatter and I can only manage a nod.

'Splendid. Let's get you inside.'

'Roddy, about Daddy ...'

'Yah, go ahead.'

'It's just Jeremy said ...'

'Not that old chestnut, it'll be fine. Everything's kosher.'

'Oh really Roddy, that's so good to hear. I've erupted ...'

'Put an extra grand on that one.'

I realise he is back on starship Enterprise and a million miles from me. He hustles me back into the drawing room. I check my reflection in a mirror and adjust my pashmina so the rash can't be seen and link my arm through Roddy's. At that moment Lecherous Leonard and his daughter Pandora Enwin enter the drawing room. That's all I need, Pug-faced Pandora and her family.

'Tra la la, we've arrived,' he calls, waving at everyone. 'So sorry we held you up.'

I'm surprised a host of angels didn't herald his arrival. Honestly, anyone would think he was God himself rather than his representative.

'Reverend Enwin, you made it,' says Lady Tarleton.

'Yes, we're here, we're here. Hello everyone, we've arrived,' bellows the reverend.

He flings his chubby arm around my shoulders and breathes heavily into my ear.

'How are you bearing up my dear? I've been praying for you. Of course we don't believe any of it,' he says leaning closer and managing to lower his arm so his hand is now clutching my bottom. Dirty bugger. I can't for the life of me think why Roddy wants him to marry us.

'Yes, we made it but the traffic was horrendous,' says Lady Nell Enwin floating into the room in her Liberty print dress. She smacks her lips and kisses the air near my cheeks, 'Such a shame you're not staying for dinner dear, but scandal is a terrible thing. We had to fight through the paparazzi didn't we Leonard. They got a good photo of Pandora though, didn't they dear?'

That's okay then. I wouldn't want Pug-face to miss out on my misfortune would I? Let's hope they emphasise her snub nose. Pug-face pecks me on the cheek, her face flushed. She sidles up to Roddy and gives him a warm hug.

'It must have been such a shock for you Roddy,' she says sympathetically, stroking his arm.

Never mind the shock to Roddy, what about the shock to me? Is that Zandra Rhodes she's wearing? God, she looks fabulous with her pearly white teeth and rich chestnut hair. A big chunky cuff sparkles on her arm and her almond shaped eyes stare evilly at me.

'Oh just look at this tree Mummy, isn't it just fabulous. Your mother has wonderful taste Roddy,' Pandora gushes.

Lady Helen Tarleton lowers her head modestly.

'Thank you dear,' she smiles while giving me a sidelong glance. I'm not leaving if that's what she's hoping and I grip Roddy's arm even tighter.

Chapter Four

'It's not fair is it? Not when you think of the real crooks out there,' says Sophie, knocking back an empty glass of champagne.

'Oh, who drunk that?' she says tipsily and looks around for a phantom wine thief.

I really can't believe this. Of all the nights why did Roddy's mother choose tonight?

'If life was fair Elvis would still be alive and all the impersonators would be dead,' says Baron De Weldon.

I'm wedged between the Christmas tree and Sophie Dumont-Smith. Roddy is chatting to Pandora and Baroness De Weldon. All I want to do is sneak out with him and talk about Daddy. I seem to be talking about Daddy with everyone but him.

'Your father always looks good on television,' says the Baroness. 'An attractive man is your father. Tell me Poppy, is he a good lover?'

The room falls silent. I feel my face turn red and the rash goes manic, and it's all I can do not to scratch myself senseless.

'I wouldn't know never having slept with him.'

Silly old woman.

'I imagine those that have will come forward now,' she says without batting an eyelid.

'Nothing like a scandal to bring them out of the woodwork, isn't that right Leonard?' says Lady Nell Enwin joining our little group.

'What's that?' asks Lecherous Leonard, knocking back the wine like it's going out of fashion.

'Are you still coming with us to Verbier?' asks Camilla handing me a glass of wine.

'I think we should all motor down this year. What a hoot that would be and you wouldn't have to worry about air fares,' says Marcus, saluting me with his finger.

'May I remind you that even that cheap option costs money Marcus, and money is something that Poppy doesn't have', Lady Tarleton declares in a voice loud enough for everyone to hear.

'But I'd be with Roddy in his car ...' I begin.

'Unsavoury business,' interrupts the Baron. 'I'm all for tax avoidance, but fraud, that's something else altogether.'

'It's just a mistake,' I mumble.

If only the floor would open up and swallow me. I get the impression I have suddenly become an outsider to the money club. Why doesn't Roddy say something? He could at least stand up for me.

'Who's up for the shoot on Sunday at Houghton Hall Manor?' asks Marcus.

I watch miserably as Pug-face Pandora leans close to Roddy and they both laugh at a private joke.

'I'll be there,' she says, seductively pulling up the strap on her dress.

'You're looking lovely tonight Pandora. You're glowing, isn't she glowing Roddy? Positively glowing,' says the Baron.

All right, I think we've got the message. Pug-face pretends to be embarrassed but really she loves the attention.

'I'm not eating carbs. I feel so fantastic,' she says. 'Don't you find that weight gain is such a problem Poppy?'

Bollocking cheek, hanging onto my fiancé and then hinting I'm fat.

'Fortunately I don't gain weight. I know some women only have to peek at carbs and they look like Dawn French,' I say sweetly.

Pandora struggles to keep the smile pasted on her lips. Her hand drops onto Roddy's arm and I feel like putting mine around her throat. She's hankered after Roddy for as long as I can remember. If she thinks she's getting him now she's got another think coming.

'I've always said you can't trust a politician who kisses babies. It's not natural. Your father did a lot of that I noticed,' says the Baroness.

Hell's bells, doesn't the woman ever stop?

'It's not a crime to kiss babies,' I say.

'It's when they're fourteen you've got to be careful,' mumbles Lecherous Leonard.

I bet he's had his hand up a few vestments, the disgusting old bugger. I must talk to Roddy about him.

'No, but it's a sure sign some skulduggery is going on,' grumbles the Baroness.

It's a madhouse that's what this is. Pug-face isn't letting up either. I throw back the wine and help myself to another.

'Will you have to get a job?' asks Sophie to gasps of shock.

I sigh and lift the wine to my lips.

'Perhaps best to lay off the sauce old girl,' murmurs Roddy.

Never mind lay off the sauce, maybe he should lay off old Pug-face Pandora. How dare he patronise me.

'That's a bit of a crashing bore isn't it, having to get a job? Can you imagine it Roddy?' Pandora laughs.

'Awful, abslootly awful,' chimes in Sophie.

God, is that all Sophie can say?

'I'd never find the time with all my charitable work,' says Pandora.

'Roddy may have to imagine it soon,' bellows Sir Henry Tarleton. 'I don't intend bailing him out forever.'

Oh dear. I must talk to Roddy about his gambling. The last thing we need is for his allowance to be stopped too.

'Roddy ...' I begin, leaning over to him with the intention of removing Pandora's offending hand. Instead I knock Lecherous Leonard's wine over his starched white shirt. I open my mouth to apologise and let out a belch instead. I'm absolutely mortified. I step back in horror only to stamp straight onto Lady Tarleton's toe.

'For God's sake,' growls Roddy, taking my arm.

'I'm so sorry,' I say.

'You've had too much vino darling,' he hisses and then more loudly. 'It's the shock, she's drunk too much. Profuse apologies, please excuse us.'

'Terrible business,' says the Baroness.

I'm marched from the drawing room and into the entrance hall.

'Don't apologise for me,' I say haughtily.

'You've embarrassed yourself,' he snaps.

'You were flirting with Pug ... Pandora,' I say childishly.

'Of course I wasn't,' he retorts, but his face colours.

'Roddy,' I begin and am appalled to hear my words slur. 'I can't stay at the flat, not now this thing with Daddy has ...'

He pushes me onto a chaise longue.

'The thing is Poppy ... Well the thing is we're going to have to put things on hold for a bit.'

'On hold?' I repeat stupidly. 'What things?'

He sits beside me and sighs. I sniff at his aftershave and feel my stomach churn. I try to look at Roddy but he keeps going in and out of focus. My eyelids are so heavy it's all I can do to keep my eyes open. Roddy licks his lips and looks around the room.

'We can't possibly go ahead with the wedding Pop, not now ...'

Oh God. Oh bugger.

'But everything is arranged and ...'

'Well, you can't possibly have your father walk you down the aisle in handcuffs can you?'

'He could hide them in his pockets,' I say stupidly.

'The thing is, Charles said ...'

'Charles?'

Who the hell is Charles?

'P'pa's chappie, knows the law and stuff,' he says vaguely. 'Thing is, he says your father could be remanded for years and ...'

'But that's Daddy not me. You're marrying me,' I say and cringe at how desperate I sound.

'But there'll be no money Poppy ...'

'But you have money,' I interrupt.

I watch his jaw twitch and he gently removes my hand from his knee.

'I can't possibly marry someone who hasn't got money. You of all people should understand that. Hopefully if everything blows over we can ...'

I jump up and wobble on my Guccis.

'Were you marrying me for my money?' I say, raising my voice.

'Keep your voice down, let's not make a scene,' he hisses. 'The thing is Poppy, I don't have a bean to my name. If P'pa cuts my allowance I'm in the shit. P'pa's become as tight as a fish's arse. I've had to take a loan from this chap Diamond. I was banking on your allowance but now ...'

I fall back onto the chaise longue.

'I do love you and I want to marry you more than anything. But you have to agree both of us being poor is rather pointless.'

'But if you don't marry me, I'll have no money. All Daddy's accounts have been frozen.'

He runs his finger around his collar and gives a little cough.

'I'm sure things will work out. You haven't forgotten the cuff have you? I'll send my man round later.'

I stare at him. Mummy was right. Roddy doesn't want me now. Oh, he wants my cuff but he doesn't want me.

'I'll get Teddy to give you a ring. You remember Teddy, he's in property?'

I shake my head. I don't seem able to remember anyone. Hopefully I'll even forget who I am by the morning.

'I'll call your driver. A good night's sleep is what you need.'

'But we've not had dinner,' I protest.

'Perhaps best if you don't stay for dinner. You're not really up to it are you darling? A good night's sleep is what you need.'

After the amount of Valium I've taken I imagine it's unconscious I'll be, not asleep. He kisses me on the cheek.

'But Roddy ...' I begin but forget what I was going to say.

'We don't have to make any announcements yet. Give it a few days, a few weeks even and ...'

'It's just a mistake,' I say.

'Yes, I'm sure it is. We'll wait till everything settles down, just put things on hold.'

'I'm so tired,' I say wearily.

I need to sleep. I'm sure Roddy's right. A good night's sleep is what I need. I'm sure by the morning Daddy will be exonerated. The wedding will go ahead and everything will be the same as it always was.

'Absolutely. Best if you leave the Verbier Christmas break though, darling. You don't want everyone harassed by the press do you? I'll call your chappie, get your car here.'

A few minutes later he kisses me goodbye and I climb into the Bentley.

'Tell you what, why don't you give the cuff to Eddie? Save you worrying about it.'

I nod and squeeze his hand. I lean my head against the upholstery and feel my temples throb. The flat is surrounded by paparazzi. Eddie fights his way through the sea of photographers and helps me into the lobby.

'Is it true Poppy?' shouts a photographer. 'Is it all over?'

Oh good, they've freed Daddy. I hurry to my apartment and turn on the television. I hand the cuff to Eddie and lock the door. A picture of Daddy pops up on the plasma screen and I turn up the sound. The picture is replaced with one of me. Ooh that's a good one. It was taken at a wedding in Oxfordshire. I prise off the tin lid of my homemade truffles and stare avidly at the TV screen.

'Poppy Wellesley, the daughter of disgraced MP Sir Rupert Wellesley has broken off her engagement to Rodney Tarleton, son of Sir Henry Tarleton and Lady Helen Tarleton. The couple were to have had a winter wonderland wedding at the Wellesley Oxfordshire home but Rodney Tarleton said this evening that although he was devastated at Ms Wellesley's decision, he understood it totally. The couple were ...'

I click off the sound and stare at the screen before throwing my Gucci at it. What a bastard. *Let's wait a few weeks* the bugger said ... he didn't even wait a few hours. Shit, I've only gone and given him the cuff too.

Jack Diamond

Roddy's heart somersaults as he looks at the invitation.

'From Mr Diamond,' says the waiter, 'If you'd like to follow me.'

The last thing Roddy needs is to have champagne with Jack Diamond and that loony son of his. He reluctantly follows the waiter into the private enclosure. From the corner of his eye he sees a hand reach out for a glass and the sight of the missing pinkie makes Roddy shudder. He reaches Jack Diamond and forces a smile. Diamond is wearing a blue silk cravat which he touches before looking at Roddy. Roddy tries to smile but feels sure it comes out more like a grimace. What had he been thinking of getting tied up with these East End thugs? It was P'pa's fault. If he'd been less stingy Roddy would not have needed to use loan sharks to pay off his debts.

'Ello Rodders, enjoying the races?' asks Diamond. 'Ave you got any tips? Jack Junior likes a little flutter don't yer lad?'

'Do what?' asks Jack Junior, looking up from his new BlackBerry phone.

Diamond sighs.

'I said you're 'aving a little flutter today. You could do with some tips.'

'Yeah,' Jack Junior sighs. 'It's this bleedin' posh food. Mum says it's too rich. It always gives me wind.'

Jack Diamond rolls his eyes.

'They do a good ole carvery 'ere don't they Rodders? Real quality.'

'I prefer pie and mash,' moans Mad Jack Junior. 'I don't like this posh tucker.'

'You got no bleedin' class that's your problem,' snaps Diamond. 'Sit down Rodders, don't be shy,' Diamond points to a chair. Roddy tries not to squirm under Jack Junior's stare.

'Where did yer get that? I need one,' he says pointing at Roddy's Bluetooth earpiece.

For one frightening second Roddy thinks he is pointing to his ear and his throat goes dry. He'd heard about Diamond's history with ears and he wants to hang onto his, thank you very much.

'Why do yer need one of them,' snaps Diamond. 'Nobody phones yer, except me and yer mum.'

'I get a lot of calls, important stuff,' snaps Mad Jack.

'Important stuff, my arse,' scoffs Diamond.

'You can buy them anywhere,' says Roddy, trying to be helpful while just wanting to escape.

'Ave you met my boy, Jack Junior?' asks Diamond, cutting into his beef.

Roddy has never seen beef so well done in his life. The man is a philistine.

'Yes, I've had the pleasure,' he says.

'Wouldn't call it a pleasure,' laughs Diamond. 'Now me other son, he's clever. Getting an education 'e is.'

Jesus Christ thinks Roddy, how can you possibly give these people an education? Mad Jack Junior suddenly lurches forward and grabs the earpiece from Roddy.

'What yer doing, you pansy? Give that back right now,' barks Diamond, jumping up and slapping Jack Junior around the head. He grins at Roddy, his gold tooth sparkling.

'I apologise for my son. I try to teach 'em manners but their mother indulges 'em. Sit yourself down Rodders. I shouldn't 'ave to tell yer more than once. Let's have some champers, that's up your street ain't it?'

He refills his glass and one for Roddy. Roddy falls into the chair as his legs tremble beneath him. He fumbles to get his Bluetooth back on.

'I should really get back ...' he begins.

'You don't like our company?' asks Jack Diamond, his face hardening.

'Yeah, you don't like our company?' repeats Mad Jack Junior.

'No I … It's just …'

Diamond pushes the champagne glass towards Roddy who picks it up with shaking hands. Champagne spills onto his shirt but Diamond doesn't seem to notice.

'So Roddy, you got a little something for me?'

'Yeah,' repeats Mad Jack, shaking his fist. 'You got a little something for us?'

'Will you stop frigging repeating everything I say,' growls Diamond.

'I'm not frigging repeating everything you say,' says Jack Junior.

Diamond sighs.

'You ain't forgotten old Jack Diamond have yer Rodders? I don't recall getting a payment from you last month,' says Diamond cleaning his fingernail with the cheese knife.

Mad Jack Junior scrapes back his chair.

'What's yer problem?' he snaps.

'I don't 'ave, I mean have a …' stutters Roddy.

Christ he's starting to talk like the nutters.

'Not you mush, *him*,' yells Mad Jack pointing to a man in the doorway to the enclosure. 'What yer looking at?'

Jack Diamond sighs and shoves his son back into his seat.

'He's our bodyguard, pilchard.'

Roddy fumbles in his pocket and produces a cheque book.

'I don't take cheques mate. You taking old Diamond for a fool?'

'No, no, of course not. It's just my allowance hasn't gone into my account. P'pa has been a bit difficult.'

'I only take cash matey, you know that. Now, you owe me ten grand and I'm not even adding the interest, which is …'

He pauses and looks at Mad Jack.

'What?' asks Mad Jack Junior.

Jack Diamond slaps him across the head and Roddy whimpers.

'The interest which is …' repeats Jack Diamond loudly.

'Oh yeah,' says Mad Jack pulling out the BlackBerry which is enclosed in a diamond-encrusted case. Roddy has never seen anything so tacky in his life. He fiddles with the phone for a few seconds and Diamond sighs impatiently.

'*Say a command*,' says a robotic voice.

'What the fuck are you doing?' snarls Diamond.

'Using the voice fing, 'ang on a minute.'

Diamond snatches the phone and taps into it.

'Wiv interest you owe me fifteen grand, Roddy ole chap.'

Roddy swallows. How can they add on so much interest? God, he'll never be out of the man's debt. He remembers Poppy's engagement ring and his face lights up.

'I'll have the money as soon as I get back from Verbier. My fiancée's engagement ring is worth eighteen thousand. I'll sell it. I just need to get it off her.'

'Ooh skiing,' mimics Diamond. 'Going on the piss are yer?' he laughs.

'It's the *piste* actually,' corrects Roddy and immediately wishes he hadn't.

Diamond gives him a mean stare.

'I'm not a bleedin' idiot. When you get off the piss you'd better 'ave me money, got it. You told me you were selling an expensive bracelet. I don't like being led down the garden path Rodders.'

'I had to give that money to another chappie and ...'

'Getting in a pickle are yer Roddy? Now I don't wanna 'ave to make you an offer you'll refuse.'

Roddy doesn't think that sounds quite right but decides it's best to keep quiet.

'I'll have it,' he says, standing up.

Diamond watches Roddy leave the enclosure and then turns to his son.

'Find out about his fiancée and stop fiddling with that bleedin' phone before I start fiddling with you.'

Chapter Five

'Oh my God, that's mine. It has to be. I've hankered after that hat, like forever. I adore the colour,' squeals Saffy as she snatches my Stella McCartney woollen hat.

'A hundred and fifty,' I say.

Her eyes widen.

'But you've worn it,' she says petulantly.

'Only once, and I paid three hundred for it,' I say firmly.

I never thought my friends would be so merciless.

'Are you selling your Jaeger suits?' asks Chelsea.

I nod miserably.

'Ooh fab,' says Georgina Troy, stuffing her mouth with chow mein.

Honestly my life is falling apart and my friends are stuffing their faces full of Chinese food.

I watch as my lovely floaty Dior evening dress is passed around. I really can't believe I'm sitting in my mother's lounge selling my clothes. What has become of me? Thank God Pandora is in Verbier or she would be rubbing my nose in it, but there's no way I will get my wardrobe onto Teddy's yacht, and I need to raise some cash. It's been a week since Daddy's arrest and I'm still splashed over the papers. I've gone from scandalously privileged to scandalously broke. I've lost all of my Facebook friends and I'm trending on Twitter. I know I've always wanted to trend on Twitter but not like this. Roddy has already changed his relationship status on Facebook to single. How cruel is that? He'll be unfriending me next. I'm not only the daughter of the disgraced MP and the ex-fiancé of top socialite but according to the papers I've also got a raging drug problem.

Fallen socialite hooked on crack is seen stumbling into The Ivy.

That's a joke. The only crack around here is the crack in my arse. The Ivy is always booked whenever I phone to make a reservation. My appointments have been cancelled at the beauty salon and my hairdresser sobbed down the phone that she couldn't possibly highlight me.

'It's all so awful Poppy but you do understand don't you?'

Actually no, I don't understand. One minute I was engaged to be married and the next it's all over. I can't believe Roddy has stopped loving me. I know I haven't stopped loving him. I've even been snubbed by the health club who cancelled my spa weekend.

'We seem to have double booked,' Marcia had said.

I'd cleared all my things out of the flat and moved in with my mother. Thankfully Jeremy has now finally 'got to grips' with my finances and has found me a new home.

'Teddy knows of a fabulous boat darling, and with a mooring, although you can sail, of course. There is enough in the bank to keep you going until things get sorted. No need to think about a job quite yet. How about selling off some of your things? That will tide you over a bit longer. Put off the inevitable.'

I was so relieved that I'd almost cried. I can live on a yacht. Daddy has a yacht moored at Cannes, or at least he did, and I have many happy memories of our times there. I'd made almost two grand by selling my designer outfits. It pained me to part with them but needs must, at least that's what I keep telling myself. Now I'm on my way to see my new home. I'm rather excited. I'll be able to sail all my friends for our yearly jaunt to Capri. Once Roddy sees the yacht, he'll come round and the wedding will be back on.

We pass carol singers murdering Good King Wenceslas and weave through the Christmas shoppers. I feel my Saint Laurent ankle boots slip on the morning frost.

'You can't be serious,' Mother says, whipping out a hip flask from her Fendi handbag. 'I can't possibly go there. What if someone sees me?'

'It's a restaurant, not a house of ill repute,' I say.

'Same thing if you ask me. God, this is unbearable,' she says, lifting the flask to her lips.

'What are you doing?' I gasp.

'You don't expect me to get through this sober do you?'

I feel agitated and my rash itches in sympathy. I'm looking more like a leper with each passing day. Why won't the awful thing go?

'You haven't got scurvy have you?' she says wrinkling her nose.

'What's scurvy?'

'It's what poor people get,' she says dismissively.

'I've only been poor for a week,' I argue. 'Anyway, you're poor now and you haven't got it.'

'I'm not as poor as you. They can't touch my capital because it was the divorce settlement. You should see a doctor.'

'I can't afford the doctor.'

'There's always the NHS, God forbid. You'll need to make an appointment soon if you want to be seen before the summer.'

I shudder.

'I can't believe you're putting me through this,' she grumbles. 'You could at least have taken me to a decent restaurant for lunch.'

'I am taking you to a decent restaurant, and we have got to get used to it. I want to live within my means.'

'I told you Roddy was a bugger. I knew he'd abandon you.'

'It's not his fault, it's his p'pa.'

I see Chelsea approaching and wave. Daddy's insisting he's innocent and that it has all been a big mistake but meanwhile his assets are frozen and so are the rest of us. Roddy has gone to Verbier and I've gone underground. Mummy spends most of her time knocking back G and Ts and giving interviews, mostly about how Daddy never changed my nappy. I imagine we'll monopolise the Sunday glossies for some time to come, at least me and my nappies will. I've spent one night with my mother and I'm already climbing the walls.

'Couldn't we have lunched at The Ivy, or The Park Hotel,' she complains.

'I didn't ask you to come. You wanted to. Besides, we can't afford The Ivy.'

I can't face the fact that The Ivy won't let us on the premises.

'I want to see the yacht you're buying and whether there's room for me. I don't believe there won't be.'

I'm making sure there won't be. Chelsea waves and weaves between the crowds. I feel a stab of envy. She's wrapped in her faux fur and smells glorious. Her Diorissimo perfume drifts across my nostrils and I sniff appreciatively. She hugs me tightly.

'You smell lovely,' I say. 'I'm so glad you're here. I thought for sure you would go to Verbier.'

'Not with that arse Roddy I wouldn't,' she smiles hooking her arm into mine. 'So, where have you booked lunch?'

'Pizza Express,' grumbles Mother.

Chelsea's eyes widen.

'Oh right,' I say, 'how exciting. I've never been to Pizza Express.'

'Why the buggery would you want to?' Mother mumbles.

'The Ivy was busy and …' I begin.

'They wouldn't let us in,' finishes Mother.

'If you carry on like this we'll be lucky if Pizza Express let us in,' I say, snatching the hip flask.

'Where is the boat?' asks Chelsea excitedly.

'Near Little Venice,' I say.

'Venice?' queries Chelsea, looking confused. 'Are you leaving the country?'

'Not *the* Venice Chelsea,' I reply patiently, 'Little Venice, the yacht is on Regent's Canal.'

Mother chokes on her gin.

'What?' she gasps. 'I thought that at least it would be docked in Richmond or somewhere decent. I've never seen a yacht on Regent's Canal.'

'It's dead exciting though isn't it?' says Chelsea. 'Have you got a photo of it?'

I shake my head.

'No, but Jeremy says it is in fab condition with all mod cons so …'

'We'll be able to sail off to Capri and Roddy can eff off. He's such an arse,' laughs Chelsea.

Mother scoffs.

'If it's Capri you want maybe you should sell the wedding dress, that'll teach your father. After all it's not been worn. Or are you planning on doing a Lady Faversham?'

'I think once Roddy sees my yacht everything will be different,' I say hopefully. 'It's not his fault.'

We squeeze through the crowds and into Pizza Express where the hot air hits us. Chelsea removes her fur and hands it to a passing waitress.

'Just a minute,' says the waitress.

'How rude,' Mother grumbles.

I spot a table and lead them over. Mother makes a big thing of wiping the table with her lace handkerchief and I fight back the tears for the hundredth time since Daddy was arrested.

'I can't believe Daddy did this to us,' I say, biting my lip.

Chelsea covers my hand with hers.

'I always warned your father about money. I told him money's not like your pecker Rupert, it won't grow in your hands,' says Mother.

I groan. The waitress places a menu in front of us.

'Can I get you drinks?'

'Let's get a bottle of red,' says Mother.

Chelsea nods while I glance through the drinks menu.

'I don't suppose you've got a bottle of *Jasper Hill's Emily's Paddock Shiraz?*' queries Mother.

The waitress gives her a puzzled look.

'I don't know that one. The house red is Sicilian.'

'Oh,' says a surprised Chelsea. 'How unusual, are you absolutely sure?'

'Yes, it's Sicilian,' says the waitress. 'I'm quite sure.'

'She meant are you sure you don't have *Jasper Hill,'* snaps Mother.

The waitress nods nervously.

'Good God,' mumbles Mother.

'The house wine is fine,' I say, 'and a jug of water.'

'Why, do you think it will need diluting?' queries Mother.

'I don't mind house wine,' says Chelsea.

'I don't suppose they have proper crystal here either,' grumbles Mother.

Chelsea hands her fur to the waitress.

'Sorry, we don't have a cloakroom,' says the waitress, looking flustered.

'No cloakroom? And no Jasper Hill? Honestly,' snorts Mother. 'You'll be telling us you don't serve pizza next.'

'Mummy,' I hiss.

'Well, this is nice isn't it?' says Chelsea, moving her cutlery around. 'I've always wanted to come to Pizza Express.'

Mother flicks through the menu and sighs. The waitress returns with the drinks and takes our order.

'Any garlic bread?' she asks.

'Good God no,' snaps Mother. 'Do we look like garlic bread people?'

I find myself wondering what garlic bread people look like and if after a few more weeks of being poor I'll become one. I sip at the wine and wince. Chelsea chokes quietly on hers and mumbles.

'This is different isn't it Poppy? It's nice though.'

'This wine tastes like petrol,' grumbles Mother as she adds some gin from her hip flask.

I could die from embarrassment and what's even worse two guys are giving us the eye from the other side of the room. Me and Chelsea that is, at least I hope it is me and Chelsea. If my mother has pulled I swear I'll kill myself. I'm so exhausted from seven days of emotional battering that I really couldn't stand a man chatting me up, as flattering as it would be. I don't think I have the energy to turn them down. Even worse, I've gained seven pounds. That's a pound a day, so maybe this is the best I can pull. If I continue like this I'll be a candidate for one of those fat programmes before the year is out. I need to get a grip but all I can think of is how I am a laughing stock, totally disgraced. I feel humiliated and the papers still seem to be full of me and Roddy.

The waitress places salmon salads in front of us.

'I might join a cult,' I say. 'It's either that or pawn my engagement ring, but I figure joining a cult would give me something to hang on to. All my friends have disowned me so I need new ones.'

Chelsea's eyes widen and she glances at Mother.

'That's a bit extreme Poppy,' she says worriedly. 'I'm still your friend.'

'Well you know what they say? Down in the mouth? It's time for a faith lift,' says Mother, knocking back her drink with a shudder. 'Your Aunty Grace found God. He was hidden down the trousers of the bishop of Shrewsbury. That caused a bit of scandal.'

'You haven't lost all your friends. Camilla texted me and said she can't wait to see you when she gets back from Verbier,' says Chelsea.

I shake my head.

'That's one person Chelsea.'

She looks thoughtful and Mother and I wait expectantly.

'I'm sure there are others. I just can't think right now,' says Chelsea finally.

Mother gestures to the waitress.

'Another bottle of petrol over here,' she calls.

I want to crawl under the table. In fact I would if it wasn't so small.

'I just don't see any future without Roddy,' I say miserably, rubbing at my arm.

'Fudge berries,' squeals Chelsea. 'That rash has got to your fingers.'

I dab at my eyes with a tissue and pull my sleeves over my hands. Roddy and I had such plans for Christmas. We were going to book a log cabin on the beach in Cape Cod. It's just too awful to think about. I fiddle with my sapphire and diamond engagement ring and fight back the tears. Who am I going to spend Christmas with now?

'He'll come round I'm sure,' says Chelsea softly. 'It's just been a shock.'

I nod.

'Yes and when Daddy is cleared everything will go back to normal.'

'Aren't you that celeb off the telly?'

We all turn to the guy hovering over our table. Chelsea blushes and my rash itches for England.

'You've made a mistake,' says Mummy.

'Nah, I know that face anywhere,' he says in an East End accent. 'Weren't you in that *Made in Chelsea* programme?'

I most certainly was not. He pulls a chair from the next table and straddles it.

'Oh dear,' says Chelsea. 'You don't get this at The Ivy.'

There's no need to remind me.

'This ain't The Ivy darling,' he laughs. 'You get a much better class of man in Pizza Express.'

'A different class certainly, we can see that,' says Mother scathingly, giving him the once over.

He scrapes his chair close and breathes his garlic bread breath over me.

'If you're free tonight I can take you for a slap up meal at the Harvester. We can share a combo.'

'Now there's an offer. How can any woman turn that down,' scoffs Mother, knocking back the wine. 'Actually, this stuff's not bad once you get a taste for it.'

'That's very nice of you,' I smile, 'but I don't like the Harvester.'

Not that I've ever been of course.

'Come back to my place instead then,' he says in a heartbeat. 'How do you like your eggs in the morning?'

I hear his friends snigger and feel my body turn hot. Mother sighs.

'Unfertilised,' she says. 'Now if you'd like to sling your hook young man, otherwise we'll have to get our bodyguard to break your ribs.'

'Ooh that's a good one,' says Chelsea thoughtfully. 'About the eggs I mean.'

'It's as old as I am,' grins Mother.

We watch him skulk away and I throw back some wine. Oh God, is that the best I can do now? If I am taken out to dinner will it be to the Harvester? Am I destined to become the combo queen?

My mobile bleeps. Please, oh please let it be Roddy. I look at the screen and see it is Teddy.

'Poppy, I'm already at Regent's Canal. I know it's a bit of a bore but you couldn't get here in the next fifteen minutes could you? It's just I've got this other client in about an hour and ...'

'Oh,' I say, 'yes of course.'

I don't want someone else getting first offer on the yacht.

'It's a fair walk to *Amelia*, about ten minutes from the entrance to the canal I'd say. You can't miss her. She's the second from the end. See you in a bit.'

Chelsea offers to pay for lunch and Mother and I make a show of protesting.

'I insist,' says Chelsea.

Minutes later we are in Chelsea's Rolls and heading to Regent's Canal.

'It's so exciting,' Chelsea says. 'We'll all come to your yacht-warming party.'

'How much are they asking for it?' Mother asks.

'I've no idea.'

Let's face it, I've never had to ask the price of anything. In my life everything was affordable. At least it was until now.

Chapter Six

'It must be a very small yacht,' says Mother. 'You're sure it's not a rowing boat you're buying?'

'Will you stop talking like I'm really really poor?' I say angrily.

'You are really really poor. You were wery wery wich. It's all you've known darling daughter. Let's be honest, you've never even washed up a tea cup. This is going to be a rude awakening for you.'

It's all I can do to stop myself pushing her in the river. I bet Chelsea doesn't have to put up with this from her mother. Then again Chelsea is still rich isn't she? God, I wish I was. I scratch my arm and sigh. Being poor doesn't agree with me at all. We've been walking along the canal for ten minutes and there is no sign of any yachts. The walkway seems to go on for ever, as do the barges. I've never seen so many boats, or dogs come to that.

'Perhaps the yachts are at the other end,' chirps an optimistic Chelsea.

'Are we in the right place?' asks Mother clapping her gloved hands together.

It's freezing and flakes of snow have begun to fall. All I want to do is get back to my lovely apartment in Belgravia, except it's not mine any more is it?

'Teddy said Regent's Canal,' I say uncertainly. 'We must have missed it.'

'And you're sure it is a yacht?'

'Well no, I just presumed that,' I say, a feeling of impending doom washing over me.

'Oh,' says Chelsea.

Surely Teddy would know I couldn't live on anything smaller than a yacht. At the very least it will surely be a big boat. Jeremy gave me the impression that the shares had yielded a nice sum.

'At least you'll be able to get something decent,' he'd said. 'Teddy will steer you right. Roddy was on the right track there.'

Yes, well now Roddy is on a ski track isn't he? No doubt Pug-face is with him.

'Where are the yachts moored young man,' Mummy asks a man cycling towards us.

'Yachts? Are you serious?' he laughs as he cycles past. 'This is Regent's Canal not the Monaco yacht show.'

'I thought it was an odd place for a yacht,' says Mother, shaking the dregs from her hip flask.

'You okay ladies? You're looking a bit lost,' calls a man from his boat. He's got holes in his jumper and cat hairs on his trousers. I wrinkle my nose. This place is so gross. I only hope things will improve as we get further down the canal.

'We're looking for *Amelia*, if you'd be so kind,' says Chelsea in her horsy voice. 'The boat that is, not the person.'

'Keep walking, you're going the right way,' he smiles. 'She's just up there.'

We step onto a boardwalk and continue.

'We must see it soon,' says Chelsea.

I am suddenly flung forward as my St Laurent heel gets lodged in one of the boardwalk planks. I feel my foot twist under me and curse.

'Shit, my ankle,' I say, losing my balance and flinging my arms in front of me. They land unceremoniously on the backside of the man walking ahead of us. He turns and catches me before I stumble to the ground. It feels like a thousand volts shoot through me at his touch and I fight back a gasp. I mumble an apology while registering his good looks before drowning in his watery blue eyes. They lock onto mine for a second and I wonder if he felt that strange something too. He then turns to my wedged foot. Without a word he grabs my ankle, his hand warm on my skin, and pulls the heel out.

'Throwing yourself at men is not the way to get a husband,' remarks Mother.

I shoot her a dirty look and turn back to the guy who I see is actually very handsome.

'I'm sorry, my ...' I begin, hearing the tremble in my voice.

What's wrong with me? It's not like he's George Clooney.

'Not the best boots for this walkway,' he mumbles, walking off.

'He's certainly got charisma,' says Mother sarcastically.

We continue passing boat after boat until my toes turn numb with the cold.

'It will be a long way for you to walk every day won't it?' says Chelsea stating the bloody obvious as only Chelsea can.

We reach the end of the line. All that is left is one solitary narrowboat.

'Is that it?' says Mother, pointing.

My heart sinks. It must be. After all, there aren't any real boats left. It's not a yacht at all. It's colourfully painted admittedly, and there are Chinese lanterns hanging outside which make it look pretty, in a barge-boat kind of way. A bike is parked at the side of it and I decide that I won't be using that. I can't possibly take this. It's way too small.

'This must be it,' I say. I spot Teddy pacing up and down. He's wearing a heavy overcoat and his mouth is hidden behind a thick striped scarf.

'Strangest yacht I've ever seen,' says Mother.

'I can't see Amanda written anywhere on it,' says Chelsea.

'I'm not surprised considering it's *Amelia* and not Amanda,' I correct.

I hitch up my skirt and lift my leg elegantly, before placing one foot on board. I'd better take a look or Jeremy will moan. I can't possibly live on this. It's far too small. I throw my Hermes bag onto the deck and feel the boat move. I wobble on my ankle boots and my foot slips from under me. I reach out and grab a pipe to steady myself. There's a ripping sound and I'm tugged back. I'm now dangling. This is too horrific for words. I hold on to the pipe for dear life while my Boden skirt rips a little more each time I move. I could cry. I hate Roddy and I hate Daddy more than I've ever hated anybody in my whole life.

'Oh fudge berries,' cries Chelsea, struggling to rescue me. 'Your skirt is caught on a hook.'

'Bugger,' says Mother, grabbing Chelsea before she also tumbles into the water. The boat sways and my hand slips from the pipe.

'Oh trollops,' shrieks Chelsea.

I groan at the sound of ripping. The Boden is an original too. I let out a scream when I realise I'm going to slide into the icy river. I feel a strong hand take my arm and steady me. I know it's him without looking because my body is again on fire. This is ridiculous. I look into the eyes of my rescuer; he's a real hottie indeed. Not as hot as Roddy of course, okay maybe a bit hotter than Roddy. I lean against his chest and regain my balance. His woollen jumper is rough against my hand.

'You've bent my pipe,' he says softly.

His sultry blue eyes lock onto mine.

'I've not heard that line before,' sniggers Mother.

'I've bent better pipes than yours in my time,' I say brushing down my clothes.

'Oh dear Poppy, your skirt,' groans Chelsea.

I pull myself from his eyes and look at the Boden.

'It's ruined,' I groan.

'Never mind your skirt, look at my pipe.'

'Never mind your pipe,' I mimic. 'Look at my skirt. Do you have any idea how much a Boden original costs?'

'As odd as it may be, I've never had cause to wonder,' he says, studying the pipe.

'Marvellous, marvellous you're here.' bellows Teddy from the bank.

'I really don't think the deck should be slippery, Teddy,' reprimands Mother.

'Well, the thing is ...'

'My daughter could have broken her neck and that would have made headlines,' she continues. 'And God knows she has enough of those at the moment.'

'Quite right, but ...' mumbles Teddy.

'However, it was just the Boden that got damaged and ...'

'And my water pipe,' says the hottie, glaring at me. He is extremely good looking. If he were to smile I imagine he could be very handsome indeed, but at the moment his eyebrows are knitted together and his blue eyes are staring angrily at me. I step carefully around him and look for a way to get inside the boat.

'How do I get in Teddy?' I ask. 'Chelsea, are you coming aboard?'

'Ooh yes,' she giggles.

'I don't where the party is lady but I assure you it's not on here. Now perhaps you and your Boden would like to leave my boat,' the hottie says sternly while plonking my Hermes into my hands.

'Teddy, can you please tell ...' I begin.

'This isn't *Amelia*,' says Teddy with an embarrassed laugh. '*That* is *Amelia*.'

He points to a tatty little tug boat further along the canal. It bobs up and down like a champagne cork. Please let this be Teddy's little joke. Let this be the boat that takes me to the yacht.

'Allow me,' says the hottie.

He smiles and despite my dazed mentality I register his hunkiness. He offers his hand to steady me and gently guides me off the boat.

'Your decking is too slippery,' I snap.

'Just as well you don't live here then isn't it?' he grins. 'And a catwalk is more suitable for those boots.'

I brush his hand off me and attempt to walk gracefully towards Teddy. I feel the ripped Boden flap against my leg.

'Here's a bit you left behind,' calls the hottie. 'If it's that expensive I imagine you wouldn't want to miss any. You might be able to stitch it back together.'

'One doesn't stitch a Boden back together,' I say irritably, catching the piece of material.

'Perhaps one shouldn't wear Boden when visiting boats. Or better still, perhaps one shouldn't trespass on other people's.' he grunts.

'What an uncultured man,' says Chelsea.

'Terribly sorry,' says Teddy. 'Please allow us to pay for the pipe.'

'Oh really,' grumbles Mother.

I stare at the real *Amelia* and feel my knees weaken.

'That's *Amelia*?' I say dumbfounded.

'Peas and rice,' says Chelsea, following my eyes.

'Yes, Jesus Christ indeed, that will just about hold my wardrobe,' I say miserably.

'It's quaint though isn't it Poppy?' says Chelsea.

I've never known anyone who can see the good in everything like Chelsea can. I'm sure if I took her to a rat infested cellar she'd be saying, 'It's nice though isn't it Poppy?'

'Well that most certainly is not a yacht,' says Mother.

She's quite right. It's as far from a yacht as anything could be. It's a bobbing wreck. I can't live in that. Where will all my shoes go?

'You can't be serious Teddy,' I say. 'Jeremy gave me the impression it was a yacht. He said I could sail.'

'It needs some work but it's very cheap. I can do it for you for ten grand.'

Mother gasps.

'Ten grand? Are you insane young man? I wouldn't pay ten pounds for that.'

Teddy leans towards me.

'I understand even ten grand would wipe you out a fair bit,' he whispers in my ear.

Oh God, why is it I have no idea how much money I have?

'Surely I can spend more than ten thousand on a boat?' I say exasperated.

'That's not what I've been told,' says Teddy. 'Look Poppy, this is a nice little mooring ...'

'It's bollocking miles from anywhere,' I say angrily. 'Who's going to visit me here?'

'From what I've been told most people have distanced themselves from you anyway, so you won't have to worry about visitors,' he says coldly.

'You're still dealing with the elite,' snaps Mother. 'I'd remember that if I were you because when the money comes back ...'

'If,' interrupts Teddy.

'Well really ...' begins Mummy before dipping into her hip flask.

'I'll be visiting, and so will Camilla I'm sure,' says Chelsea. 'Let's have a look inside Poppy.'

Teddy tries to pull the boat in without dirtying his suit and fails miserably.

'I'll get someone,' he says looking at his watch. 'I've got a big client in a bit.'

He marches off and my rash starts to itch.

'That's getting worse,' remarks Mother. 'In fact everything is getting worse.'

I see the hottie strolling towards us and I groan. He walks confidently and has an irritating smile on his face.

'You need pulling?' he asks.

'Is it a combo you'd be offering?' says Mother.

'Mother,' I say, giving her a nudge and then turning to the hottie. 'No thank you. I managed very well in Pizza Express. I feel quite sure I can do it again,' I say rubbing at the rash. Although I have to admit if anyone is worth pulling he most certainly is. He really is quite gorgeous. Before I know what is happening he has leapt onto the boat and is tying it closer to the walkway.

'Impressive,' says Mother. 'Now if I were twenty years younger.'

He pulls the sleeves of his jumper up to his elbows and looks at us.

'Do you need help to get on board,' he asks brusquely.

'We can manage thank you,' I say lifting my nose in the air.

'You'd better mind this funny penisy hook thing,' warns Chelsea. 'You don't want to rip more of your skirt.'

Penisy hook thing? The last thing I need is to get caught on another bloody hook, especially one that looks like an up bent penis. I gingerly step over the strange red extrusion that pokes up from the deck.

'That's the horn cleat,' he smiles. 'I'd replace that if I were you, it's for tying the mooring rope but it slips on that one. Are you sure you don't need a hand getting on board?'

'We can manage thank you very much.'

'Whatever,' he says, jumping down. 'Don't bend any more pipes.'

He winks at me as he walks past.

'Thank you,' calls Chelsea.

'Chelsea,' I reprimand.

She lowers her head.

'He did help. Teddy is useless, you have to agree.'

She hitches up her faux fur and clambers clumsily onto the boat, wobbling slightly as it moves on the water. She holds out her hand to help me up. I check the hottie isn't looking. The last thing I want to do is fall arse over tit in front of him. Fortunately there is no sign of him so I clutch her hand and pull myself up. Teddy returns with a big burly man who lifts Mother onto the deck. We stand with the wind blowing around our ankles and the snow stinging our faces. I'd like to say it feels festive but the truth is it doesn't.

'Jed will show you the hold,' says Teddy stupidly, before slapping his gloved hands together. 'The thing is I've got to get off. Let me know if you decide to take it.'

I've most certainly already decided *not* to take it.

'Right, this way ladies,' smiles Jed. 'Chilly today isn't it? You've got a little wood burner here,' he says cheerfully. 'Of course it's not on. Bleedin' mental to have that on when no one is living here,' he laughs.

'Yes quite,' says Mother dryly.

'But they throw out a lot of 'eat these burners,' he continues.

'Where's the kitchen?' Chelsea asks.

'You're standing in it darling. It's all open plan on these narrowboats and ...'

'As long as the loo isn't open plan,' says Mother. 'I know it's intimate to have your friends watch you cook. But having your friends watch you pee is a whole other matter.'

I don't say anything because I'm bollocking speechless. He opens a door into a tiny cubicle.

'Here is the loo.'

It is then I want to die. I can't pee in there. And I can't possibly do the other. There's barely room to sit down. This is too awful for words.

'I can't do it,' I say. 'I just can't.'

The whole boat is the size of my Bentley. Come to think of it I'd be better off living in the Bentley. At least it has a minibar.

'It could do with a lick of paint,' agrees Jed.

I turn and climb the steps to the deck.

'I'll kill Jeremy,' I say, pulling out my phone. At that moment a movement near the edge of the boat catches my eye and I shriek.

'Rat, rat, look, can you see?'

'Don't be silly,' tuts Mother. 'Roddy wouldn't be seen dead around here.'

Nor would I normally, this is just too awful for words. In fact there aren't any words for this.

'You'll see plenty of them,' laughs Jed.

Oh my God. The boat dips to the side as Mother mounts the steps and I grab Jed's arm to steady myself. My iPhone slips from my hand and slides across the deck and over the edge. There is a plop as it hits the water.

'Oh buck it,' says Chelsea.

'You'll need to get your sea legs if you're going to live on a boat,' laughs Jed.

Never mind my sea legs, what about my iPhone?

'I'm not going to live in a bollocking sardine tin,' I snap. 'Get me off this piece of junk.'

'Where now?' asks Mother. 'Carphone Warehouse?'

Harrods more like, for a crate of truffles.

'Oh buck it,' repeats Chelsea.

'Right, let me know if you're interested in my sardine tin won't you?' Jed says.

'I won't be,' I say under my breath before slipping on the boardwalk.

Chapter Seven

I fiddle with the stem of my glass and take a deep breath to calm my nerves. Jeremy returns with two prawn salads and places one in front of me.

'Sorry it took so long. It's insane, Christmas bloody parties, everyone's at it,' he says apologetically. 'Have you gained weight?'

Shit, is it that noticeable? I must lay off the truffles. But it's my only comfort. Some people smoke to relax don't they? I eat truffles.

'I don't think so,' I lie.

And I'm most certainly not at it. I haven't been at it since Roddy and I celebrated my thirty-second birthday, which means I haven't been at it since I turned thirty-two. I know that was only a few months ago but it feels like forever. I most likely will never be at it again.

'So, making plans for Christmas?' he continues.

'Yes, I thought I'd slash my wrists after the Queen's speech. I'm living with Mummy remember.'

He tuts and launches himself at the prawn salad.

'Why don't you go away?'

'Good idea Jeremy. How about two weeks in The Priory?'

He continues molesting his salad.

'It's not my fault you know,' he says petulantly.

We're in a small restaurant off Oxford Street which is heaving with Christmas shoppers and I couldn't be more miserable. Everywhere I go there is that festive feeling. You know the kind of thing. People bashing into you in the street like you've become invisible. Car radio aerials covered in stupid tinsel and what's worse the shelf that used to hold the truffles in Harrods suddenly disappears and is magically replaced with every kind of mince pie imaginable. Don't get me wrong, I love Christmas. I love it even more when I have money. I've never had a poor Christmas. Visions of soup kitchens enter my brain and I shudder. Mother is apparently buggering off to Long Island to spend the holidays with her sister and Daddy has flown to the Bahamas, courtesy of a friend.

'He needs the rest,' Jeremy had said. 'He's been under a dreadful strain.'

Never mind Daddy, what about me? I'm the one who has had her whole life frozen.

'Ah yes,' he says, digging into his jacket pocket. 'I've a new phone for you. I've taken the liberty of adding the relevant numbers for you, mine included. I phoned Roddy just in case he was trying to get through to you.'

'Did he ask about me? Is he coming back from Verbier soon?'

'He misses you and hopes this embarrassing business is over quickly.'

He looks longingly at my prawn salad and I hand it over. I look pointedly at my glass and he orders another bottle of wine.

'I've had someone from the *Daily Mail* get in touch,' he says quietly, pushing a card towards me. 'They'll pay for your story. Riches to rags, you know the kind of thing.'

Great, I'm a Cinderella in reverse. All I need is my Prince Charming. Remind me to buy some glass slippers.

'I'd need to be desperate to sell a story to the *Daily Mail*,' I say scathingly.

He grimaces before saying, 'You *are* desperate.'

'How much money is there Jeremy?'

'Ah,' he says, through a mouthful of lettuce, 'If you're talking about available funds, then not much.'

I throw back my wine and top up the glass.

'Perhaps best to go steady on the old booze,' he advises.

'How much money do I have Jeremy?'

'It's not good Poppy,' he says pushing his plate away. Oh God, if he's not eating it must be bad. I hold my breath.

'If you don't want to live with your mother then I'd suggest you take the boat. There should be enough for you to tidy it up, but you'll have to think about getting a job Poppy.'

I feel a lump in my throat.

'A job? You want me to get a job? What kind of job? I'm thirty-two and not qualified to do anything. I should be a socialite wife.'

'There aren't many vacancies for those and especially not for women without money I'm afraid.'

I slump in my seat.

'I can't possibly,' I say, swallowing a Valium and washing it down with wine.

He clicks his tongue nervously and glances at his watch. Why is it everyone I meet needs to be somewhere else these days?

'That boat is so tiddly, Jeremy. Where am I supposed to put my clothes? There's all my make-up and shoes, and ... The thing is, it's just too small.'

'Put them in storage. I don't see you have much choice Poppy. This is your situation right now.'

I fight back my tears.

'Poppy Wellesley, well I never,' thunders a voice from behind me.

I cringe as a hush pervades the room and Lord Balthazar Wyndham-Price, affectionately known as Barmy Balls, marches towards us.

'Oh no,' I groan. 'Balls has hankered after me forever.'

'You could do worse,' whispers Jeremy. 'Surely better than getting a job. *Lady Balls Wyndham-Price*, that has a nice ring to it.'

'I could fire you, you know that,' I say.

Balthazar strides arrogantly towards us. He's wearing a lime-green suit with a multicoloured tie. His jet-black hair hangs from beneath a tweed cap.

'Balls,' I say as he approaches.

'Pops,' he cries sucking at my cheeks. God, it's like being attacked by an overeager Labrador except a Labrador would be preferable.

'Terrible state of affairs darling, you must be beside yourself. What's that you're drinking? Oh no, that's not cricket,' he says, glancing at the bottle.

'Waiter, a bottle of Dom Pérignon,' he calls.

Oh now, this is more what I'm used to.

'Tell me darling, is it true you broke off the engagement?' he asks pulling up a chair beside me.

'Well ...' I begin.

'She felt it was only fair on Roddy. You know how selfless Pops is,' interrupts Jeremy.

I glare at him. It's bad enough Balls calls me Pops. God, can you imagine if I did marry him. People would call us Balls and Pops. It sounds like a comedy duo. Mind you, I'm not far off being a comedy am I?

'Good news for me,' he bellows.

The waiter uncorks the champagne and Balls orders lobster.

'They have the best lobster here. The absolute best,' he smiles, resting his hand on my knee.

'It's been a difficult time,' says Jeremy, helping himself to champagne.

'You've got the flat in Belgravia surely Truffles?'

'Sir Rupert had that on expenses, second home, you know the kind of thing,' says Jeremy.

'Good God, don't tell me you lost the flat Pops?'

Doesn't he read the tabloids? According to them I'm not only homeless but lying in the gutter with a hypodermic in my arm.

'It's great you're here for her Lord Wyndham-Price. You know how people disappear off the radar at times like this,' says Jeremy.

'Good God man that's scandalous. It's at times like this that one should stick together, what?'

'That's very charitable of you Lord Wyndham-Price. Most have just turned their backs.'

Hello, has Jeremy forgotten I'm here?

'She's all alone over Christmas,' he mumbles, pulling a sad face and then giving me a sly wink.

Oh no, why did he have to say that?

'What, all alone at Christmas? No one should be alone at Christmas. I'm not having that, by Jove I'm not.'

'Honestly I'm fine,' I say quickly.

'You'll come to Balls' and be damned,' he says, thumping his fist on the table.

I'll be damned all right. I rack my brains for an excuse to get out of Christmas at Balls' house.

'In fact,' Balls adds thoughtfully, 'come and stay at my place until you get back on your feet.'

He bites noisily into the lobster.

'I bloody love the lobster here. Bloody love it.'

'Actually, I'll be working on my new place over Christmas so I can't possibly,' I say impulsively.

Jeremy looks at me over his champagne.

'Is that right? You want me to put that offer in do you?' he smiles.

Seriously, what choice do I have? Put yourself in my Guccis, Christmas at the Balls' luxurious mansion or slumming it in a cold damp narrowboat. It's a no-brainer.

'I'll get onto it immediately,' says Jeremy.

Peas and rice, how did that happen? Sardine tin, here I come.

Chapter Eight

'Right, that's your lot,' pants Trevor, dropping my last box with a thud.

I struggle onto the boat, tripping over the mooring rope as I do so.

'I'd like the boxes in the right rooms please,' I say, 'If you could start with the bedroom boxes first.'

'Is that right? You got a map of this mansion have you? I wouldn't want to get lost,' laughs Frank.

Oh yes, very funny.

'That's it I'm afraid darlin,' says the other man. 'We've another job to get to.'

Never mind another job, what about my job?

'But you haven't finished this one,' I argue.

'By rights lady, we aren't supposed to carry things further than a few metres, ain't that right Frank?'

'That's right,' agrees Frank. 'Ealth and safety.'

Health and safety, they surely aren't serious. How can walking along a boardwalk be dangerous?

'I've near given meself an 'ernia carrying this stuff along that boardwalk,' says Frank. 'By rights we shouldn't have done that.'

'But you can't leave my things out here,' I say, pushing a stray cat off a hat box. 'They'll get ruined.'

They both look at the boat.

'We ain't insured for no boat,' says Frank.

'But …' I begin.

'Rules are rules you see.'

What rules are we talking about?

'Ealth and safety. If one of us gets injured … well,' says the other.

I'll injure them in a minute, insurance or no insurance. I clench my teeth and watch helplessly as they pocket my two hundred and fifty quid and stroll back along the boardwalk.

'You can't leave me,' I call, falling miserably onto one of the boxes only to jump up when I see something scuttle along the bank. Oh no, not a rat, what if it gets into one of the boxes. This is awful. My heart aches for Roddy and all I want to do is wallow in self-pity but if I don't do something about these boxes they'll be wallowing in rain. I grab a box and drag it towards the boat. Twenty minutes later and wisps of hair have escaped my neat bun and I've stripped down to my silk poncho and leggings. I exhale and grab another box when a large gust of wind blows up and I'm hula hooping my top around my neck. I'm going to be throttled by my Calvin Klein poncho, although on reflection it's not a bad way to go is it?

'Oh, look Sheridan. Isn't that quaint? Quick get a picture,' says a voice with an American accent.

I struggle to free myself from the poncho to see Sheridan snapping away with his shiny Nikon.

'Can you pose with Mildred?' he asks. 'You know to show the folks back home?'

Perhaps he'd like me to re-enact the *Titanic* sinking scene for the folks back home too. We could even make our own little home video.

'Sod off,' I say, dragging another box onto the boat.

'I heard they were rude,' grumbles Mildred.

Two hours later and I can't move on the boat for all the boxes. Come to think about it, I simply can't move. I can't lift another box if I tried and there are still three on the boardwalk. My poncho is all scrunched and my leggings are ripped. I pull my mobile out of my bag and attempt to search for another removal company except there is no signal. Oh, what? I climb back onto the deck and wave the phone around. Come on, come on, just one bar that's all I need. I lean over the boat and yes one bar, only to have it cut out.

'Bugger.'

I go to the other end of the deck and try there but still nothing. This is madness. Don't tell me I have to take the stupid boat for a sail every time I need to call someone. I go to the helm, lean over the boat and hang on for dear life. Yes, hurrah, three bars.

'Don't do it,' yells a voice.

I turn and feel myself wobble.

'What?'

I see the hottie smiling at me. This is great, just great. Why is it every time I encounter him I'm making a fool of myself?

'You let go, and I'm going to have to come in there after you.'

'I assure you I'm not going to jump,' I say, carefully putting one foot back onto the deck. 'And this isn't the movie set for the *Titanic*.'

Famous last words, for at that moment my foot gets tangled in a piece of rope and I go head over heels. I cling to the helm for all I'm worth. I bet I'm getting good signal now. My nose is almost touching the water.

'Help,' I shriek, feeling the phone slip from my fingers. Not again.

I feel the hottie's arms go around me, lifting me back onto the deck. I'm trembling so much that my muscles hurt.

'What were you saying?' he says grinning.

I could happily push him in.

'My phone,' I say breathlessly.

He hands me the iPhone.

'You dropped it on deck,' he says.

I take the phone off him while trying to avoid his eyes.

'That was your fault,' I say angrily.

'What did I do?'

'You distracted me.'

'Ah,' he says. 'Do you want these boxes on the boat?'

'I'm not staying here. It's barbaric living on a boat. I'm leaving.'

'Right,' he smiles. 'All the same, I'll put these in the boat shall I? They can't stay on the boardwalk, health and safety and all that.'

'Huh,' I scoff. 'If there were phone masts here we wouldn't have to worry about health and safety would we?'

'Where would you have them, bang slap in the middle of the Thames?' he asks.

I ignore him and walk to the hatch.

He picks up all three boxes and lifts them easily onto the boat.

'Anything else I can help you with?'

'No,' I say sharply, trying not to look at his rippling arm muscles.

'I'll be leaving in a bit,' I say determinedly.

He nods and wanders back to his boat.

I climb back into the warm and burst into tears. I stare at the hideous mess around me and pour a large glass of wine. I sip the wine and nibble a truffle. I can't stay here. How am I supposed to contact people without phone signal? How will I phone the Samaritans in my moment of desperation? Actually, this is my moment of desperation. See what I mean? Another glass of wine later and things are looking a little better. I still need to make it homely but Jeremy had made sure that it was clean although it's now cluttered with all the boxes and these are just my essentials. The coal bucket is full and I have kindling for the log burner. Jeremy had arranged a full gas bottle for the cooker and I'd been given the phone numbers of all the important boat people although how I'm supposed to phone them is beyond me. *I've got everything in hand* he'd said, *someone will come and sort the loo out when ness.*

Fortunately he hasn't mentioned the job thing again.

I peek into the loo and debate whether it is safe to have a pee. I can't hold it in forever can I? At that second there is a tap on the hatch.

'Harrods delivery,' calls a voice.

Oh goodie, my Harrods shop. Well let's face it, I'm not going to shop anywhere else am I? At least not while I have *some* money in the bank. I open the hatch and allow him in. Of course by the time he leaves the place is even more cluttered. By seven I'm knackered. I pour myself a third glass of wine and make a smoked salmon sandwich and play *All by Myself* on my iPhone. If Bridget Jones can survive then so can I. The next thing I know I'm clambering into the tiny bed and watching videos of me and Roddy on my phone while comforting myself with a box of dusted strawberry truffles. It takes me ages to get comfy in the little bed and forever to fall asleep but in what seems like no time at all I'm wide awake again. The room is brighter than the Blackpool illuminations and to top it all I've got Kings of Leon as an accompaniment. What the hell? I'm starting to feel like I'm on Blackpool pier. I pull the curtain back to see the light is coming from the hottie's boat. I fumble for my phone and check the time. God, what is he doing? It's one in the morning, doesn't the bugger sleep? I turn over and cover my eyes with my hand. It's just my luck to have a neighbour with insomnia. How can he be so inconsiderate to play music so late, and Kings of Leon at that? He knows there is a boat right next to him. I pull the covers over my head and try to think of other things, except all I can think of is my lovely penthouse flat in Belgravia and Roddy's warm arms around me. I'm starting to drift off again when the fragrant smell of curry reaches my nostrils. Oh what? Most people have a hot drink when they can't sleep, not a bloody hot meal. Why is this happening to me? I pull my silk kimono towards me and feel tears prick my eyelids. Roddy had bought me the kimono for Christmas last year and had dropped a pearl necklace into the pocket. Oh, Roddy, I miss you so much. My mind is pulled back to the present at the sound of the hottie's voice.

'Come on, there's a good girl, up you go.'

Oh no, he's brought a woman back. I'll hear them humping next. I peek nervously out of the window and see his boat rocking. God, they're at it already. How disgusting. I should have known. He looks the type, a girl in every port and all that. Don't you just hate that kind of guy? Well, this will soon stop. I don the kimono and wrap my fur around me before pushing my socked feet into my boots and grabbing my phone. After all I may have to call the police. Who knows what these boat people are capable of? I climb warily from the boat and gasp as the cold air hits me, almost knocking me back through the hatch. I slip and slide tipsily towards the hottie's. It sounds like he's having a party. I look around nervously and check there are no rats about. They come out at night don't they? Or is that just vampires? My phone bleeps as it gets signal and I strain to see the message. It's a text from my mother.

I'm at Raffles with Lady Haughton. We're tossing back cocks like there's no tomorrow.

How I'm not in therapy I'll never know. There's another bleep and I can barely look.

COCKTAILS, she corrects. Why don't you come over? Get some money from Jeremy.

The text was sent four hours ago, that's about right. I'll miss everything living on this boat. The end of the world will come and I'll only get the texts when I surface. I sigh and turn back to the hottie's boat. Something tugs at my kimono and I slap madly at my thigh.

'Oh God, get off me, get off me.'

My eyes vaguely make out the outline of a cat and I sigh with relief. I lean towards the hottie's boat and perch my hands on my hips.

'Hello, sorry to bother you but you're making quite a lot of noise,' I call.

Not to mention a lot of smell. The curry odour is stronger now and I feel my stomach rumble.

'Hello, 'I shout again.

I attempt to clamber aboard his boat but at that moment the cat decides to play with the tassel of my kimono and I lurch backwards landing with a thump onto my bum.

'Holy shit balls. I hope you're having the greatest sex of your life in there while your neighbour freezes to death?' I yell angrily.

What's happening to me? I never used to be like this. I need to get a self-help book. God knows I can't afford to see a shrink. I push the cat away and struggle to my feet.

'Need a hand there?'

I look up to see the hottie standing on the deck. He's wearing glasses and looks both studious and sexy. Even his voice is lovely. Not as cultured as Roddy but well-spoken nevertheless.

'It depends where it's been' I snap haughtily.

I push the annoying cat away and reach for his hand.

'I thought you'd left' he says, releasing my hand and pulling on a jumper.

'No,' I say sharply.

'Ah, so you are living on *Amelia* then?'

'I'm trying to,' I say haughtily.

'Sorry didn't mean to disturb you,' he smiles. 'There hasn't been anyone on *Amelia* in years and you did say you weren't staying.'

'That maybe so, but there is someone on *Amelia* now,' I say primly.

'Uppity aren't we?' he says squinting his eyes and meeting mine.

'Noisy aren't we?' I respond. 'If you could please turn the music down and lower the lights. They're shining right into my bedroom.'

'Yes ma'am.'

I ignore his sarcasm.

'And maybe you could cook something other than curry at one in the morning?'

'Right, any other orders? Because if there isn't anything else I'd like to finish having the greatest sex of my life,' he says with a wink.

I feel my face grow hot.

'Oh ...' I stammer. 'Yes right, of course.'

'Are you okay to get back?'

'Yes, of course, I'll just ...' I trail off and slide on the slippery boardwalk.

'Are you okay?' he says.

Yes, I'm fine … I'll leave you to …' I trip over the cat and curse. 'You just erm, yes, well goodnight.'

Oh God, this is awful.

'I'll keep the orgies down now I know you're next door,' he smiles.

I realise he is teasing me and could kick myself.

'Goodnight,' I say primly, tugging the kimono from the cat's paws for the final time.

'Off you go girl,' he says and I'm about to give him a sharp retort when I realise he is talking to the cat.

'Welcome to the canal by the way. We're a nice bunch when we're not disturbing the peace,' he says and I hear the smile in his voice.

I give a backward wave and climb back onto *Amelia*. Tucked in my bed a few minutes later I remember his warm hand in mine and feel a little tingle. The room turns suddenly dark and there is silence. Minutes later and I'm asleep.

Jack Diamond

Jack Diamond slices into his meatballs and sighs with satisfaction. You can't beat meatballs and pasta in his opinion. No fancy posh food matches up to the old meatballs and pasta in his favourite restaurant. He likes the respect he gets here. The Valentino suits help of course. They know a bit of class in this place. His mind turns to Roddy Tarleton and he smiles. He might be upper class but he hasn't got brains. Who bets on lame horses? The prick doesn't know a runner when he sees one. He's just about to tuck into his dessert when Mad Jack Junior bursts in, bumping into a waiter as he does so.

'Watch where yer going,' Jack Junior says loudly.

'What's the matter with you?' snaps Diamond. 'You're always giving me bleedin' indigestion.'

'Look I don't need to hear this crap,' retorts Mad Jack.

Jack Diamond chokes on a spoonful of tiramisu.

'What the ...?' splutters Diamond.

'I want some respect from you,' continues Mad Jack. 'I've taken enough crap these past few months and it's time you came up with the goods.'

Diamond can barely believe his ears and slams his hand down on the table.

'You cheeky little git. You'll get more than respect if you ...' Diamond stops on seeing the Bluetooth earpiece sticking out the side of his son's head. God, give him strength. Mad Jack fumbles with it for a moment before sitting down.

'Vodafone, I hate the bastards.'

'Say a command,' says a robotic voice.

Mad Jack pulls his BlackBerry from his pocket.

'Say a command,' the voice repeats.

'For Christ's sake, what's wrong with you?' Diamond sighs.

'Say a command.'

'Ello, ello,' yells Mad Jack into the Bluetooth angrily.

Diamond grabs the phone.

'Say a ...'

'Sod off, there's a bleedin' command for yer,' he says, turning off the phone and throwing it at Mad Jack. 'You're going to give me a bleedin' ulcer.'

Mad Jack whips the Bluetooth off.

'There's something missing with this,' he says.

'There's something missing in your 'ead all right,' says Diamond.

Mad Jack touches his head gingerly.

'I knew it,' he grumbles. 'They've fiddled me.'

Diamond scoffs. Mad Jack throws a crumpled magazine at him.

'Something fishy going on with Rodders too,' he says proudly. 'I've been looking into it. That's his bird. She looks different in real life though. She lives on a boat. It's really tiny as well. That's them on the piss.'

Diamond studies the photo of Pandora and Roddy on the ski slopes.

'Where's the bleedin' ring?' he asks.

'I dunno. I ain't seen no ring. On the boat I suppose,' he says fiddling with his Bluetooth.

Diamond wipes his mouth on a serviette.

'Right, let's go get our money,' he smiles. 'You lead the way and I don't wanna end up on bleedin' Southend pier.'

Chapter Nine

'Is it much further?' Chelsea asks.

'I can't remember,' I say honestly.

We'd been shopping in Regent Street and I'd bought new bed linen for the sardine bed in my sardine home, along with candle holders, vases, glasses, flowers and curtains. Chelsea had bought a floral tea set for me and now we're both desperate for a pee.

'I'm sure it wasn't this far,' Chelsea says worriedly, glancing behind.

'Why do you keep looking back?' I ask.

'I keep seeing this guy. Everywhere we go he seems to be there.'

'That will be the day when guys start following us,' I laugh.

Her perfume floats on the chilly air and I sniff it appreciatively.

'Are you really going out with Barmy Balls?' she asks, changing the subject.

I stop and pull on another pair of gloves.

'No, I'm not. We had one dinner together, that's all.'

'I couldn't bear it if you became Lady Balls.'

Nor could I. We pass a couple who are hanging festive lanterns on the outside of their boat and Chelsea stops to stroke their dog.

'Lovely day isn't it?' the woman says.

It's bollocking freezing. I wonder if these boat people feel the cold. They always seem to be outside.

'Yes lovely,' agrees Chelsea, who hasn't stopped moaning about the cold all morning.

'Settling in?' asks the man.

'Getting there,' I say, hurrying past.

'I wish you wouldn't talk to them,' I whisper to Chelsea.

'It's hard not to,' she says while waving to the man with the holey jumper.

'Hello,' he calls. 'Are you settling in okay? Holler if you need anything. I'm Jim by the way.'

I step around his cat as it rubs itself on my ankles.

'We will thank you. I'm Chelsea and this is Truffles.'

I huff and continue past.

'You shouldn't be so stand-offish,' she says.

It's easy for her to talk isn't it? She doesn't have to live here with the riff raff.

'Ooh look there's Camilla,' she squeals.

I feel a rush of warmth at the sight of her. This means they're back from Verbier.

'I've been dying to see you. It's a long walk isn't it? How do you cope?' she gushes. 'Which is your boat? Pandora said you're living in a septic tank these days. She's such a bitch. I hate her.'

'We seem to have forgotten where the septic tank is,' says Chelsea worriedly.

With friends like Chelsea who needs enemies?

'How does Pandora know where I'm living?' I say angrily.

'Everyone knows.' she says looking around. 'I'm not sure how.'

I'll kill Jeremy. I point ahead where my sardine tin is bopping on the water.

'Unfortunately it's still there,' I say.

Camilla spins round, whipping us with her Marc Jacob pashmina. I get a quick waft of Jo Malone Grapefruit before she is skipping along to the boat, her ash blonde hair swinging under her beret. She stops outside the hottie's boat and turns to wave to us.

'It's small but rather fab,' she calls.

'Oh dear,' says Chelsea.

We reach her as she is about to clamber on board.

'No, not this one,' I say and point to *Amelia*. 'That's it.'

'Oh Golly, you're living on *that*?' she gasps.

'Yes, she's living on *that*,' confirms Chelsea.

Honestly, Chelsea is the limit sometimes. I feel myself bristle.

'It's not that bad,' I say.

'Quite right,' says Chelsea.

'Yes, and it's not like it's forever. It's only until everything gets sorted and I get the money back,' I say confidently.

'Everyone was talking about it at Verbier. I can't believe you broke off the engagement Poppy,' says Camilla. 'Surely Roddy's money would have been the answer to all your problems.'

Yes, well one would have thought so.

'I didn't break it off,' I say. 'Is that what Roddy's telling everyone?'

'I suppose he's embarrassed. He's got no money either. His father is horrid sometimes,' says Camilla.

She hitches up her coat ready to board and looks around. If she's expecting a Jeeves to pop through the cubby hole, she'll still be here at Christmas.

'Don't you have staff?' she asks stupidly.

'Of course, I've got a whole other boat for them. What do you think Camilla? I've got no sodding money.'

'What happened to them?'

Never mind the staff, what about me. It comes to something when your friends are more worried about the staff than they are about you.

'I had to let them go. Don't worry I gave them excellent references.'

'It's simply staggering what's happened to you,' she says hugging me. 'I couldn't have coped. I'd have been whisked into The Priory.'

If only someone would whisk me into The Priory. I could do with free drugs and lots of sleep.

'Mind the penis hook,' says Chelsea.

'The what?' Camilla laughs.

We point to the hook.

'The cleat hook,' I say, sounding very boat knowledgeable.

We climb carefully onto the deck.

'She's going out with Barmy Balls,' confides Chelsea, dropping her voice to a whisper and mouthing Barmy Balls like it's some kind of filthy word. Although, I suppose it is. No one would openly admit to dating Barmy Balls. He really is the most boring person on earth and most certainly barmy.

'Barmy Balls? Oh my God, you're not,' says Camilla, looking horrified. 'Are things *that* bad?'

Yes they are actually, but I'm not, most certainly not going out with Barmy Balls.

'We had dinner once that's all.'

I so want to ask her if Roddy talked about me in Verbier but feel too scared. We stare at the river for a few seconds before Camilla says,

'I bought you some plonk and a box of Harrods truffles, the ones you like.'

She hands over the wine and truffles and I sigh with pleasure. There is a tinkle behind us and I turn to see a man on a bicycle, trailing gas cylinders in a little cart behind him. He's wearing a baseball cap and a coat that looks at least two sizes too big. His cheeks are rosy red and his eyes bright blue.

'Hello ladies, looking very lovely on this cold winter's day. Dusty at your disposal. Enjoying *Amelia* are you?'

We look at him. Camilla smiles nervously and Chelsea juggles her parcels.

'Right,' I say, 'I need a drink.'

He jumps from his cycle, bows gallantly and starts to recite a poem. It's all I can do to stop myself leaping into the river. What am I doing here? I'm rich, I'm very very rich. I should be having tea at Claridge's with my friends, not listening to some nutcase reciting poetry. And it's not exactly the best poetry either.

Anything dirty, dingy, looking a touch rusty
There's only one person to call and that's Dusty.
Need to warm up your ass
Dusty can get you the gas
No job too big or too small
Just give Dusty a call.

Chelsea stares open-mouthed and Camilla looks like she's just come face to face with an escaped mental hospital inmate.

'Crab apples,' mumbles Chelsea.

'Jesus,' exclaims Camilla. 'This is a real education.'

'I've never been credited with giving anyone an education,' says Dusty proudly.

'It's not exactly Keats is it?' I say.

'No, it's more Pam Ayres, I agree, but its novel ain't it?' he grins.

I wince at the word *ain't* and usher Camilla onto the boat.

'Thanks very much but I won't be needing your services today or come to that, any day.'

'Her man Jeremy takes care of everything,' snorts Camilla, handing him a ten pound note. 'Here's for your trouble. Now please be off.'

He raises his eyebrows.

'I didn't know you had a bloke,' he says climbing back onto his bike.

'Jeremy is not my ... bloke.'

God, I'm starting to talk like them now.

'Jeremy is staff,' says Chelsea.

'Ooh staff, that's new around here,' he laughs. 'Bunking it with the butler can't be bad.'

He ignores Camilla's ten pound note and turns his cycle around.

'Good luck to you,' he says and rides off.

'Let's have some wine,' says Camilla. 'I reckon you need it.'

We step carefully into the boat and Camilla squeals.

'Oh God, it's just too cute. Shame about the pong from the river, it smells like someone has dropped a beast.'

Chelsea unpacks my new glasses and we struggle not to bump into each other as we prepare the drinks. Camilla tries out my bed and squeals again.

'It's proper slumming isn't it? I say, where are you going to put your clothes and stuff?'

I open the shoebox of a cupboard that is called my wardrobe.

'Tra da,' I say without any trace of joy in my voice.

'Holy fuck.'

I couldn't have said it better myself. I down half a glass of wine while wondering how much longer I'll be able to enjoy the good things in life.

'I'm storing all my best things at Chelsea's,' I say.

'We all know where to go if we want to borrow them,' laughs Camilla.

'Shall we put the new bed linen on?' says Chelsea. 'There's no one else to do it is there?'

'No, I gave everyone the day off,' I quip.

How can I live without staff? It's totally ridiculous. I make a mental note to phone Jeremy. Surely there is enough for a cleaner at least. They can come in on a daily basis. The boat will need cleaning and there are my clothes to be laundered. I look around the boat despondently and back to my suitcases piled in a corner. Where am I going to put all my clothes? They'll be ruined if I leave them in the suitcase and God knows what's lurking in this cupboard. They'll be chewed by moths if they go in there. I'll be looking like the man in the holey jumper before the week is out.

'Marcus said he might mosey down later. We can have a party,' Camilla says clinking her glass against mine. 'A boat-warming party,' she adds.

I look at her hopefully.

'Is Roddy coming?'

She avoids my eyes.

'I think he is driving down to his parents with Pandora. Its pheasant season, but you know that.'

'I'd forgotten,' I mumble.

Camilla sits cross-legged on the floor and rummages through her shopping bag.

'Charvet dress shirt, isn't it delicious?' she says holding it up. 'Daddy's Christmas present, I can't wait. We're going to Vienna. It's going to be fabulous. Hugo's coming too,' she says dreamily.

'Super,' says Chelsea.

I polish off my glass of wine and pour more. We still have our coats on. I swear it's colder in the boat than it is outside.

'Shall I text Marcus and get him to bring some food,' says Camilla, rummaging through her Dolce and Gabbana bag.

'You'll need to go up on deck to get signal,' I groan.

'I've got four bars,' says Camilla.

Great it's just my phone that's useless.

'It's a bit cold Poppy,' says Chelsea studying the wood burner. 'Do you know how to use this?'

'You just put burnable stuff in it don't you,' says Camilla, tapping into her phone.

Chelsea hunches down by the log burner and fills it with kindling wood while the wind howls outside.

'Okay girls, are you ready? I'll show you these before the guys come and then I'll tell you about my little surprise,' she says, her voice quivering with excitement.

Chelsea and I exchange glances. Camilla's surprises have always managed to get us into some kind of bother. Chelsea gasps and I stare in fascination at the leather wrist cuffs that Camilla pulls from a carrier bag like a magician with his hat.

'Ooh,' I say.

'And ...' she makes the sound of a drum roll and produces ankle cuffs and a riding crop.

'Frogs' knickers,' utters Chelsea.

'No, I haven't got any of those,' laughs Camilla, 'but we can get some really sexy undies when we go.'

'Go where?' I ask.

'Coco de Mer,' she whispers excitedly.

Oh no, not the sex shop.

'I didn't know Hugo was into that kind of thing,' I say.

'He isn't yet,' laughs Camilla. 'I've booked us girls on a course, it's on me. I thought we'd have a girls' night out.'

'Fudge berries,' says Chelsea nervously, taking a sip from her glass.

'They have a spanking skills salon with Miss Tits and Tease.'

Chelsea chokes on her wine.

'Cripes,' she says hoarsely.

'Most girls' nights out are dinner and a club,' I point out.

'We're not like most girls are we?'

'I am,' says Chelsea.

Camilla pulls out some leaflets. Chelsea stares wide-eyed at a half-naked woman who is getting the spanking of her life and enjoying it by the look on her face.

'Fudge berries,' groans Chelsea in a lower tone. I am sure Chelsea could construct an entire language by saying *fudge berries* in a multitude of different ways.

'Focusing on decadent kink and spanking, this salon will teach you the history behind the art, how pain can translate to pleasure, and how to safely invigorate your bedroom play. You will discover various positions, how and why controlling the speed and force is important, and how not to spank. Be prepared to leave your inhibitions at home ...' reads Camilla.

'Decadent kink?' I query. I pick up the riding crop and fiddle with it. Roddy always wanted me to spank him. I just didn't like pretending to be his nanny and spanking him for being a bad boy. I never got it right either. He always complained I either didn't spank him hard enough, *You need to be firmer with the discipline,* or spanked too hard, *I like it when you're in control Pops, but not too much,* he'd moan. There's no pleasing men is there? Maybe the workshop would be a good way to brush up my skills, well not brush up exactly. It's not like I'm a professional at bondage is it, but you get my drift. I wonder if he's got Pug-face spanking him? No, Pug-face hasn't got a kinky bone in her body. Yes, this is the way to win Roddy back. I'll be the perfect dominatrix.

'I really don't think there is any point. I don't have anyone to spank,' says Chelsea lowering her eyes.

'Who do we spank at the workshop?' I ask.

'Each other I suppose,' says Camilla thoughtfully.

'Oh dear,' mumbles Chelsea.

There is a tap at the door. Not that you can actually call it a door, it's more of a hatch with steps. Camilla throws the riding crop and cuffs back into the bag. I pull open the hatch and come face to face with a bright cheery woman with bits of red hair sprouting under her woolly hat.

'Hiya,' she says, jangling an assortment of cheap bangles as she hands me a bunch of flowers. 'I'm Ruby. I just popped by to say hi.'

I force a smile.

'I brought you these. It's just to say welcome to the boat club. They're only carnations but it brightens up the place don't it?'

Her South London accent is already grating on me.

'That's very kind of you, thank you very much.'

'Dusty said you was a bit posh,' she says with a smile.

I'd like to think I still am.

'Right yes, anyway, must scoot.'

She pokes her head in a bit more and I see she is wearing long dangling earrings.

'Yeah, of course, it's nippy with the hatch open. If you need anything, anything at all, I'm in *Honeybee,* just a few boats upstream. If you want me to do the walk of shame with you the first time just say, you know, it's not a problem.'

The walk of shame? How dare she? I don't know what kind of shame walk she does but I'm a whole other world away. I don't do walks of shame. Honestly, what a dreadful woman, even mentioning such a thing. I'm not in the least ashamed, why should I be? Daddy didn't do it, I feel quite sure. How dare she insinuate such a thing? What kind of people are they around here, doing walks of shame? Well, they're not pulling me into their stupid club. After all, I won't be here that long.

'I'm not in the least ashamed. Now, if you'll excuse me I have company.'

I slam the hatch angrily.

'Marcus is bringing an Indian,' says Chelsea, throwing coal into the wood burner.

'Food that is,' laughs Camilla. 'I say Poppy I just used your loo. What an experience. Do you have to empty it?'

'Someone does that,' I say vaguely.

'How bloody quaint this all is. I can't wait for Hugo to see it. He's coming with Marcus, that's okay isn't it? They're all keen to see what your boat is like.'

Oh yes, very okay. It feels just like old times, apart from the frightful boat of course. If only Roddy were coming. I flop onto the bench that passes as a couch. The barge lurches to the side as a tug boat passes on the river and we all slide to the left. Chelsea catches her glass in the nick of time.

'I'll throw some more coal on shall I?' asks Camilla.

By the time Marcus arrives with Hugo and Sophie the boat is as warm as toast. Sophie clambers on board and looks around in astonishment.

'How the devil do you cope?' she asks, accepting a glass of wine from Camilla.

'It won't be forever,' says Chelsea, 'I think it is fab.'

'It's a humongous change,' says Marcus, checking his reflection in the tiny mirror. He straightens his navy velvet suit and fingers his moustache.

'Well, what do you think of the new Marcus Bellamy?'

I don't like to say it looks exactly like the old Marcus Bellamy.

'Very nice,' I nod. 'The tash suits you.'

'Pandora's idea, she said it would dignify me.'

I try not to pull a face. I suppose Roddy will have a beard the next time I see him.

'This boat is dinky isn't it?' giggles Camilla.

'Better not pop some champers,' laughs Marcus. 'Don't want the cork ricocheting off the walls.'

'I'll open it outside,' says Hugo, clumsily climbing through the hatch while Camilla and Sophie fall about giggling.

Sophie throws herself onto the bed. The boat rocks as Hugo fumbles about on the deck.

'Hell's bells,' cries Sophie. 'Everyone will know when you're having nookie on this.'

I can't help wondering who Sophie thinks I'm going to be having nookie with.

'Roddy would roar if he could see us,' says Hugo as he descends the steps from the hatch.

'Do you think?' I ask hopefully,

'Why are you still wearing your engagement ring?' Camilla asks, handing me a plate.

'I'll pop more coal in this thing shall I?' ask Hugo.

'Well ...' I begin, but he is chucking in coal like it's going out of fashion.

'She's still engaged,' says Chelsea, rescuing a vase as it slides from the shelf. 'They've only put it on hold until things get sorted.'

There is silence apart from the clattering of plates as Marcus piles rice and chicken balti onto them.

'Right,' says Hugo. 'It's just we thought ...'

'You thought what?' I ask, feeling my breath catch in my throat.

'Well, we just thought with Pandora spending Christmas at Dunbarton Hall that ...'

'What?' I squeal. I leap up and send the boat rocking. 'She's spending Christmas with Roddy's parents?'

'Have another glass of Moet darling,' says Marcus. 'It's jolly good.'

'Don't you have music?' asks Hugo.

Never mind music. I need to hear more about Pandora. I don't believe this. *I was* spending Christmas with him at Dunbarton Hall.

'Are you absolutely sure about that?' I ask.

'Abslootly,' says Sophie. 'It was all Pandora talked about.'

I could cry. Things couldn't get any worse could they?

'Hello Pops, are you in residence?' bellows a voice.

Then again maybe it can.

'Balls,' says Chelsea with a groan.

Jack Diamond

'It's a bleedin' long ball and chalk,' says Jack Diamond.

Mad Jack Junior feels ill. The last time he felt this rough was after eating some dodgy jellied eels. He hasn't had the pleasure of eating anything this time which just makes it worse.

'I'm bleedin' seasick,' he groans. 'Mum always said I was bad on boats.'

'You're not on a bleedin' boat yet, you pilchard.'

'Do we 'ave to do this? I can't feel me toes, it's so cold.'

'If you don't shut it, you won't feel your ears either. Yes, we gotta do this. I want that ring. I don't trust Rodders.'

'I don't think I can get on the boat,' whines Mad Jack.

'Don't be bloody stupid. It'll be a piece of piss. I can't believe you came from my loins sometimes, I really can't.'

'I 'ate boats. It ain't natural living on water,' complains Mad Jack.

'Jesus Christ,' mumbles Diamond. 'You're a bloody girl's blouse that's what you are.'

'That looks like it,' Mad Jack says as he points to the boat with the lanterns.

'Looks like it?' repeats Diamond. 'Don't you bleedin' know?'

'It all looks different in the dark,' he replies, kicking a cat.

Diamond carefully clambers onto the boat and waits for his son who gingerly follows. The boat rocks and Mad Jack falls to his knees and crawls along the deck nervously.

'Jesus Christ,' mutters Diamond. 'What the fuck yer doing on yer knees?'

Below deck is in darkness and Diamond shines a torch through a window.

'This can't be it,' he says looking around the room. 'It's all blokes' stuff in there, and the toilet seat's been left up.'

He swipes his hand around Mad Jack's head.

'Can't yer get anything right, you dipstick?'

'What did yer do that for? I'm dizzy now and I feel sick.'

There's loud laughing and shouting from the boat next door.

'Keep your voices down. We don't want Poppy thrown off the boat in her first week,' someone says.

'It must be that boat,' whispers Mad Jack. 'She's been on it a week.'

'I thought 'er name was Pandora.'

'Poppy must be her nickname,' says Mad Jack thoughtfully.

Once the noise has died down, Diamond climbs off the boat pulling Mad Jack after him.

'See if the door is unlocked on that one,' he says pointing to *Amelia*.

He leans against the mooring post while Mad Jack gently tries the hatch door.

'It's locked,' he says miserably, tripping over the mooring rope as he gets off the deck.

'Girl's blouse,' says Diamond, marching off.

'Wait for me,' cries Mad Jack. He'll do for that pilchard Roddy Tarleton for putting him through this.

Chapter Ten

It's not until one in the morning that the boat-warming party comes to an end and my guests stumble off *Amelia*. I only wish I could stumble off with them.

'It's been fun hasn't it?' laughs Camilla.

'Balls, don't touch that doobry,' slurs Marcus.

'Yes mind the penis hook,' giggles Camilla.

'What?' yells Hugo. 'He's not banging his bishop on the boat is he?'

Marcus roars with laughter.

'Keep your voices down,' hisses Sophie. 'We don't want Poppy thrown off the boat in her first week.'

Oh I don't mind. As long as they throw me off the deep end and it's over quickly. How dare Roddy invite Pug-face Pandora to Dunbarton Hall for Christmas?

'Fanbloodytastic evening, Pops,' bellows Balls.

'Mind the doobry,' hiccups Marcus.

Chelsea plonks her warm lips onto my cheek.

'Thanks so much Truffles. It's been a hoot.'

I shiver as the wind cuts through me.

'Yes yes, jolly good,' says Balls, pulling me into a bear hug and squeezing my buttocks. I so wish they could stay. I'm already feeling lonely. The lanterns from the boat next door swing in the wind and make the mooring look rather spooky.

'I'll be in touch and we'll have a spanking good time in a few weeks,' laughs Camilla.

Balls lurches towards me again and pulls me into an embrace.

'Shall I stay Pops, keep the wolves from the door, what?'

Chelsea rolls her eyes.

'Terribly sweet of you Balls but I'll be fine.'

Although I have to admit even Balls' company feels preferable to being alone on the boat again.

The boat rocks as they climb off. I wave as they stroll along the walkway. Finally they disappear into the darkness and I clamber back into the boat, locking the hatch behind me. I shiver and warm my hands in front of the log burner. The place is one big muddle and I sigh. I shove the glasses into the tiny sink and pull my phone from my handbag. I text Jeremy, knowing full well he won't get the message until the morning.

This isn't working Jeremy and Daddy would be appalled if he knew. You need to find me somewhere else ASAP. If you can't, then I'll have to hire someone who can. I'm sure Daddy, who is paying your salary, would be livid if he knew.

I click send and sigh with satisfaction. I tidy up some of the mess and then use the atrocious loo which smells disgusting. How can that be? Am I supposed to put something down it? For God's sake, someone of my class shouldn't be doing this. My father is a *Sir* for goodness' sake. As I fall onto the bed I spot Camilla's Coco de Mer carrier bag. I pull on my nightie and slip between the covers hugging the riding crop. Please God, make Roddy phone me. I'll work really hard at being the best dominatrix ever. Please let me have money again, I can't be poor. I'll end up going insane. The boat rocks gently and I feel my eyelids grow heavy.

I wake with a jolt and pull my feet under the duvet. God, it's freezing. My nose feels like an icicle. I check the phone and see it is 3 am. Why is it so cold? I pull the duvet up to my chin and struggle to get warm. The boat is rocking. The wind must have come up. There is a thump and I jump out of my skin. Oh God, someone is on the boat. I'm shaking but I can't tell if it is from the cold or fear. I'm going to be murdered on my second night. I strain to hear but all is silent now. I throw the duvet off as quietly as I can and peek into the living area. There's nobody there. I sigh and look at the wood burner and the empty coal bucket sitting next to it. Shit, they used all the coal, and now the loo stinks more than ever. I'm going to bloody murder Jeremy, that's if I don't die from hypothermia first. The boat rocks and there's another thump. Honestly, how can anyone get any peace with this going on? I bet it's the hottie again. Doesn't the guy ever sleep? I pull back the curtains and peek out of the window. It's so dark I can barely see a thing but I can make out the hottie's lanterns swinging in the wind. They look so much further away tonight. I look again and feel my heart flutter. Hang on, this can't be right. I'm sure his boat was on the left side. Why are they now on the right? Has the hottie moved his boat? What's he playing at doing that in the early hours? I wrap my fur around me grasp a torch and step outside. The icy air hits me and then I see exactly where the other boat with its swinging lanterns is. Oh buggery bollocks. I'm the one that has bloody moved. I've only gone and drifted off.

Taylor

He nurses a whisky, turns on some music and glances at the Christmas card again. His mind unwillingly travels back to a year ago, to the worst moment of his life. Funny it should be snowing tonight exactly the way it was then. That night he'd walked into his flat to find Simon and Lisa humping away to Elton John's *Bennie and the Jets*. Simon's bum was wobbling like jelly and he couldn't help but notice the tattoo on his right cheek which said *Mum*. Somehow that just made things worse. The remains of a Kentucky Fried Chicken bucket sat by the bed and in that moment he saw red. Simon's head turned and his eyes widened before Taylor's fist connected with his chin, sending him sprawling off Lisa. She screamed and pulled the duvet over her naked body.

'What are you doing here?' she shouted. 'I thought you weren't getting back until the morning.'

'That's clearly obvious.'

Simon had attempted to stand just as Elton John began to sing *I'm still standing* and Taylor shoved him back. Simon of all people, hadn't Lisa always said what a wanker he was?

'I'm back now aren't I?' he'd said caustically, throwing Simon's clothes at him.

Simon tried again to get to his feet and Taylor had stepped towards him menacingly.

'Leave him alone,' Lisa screamed. 'He won't hit back. He's more a man than you are.'

A wobbly arse and a *mum* tattoo? He doubted that made him a man somehow, but was in no mood to argue with her.

'I love her,' Simon said shakily.

Taylor rolled his eyes.

'How long has this Elton John, Kentucky Fried Chicken love fest been going on for?' he asked.

'Long enough,' Lisa said, wrapping herself in a robe. 'You're never here. You're always working.'

'Why didn't you talk to me if it was a problem?'

'Huh,' she spat. 'I mean, when do we ever have Kentucky Fried Chicken?'

Simon was struggling into his trousers without taking his eyes off Taylor.

'It's over,' Lisa said miserably. 'You're too busy being the best at what you do.'

'Looks like you've been busy doing that too,' he retorted.

Her face turned red and she grabbed the Kentucky bucket and threw it at him.

'I want a divorce,' she said.

'My pleasure.'

He'd given Simon one last stare before storming from the flat for the final time.

He pulls his mind from the past and picks up the Christmas card and reads the flowery writing inside. *Happy Christmas Taylor, been thinking of you lately. Much love Lisa x.*

He removes his glasses and rubs his tired eyes. Heavy snowflakes streak past his window and he looks as some collect on the edge of the frame. It is then he sees something flashing in the distance. He shakes his head and climbs onto the deck where he sees *Amelia* is no longer moored alongside him. That spoilt rich girl is going to be trouble, he sighs as her panicky cries echo around the canal. He unties his boat from its mooring, starts the engine and sets out to rescue her.

Chapter Eleven

'Shit, oh bollocking shit.' I groan, feeling my body tremble.

How did the rope get unhooked? It must have been that Barmy Balls. I peer over the side and see I'm bumping against a bank. God, I could drift off into oblivion. I'll simply disappear. I'll be shipwrecked. I can almost hear James Horner's haunting *Titanic* music playing in the background. I must not panic. I slam the hatch shut and step back to the bedroom. I have no bars on my mobile so can't even call for help. I'm going to drift out into oblivion. Oh my God, what if water comes into the boat. I'll probably capsize and that will be the end of me. Daddy will be beside himself. Why didn't someone teach me Morse code? Stupid finishing school, it didn't teach me anything useful. I could at least have been taught the right bollocking etiquette for how to behave in a sinking narrowboat. If I don't capsize I'll most likely freeze to death. Panic rises up in me. I must keep calm. No need to panic. Take deep breaths. I slide my arms into the sleeve of the fur and button it up before tying a white pillowcase to one end of the riding crop. I then open the hatch and attempt to climb onto the deck but the wind blows the hatch back at me. I grab it quickly and feel my nail snap.

Oh no, not my nail. I so hate this bollocking boat. I look down at the nail miserably to see the gel has also chipped on two others. Oh, this is just terrible. I'm going to the dogs. Soon my own mother will disown me. I'll be an embarrassment.

I lift the riding crop and wave like a loony while screaming at the top of my lungs.

'Help, help, I've drifted off. Someone help me please.'

My shouts echo around the canal and the boat rocks with my movements. Maybe I should offer a reward. I try to think how much would be acceptable. Then I work out how much I can afford. God, I so hate being poor.

'Help, please help,' I cry in panic. 'I'll pay a reward, please rescue me. My daddy is a Sir.'

I should have flares. Just wait till I see 'I've got everything in hand' Jeremy.

I see a movement by the boat with the lanterns. There is a flash of light and I think I hear someone call. If only I had a whistle like Kate Winslet in the *Titanic*.

'Hello, is there anyone out there?' I shout.

The lanterns on the boat seem to be moving and I realise the boat itself is coming towards me. Oh thank God.

'Hello,' I yell waving the riding crop. 'Can you hear me?'

'I think the whole canal can hear you,' someone calls back. 'What are you doing out here?'

Well I'm not taking the air am I? What a stupid question.

'I think the mooring rope came off the penis hook,' I call back, without thinking.

'You need pulling?' he shouts.

Not that again.

'Yes, this time I most certainly do.'

I can just make out the hottie now. He's wearing an oilskin jacket and his hair is windswept. I watch as he steers his boat close to mine. He then leaps on board. Soft blues music reaches my ears and I realise it is coming from his boat. He turns and looks at me.

'I seem to be forever pulling you,' he says his blue eyes looking directly into mine. I pat at my windswept hair. I must look like a scarecrow.

'Please don't flatter yourself,' I retort.

'You should check your mooring regularly,' he says brusquely. 'I did tell you to get that hitch cleat fixed.'

'I had people over and they must have touched it without realising.'

He looks at the riding crop and I blush.

'A friend left it,' I say and then realise how wrong that sounds. I feel myself come over all hot.

'Really? Interesting friends you have,' he says, glancing down at my nightie.

I pull the fur around me and feel my nipples harden. It's the cold, I tell myself.

'Can you please tow me back? I'll make it worth your while.'

Oh no, did I really say that? He raises his eyebrows.

'I'm not into bondage,' he smiles. 'But thanks all the same.'

I blush even more and am grateful it is too dark for him to notice.

'I didn't, I meant ...' I stammer.

Oh God, how embarrassing. He grins and ties a rope onto my boat.

'I'll need you to steer. Preferably back to the bank. Can you manage that?'

How dare he? Of course I can manage it.

'I'm not silly, I do know how to helm a yacht,' I snap.

'Yes right,' he mumbles.

'This is the rudder,' he says, placing my hand on it and giving me a wink. 'Just shout if you're not sure what to do.'

He stands close and I can smell the fresh fragrance of him. He smells clean and manly. His hand brushes my hip as he moves past and I feel that weird sensation again.

'I've handled many a rudder,' I say looking down at it.

'I'm sure you have,' he retorts.

What does that mean?

'Okay, are you ready?' he asks.

More than I've ever been in my life. How can this stranger have such a powerful effect on me? He gives the rope one last tug and leaps back into his boat. I glimpse through his windows and see his cosy living area and feel envious. He starts his boat and within seconds I am chugging along behind him. I could cry with relief. Tomorrow I'll phone Jeremy. I'm not putting up with this. My hands are blue with cold and I'm shivering for England by the time we reach the bank, and it is all I can do to pull my freezing hands off the rudder. He ties me to the mooring. The boat that is, not me. This bondage thing has gone to my head.

'Th ... tha ...' I begin, but my teeth are chattering so much I can't get the words out.

'You need a brandy. Come on,' he says, holding out his hand. I take it gratefully and clamber from the boat. He helps me onto his and I climb carefully inside. Music is playing and there is a roaring log burner. I feel myself thaw and gratefully sit on one of his couches. It's a far bigger boat than mine and I try not to feel too envious.

'Brandy, or do you prefer something else?'

'Brandy is great.'

He hands me a glass and I throw it back feeling the warmth of the liquid run down my throat and into my stomach. I glance at a clock on a side table and see it is almost 4 am.

'Thank you so much for helping me,' I say, standing up.

'It was just lucky that I arrived home when I did,' he smiles.

I see a full basket of wood and look at it longingly.

'You couldn't spare me some of your wood could you? I'll pay for it,' I say hopefully.

He opens a cupboard and pulls out a bundle of logs.

'Dusty sells them. He's a handy guy to have around. I hear you weren't very impressed with his poetry.'

For God's sake, am I getting told off for not befriending the staff now? That's a first. I take the logs and turn to the door.

'I'm really too busy to listen to a bad rendition of Pam Ayres,' I say.

'His poetry is original actually. Writes it himself,' he says quietly.

'I could tell.'

'The boat people are extremely helpful. Ruby in particular and …'

I sigh heavily.

'I suppose you're going to tell me off for not doing the stupid walk of shame. I'm from a good background and …'

'We're not good enough for you?'

He said it didn't he? I push open the hatch and climb the steps.

'Thank you very much. Goodnight.'

Before I know it he has jumped off his boat and onto the walkway. He offers his hand and I know I have to take it if I'm not going to break my neck climbing off his boat as the deck is slippery with fresh snow. He walks behind me and then offers to help me onto *Amelia* before throwing the logs onto the deck.

'I've got no idea what you do,' he says, turning his back to me. 'But if you insist on entertaining men on your boat late at night, at least make sure the mooring is tied. Just think of it as part of the bondage games you play.'

I watch open-mouthed as he walks back to his boat. By the time I find my voice he has disappeared through the hatch. How dare he insinuate I'm a prostitute? I throw a log into the wood burner and watch it smoulder on the hot embers and then climb back into the bed still wearing my fake fur and fall asleep immediately. I dream of Roddy and it is oh so lovely.

Chapter Twelve

I stare at the loo and feel tears prick my eyelids. It was in full swing last night with everyone using it and it is now overflowing. I have no idea when the domestic will come to empty it and Jeremy still hasn't texted so I'll have to humiliate myself, yet again, and ask the pain in the arse next door. I curse as I kick the boxes out of my way. A tinkle of bells from outside distracts me and I pop my head through the hatch. A man roasting chestnuts over a brazier stands on the towpath.

'Lovely chestnuts?' he calls.

'You don't know when they come to do the loos around here, do you?' I ask.

'Do what?' he grins, showing two crooked teeth.

'When do they come to do the loos?'

I really can't be any clearer can I? He shrugs and rings his little bell again. I pull on my jeans, wrap myself in two jumpers and head out into the cold. Why did Daddy get done for fraud in the winter? I clamber from *Amelia*. The curtains in the hottie's boat are drawn and there is no sign of life. He must do night work, some kind of security guard no doubt. He looks the type with those rippling biceps and firm thigh muscles, not that I would normally notice you understand. It was just difficult to avoid looking at them yesterday. I trudge back to *Amelia* and spend the next hour going through my organiser. I delete the spa weekend and the committee meetings for Help the War Victims. I depressingly delete my hairdressing appointment. I'm so overdue a blow dry and I badly need waxing. My underarms are that bad I'll need to take a chainsaw to them. My phone rings and I grab it, only to have the thing die as the signal drops out. I so hate this boat. I clamber on deck and wave the phone about. Honestly, you have to be dangling over the Thames to make a call. It rings again. I rush to the helm and lean over the edge.

'It's me,' says my mother. 'How are you finding the boat? Everything ship-shape?'

Ooh listen to my mother getting into the boat lingo. I'm not going to tell her I drifted off am I? Put yourself in my Jimmy Choos. She'll never let me forget it if I do.

'Of course it is,' I yell. 'Everything is fine.'

A gust of wind rocks the boat and I struggle to hang on.

'Are you still there?' I shout.

'Why are you shouting?'

'Because I'm hanging off the end of the boat and it's blowing a gale out here.'

'Hanging off the boat, good Lord what on earth for?'

Honestly the questions some people ask.

'It's good for my core muscles.'

'Good God Poppy, you're surely not doing your *I'm the King of the World Titanic* impression? That's all very well on your father's yacht but not the thing on a little poxy barge. You might fall in.'

'Of course not. There's no phone signal in the boat. You practically have to throw yourself over to get two bars.'

A dog swims by and I stare at it open-mouthed.

'Why didn't you come to *Raffles* the other night?'

'I didn't get the text until the middle of the night. By the way, you really should check your texts before you send them. It's really not good for my blood pressure to read that my mother is throwing back cocks like no tomorrow. If I hadn't seen your second one I wouldn't have slept a wink.'

'You're far too sensitive. I only wish I had been throwing back cocks like no tomorrow.'

I blame the menopause.

'Did Jeremy tell you that I'm off to Long Island? Of course your father's gone to the Bahamas. Crime pays if you ask me. So what are you doing today?'

'After my Kate Winslet impression, I thought I'd sell some drugs. There's money in that I hear. Or maybe prostitute myself. After all, my neighbour already thinks I am one, some kind of bondage expert no less.'

'Your neighbour is a bondage expert?'

'No, he thinks I am.'

'Good God, why would he think that?'

'The last time he saw me I was waving a riding crop,' I shout as a passing barge chugs by.

'This just gets worse Poppy. Why in God's name were you waving a riding crop?'

'It's a long story.'

'That's not the way to get a husband you know. Is he that good-looking one?'

'That's a matter of opinion,' I say scathingly.

'Don't you have a charity to attend to? Or a lunch date?'

'No. Everyone has cancelled me out. I can't even get a hair appointment.'

'That's no good. I'll phone Dudley. He highlights wonderfully and gives a fab blow job.'

'Blow dry,' I correct.

'You call it what you like. All I know is he's hung like a horse. Makes all the difference darling. I'll call you back.'

I step back into the boat and open the teeny fridge and find two bottles of wine left over from last night. What a bonus. I turn the squeaky bath tap and let the tub fill with water while I search through my wardrobe. It's full of shoes and handbags and, oh God, what's that. There's a black thing in the corner. Oh shit, shit. What kind of creepy crawlies do you get on boats? Why didn't Jeremy warn me? I'll never get any sleep tonight with that thing on the boat. A little eye seems to glint at me and I slam the door shut. What if it is a rat? God, a rat in my bedroom. I shudder and turn the lock on the door. Best to keep these things confined. I turn the squeaky bath tap off and test the water. Oh no, the water's cold. Please don't tell me there is no hot water. What is wrong with Jeremy putting me on this stupid, only fit for a midget, boat? And then the tears come. It's not just a little shower either. It's a full blown downpour. I have no food, no money, no events to attend, no lunches to rush to. Not even coffee with a friend. The love of my life has decided I'm not even good enough to be put on hold. Even love has cancelled me and to top it all my nails are a disgrace. It can't get any worse can it? Life as I once knew it is well and truly over. I pull my engagement ring off my finger angrily. My new neighbour thinks I'm a prostitute and the boat people think I should do a walk of shame. Maybe they're not wrong. I drop the ring into a pot and pull a tissue from my Hermes; I exhale and pull myself up in time to see the hottie walking past. My head is now throbbing. That will teach me to cry with self-pity. I check my reflection and groan. I'm one big blotchy mess. I don my sunglasses, grab my phone and pull open the hatch.

'Hello, excuse me.'

He turns to look at me.

'Could you tell me when they come to empty the, the ...' I hesitate and curse myself. I've never had to ask anyone about emptying a loo before. 'The bog,' I say, finally.

He fiddles with my mooring rope on the penis hook.

'Hang on a sec. I just want to make this more secure. I can't spend my nights pulling you,' he smiles.

'It's just I think they may have forgotten me,' I say worriedly.

'They?' he repeats.

He may be handsome and all that but he's clearly as thick as two planks.

'Yes, when do they empty the bogs?'

'Do you want me to do the walk of shame with you?'

Oh for Christ's sake. What is it with these people? What makes them so arrogant to think they are better than me? What happened to the concept of innocent until proven guilty?

'What is it with you boat people and the walk of shame? I'm not ashamed. I've done nothing to be ashamed of and neither has Daddy.'

He looks at me oddly.

'I'm not sure what your father has got to do with it,' he smiles. 'You asked me about emptying the loo.'

'Yes, when do they come? I can't have a stinking loo for the next week. How often do they come? Do I need to phone them?'

He shrugs.

'I've no idea who *they* are.'

I struggle to keep my temper.

'But,' he says, leaping onto the boat, making me step back. 'This is your spare loo cassette. Do you want me to change it over for you?' He takes something from the roof of the boat.

'Oh,' I say.

'We've not properly introduced ourselves have we? I'm Taylor Havers,' he says, stepping closer. 'Do you normally wear sunglasses in the winter?'

I pull them off.

'I have a headache.'

'Ouch, you do look rough.'

He certainly knows how to compliment a woman doesn't he? He clambers into my cabin. He might wait until he is invited. I follow him in and he clicks a switch above the sink.

'That will give you hot water. Hasn't Jed showed you around?' He asks, pushing past me to check the log burner.

'Well ...' I begin.

'You need to keep this cleaned out if you want to get the benefit. This weather you'll need it. I'd invest in a hot water bottle unless you've got another body to keep you warm.'

He looks into my eyes and I find myself thinking how his lovely hot body would do and blush.

'No ... that is ... I don't and ... I'll get a bottle.'

'I may have a spare.'

Is that his way of telling me that he doesn't have another body keeping him warm? Or is it spare because he does have somebody?

'You'll need a wheelbarrow,' he says, his back to me as he fiddles in the loo.

'A wheelbarrow?' I say stupidly, moving closer to see what he is doing. 'How large is your hot water bottle?'

He grins and gives a sly wink before standing up abruptly. I step back. He's holding what I presume is a full cassette and I frown.

'Wise move. You certainly don't want this over you.'

I grimace.

'Did I miss your name?' he asks, climbing back onto the deck.

I follow him cautiously.

'No, I never said it, but it's Poppy.'

He jumps off the boat and washes his hands under a tap on the walkway.

'Right, I'll drop the hot water bottle in to you later, Poppy. Do you want to borrow a wheelbarrow until you get your own?'

I shrug.

'That's very nice of you but I'm not sure I actually need a wheelbarrow.'

It's not like I'll be taking on an allotment in the near future is it?

'For the walk of shame, it's a long way.'

Not that again, and what the hell has a wheelbarrow got to do with anything?

'I won't be doing your stupid walk of shame so you may as well stop pushing it. I'm not in the least ashamed and ...'

'This is your walk of shame,' he says, holding up the full cassette. 'You have to empty it. No one else will do it.' He places it on the roof of the boat.

He is surely not serious.

'I can't ...' I stammer.

'I'm afraid you have to,' he smiles. 'It's either that or stop going. It can be quite heavy and the walk to where you empty it is a fair trip and ...'

'Oh please,' I say covering my ears. 'Surely there is someone who will do it if I pay them.'

'Used to paying people to do things are you?' he says.

'Actually yes, I am,' I say haughtily.

He nods.

'Well it's not my business. Like I said, I'll drop the hot water bottle in and if you want a wheelbarrow I can get you one and if you need someone to show you where to go, I'm happy to do the walk of shame with you the first time. I think Ruby offered too. Just let us know. By the way, we all meet for a drink at the local every Friday. The pub is opposite the entrance to Regent's Canal. Tomorrow at nine, if you want to pop along.'

'I feel sure I'm busy,' I say.

'Of course,' he smiles, looking at my neck. 'Have you got anything for that rash?'

I shake my head and pull my jumper up a bit higher.

'It's nothing,' I say.

'I've got stuff. I'm sure something will help.'

Stuff, oh my God, he's not a drug pedlar is he? Daddy would be appalled if he knew what kind of neighbourhood I am living in.

'Thank you, but I don't need anything.'

I then remember the black thing in the wardrobe.

'There's something in my wardrobe,' I say.

'That's nice,' he says, walking away.

'It's black and alive.'

'I'm sure he will be very helpful in sorting out your rash,' he retorts.

I gasp.

'How dare you. I think it's a rat and I don't want it there all night.'

He sighs.

'You want me to get rid of it, is that what you're asking?'

'I'd be grateful,' I say.

He shrugs and climbs back onto the boat. I lead him into the bedroom. This is probably the closest I'll get to leading a man into my bedroom for a while.

'In there,' I say pointing.

He opens the door and I jump back. He fumbles around for a bit and then turns to me.

'I can't see anything.'

'It's there,' I say nervously. 'In the corner.'

I step closer to him and feel the warmth from his body.

'There,' I say, pointing.

The boat rocks and we fall onto the bed.

'This isn't just a ploy to get me into your bedroom is it?' he smiles.

'There, there,' I point as a glint catches my eye.

He reaches out and grabs the creature.

'You mean this?' he says holding the button from my Burberry French coat. 'This very dangerous button?'

'It looked different before,' I say.

He gives me that arrogant grin of his and strolls to the hatch. I watch him jump off the boat leaving it rocking. The boat feels strangely empty without him.

The walk of shame, my arse. There is no way, absolutely no way I am going to walk with my shit in public along the canal, and there is absolutely no way I will be seen in a pub with these boat people. I am about to phone Jeremy to tell him that when my phone rings. I dash onto the deck before it cuts out and answer it.

'Darling it's Balls, fanbloodytastic time last night. Are you free this evening? The Landales are doing Christmas and you know how bloody brilliantly they do it? I want you on my arm. No, I won't take no for answer.'

I had no intention of saying no. Roddy will be there. He always goes to the Landales' Christmas do. I feel my heart flutter at the thought of seeing him.

'I'd love to,' I say and feel a hundred times better.

Chapter Thirteen

Heads turn as Poppy Wellesley enters. She looks stunning in a Prada dress and floats confidently into the ballroom on the arm of Lord Wyndham-Price. Roddy can't take his eyes off them and feels anger well up inside. He's not sure if it's because Poppy has the nerve to be here or because she is here on Balls' arm. He gives Lord Wyndham-Price a scathing look. What does that idiot look like? Only he would wear a multicoloured bow tie with a purple waistcoat. What on earth is Poppy doing with him? The Landales' London home in Maida Vale is heaving with people. It's the social event of the year and anybody who is anybody is here. Mannequins dressed as snowmen surround the ballroom and waiters dressed as elves serve the guests. Roddy accepts a drink from a miserable looking elf and allows his eyes to follow Poppy and Balls as they are greeted by Lord Charles Landale and his wife, Lady Isabella. He had stupidly thought Poppy wouldn't come. The band play *Driving Home for Christmas* and he watches as Balls spins Poppy around to the music. Roddy's eyes meet hers across the room and he smiles nervously. She gives a little wave and he sees that she is no longer wearing his ring.

'Oh God,' groans Pandora, tapping him on the shoulder. 'I can't believe she had the gall to come here. I'd be too embarrassed if it were me.'

'Is that Poppy?' cries Camilla, nearly spilling her drink in the excitement. 'I must say hi.'

She pushes past Pandora and hurries towards Balls and Poppy.

'Honestly,' mutters Pandora, staring enviously at Poppy's dress. 'Is that Prada she's wearing? I'm surprised she can afford it. And what is he wearing? That man is a total eccentric. They're both an embarrassment.'

'Ooh it's Truffles. Doesn't she look fab?' chirps Chelsea, joining them. 'I'm just going to pop over and say hello. I say, how marvellous that Balls brought her.'

Pandora makes a clucking sound with her tongue and fidgets uncomfortably. Lady Nell Enwin pulls her eyes from Poppy and hooks her arm through Roddy's.

'I hope you'll escort this old lady into dinner,' she smiles, pulling him around so he can no longer eye up Poppy Wellesley.

The audacity of that woman, she thinks angrily. Here of all places. The fact that Roddy had even considered bringing Pandora here showed he was serious about her. How dare Poppy Wellesley come here and upset the apple cart. At least her mother had had the decency to stay away.

'Good Lord, is that Poppy Wellesley,' cries Baroness De Weldon. 'Well I never. What the buggery happened to her father? I can't for the life of me remember.'

'He was arrested for fraud,' says Pandora smugly.

'Yes, I know that stupid girl. What's happened to him since?'

Pandora grips Roddy's arm.

'That pinches, Pandy,' Roddy says, pulling his arm away.

'Don't be too clingy, dear,' Lady Enwin admonishes. 'The men don't like it.'

'Is he here?' asks Baroness De Weldon.

'Who?' asks the Baron.

'The fraudster, the one who kisses babies,' she snaps.

'He's in the Bahamas,' says Roddy.

'Just as well,' mutters Lady Enwin. 'It's all very embarrassing.'

Dinner is announced and Lady Enwin sighs with relief.

'Did you put our presents under the tree?' she asks Pandora.

Roddy's stomach churns when he realises that he has no present under the tree for Poppy. She was the last person he had expected to see. Damn, what a bad show. Hopefully no one will notice. He imagines bollocking Balls has got her a present all right. What is the old fella playing at? He and Poppy broke up only two weeks ago. Balls is a bloody fast worker. God, she looks fabulous. He finds himself hoping he will be seated close to her so he can drink in the beauty that is uniquely Poppy's. Lady Tarleton watches her son as he feasts his eyes on his ex-fiancée and fights back a sigh.

'Don't make a fool of yourself will you, not here of all places,' she whispers into his ear. 'She's living on a barge for heaven's sake.'

'He should ask for the ring back,' whispers Lady Enwin.

'Absolutely,' agrees Lady Tarleton.

Roddy rolls his eyes and wishes they would all bog off.

'She's probably only going to sell it,' says Pandora.

'Sell what?' says the Baroness.

'The ring.'

It occurs to Roddy that they could well be right. After all, she's desperate for money and the ring will fetch a bit, more than enough to pay his debts in fact. He'll need to get it soon. Damn Jack Diamond and his interest. It's criminal that's what it is.

'I recognise that arse,' bellows Reverend Enwin. 'Poppy Wellesley is here,' he roars.

Chapter Fourteen

'Don't you just love Christmas?' cries Sophie, pulling a cracker with me. 'I love you in that dress. Prada is just the best isn't it?'

I glance down at my dress and sigh with pleasure. Thank God I didn't sell this one. I was tempted, thinking I would never have the occasion to wear it again, but thank heavens for Chelsea and her walk-in wardrobe. Roddy had blanched when he'd seen me. Honestly, you'd think I'd risen from the dead the way everyone is carrying on. If only Roddy and I were spending Christmas together. The thought of Christmas fills me with despair. I imagine I'll be spending it alone on my little boat, or even worse at the Balls' residence. God, that boat, that boat, it's enough to drive someone insane. Oh well, at least Balls has a loo that empties itself. What am I thinking? Everyone has a loo that empties itself, everybody who is bollocking normal of course. Mind you, the hottie seems reasonably normal doesn't he? There is a crack and our paper hats fall onto the table.

'So where are you going for Crimbo?' asks Sophie, as though reading my mind.

I raise my eyes in a thoughtful pose. After all I don't want her knowing that I have absolutely nowhere to go do I?

'I'm not sure yet. So many invites, you know what it's like?'

Thankfully Camilla is sitting one side of me and Sophie and Chelsea are opposite. It's unfortunate that Lecherous Leonard is also sitting opposite albeit a few seats down. I glance at Roddy and wonder if he has bought me a present. I'd had to fly to Harrods after Balls had phoned. I'd put the purchases on my Harrods account with my heart beating nine to the dozen but nobody had batted an eyelid. After all, I couldn't have come without gifts for everybody. Oh well, if there are any problems Jeremy can sort them out, after all he's doing very little else these days.

Bowls of cranberry sauce are placed on the table and I feel my mouth water. I'd not eaten since the Indian takeaway last night.

'Fab night last night,' says Chelsea. 'How do you find sleeping on a boat?'

'What's that I hear about a boat?' asks the reverend, stealing a slice of turkey from the platter in front of him. God, did he just pick that up with his hand?

'Poppy has a boat now,' pipes up Camilla. 'It's just too divine for words.'

'We had a scream last night, didn't we Cami? I nearly fell in the water,' giggles Sophie.

I feel Roddy's eyes on me and laugh along with Camilla and Sophie.

'It was a hoot,' I say.

Balls throws an arm around my shoulder.

'You weren't too cold in that little bed of yours, were you?' he says sexily and loud enough for Roddy to hear.

'I can't even begin to imagine how you cope with it,' says Pandora resting her hand on Roddy's arm. 'It's okay for everyone to joke about what a hoot it is but it must be a terrible shock to the system. Is it true you're looking for a job? What on earth will you do Poppy? It's not like you're skilled is it?'

I swear that's an evil glint in her eye. The table goes silent and everyone looks at me. You'd think I was about to announce the winner of a Bafta such is the tension in the room.

'Daddy's financial adviser said that's not necessary.'

It's only a white lie isn't it?

'I can't imagine what job you'll do,' prattles on Pandora, wiping a chapstick across her glossy lips.

'She hates me,' I whisper to Camilla.

'I wish I could swap a glue stick for that chapstick,' says Chelsea under her breath.

'What did you say?' snaps Pandora.

'Nothing,' Chelsea shrugs.

'She's never liked me,' I say.

'I wouldn't worry about it. You're not a Facebook status are you?' grins Camilla.

I accept the plate of turkey breast from Balls, who bizarrely looks perfectly normal wearing a bright yellow Christmas hat. I help myself to roast potatoes and stuffing. After all, who knows when I'll eat again?

'I saw you in that cheap tabloid's Christmas rich list,' shouts Baron De Weldon. For one wonderful moment I think he means me. Balls shrugs.

'It's wrong. I'm the 10th richest man, not the 12th.'

Camilla nudges me.

'Just think,' she whispers.

I really don't want to think about it at all

'Pull your crackers everyone,' Lord Landale calls. 'We can't have anyone without a Christmas hat.'

Before I know it dinner is over and we're ushered into the lounge with its huge Christmas tree and roaring log fire. I so much want to talk to Roddy but Pug-face seems to be constantly clinging to his arm.

'She's worse than vine weed,' says Camilla, sitting beside me on a couch.

The present-giving ceremony begins and I sip champagne, grateful to be back in the world I know so well. I forget my little boat with its mooring ropes and walks of shame, and enjoy life as I had always known it. I allow a butler to top up my glass and accept a small bowl of chestnuts. The room is warm and I feel happy. Camilla hands me present after present. There is a bottle of Dior perfume from Chelsea. Two tins of Penhaligon Bluebell talcum powder from the Landales and a lovely bouquet of roses from Balls.

'There's a bottle of Oudinot Rosé to go with that,' he whispers into my ear and managing to lick it with his tongue. I shudder. I watch Roddy as he is given my present. Pandora practically shakes with anger as he opens it. Honestly, this is ridiculous; two weeks ago he was my fiancé. I'm not letting him go that easily. I'm certain he only broke off the engagement because his father put pressure on him. His face lights up as he opens the box and sees the cufflinks. His eyes meet mine and I feel my heart somersault. The presents are given out one by one and I realise that Roddy hasn't brought me anything. I watch miserably as Pandora shrieks with delight when she opens hers and have to swallow several times to stop the tears. He'd given her a Tiffany bracelet. What an arse. I wonder when he'll want that one back to pay his debts. The band strike up and play *Do you hear what I hear*, and Balls swings me onto the dance floor.

'Woo hoo, it's Christmas,' he bellows and I almost trip over my Prada as he spins me around.

My eye catches Roddy heading towards us.

'Do you mind old chap?' he asks.

Balls jaw twitches and he releases me gently.

'Yes I do actually. It's entirely up to Pops.'

'It's fine Balls,' I say and am surprised to hear my voice sounds normal.

'I'll see you in a few minutes,' he grunts.

Roddy pulls me into his arms and I feel like I've come home. The music changes tempo at that exact moment and he pulls me even closer. This couldn't be lovelier.

'God Pop, you look delicious. Good enough to bloody eat in fact.'

I try to avoid Pandora's piercing glare.

'Roddy, why did you break off our engagement?' I ask bluntly.

He sighs.

'I didn't want to. P'pa was adamant and I didn't know what else to do. He was threatening to cut me off. Says I spend too much. God, you smell fabulous Pop. Look, why don't I come over to the boat later and we can ...'

I snap my head up and meet his eyes.

'I don't think so Roddy,' I say, while wanting desperately to say yes.

'No no, of course not,' he says quickly. 'It's just I was wondering about the ring. I've got myself in a bit of a fix and it's not like you're wearing it ...'

I see Pandora heading towards us and lead Roddy into the centre of the dance floor.

'It's still my ring Roddy.'

'Yes, yes of course. By the way the cufflinks are divine, thank you darling,' he says, twirling me around expertly before pulling me back into a tight embrace. 'I didn't know you were coming otherwise I would have ...'

'It doesn't matter,' I say quickly, not really wanting to hear his excuses.

'You're not serious about old wanking Wyndham-Price are you? I'm not sure if he even knows he's got a dick, let alone how to use it,' he laughs.

'He's been very kind,' I say, feeling a strange loyalty to Balls. After all, he has been there for me when no one else had.

'Yes, yes of course,' mutters Roddy. 'I can't help feeling jealous. Look, let me come to the boat and we can, you know, have a drink, go for a little sail. I'll bring lunch. Say yes Truffles?'

This must be Roddy's killer line. Go for a little sail? In my boat? He hasn't got a clue has he? The only little sail my boat does well is to the other side of the river.

'It wasn't the same in Verbier without you. The whole holiday dragged.'

Pleased to hear it, I think bitchily. The music changes to something Latin and I find myself being propelled towards the doors. Moments later we are in the library and Roddy is pushing me appropriately against the D.H. Lawrence section while his hand travels roughly up my thigh. I feel like Lady Chatterley. His hand grips my buttocks and he groans.

'Christ Pop, you've got those sexy sailor panties on haven't you? You dirty little bitch.'

He's not wrong, about the panties that is, not me being a dirty little bitch. I'd been so late back from Harrods that I'd grabbed the nearest pair of panties in the suitcase. I'm not normally in the habit of wearing crotchless sailor knickers to dinner parties but the light was so bad on the boat.

'Seeing you with Balls really got my gander up,' he whispers, one hand stroking the inside of my thigh while the other caresses my breasts through a layer of chiffon.

I can most certainly feel that his gander is up. We bump along the books in our passion and I stretch my hand out for support and lean heavily on Mark Darcy. Well a leather bound copy of *Pride and Prejudice* that is, which is as close to Mark Darcy as I'll ever get. Roddy's lips trail kisses along my cheek before reaching my lips and devouring them. I melt into his arms and all I can hear is Roddy's heavy breathing and the ticking of a grandfather clock. It feels like nothing has changed at all. I can almost forget that Daddy has been frozen.

'It's always been good with us hasn't it Pop?' he says huskily shoving a hand through the hole in my panties. I gasp in shock. Maybe I should mention the spanking session that Camilla has organised.

'Roddy ...' I begin but his hot lips cover mine again and his pulsating gander shoots between us like a loaded gun as he frees it from his trousers.

'Ooh,' I gasp.

'God Pop, I want you so badly.'

'Maybe not here,' I whisper. 'Not against Jane Austen.'

He lifts his head and looks over my shoulder.

'Quite right,' he sniggers. 'Let's find the Karma Sutra. Much more fitting don't you think? I'm sure that dirty old bugger Landale has a first edition knowing him.'

'This dirty old bugger may well have. But I prefer not to have your spunk over it, Rodney Tarleton,' barks a voice.

I freeze. How did we not hear the door open? There is a sharp intake of breath from Roddy and he quickly pulls away from me. I stare at his erect gander and blush. Oh God, there must be a quick way of deflating that surely. I step in front of him and feel it poke against the cheek of my bum. I hastily pull down the Prada and attempt to look dignified, which is easier said than done with Roddy's pecker jammed against my arse and my crotchless knickers creeping up the crack in my bum. The door is wide open and standing in the doorway is Lord Landale and to the side of him is Pug-face. I hear the sound of Roddy's zipper before he stands at my side.

'We were, erm. Yes, we were looking at your wonderful collection of D.H. Lawrence weren't we Pop?' he stammers as Pandora bursts into the room with tears streaming down her face.

'How could you Roddy?' she cries.

'We are engaged,' I say, totally forgetting I'd taken off the ring.

'Were engaged,' snaps Sir Henry Tarleton walking into the room and grabbing Roddy by the arm. 'What the hell are you playing at?'

'Well I, the thing is ...' mumbles Roddy.

'Man up Roddy,' I snap.

'Yes, the thing is Pop and I are, well we were ...'

I sigh.

'Doesn't she live on a little tug boat on a canal? ' I hear someone say.

Lady Nell Enwin rushes to her daughter and places a protective arm around her before giving Roddy a scolding look. Honestly, anyone would think he was engaged to Pandora instead of me.

'We are engaged,' I repeat, although I don't know why I'm bothering as no one seems to be listening to me.

I so wish I hadn't taken off the ring.

'You were engaged,' repeats Sir Henry loudly.

Roddy bites his lip and avoids my eyes. His mother takes me by the arm and leads me past the guests that have crowded around the doorway. I'm led into the grand hall and the door is slammed behind us.

'We are very much hoping that Roddy and Pandora will make an announcement in a few days,' she says calmly.

'An announcement?' I question.

What does she mean an announcement? It's clearly not to announce that it's Christmas is it? There can be only one announcement she's referring to.

'But Roddy is engaged to me,' I say.

'That engagement was broken off Poppy.'

Not by me. I feel my stomach churn and wonder if I'm going to throw up over the Prada. I open my mouth to speak but nothing comes out.

'Roddy needs a wife with money. You know how he gets through it. We can't possibly wait for things to settle down where your father is concerned. God knows, it could be years. You know how things are. I'd much prefer he married you, but what can we do? We can't keep bailing him out. I don't know what he does with the money.'

He puts it on the gee-gees I want to say but decide I'm in enough trouble already. The doorman comes forward with my coat and handbag.

'It's the perfect arrangement. You surely understand that. Of course there's nothing to stop Roddy visiting you for, well you know. Men have their little flings. God, we all know about those. Just give them time to settle and ...'

I snatch my handbag from the doorman.

'Are you seriously suggesting that I become Roddy's mistress?'

She steps back in shock.

'Well you don't seriously think you can marry him now do you? In fact, do you really believe you can marry anyone from our class? You're gutter news these days darling, or haven't you noticed.'

Balls strolls into the grand hall and gestures to the doorman for his coat.

'I've challenged your son,' he says loudly and I can hear the gasps of shock from the guests in the other room. 'Saturday at noon.'

Jane Austen eat your heart out.

'Are you mad Balls? That kind of thing went out with Jack Sparrow,' I whisper.

'Your honour is at stake.' He turns back to Lady Tarleton, 'Your son has choice of weapons.'

Oh God, this sounds like a re-run of Downton Abbey.

'Lord Wynd ...' she begins.

'I really would prefer you didn't,' I say, feeling like I've progressed from a Jane Austen novel to a Jane Austen movie. I'll be back in the headlines next.

'It's done,' he says firmly, lifting his chin in the air.

'Balls, I really think you're getting carried away ...'

'It was you that got carried away,' screams Pandora. 'You're nothing but a slut.'

She spits the word at me and coughs. Camilla and Chelsea follow her in and I look at them despairingly. Camilla pretends to slash her throat with an imaginary knife.

'Cripes,' says Chelsea, her eyes so wide I think they may pop out.

'Call my driver,' Balls instructs the doorman.

'Lord ...' begins Lady Tarleton.

He waves his hand.

'Please don't have the duel, Balls,' I whisper. 'I really couldn't bear it.'

He puts a comforting arm around my waist.

'Only if you're sure? I don't want you to be upset.'

I'm sure all right. I nod.

'If he insults you again, I'll have to call him out,' he says firmly.

'Thank you Balls.'

'We're coming with you,' says Camilla. 'There's too much horseshit around here.'

She grabs Chelsea by the arm.

'That's because too many people are up their own arses,' says Chelsea.

Balls takes my arm and walks me to the door. I see Roddy watching us and he looks shaken. He's probably scared he'll be killed in the duel. I really don't believe this is happening. Perhaps I'll wake up soon in my little sardine bed and realise it has all just been a bad dream. I meet Roddy's eyes and he shrugs.

The four of us walk towards Balls' Rolls-Royce. When I turn back the doors are already closed. That will teach me to wear crotchless knickers to a dinner party.

Chapter Fifteen

'I can't talk. I'm meeting the girls. We're supposed to be getting spanked.'

'I'm pleased to hear it. It's no good pining over a man?' says Mummy. 'There's plenty more fish in the sea you know. Just don't let your rod get rusty.'

'Huh, I think my rod will need a lot of oil. It's not been used in yonks.'

'You can do better than Roddy. He has a face like a battered cod anyway,' she laughs.

'I'm not so sure spanking is the answer. Maybe I won't go.'

'Of course you're going,' says Mummy. 'Your rod needs some stimulating if you're going to remove that rust.'

'I don't know.'

'You've got to get back to normal.'

I'm not sure how many mothers would consider a spanking session as normal but then my mother isn't like most mothers is she?

'And what's this I hear about the Landales?'

'Oh that.'

'You could do a lot worse than Balls Wyndham-Price, you know?'

'Are you sure about that?'

'Okay, maybe you're right but let's face it, you're in no position to be choosy are you?'

'Anyway, I'm not so sure I want to get back to normal. In fact I'm not even sure I remember what being normal was like and I don't actually think spanking sessions are normal.'

'Living on a tiny boat with a loo the size of a shoebox is not normal, that much I can assure you. Being disgustingly rich and having staff is very normal and there is nothing wrong with spanking sessions, why your father and I ...'

'Yes well telling me those things isn't normal. I really don't want to hear what you and Daddy did with a riding crop.'

'Oh, it wasn't a riding crop,' says Mummy. 'In fact ...

'Enough I've got to go. I can't take any more traumas. I'm still recovering from Daddy not changing my nappy.'

Thirty minutes later and Chelsea, Sophie, Camilla and I are strolling confidently down the street, swinging our designer handbags like the cast of *Sex and the City*. We stop nervously a few feet from Coco de Mer.

'Ooh I'm really not sure about this,' says Chelsea touching her backside self-consciously.

'It'll be a hoot,' says Sophie.

'I didn't wear my best knickers,' whispers Chelsea.

'You have best knickers?' I say, surprised.

She shrugs.

'Special occasion ones, yes. What's wrong with that?'

'Nothing, anyway we're not stripping,' I say and add quickly. 'We're not are we?'

God, I hope not. I'd have worn a lacier pair if I'd known.

'I don't think so,' says Camilla in an uncertain voice.

'Let's do it,' says Sophie, striding into the shop with the rest of us tagging nervously behind. Miss Tits and Tease greets us. She is wearing a black leather zipped-up catsuit with her firm breasts swelling over the top. We all pretend not to notice the riding crop in her hand and look straight ahead instead.

'Maybe we were supposed to dress up,' whispers Camilla.

'Welcome, to the world of pain and pleasure,' Miss Tits and Tease smiles. 'Outfits are through here,' she says guiding us into a room full of cat suits, suspenders and frilly underwear.

'Cripes,' groans Chelsea.

'Don't be nervous,' says Miss Tits and Tease. 'It's all perfectly natural. This will heighten your sex life. You'll be amazed at the difference.'

I'll be very amazed at the difference indeed, considering I don't actually have a sex life. Chelsea grimaces and hooks her arm in mine before saying,

'I don't have a sex life.'

'I don't either, at least not much of one. Hugo is ... well is ...' stutters Camilla.

'Make that three,' I say, holding up my hand. 'My rod is well and truly rusty'

'Well I do,' says Sophie.

Oh, well, that's that then. We're all going to get sore red bums because Sophie has a sex life.

'I see. All the more reason for a spanking workshop, the more experienced you are the more confident you will be,' says Miss Tits and Tease. 'A confident woman is a sexy woman. Follow me.'

Ten minutes later and we're decked out and looking like something out of *Secret Diary of a Call Girl.* Chelsea is a bunny, Camilla a French maid, Sophie the naughty school girl while I chose to be the sexy secretary. I feel a little nervous when Camilla takes some pictures of us with her phone. I'm already in enough trouble without sexy pictures of me popping up on Twitter.

'Follow me to the punishment room,' orders Miss Tits and Tease.

'I feel like Anastasia Steele,' whispers Camilla.

'I hate to tell you this but Hugo is far from being a Christian Grey,' says Sophie.

We all follow to the spanking room. Chelsea lets out a small whimper and I feel sure if I wasn't hanging onto her arm she would have made a run for it.

'So this is what a red room of pain looks like,' says an amazed Sophie.

'I'm not into pain,' says a worried Chelsea.

'Spanking isn't about pain,' corrects Miss Tits and Tease.

That's a matter of opinion.

'I need a drink,' says Camilla.

Now I'm not a prude, but practising spanking your best friend is just a touch embarrassing. I'm not sure how this will give me confidence.

'Let's have a look at the table,' says Miss Tits and Tease. 'We'll start with this and work our way up.' She leads us to the spanking table and removes a hairbrush. I stare at the table. I feel like I've entered a medieval torture chamber. She hands me the hairbrush.

'Chelsea, over on the horse please.'

'Horse?' she croaks.

'Not a real horse, Chelsea. It's not that kinky,' I say.

'Oh good,' she sighs before walking warily to the leather horse. I honestly never thought I would be having carnal knowledge of Chelsea. It all seems so wrong. Chelsea stands against the leather horse and gingerly pushes her backside out. I stare at it and shake my head. If I thought I should have been sectioned before, there is no doubt I should be now. I'm spanking a very bunny looking Chelsea. If this doesn't cement our friendship nothing will.

'Chelsea, that's not provocative enough,' clucks Miss Tits and Tease.

'It's provocative enough for me,' I say.

'Oh,' mumbles Chelsea, 'okay.'

She leans further over the leather horse and blushes profusely. If she says 'Isn't this lovely Poppy,' I swear I'll beat her to death. I tap her lightly with the brush.

'A little harder Poppy. That won't get you what you want,' instructs Miss Tits and Tease.

I exhale and bring the brush down again. Five strokes later and I'm really getting into it.

'A little softer Poppy, always remember that spanking is not about punishment.'

I wish she'd make up her mind.

'It's lovely and all that, I think,' mumbles Chelsea. 'But a bit softer would be nicer.'

Am I really spanking Chelsea?

'Don't start enjoying it,' I say. 'We're not doing this when we get home.'

My mobile trills and Camilla looks wide-eyed at the screen.

'It's Roddy,' she says.

My heart beats a little faster. Please say he wants to see me. If he asks about the bloody ring again I'll scream.

'Can you ask him to hold on?'

'I'm really supposed to be spanking Sophie.'

'I don't mind if you stop,' says Sophie, rubbing her backside.

And my mother thinks this is normal.

'That was too hard Poppy,' reprimands Miss Tits and Tease.

I grab the phone with my other hand and click it on.

'Hello.'

'Can we talk?' he asks, 'about the other night at the Landales'.'

'Roddy ...'

'Can we meet Pop? I really want to see you?'

'I'm spanking someone at the moment and then I'm getting spanked so it's a bad time actually.'

'What do you mean you're getting spanked? Who's bollocking spanking you?' he asks and I can picture his red face. 'I'll do for that Balls.'

'Well …' I begin.

'I'm coming over, where are you. If there's any spanking to be done. I'm doing it.'

Ooh now he's talking.

'By the way Pop, you do still have the ring don't you?'

I don't believe this.

'Don't keep calling me Pop,' I yell.

'Ouch Poppy, that was my hip,' cries Chelsea.

'This boat lark has really turned your head. Who the hell is spanking you Pop? I'm not putting up with this,' demands Roddy.

'Not putting up with what?' I snap.

'Ouch Poppy, spanking isn't about punishment remember,' says Chelsea.

'Why don't you come over to Miss Tits and Tease and we'll see how much you can put up with,' I say angrily.

'Miss Tits and Tease?' says a shocked Roddy. 'Good God Poppy. I really don't know what's happened to you since that boat business. I know you're angry about the ring and the engagement but you've got to put that behind us.'

Behinds are all I'm thinking about right now. I hand the hairbrush to Chelsea and fall across the horse.

'Roddy are you forgetting that you're now seeing Pug-face Pandora?'

'What did you call her?'

'Pug-face Pandora.'

'Go gently Chelsea, lower the flogger a little bit,' says Miss Tits and Tease.

'Flogger,' I gasp.

What happened to the hairbrush?

'Flog her, what is wrong with you today? Have you been drinking?'

I wish.

'I really can't believe you called her that.'

'Well I did and …'

Chelsea whacks me so hard with the flogger I slide forward on the horse and gasp,

'Ouch, bloody hell Chelsea, what happened to the spanking isn't about pain stuff?'

'Chelsea is spanking you?' says a stunned Roddy.

This is all I need. This is how rumours start isn't it? I knew this was a bad idea.

'Yes, but it's not ...'

'Christ Poppy. I don't know you any more.'

'I don't know you either,' I say feeling myself well up.

I click off the phone before he can hear me cry.

'It's just beastly the way Roddy has treated you,' says Camilla gripping the end of the table.

'Let's change the pace a little Sophie, enhance the pleasure,' instructs Miss Tits and Tease.

'What pleasure?' Camilla grumbles.

'Shall I use the paddle now?' asks Chelsea.

'No, I snap.

'Do you think you'll end up with Balls?' asks Sophie.

'She likes the hottie,' says Chelsea.

'I do not,' I deny.

'What hottie?' says Camilla, her eyes as bright as light bulbs.

'He lives on the next boat,' pants Chelsea. I rather think she is enjoying this despite being breathless from her exertions.

'He rescued Poppy when her boat drifted off.'

'Enough,' shouts Miss Tits and Tease, her breasts wobbling. 'Spanking should be taken seriously. Poppy, sprawl across the horse and visualise. Robert is ...'

'It's Roddy actually, but ...' interrupts Chelsea.

'I don't think ...' I begin.

'Give me the flogger Chelsea,' snaps Miss Tits and Tease.

'Roddy is approaching you, his tool firm and erect. Visualise, Poppy. Roddy is in charge.'

'Oh dear,' says Chelsea.

'Picture yourself surrendering to Roddy.'

I try, I really do but all I'm picturing is the hottie with his rippling biceps and firm thighs and his warm hand on mine on the rudder. I'm really getting into it when Miss Tits and Tease brings down the flogger with a swish.

'Ouch,' says Sophie.

'*This* is giving pleasure. You need to visualise, Poppy,' says Miss Tits and Tease who is beginning to sound just slightly insane.

I'm visualising all right. A large glass of wine and Arnica to be exact.

'Four more strokes and ...'

I hear a swish and slide to the left. The flogger lands with a crack on the leather horse.

'Frogs' knickers,' gasps Chelsea.

'You moved,' says Miss Tits and Tease breathlessly, her breasts heaving.

'Ooh is that the time,' says Camilla. 'We ought to be getting off.'

My phone bleeps and I grab it gratefully.

'Ballsey is free to play. Let's be at, what!'

Someone please kill me.

'It's Balls,' I say.

'Well, if it's truly off with Roddy, you might as well,' says Camilla.

'Yes, you have to remember you're not in your twenties now,' says Sophie, 'which makes your situation pretty dire.'

Hang on a minute.

'What about you lot?' I say defensively.

'I'm only twenty-nine and Cammy's not yet thirty. How about you Chelsea?'

'Twenty-eight.'

They make me sound like an OAP.

'As lovely as this is Camilla. I think half an hour with a punch bag would be better for all of us,' I say. Much more preferable than me being the punch bag anyway.

'Hear hear,' says a relieved Chelsea.

'A couple of drinks would be even better,' says Sophie.

With that we thank Miss Tits and Tease, and her heaving breasts, and make our exit.

Chapter Sixteen

'I'm not sure about this,' whispers Chelsea.

I look through the window of Chelsea's Porsche and try to gauge the type of person going into the pub.

'They don't look at all our type,' she says nervously.

'Of course they're not our type. *Our type* are at Annabel's,' I say. 'But I've got to do something and he's the only person I know.'

Chelsea shivers.

'But you said he was a drugs dealer,' she says wringing her hands.

I exhale and grip my Hermes handbag.

'I'm not *sure* if he's a drug dealer, it's just everything points to that.'

Three scruffy men enter the pub, followed by what looks like the girl from the boats. I sit up and strain to see if it is her. She approaches the pub entrance and shakes her umbrella.

'That's the girl, Randy, or Roody or something,' I say excitedly.

'So, it's the right pub then?'

I nod.

'Are you absolutely certain there isn't anyone we can phone?' says Chelsea, turning the car heater up higher. 'I really don't want to go in there unless we absolutely have to.'

I'm not exactly sure who Chelsea thinks we can phone. There is barely anyone left in my phone contacts. It's undergone a short back and sides in the last few days. Sophie had sent a text saying it would be abslooty fab to stay in touch but it was a bit difficult now that Roddy was with Pandora. Marcus had not invited me to his Christmas fancy dress party which I've been going to for as long as I can remember. Camilla phoned and said that she and Hugo had had *the most awful to do about you and Roddy* and that the upshot of it all was that they really couldn't see me. *I think it's all pretty grisly*, she'd cried down the phone.

'How about Balls?' Chelsea says.

I roll my eyes.

'I so wish you'd engage brain before opening mouth Chelsea.'

'Sorry,' she mumbles.

It now seems Christmas at Balls' residence is out of the question.

'Mother is coming after all,' he'd said apologetically. 'She's put her foot down I'm afraid.'

That's that then. Everyone knows that Balls' mother rules the roost. It's only a matter of time before she puts her foot down a bit harder and tells him he can't see me any more.

I pull off my Marc Jacob poncho as warmth from the heater fills the car and feel my hair get tangled in the needles of a Christmas tree that is wedged on the back seat. I wince. God, is it not enough I have this rash. Bollocking Christmas, honestly it's more trouble than it's worth. Jeremy, it seems, has also buggered off to the Bahamas. He sent me a text saying he wouldn't be back until the New Year and had the gall to wish me a happy time over the festive season. I've never hated Christmas more in my whole life. I'm struggling to disentangle my hair when a rapping on the window makes us both jump. I feel my rash itch like crazy and it's all I can do not to scratch for England. Chelsea pushes a button and the window winds down. Cold air pours into the car along with the head of the red-faced traffic warden.

'Yes?' I snap.

'You're on a double,' he says flatly while chewing on some gum.

He makes it sound like a card game. Double or twist.

'Ooh, do we win something?' I say sarcastically.

'You get a ticket,' he growls.

My hair is full of pine needles and trying to remove them is agony. I've never experienced so many pricks in one go. The smell of a rotisserie chicken that Chelsea had bought for our dinner has gone decidedly sour and I wrinkle my nose.

'Hello,' says Chelsea in her cheery voice. 'We have a bit of a problem.'

I look back at the red face and want to add *and you're it*, but I don't. His face is very close to me and I can't really move away without pulling a handful of hair from my scalp. I'm feeling very hemmed in. I never did like Porsches with bucket seats; they induce cabin fever if you want my opinion. He pokes his head further in and the smell of cheap aftershave overpowers me. God, did he spray a whole tin over himself?

'Nice aftershave,' I say as he invades my personal space.

'From Aldi,' he says proudly. 'Form an orderly queue ladies.'

My God, he's deadly serious too. He spits on his finger and flattens his eyebrows. I've never seen anything so nauseating in my life.

'We'll try to resist you, won't we Chelsea?'

'Oh yes.'

'What's cooking?' he asks, peering suspiciously into the back seat.

Chelsea shrugs.

'Champagne, huh?' he says, craning his neck and spotting the booze.

He'll be transforming into Mr Stretch of the fantastic four and joining us in the car any minute. I nudge Chelsea and say.

'I'm sure we have a bottle to spare, don't we Chelsea?'

She widens her eyes.

'What?' she squeals.

He pulls his head back quickly.

'Are you trying to bribe me madam?'

Abslootly, as Sophie would say. I lean into the back seat, ricking my neck in the process so as not to get stabbed by the bollocking Christmas tree, and grab a bottle of champagne.

'The thing is, we need to go into that pub for a bit and there's absolutely nowhere to park. You know how hard it is to get parked around here.'

'Like your drink don't ya?' he quips.

'Like giving out tickets don't ya?' I say mimicking him.

At that moment I see the hottie strolling towards the pub.

'That's him,' I cry.

'I really don't think so madam,' says the warden firmly.

'No it is,' I say, opening the car door and banging it against his thigh.

'Cripes,' groans Chelsea.

'Here have this on us,' I say handing him a bottle of Moet.

He takes it with one hand and with the other hands me a parking ticket.

'Have this on me,' he says with a smile and walks off with the champagne.

'Pig, you're all pigs,' I call.

'That's the police,' says Chelsea.

'What?'

'The police are the pigs not the traffic wardens.'

I take her arm and we push against the bitter wind towards the pub door.

'Are you sure about this?' Chelsea asks for the umpteenth time.

'No I'm not at all sure but the boat's drifted off and I don't know anyone else who can pull it back'.

We'd arrived back from late night Christmas shopping over an hour ago with great plans of decorating the Christmas tree and enjoying a dinner of chicken and salad only to find said boat was no longer there. Chelsea had spotted it bopping on the water some way in the distance. The fact that it was bumping against the same bank as the last time it drifted off filled me with some comfort and I just hoped it would stay there. I can't believe it's done that again, it's like it has a mind of its own and prefers to sit there rather than its proper mooring. I'd fished out my phone and rung everyone I could think of from a plumber to a locksmith. None of them retrieved boats or knew of anyone who did. The hottie, whose name I had forgotten, wasn't at home. The man with the cat haired trousers apologised for not being able to help.

'My old boat doesn't move, else I'd help you out. Why don't you pop to the Queen's Head? We all meet there on a Friday. You'll find someone who can help you out.'

I remembered the hottie's invitation and we had zoomed down to the local only to sit outside it for thirty minutes trying to get up the courage to go in. I take a deep breath, push open the doors and shove Chelsea inside. The place is heaving and the smell of stale beer wafts over us. Christmas music thumps loudly and I strain to see the hottie and the Randy girl.

'Can you see them?' I shout above the laughter and hubbub.

Chelsea pulls a face and squeezes into a corner like a frightened rabbit.

'It's not like our usual haunts is it?' she says nervously.

I can't disagree and frown as I step in a puddle of spilt beer. I rub my eyes and struggle to find the hottie. It's almost impossible to see anyone it's so crowded.

'They must be here,' I say.

'They're probably in a corner doing a drug deal. I think we should go,' quivers Chelsea. 'We don't want to get stabbed.'

'That's a bit extreme Chelsea.'

I take her arm and lead her to the bar where I have a better view of the other side of the pub. It is then I spot the Randy woman.

'There she is,' I say, lifting a hand to point and almost taking out the eye of a passer-by.

'Oye, what ya doing.'

'I'm so sorry, I was ...'

I pull Chelsea towards Randy, who is juggling a tray of drinks.

'Randy?' I say.

She stares bewildered at me.

'I'm sorry,' she says dubiously.

'Are you Randy?'

'Sod off and find someone else to pull,' she says sharply, brushing past me.

'I think she thought you were chatting her up,' mutters Chelsea.

That's wonderful isn't it? I'll go from a druggie to a lesbian. I can see the headline now, *Shamed socialite turns to other women in her moment of desperation.* Let's face it, I haven't had much luck with men have I, so it's not altogether a bad idea.

'Hang on a minute,' I say, following her.

'We should be careful,' Chelsea shouts in my ear. 'They're not like us. We don't want to get into trouble.'

She makes it sound like we've just strolled into a pub full of vampires.

'This isn't *Twilight*,' I remind her.

Randy stands with her back to us, handing round the drinks.

'Do you not recognise me? I moved onto *Amelia*.'

She studies me.

'Oh yeah, you're the snotty one. My name's not Randy, it's Ruby,' she says loftily.

Snotty? What a cheek.

'Sorry, I knew it began with an R. I'm looking for the hot ...'

Chelsea nudges me in the ribs.

'For the guy who lives in the boat next door,' says Chelsea.

'He's there,' she says, pointing.

I turn and recognise the hottie's jacket. He takes it off and I watch mesmerised as he tugs off his jumper revealing a light blue shirt and those rippling biceps. Recognition sparkles in his eyes and he waves.

'He's seen us, come on,' I say, pulling a reluctant Chelsea.

We reach the table where I recognise some of the faces from the boats.

'Hi, glad you could make it. What can I get you to drink?' asks the hottie, whose name I am still struggling to remember. Was it Tyler or Tyson? I fiddle with my hair self-consciously and feel the prick of pine needles. Oh hell. I must look like a blonde highlighted Christmas tree. I discreetly try to remove them but find myself yanking out strands of hair. This is just great isn't it? Just bollocking great. Talk about make a good impression. He'll no doubt think I suffer from compulsive hair pulling as well as eczema.

'He's gorgeous,' whispers Chelsea. 'I can see why you fancy him.'

'I don't fancy him,' I correct.

'The thing is ...' I begin, turning back to the hottie. I stop when a groan emanates from Chelsea. I follow her wide eyes to a holdall by the hottie's foot. Oh my God, are those hypodermics? She clasps my hand and squeezes it. He *is* a drug dealer. Jesus, this is worse than I thought.

Chapter Seventeen

'What's your poison?' asks another man who sits with his legs so wide apart that I have to force my eyes from his crotch, and let me tell you his jeans are that tight that I can see the outline of his testicles.

'My poison?' I repeat in a shaky voice. Is he talking about drugs? 'I don't really have one,' I stammer.

'They do cocktails on Friday evening,' he grins and I have to fight off the image of my mother throwing back cocks like no tomorrow.

'Half price happy hour,' continues Mr Crotch, who widens his legs even further. He's like a proud cock without the feathers. I'm beginning to wonder if he's double jointed.

The hottie pulls out two stools and Chelsea falls onto one. Ruby hands us a menu and I stuff strands of hair into my handbag. I hope I'm not displaying a bald patch. That will really be the last straw.

'Here's the list, or you could have a glass of wine.'

Honestly, do we look stupid? I have been into a club during happy hour. I do know you don't have to have a cocktail. Chelsea studies the menu intently, chewing her lip thoughtfully.

'The slow comfortable screw is nice,' says Ruby.

'If I'm giving it,' drawls Mr Crotch.

I snap my head up and hear something crack. Great that's all I need. I've done my neck in. I then see that Mr Crotch is cracking walnuts, not between his legs I hasten to add.

Ruby gives him a sharp look.

'Not that I've ever given *you* one,' he stutters trying to avoid her eyes.

I look down at the cocktail menu and catch Chelsea's eye. There is no way I am going to order anything from this.

'I'll have an *Angel's Tit*,' says Chelsea and giggles. 'I've never had one of those before.'

'I'm sure you have darling,' laughs one of the men. 'You're a real angel if ever I've met one.'

He jumps from his seat to beside her in one move.

'I'm Geoff. So what's your name gorgeous?'

'Chelsea,' she says, blushing profusely.

I stare at her open-mouthed. I can't believe she asked for an Angel's Tit. The hottie looks at me expectantly. I look back at the menu and feel everyone's eyes on me.

'I'm spoilt for choice,' I say with a false laugh.

I struggle to find the least obscene name on the menu. I don't want to ask for the *Red Headed Slut,* not with red haired Ruby standing so close and *Screw Me Sideways* seems a bit blatant, what with the hottie standing at the side of me. You get my drift. I'll leave *Leg Spreader* to the guy opposite.

'I can recommend *Between the Sheets*,' says the hottie with a wink.

'Really?' I say.

'But then *Sex Machine* is very nice,' he says his eyebrows rising.

'I'll go for the *All Night Long* I think,' I say and realise we are flirting.

He grins.

'Good choice. I'll get a bottle of wine too,' he says moving to the bar.

'Have a walnut. I'm Pete by the way. My boat is a long way from yours,' says Mr Crotch.

There is a God and he does love me.

'I'm in house clearance,' he says, widening his legs even more.

The couple with the dogs arrive and pull up more stools. It's getting packed at our little table. Chelsea chats to Ruby as she spreads an assortment of handmade earrings onto the table.

'Ooh these are lovely,' coos Chelsea.

Has she completely lost the plot? They're total rubbish. I watch as Chelsea tries them on. Taylor returns with the cocktails and sits next to me. His soft fragrance wafts across. He smells of musk and something else I can't quite identify. He pushes the cocktail across the table and looks into my eyes.

'Your *All Night Long*,' he says softly.

'The pearl ones suit you,' Geoff tells Chelsea.

I need to get her out of here before she succumbs to the charm of the delightful Geoff.

'Tyler,' I begin, turning to the hottie.

'It's Taylor,' he says.

Wasn't that what I said?

'Yes Tyler the thing is ...'

'It's Taylor, my name is Taylor,' he interrupts again.

'I thought I said that.'

'No, you said *Tyler*.'

'Hello,' says the woman with the dogs, plonking her face between us. 'I'm Rose and this is my husband Jack.'

It's like the *Titanic* all over again.

'We're getting a round. What would you like dear?'

I shake my head.

'Nothing really, thank you, we'll be going soon.'

'You've only just arrived,' says Taylor. 'Fed up with us already?'

I sigh.

'No, it's just Chelsea's Porsche is on a double line and ...'

'You've got a Porsche?' says Geoff excitedly.

Oh God, me and my big mouth.

'You can park at the back of the pub,' says the dog lady.

Actually we don't even want to be in this pub, let alone park near it.

'No, we won't be ...'

'Let's move it Chels,' says Geoff.

Did he really just call her Chels? Jesus, whatever next?

'No, really ...' I begin.

'Okay,' says Chelsea, standing up.

Honestly, that Swiss finishing school was wasted on her.

'You've got a ticket now so it doesn't really matter,' I argue.

'But you said that's why you have to leave early,' queries Geoff, whom I'm going off big time.

'Unless of course we're not good enough for you?' says Taylor.

For goodness' sake, I just want my bollocking boat back that's all. The dog lady sits next to Chelsea and begins trying on the earrings. That's how you get AIDS isn't it? I look at Taylor as he hands over the hypodermics to someone. Oh my God, there is drug dealing going on, right under my nose. Oh shit. The rash goes crazy and I itch like mad. We need to get out of here. I wouldn't put it past them to put Rohypnol in our drinks. I most certainly wouldn't put it past crotchless Pete, who hasn't stopped talking to my breasts for the past five minutes.

'I know you from somewhere,' he says.

I'm not sure if he means me, or my breasts.

'I assure you we don't go to the same places,' I say politely, sipping at my *All Night Long.*

He laughs and continues talking to my breasts and I fight the urge to kick him between his splayed legs.

'Can I offer you some wine?' says Taylor, pushing a full glass towards me.

I'm not stupid, that'll be spiked with Rohypnol for sure. Chelsea turns, swinging a pair of hooped earrings.

'What do you think?'

'I think you're losing your mind. I can't believe you considered wandering off with some weirdo. At least let me memorise what you're wearing so I can describe your dead body to the police,' I snap. 'And don't try those earrings or you'll end up with hepatitis or something worse. Make some excuse. We have to go. He was doing a drug deal right under my nose. I wouldn't put it past them to spike our cocktails,' I whisper in her ear.

'Another cocktail Chels?' Geoff asks.

'See what I mean,' I whisper.

'How's the boat?' asks the hottie.

'It's drifted off again,' says Chelsea.

Taylor looks at me and raises his eyebrows.

'Why didn't you say?'

'Well, I was going to but …'

'Where is it?'

'On the other side like before,' I say feeling like a scolded child.

'You should have said. Throw your blanket on,' he says sharply, pointing to my poncho. 'We should go and pull it back before it gets damaged. I don't want to spend my Friday night bailing her out.'

'I'll help,' offers Geoff.

'That's kind,' says Chelsea. 'Isn't that kind Poppy?'

Before I know what's happening we're all heading back to the canal with Ruby following on her bicycle.

Chapter Eighteen

Thirty minutes later and *Amelia* is back in her rightful place. Geoff had helped to pull her back and Chelsea had watched him admiringly.

'It's like *Pirates of the Caribbean* isn't it?' she says dreamily, watching Geoff leap from boat to boat.

I shiver and pull my cold hands under the poncho.

'Not quite,' I sigh. 'More like *Carry on Boating*.'

I watch appreciatively as Taylor fixes the horn cleat.

'That should do it. Hopefully you won't drift off again and if you do I'll have to see it as a cry for attention,' Taylor grins.

'I'm not the attention seeking type,' I say in my best uppity voice.

'We're getting a takeaway,' says Geoff. 'Do you two want to join us, on my boat?'

I shake my head.

'Ooh, that sounds lovely, doesn't it sound lovely Poppy?' says Chelsea.

I'm sure they've put something in Chelsea's drink that makes everything look lovely. I'm sure if they said they were all going to get pie and mash and have an orgy afterwards, she'd be saying *Ooh that sounds lovely. Don't you think an orgy sounds lovely Poppy?*

'An orgy is not really our thing Chelsea,' I say without thinking.

There is silence.

'Being hopeful are you,' laughs Taylor.

'No, I erm ...'

Oh God, I sound like a sex maniac every time I see him.

'It's not our thing, Chelsea.'

'Oh,' she says, looking disappointed.

'What's not your thing?' asks Taylor. 'The orgy, the takeaway or us?'

What is it with this guy? He looks into my eyes. Geoff coughs nervously and Ruby jumps back onto her bicycle.

'I'll get the plates ready,' she says, cycling off.

'Shall we get the takeaway and meet you back at the boat?' asks Geoff uncertainly. 'We can pick up the Porsche.'

Taylor nods without taking his eyes off me and I feel the rash go manic.

'I'm just going to give Poppy a hot water bottle.'

God, for a moment I thought he was about to say *I'm just going to give Poppy one.*

'I'll go then shall I?' says Chelsea nervously.

I nod, still unable to pull my eyes from Taylor's. I hear her heels clip clop on the walkway. I wait for him to speak.

'Let's get that bottle then,' he says, jumping onto his boat and holding out his hand. I take it and feel my heart race the moment our hands touch. What am I doing? He's not my type in more ways than one. I've never gone for the outdoor type and let's face it I'm way out of his league. I'd never dine with someone like him, or Geoff come to that. Roddy would have a fit if he knew. The boat is lovely and warm and I hate him for it. In the corner is a little Christmas tree. That wasn't there before, nor were the two crates of booze to the side of it. He's planning a wild Christmas obviously. I feel a small pang of envy when I think of my lonely Christmas looming ahead. I'll stuff myself full of Quality Street and mince pies no doubt, and then hopefully fall drunkenly into the Thames. I can't even watch boring re-runs of *Only Fools and Horses* as the boat is not graced with a TV.

'Here's the bottle,' he says. 'Let me know if it's not enough and I'll see what I can do.'

Ooh, that sounds promising. I take the hot water bottle gratefully.

'I'll see you onto your boat,' he says briskly. 'I really don't expect you to join us lowlifes for an Indian. Besides, I'm sure you've got better things to do with your time.'

Oh yes like twiddling my thumbs. I should be thankful for the excuse but instead I'm disappointed. The truth is I'm absolutely starving and the last place I want to be is on stupid *Amelia* freezing my tits off. I don't even have the bollocking rotisserie chicken do I? It's probably been pounded by now. The car that is, not the chicken. It's my own fault of course for being so stand-offish. I wish Roddy hadn't been such a spineless git. Surely he isn't really going to get engaged to Pug-face. She's frumpy and she's a vegetarian, and her breasts are too big. Seriously, who wants breasts that slap you in the face when you're jogging? I look wistfully at my breasts and sigh. It's quite absurd isn't it? All this marrying for money lark. I'm sure Roddy will be desperately unhappy with her. How can he be anything else with Pandora? I wonder what he's doing now, having mad torrid sex with her no doubt. I hope he spanks her arse till it's raw. I sigh.

'Actually I'm starving. Do you mind awfully if I come along?' I ask timidly.

He smiles and my heart dances. He really is lovely. What a shame he's a drug dealer.

'Sure. It'll be nice to have you.'

'You haven't had me yet,' I say boldly, feeling a little tingle in my loins.

Note to self: stop thinking about mad torrid sex, especially mad torrid sex with Taylor. I wonder if *he* likes spanking? After all I'm a bit of an expert now, aren't I?

'I doubt I can afford you,' he says leaping from the boat.

I perch my hand on my hip. Did he really say what I think he said? What a nerve.

'I don't ...' I begin angrily.

He raises his eyebrows.

'You don't?' he asks.

'No I don't, actually. One riding crop does not a prostitute make. How dare you.'

There I've said it. Perhaps a bit too loudly, but I've said it.

'Right, I think that's clarified things for everyone on the canal,' he says, his eyes twinkling and his lips curling into a smile.

'Good,' I snap. 'I'm glad it has.'

He nods at the hot water bottle.

'Do you want to get rid of that? It will be warm enough on Geoff's boat.'

He waits while I throw the hot water bottle through the hatch into *Amelia* and then hooks my arm through his. We walk silently along the canal until we reach Geoff's colourful barge. Taylor taps on the hatch and Ruby opens it with a smile.

'Hi, everything's ready.'

There are no chairs, just lots of scatter cushions in front of a log burner. Candles burn brightly and the place is wonderfully warm. Ruby has put plates and cutlery on a table and is fetching glasses.

She's taken off her bobbly hat and her hair is tied in a rough bun. She points to a cushion.

'Don't stand on ceremony, we're not posh here,' she says and then claps a hand to her mouth. 'I didn't mean …' she begins.

Chelsea strolls down into the cabin then and I'm saved from saying anything.

'Oh, isn't this nice?' she says, looking around.

Geoff hands Ruby an armful of brown bags and clambers over cushions. He pulls a crate towards him and produces two bottles of wine. He throws a corkscrew to Taylor and gives Chelsea a glass.

'Taylor's good with a corkscrew,' Geoff laughs.

There is a pop as Taylor pulls the cork and I recognise the wine as a good one. Not the cheap Spanish plonk which I had been expecting.

'The wine is super,' says Chelsea, obviously also pleased with the quality.

'There's more where that came from if you want me to get you some. Three quid a bottle,' says Geoff proudly.

'Three quid?' Chelsea and I say in unison.

'Yeah, do you want me to get you some?'

'But this wine is about twenty-five pounds a bottle,' I say.

'You can give him twenty-five quid for it. I don't think Geoff will complain,' says Taylor mockingly.

So that's where Taylor's two crates of booze came from. They're thieves as well as drug dealers. Ruby hands me a plate of chicken korma and I take it gratefully while trying not to look at Taylor's bag where the hypodermics are hiding. I hope they don't shoot up after dinner. That's all I need. It's bad enough I have the image of being a druggie, without actually being seen with some. I'll have to keep a close watch on Chelsea or she'll be shooting up too and saying how lovely it all is. Mind you, they don't look spaced out or anything. Ruby's eyes are clear and bright and Taylor seems on the ball. Then again, he could just be a pusher. I really have to get off the boat and off this canal. Daddy's hair would curl if he knew.

'Here take a bottle,' says Geoff.

'That's generous, thank you Geoff,' says Chelsea.

'We'll pay you,' I say primly.

'You can have that one on us,' says Geoff.

'That's nice of you, isn't that nice of Geoff, Poppy?'

I really don't know what I'm going to do with Chelsea. This is all I need isn't it? Chelsea falling for some wide boy who sells cheap booze.

'Very generous,' I say.

I sit stiffly on the scatter cushion and discreetly wipe my fork on a tissue. Well, you don't know do you?

Geoff excuses himself to use the loo and Chelsea leans across to me.

'He's nice isn't he?' she whispers.

'He's not really your type is he?'

'No, I suppose not,' she says, looking disappointed.

'Is the food all right?' Taylor asks, studying me. 'The cutlery up to standard is it? Sorry we didn't get the silver out.'

'It's fine,' I say stiffly, feeling myself sweat under the poncho.

'Aren't you hot in your shawl?' asks Ruby.

Yes, I'm roasting but I want to be able to make a quick exit should they get busted or get out their credit cards to cut the crack. Just thinking of credit cards fills me with despair. I can't remember a time I didn't have my American Express.

'I'm fine, thank you,' I say.

'It feels like you're going to leave any minute,' says Taylor.

Yes, well that's most likely because I am.

'I'm sure you'll feel more at home without it,' he adds, attempting to help me off with my poncho.

'Really, I'm perfectly fine,' I say haughtily, hanging onto the poncho for dear life.

He gives a tug and the next thing I know he has yanked off not only the poncho but my blouse too. I find myself sitting in my pink bowed Chanel bra. I swear my face turns redder than the glowing coals on the log burner.

'Frogs' knickers,' squeals Chelsea, holding my Hermes bag in front of me with one hand while trying to pull my blouse over my head with the other. The only person I'm aware of is Taylor. Now he'll know I'm small breasted, not that I'm that small you understand. 34a isn't *that* small is it? But if I am going to strip down to my undies in the middle of dinner with a hottie like Taylor it would be better to be a size 36D don't you think? There is one consolation; at least I'm wearing a Chanel. Mind you, if he didn't recognise a Boden skirt he's not going to recognise a Chanel bra is he? God, what am I thinking?

'Everything okay?' asks Geoff, returning from the loo.

'Oh yes. Poppy accidentally removed her ...' begins Chelsea.

'Chelsea,' I interrupt.

'Sorry about that,' smiles Taylor. 'I don't normally undress women in public.'

'I'm glad to hear it,' I say.

'I don't think anyone noticed,' says Ruby, nibbling a poppadum.

'Blimey, what did I miss?' asks Geoff.

'What do you do Poppy?' asks Ruby in an attempt to change the subject.

Aside from strip off in public does she mean?

'Do?' repeats Chelsea.

I sigh.

'For a living, what's your job?'

'Well, she doesn't really do anything, do you Poppy?' says Chelsea

'You must have a job. What about you Chelsea?' asks Ruby, topping up our glasses.

'Oh, I help out at an art gallery. A friend owns it you see,' says Chelsea proudly.

'How decadent is that,' chirps Ruby excitedly. 'What about you Poppy?'

Chelsea bends her head and studies her Bombay potato. I toss back the remainder of my wine and say,

'I'm a rich socialite, at least I was until my father got done for fraud and had all his bank accounts frozen. So, I don't have any money now and because of that my fiancé broke off our engagement. We were going to have a winter wonderland wedding and *HELLO!* were going to feature it but of course that's now been cancelled. I sigh. 'My apartment, which was huge by the way, I had to leave because my father put it on expenses. I've just sold my designer clothes and I will probably throw myself in the Thames on Christmas Day because I've got nothing else to do. Oh, and no, I don't have a job because I'm not skilled in anything.'

When you say it out loud it sounds even worse. I may as well throw myself in the Thames right now. There is silence. Not even the crunching of a poppadum can be heard.

'Holy fuck,' says Ruby finally.

'I knew you looked familiar. I said she looked familiar, didn't I Rube?' says Geoff excitedly.

'She was in the papers,' says Chelsea.

'Your fiancé chucked you?' says Ruby incredulously.

'He's an arse,' says Chelsea.

'I'd love to see your designer clothes someday,' says Ruby shyly.

'Mushroom bhaji?' Taylor asks, thrusting a carton towards me.

Is that all he has to say? I nod stupidly and let him tip some onto my plate.

'Christ, the boat must be something of a shock,' says Geoff.

'It's taking some getting used to,' I say miserably.

'What a bastard to dump you because you have no money. That's terrible Poppy. Did you have the wedding dress and everything?' asks Ruby, flopping onto a cushion in front of me.

'It's a Valentino,' nods Chelsea. 'Her mother thinks she should sell it and go to Capri with the money.'

'That was a joke Chelsea.'

'No I wasn't joking.'

I sigh.

'Mummy was joking.'

'Oh,' says Chelsea.

'What about your friends?' Geoff asks.

'They've all dumped me, apart from Chelsea.'

'And Lord Balls Wyndham-Price who wants to marry her,' pipes up Chelsea.

Chelsea will be springing a red book on me any minute, and chiming *Poppy Wellesley, this is your life*.

'Lord Balls?' giggles Ruby.

'What a fascinating life you do lead,' says Taylor emptying the last of the jalfrezi onto his plate.

'I think it's really sad. They can't have been real friends Poppy, not if they dropped you just because you didn't have money,' says Ruby.

'Well you're in good company because we don't have any money either, well Tay does ...' begins Geoff and stops when Taylor gives him a sharp look.

Yes well, I expect as a drug pedlar he makes pots of money.

'You have money, Geoff,' says Taylor.

'Oh yeah. I don't think I'm in Poppy's league,' laughs Geoff as he fiddles with the music player.

The sounds of Nina Simone fill the boat and I feel myself relax. Of course it could be the wine or come to that the Rohypnol. He's

Chelsea's type, I can see that. She's always liked the boy-next-door look and if I'm honest she's been after a bit of rough for years.

'You can afford good wine,' laughs Taylor, uncorking another bottle.

'I don't read the papers,' says Ruby, pulling her handmade earrings from a huge beaded bag. 'I bet they wrote loads of lies about you.'

'What do you do?' I ask Geoff.

God, I'm like Chelsea's mother. I'll be asking if he has a good income and what his prospects are next.

'I'm an anaesthetist.'

'Ooh that sounds grand,' says Chelsea. 'What do anaesthetists do?'

I roll my eyes. Chelsea is the sweetest friend but I sometimes wonder if she was dropped on her head as a baby.

'I'm a junior doctor. I'm learning how to put people under,' he grins.

It gets worse by the minute.

'I've never been put under,' says Chelsea.

There's still time. You've got to admit Chelsea does ask for it. Taylor holds up a tub of Ben and Jerry's.

'Who's for ice cream?'

'Ooh me,' says Ruby, raising her hand. 'I'll get the dishes.'

Taylor smiles at me. He looks very handsome or is it the effect of the wine? But he isn't as handsome as Roddy, and I do miss Roddy.

'We ought to get going really,' I say, attempting to stand up but the effects of the wine and the lowness of the cushion make it impossible.

'You can't go before the ice cream,' says Ruby. 'And besides, I want to show you my jewellery. I would really appreciate your opinion. I imagine you've only ever bought the best.'

An hour later Chelsea and I have purchased a pair of earrings and a bracelet each, all for the princely sum of five pounds.

'Do you really have nowhere to spend Christmas?' Taylor asks, pulling a scatter cushion close to me. He smells lovely and I inhale the fragrance. It's much softer than Roddy's aftershave. I sigh at the thought of Roddy.

'Nowhere. Nobody wants me in their home. I'm an embarrassment.'

'Yes, I had noticed. Stripping off in other people's homes can be a bit disconcerting.'

I widen my eyes.

'That was your fault.'

He grins wickedly.

'Yes, I suppose it was. I'm sorry for the *on the game* comment earlier by the way.'

I sip my wine and feel my foot touch his calf.

'Oh that's okay. Pulling my clothes off was by far worse.'

A flash through the window makes my stomach churn. The sound of a paparazzi camera and the distinctive flashing that accompanies it is all too familiar. Ruby naively opens the curtains to a volley of flashes.

'People are photographing the inside of the boat,' she squeals.

'Oh no,' I groan.

'Oh dear,' mumbles Chelsea. 'Do you think the paparazzi have found where you're living?'

I jump up and wobble with the movement of the boat.

'I've had enough of this,' I slur, ambling through the hatch and feeling something catch on my Versace blouse.

'Christ,' I moan as the freezing air hits me in the face. It must be minus four out here. Shit, what was I thinking of? I pull myself up and feel the blouse rip.

'Poppy come back into the boat,' calls Chelsea.

'Bollocks. Bollocks to everything,' I groan, and am blinded by a hail of flashes.

'Poppy, what it is like slumming it on the boat? A bit of a comedown for a posh girl like you?' yells a voice from the darkness.

I feel a hand on my arm.

'Poppy, you should go back down. Your blouse is torn,' Taylor whispers.

Wanking tit basket, that's all I need.

'Is this the new boyfriend,' shouts another to a shower of flashes.

'No it isn't,' I say firmly.

'Look mate, you need to push off. I don't know how you got in because the gates are locked at eight. You're on private property,' says Geoff.

'Just doing our job, don't get involved,' says the photographer.

I clutch the side of the boat as I feel myself wobble.

'Is this your bit of rough Poppy? Does Roddy know?'

'Oh just go away,' cries Chelsea. 'You're all horrid.'

'Okay, time for you to move on,' says Taylor. I feel Chelsea tremble beside me and grasp her hand.

'It's ripped Poppy, you can see ...' she says.

'Nice tits darling, let's get a shot of those.'

I gasp when I realise my bra is on show again. I'm becoming an accidental exhibitionist. Taylor grabs the photographer by his coat collar.

'Push off mush,' growls the photographer.

'I don't think you heard me, mush,' mimics Taylor. 'It's time for you to move on,' he snatches the camera and throws it to the ground.

'I didn't give you permission to take photos of me and you're trespassing. Now get off the canal before I call the police.'

'That's a bloody expensive camera mate. I don't think much of your new boyfriend Poppy. 'E's not got old Roddy's class 'as 'e?'

The other pap sends a volley of flashes before they both hurry off. I pull my blouse together and stand shivering.

'Get back in the warm, you'll freeze to death you two,' grins Geoff.

'I'm so sorry,' I say.

Ruby stands with her hand over her mouth.

'That was awful. I was about to phone the police,' she says breathlessly. 'I've never known such excitement before.'

We obviously have different ideas of excitement.

'I'll walk you to a get a cab,' Geoff says to Chelsea. 'See them off if they're still hanging around.'

'I'll walk you to your boat. Get that log fire going,' smiles Taylor.

'I'll join you Geoff,' says Ruby, donning her hat, scarf, and coat. She grabs me, almost knocking me over and gives me a huge kiss on the cheek. I'm so taken aback I can't speak. I think it has been years since another woman actually kissed my cheek. I'm far more used to air-kissing.

'I think you're lovely Poppy. A bit stuck up maybe but you can't help that. I was thinking you could come and work for *Blundell's.* You know, help make the sandwiches. They need someone else and we'd be working together. It would be great.'

I gape at her. That has to be the worst idea ever aside from declaring war on Iraq.

'And they'll be lots of Christmas perks too,' she adds excitedly.

'I'll give it some thought,' I say, knowing with absolute certainty that I won't.

'And I was thinking, you can spend Boxing Day with us, can't she Taylor? We're all getting together on Boxing Day. It's Dusty's birthday you see.'

It's just gets worse.

'Oh, my tree is in the car,' I say after they've left.

Taylor hands me my poncho.

'Just as well, there is only so much excitement you can take in one evening. You can collect the tree tomorrow.'

He is mocking me but I don't have the energy to fight back. He helps me onto the deck and I look around nervously.

'The photographers have gone. Don't worry. Do you want to wait in mine while I get the log burner going for you? Get the place warmed up.'

I hope he doesn't think I'm easy pickings now I've shown him my breasts, and not just once but twice. I think of Roddy and get a sinking feeling in the pit of my stomach. He can't marry Pug-face he just can't and I mustn't get involved with someone like Taylor. Life with Taylor would mean a lifetime of Nivea face cream in place of La Prairie, and I can't imagine ever flying economy. I never want to get up close and personal with anyone in economy other than Roddy of course. Just the thought of Roddy makes me feel all frisky. It's having those Coco de Mer goodies on the boat that's doing it. It's no good; I just can't become one of the lower classes. I simply can't and there is no way I can get involved with anyone other than Roddy. I just know Daddy will get things sorted. Everything will be tickety-boo by the New Year. I'm thirty-two; I know Roddy said we wouldn't rush into having sprogs too early but this is getting ridiculous. By the time Daddy gets sorted and Roddy and I set the wedding date again, not to mention getting pug-faced bloody Pandora out of the way, I'll be thirty-four. God I'll be middle aged.

'Thanks but I'm really tired,' I say. 'I think I'll hop straight into bed.'

Not that there is much room to hop anywhere in that buggery boat. I can't do my morning Pilates without risking fracturing a body part on the side of the boat. Who lives like this? Poor people that's who. I can't even stretch out in the bath it's that small. I had a Jacuzzi in the apartment. If I want bubbles now I have to fart in the bath. Oh, what a come down.

'No worries, I'll see you to the boat and get the log burner going.'

Fifteen minutes later and he's gone. Not a whiff of marijuana or a polythene bag in sight. I don't know what I was expecting but I certainly didn't expect him to leave without making at least a small pass. Seems I can't pull anyone these days. With that thought, I climb fully clothed into the bed and fall asleep.

Chapter Nineteen

I can't decide whether to wear Boden or Jaeger to an interview at Blundell's. I finally choose Boden, only to find I can't zip up the skirt. When did that happen? Bloody truffles. I rummage through the cupboard for my spanx and struggle into it. It's like squeezing my body into a king-size condom. After holding my breath until I turn blue I get the thing on. I'm finally studying myself in the tiny mirror when there is a tap on the door.

'Pop, it's me. Are you home? I've something I need to tell you.'

Oh no, it's Roddy. I don't want him seeing me looking fat. I dash into the bedroom and rummage around for my kimono.

'I can hear you. I'm coming in,' he calls.

I lean across the bed to reach for the kimono and hear a groan from behind me. I'm only sticking my fat arse in the air.

'Christ Pop,' he groans.

'I know, I know. I've gained weight,' I say grabbing the kimono.

'What a turn on. I've got to have you.'

Oh, what. Not now, I have an interview to get to.

He throws his body on top of mine and I'm squashed flat on the bed. If I couldn't breathe before, I certainly can't now.

'Jesus Pop, this new you is driving me insane,' he moans, pulling at the spanx.

What new me? He can't surely mean the poor new me can he?

'Which new me?' I ask.

'The sexy, voluptuous, with big tits, new you.'

Ooh big tits. Goodie, that's a bonus. Shame about the big arse though.

'Roddy,' I say, trying to turn over and feeling the spanx cut into my nipples. 'This isn't the time.'

'I want you, you filthy little filly. Come on spank me for being a naughty boy climbing onto your boat like this. You like spanking don't you? I don't mind if you spank your friends. It's exciting.'

'It was a spanking lesson Roddy. I don't want you telling the whole world that Chelsea and I spank each other. I don't need any more bad publicity.'

I wriggle onto my back and am attacked by his hot wet lips and oh it feels so lovely. I fight the overwhelming urge to pull him even closer.

'Where's that little sailor outfit I bought you,' he whispers huskily. 'Do you still have it?'

'Well, yes ...'

'Say aye aye Captain.'

This is getting ridiculous. I know I said I'd be the best dominatrix ever but there is a time and place for everything isn't there?

'Roddy, I can't do this not until you break things off with Pandora.'

'Shush,' he says.

'But Roddy ...'

'Hi, yah, I'm here,' he says. 'Of course I'm missing you darling.'

I stare at him.

'I'm looking for a special Christmas present,' he says before smacking his lips down the phone. It's nauseating, it really is.

'Of course I will. Yes, absolutely. No, of course. Yes, yes I will. Bye darling.'

He clicks off his Bluetooth.

'Pandora,' he mumbles.

'I'd never have guessed. You're pathetic at times Roddy,' I say, struggling off the bed. 'What is it you've got to tell me?'

He shakes his head.

'Oh, it's nothing. Poppy, when can I visit you? You know ...' he says, looking pointedly at my breasts.

'Roddy, you broke off our engagement, just when I needed you most and ...'

'I know Pop and I'm sorry but I'm in this really sticky fix and ...'

He should be in this spanx.

'I was wondering about the ring Poppy.'

It seems the bloody ring is all he wonders about.

'I've got an interview. You have to leave,' I say firmly, while so much wanting him to stay.

'But Pop ...'

'Now, or I'll phone Pandora and tell her you're here and not Christmas shopping at all.'

He walks dejectedly to the door.

'Jesus, I can't believe you're living on this. It's demeaning,' he says clambering up the steps and catching his Bluetooth earpiece on the side of the hatch.

'I won't give up,' he says climbing onto the deck.

I sigh and quickly change out of the spanx into a black body thong. Of all the days, Roddy sure chooses them.

I make my way along the canal and wait by a half-melted snowman for Ruby. She jumps on me from behind.

'I thought that was your new boyfriend,' she laughs, nodding to the snowman.

'Ah yes. This is him. He doesn't say much, and between you and me he's a bit cold, nice carrot though.'

She laughs and takes my arm.

'It's along here,' she says pointing ahead.

I see the baker's and feel a wave of panic. What am I doing? I'm Poppy Wellesley; my father is Sir Rupert Wellesley. I'm rich, I'm very very rich. I can't possibly take a job in a baker's.

'Ha,' whispers my mother's voice, like a modern day Jacob Marley. 'You're poor now and all that's left for you is sandwich making.'

I picture Mummy with her special chin apparatus. When she wears it she does seriously resemble Scrooge's business partner.

'Keeps the wrinkles at bay,' she'd said.

Personally I think the only thing that will keep them at bay is La Prairie night cream.

'And how long can you afford La Prairie?' hisses Mummy, dragging her chains behind her. Christ, I'm having a mental breakdown. This is what losing all your money does to you.

'Come on,' says Ruby.

Inside the shop the heat hits us. A red-faced girl with a white cap is serving behind the counter.

'Hiya,' she says. 'It might be cold enough to freeze the balls off a brass monkey out there but I'm sweating like a turkey on Christmas Eve. Oh hello,' she adds on seeing me. 'I like your coat.'

'Is that bloody Ruby here yet, with the posh girl?' barks a voice from the back.

Ruby grins at me.

'Here she is Bill,' she says and shoves me through a beaded curtain.

'Come in,' Bill shouts.

I try to, I really do, but the stupid beads in the curtain are caught in my earring and one false move could see me earless.

'Come in then,' calls Bill.

'I'm trying to,' I say, battling with the curtain.

I must seem so hesitant. Ruby, realising what's happening rushes to my aid.

'Oh bollocks,' she says. 'I always said this thing would take someone's eye out but I never imagined it would be an ear.'

'Are you coming in or what?' bellows Bill.

'I'm almost there.'

'It's not a bleeding obstacle course,' shouts a mystified Bill.

It feels like it right now. Just as Ruby frees my earring Bill whips the curtain to one side.

'What the bloody 'ell's going on?' he snaps.

'This is Poppy,' says Ruby pushing me forward. He steps back and looks at me.

'You look like you're wearing half of Whipsnade zoo around your shoulders,' he snorts.

Mummy rattles her chains and mumbles, 'She's not rich any more.'

'It's not real fur,' I say as I take off my coat.

'Ruby says you want a job.'

No, I don't want a job. I just want to be able to eat.

'Right,' he appraises me. 'This is a bakery, not a film set. You won't need your pearls 'ere. The closest we get to the movies is Disney party cupcakes.'

'She can make sandwiches, can't you Poppy?' says Ruby.

'Anyone can make a sandwich,' says Bill.

Oh dear, I'm destined to disappoint.

'I can make truffles too,' I say, trying to impress.

Bill snorts.

'Ain't no call for posh mushrooms around here.'

'Chocolate truffles,' I correct. 'Do you want to try some?'

'They're lovely,' says Ruby licking her lips.

He looks at the truffles and hands them to Ruby.

'Put them by the till with the mince pies. So what's your size Poppet?'

'My size?'

What has my size got to do with the price of bacon?

'For the overall,' says Bill, yawning.

I stare at him. Do I look like the kind of woman who would wear an overall?

'I don't need an overall,' I say. 'And my name is *Poppy* actually.'

His eyes dart from me to Ruby.

'If you're making sandwiches for Bill Blundell, you wear an overall Poppet,' he says firmly. 'You'll have the food standards agency onto me if you don't. Two hundred and fifty a week, that's before deductions. I'll need a P45 if you've got one, and you can start Monday on a week's trial.'

Two hundred and fifty a week? That wouldn't even cover my highlights. He cocks his head to one side and studies me.

'I've got a size fourteen, that should fit you.'

Size fourteen?

'Any questions?' he asks lifting his glasses and rubbing his eyes.

'Do you have a size 12?' I ask.

'Thanks Bill,' says Ruby, pulling me away. 'You've got it,' she whispers dragging me through the beaded curtain.

'Does he call everyone *Poppet* or does he really think that's my name?' I ask.

I should celebrate really but there is no one to celebrate with apart from Chelsea and she's doing her stint at the art gallery today. I hail a cab and allow Ruby to kiss me on the cheek before climbing in. I pull my vibrating phone from my bag and click it on.

'Hello.'

'Poppy it's Marcus.'

I feel a flutter of excitement in my stomach.

'Marcus, how are you?'

Please be phoning to invite me to a party, or a fun weekend, or just anything.

'Yah, I'm great. How erm, how are you doing? How's the old barge?'

'It's looking great actually; you should come over again with the gang.'

I hold my breath and wait for him to agree but he clears his throat.

'I'd love to mosey down to the canal, old girl but it's all cringingly embarrassing isn't it? I just thought you should know, because I don't suppose any other bugger will tell you.'

Tell me what?

'Roddy and Pandora have got engaged. They'll be announcing it in *Country Life* and no doubt the damn nationals will pick it up and ...'

My head spins and there's a buzzing in my ears. But wasn't Roddy just with me? Oh, how could he?

'I thought as you had a new boyfriend ...'

Roddy is engaged to Pug-face Pandora? Is he insane? He always said he couldn't stand her.

'I don't have a boyfriend,' I say, feeling my throat close up.

'Oh, I thought the papers said some guy on the boats or ... Oh golly, never believe the papers right?'

I click off the phone.

'Can you stop please?'

'What 'ere, Buckingham Palace?' says the cab driver.

He brakes sharply and I open the door and lean out, feeling the body thong ping undone at the crotch as I do so. I then throw up on the Queen's doorstep. That's how us rich do it.

Chapter Twenty

'I come bearing gifts, mistletoe to be precise.'

Taylor peeks through the hatch and I try to smile.

'Come in,' I say, when all I want is to be alone. 'I'm not quite sure what I'll do with it,' I shrug.

He boards holding the mistletoe aloft. Before I know what's happening I am embraced in his arms and his lips are on mine. My shoulders tense. How dare he? What is it with men, thinking they can take advantage of your body whenever they fancy. He releases me and I exhale.

'How dare you,' I say. 'I'm not some kind of sex object.'

While rather wishing I was. He sighs.

'You're one uppity madam aren't you? Just for your information that's what you do with mistletoe.'

'I didn't ask for a demonstration,' I say, realising I sound very ungrateful.

'Where do you want it?' he asks, looking around.

I open my mouth and close it again.

'You look shell-shocked,' he says. 'Was my kissing that bad? Or are you just in a filthy mood.'

'It wasn't that bad but I've had better.'

'So have I,' he says not missing a beat.

I try not to smile. The truth is it was the nicest kiss ever but I don't want him to know that do I?

'My fiancé got engaged today,' I say.

He puts the mistletoe down.

'Your fiancé?' he repeats.

I nod.

'Unfortunately he can't be your fiancé can he? Not if he's just got engaged to someone else, unless he got engaged to you, which from the look on your face isn't the case,' he says.

'Smart arse.'

He raises his eyebrows and I smile.

'How about if I take you to a really decadent Christmas party where I can guarantee there won't be any rich people? I'm off duty tonight and I've got no one to go with.'

'Well ...' I say, while wondering how a drug dealer can be off duty.

'Great, you've got forty minutes to get ready.'

It won't take that long to find something in my stupid wardrobe but it will take forty minutes to get the creases out. He hangs the mistletoe and with a thumbs up informs me he'll be back. I rummage through my clothes and settle on a simple black dress I'd bought in Paris. I find my Donna Karan cashmere blanket coat and tuck a scarf into my Mulberry handbag. Finally I clip on the matching pearl necklace and earrings that Daddy had bought me in Cannes. I leave my hair down and brush some soft peach blusher across my cheeks and am just applying lipstick when Taylor peeks through the hatch.

'Permission to come aboard Captain?' he asks.

He looks appealing in a white shirt. His hair is still slightly damp and I envy his shower. My little tub is so small I get cramp when I use it. His gorgeous eyes survey me and I try not to fidget under his gaze.

'Feeling better now?' he asks.

I grit my teeth.

'I wasn't unwell,' I say.

'Just in a filthy mood?' he grins. 'By the way, you look really lovely,' he adds, surveying my dress. 'Roddy's lost a good one.'

'A poor one,' I say.

'Money isn't everything. Let's go, I booked a cab, it should be waiting.'

We travel in silence and I enjoy the sights of London at Christmas with its twinkling lights and Dickensian atmosphere. There is nothing like Christmas in London. We drive along the Embankment passing rows of party boats bursting with revellers. I crave my old life. The drunken nights strolling along the Embankment with my stilettos in my hand while Roddy serenaded me. The cab stops in Chelsea Walk and I'm pulled back to the present.

'Here we are,' says Taylor, taking my hand.

We approach a brightly lit town house with sounds of laughter above the thumping music. The door bursts open and we are greeted by a smiling man.

'Tay, happy Christmas mate,' he says.

'I've brought a friend. Poppy this is Richard, a work colleague.'

He doesn't look in the least like a drug dealer. Mind you it's all very sophisticated these days isn't it? I imagine Howard Marks had parties just like these. After all, he wasn't known as Mr Nice for nothing, and Taylor Havers is also very nice, if I do say so myself.

'Hi Poppy, great to meet you. Glad you could come.'

I walk along the hall and brush past a skeleton.

'Mind Bones,' laughs Richard.

'Tay,' shouts a woman from the kitchen 'Merry Christmas.'

Taylor kisses her on the cheek. No air-kissing for these people it seems.

'Hello,' she says looking at me keenly. In fact quite a lot of people are looking at me keenly.

'This is Poppy,' says Taylor. 'She's just bought the boat next to me.'

'Hi Poppy,' says Molly, pecking me on the cheek.

She pushes us towards a buffet table.

'Have some food. There's plenty.'

A plate is pushed into my hands and I stand uncertainly at the table. *Love is here to stay* strums through the speakers and I sway to the music. I sip my wine and feel Taylor at my side.

'The food not up to scratch?' he asks.

I look at the quiches and salads and sausages on sticks.

'I'm waiting to be served,' I say.

He laughs.

'Ah, then you may wait quite a while I'm afraid. It's self-service. Unless, of course, you were hoping I'd do the honours.'

'Oh,' I say, feeling stupid.

I watch as he piles coleslaw and quiche onto his plate and follow suit. He holds a sausage on a stick towards me and I could die from embarrassment.

'Go on, be common,' he urges with a smile.

I bite the sausage and feel myself blush. I chew it nervously, expecting it to taste foul but it's actually quite good. I place a few more onto my plate and help myself sparingly to quiche and salad. After all I'm still smarting from Bill's size 14 comment. A man in a faded grey shirt heads towards us. He is smoking a cigarette, and is that a spliff in his hand? I knew it. This is a drugs party and I've come in my Donna Karan cashmere blanket coat like your typical upper-crust junkie. Talking of which I'm now sweltering in the thing. There is so much body heat here. The guy reaches us and I see the spliff is in fact a Chinese spring roll and the cigarette is electronic. He is sucking the cigarette with all the gusto of a baby at the nipple. He's a breastfed baby that's for sure. You can always tell can't you?

'Across a crowded room and all that ...' he says mysteriously. He winks at me, and then winks again, and again, and I realise he has a twitch. I try to ignore it and avoid eye contact. He sips at a beer can and sucks at the cigarette again before saying,

'I just knew we had to connect, it's like our bio-rhythms were in sync, do you know where I'm coming from?'

From planet Krypton by any chance? For some reason I find myself wondering what Roddy is doing at this moment. I don't know why. Maybe it's the twitching. Roddy twitches when he comes. The first time it happened I thought he was having a seizure and threw him off me to phone 999. That went down like a lead balloon as did his erection. I never really got used to it. It was like watching his eye orgasm. I wonder if he's twitching now. I hope not. I turn back to the guy in the faded shirt who, by the way, is not orgasmic. At least I hope he isn't.

'Did you feel it?' he asks.

Then again maybe he is.

'I'm sorry did I miss something?'

I look for Taylor but he has moved to the other end of the table.

'You like a sausage on a stick do you?' the guy asks between puffs and sips and not forgetting the twitching.

'Because if it's sausage you want, look no further. Darren Roberts at your disposal and I have just the toad for your hole.'

Am I really hearing this or is the food drugged and I'm tripping.

'Thanks very much but if I am going to have a sausage then I prefer a nice big juicy one not a chipolata.'

I see Taylor approaching and sigh with relief.

Darren takes a gulp of beer and wipes his chin with his hand.

'Yeah well to be honest you're a bit too thin for me,' he says nastily.

Oh good. That's the best insult I've had for weeks.

'And you're a bit thick for me,' I retort, feeling Taylor's hand on my hip. His touch seems to bring my body alive.

'Hi Darren, you've met Poppy I see,' he says calmly.

'Yep,' says Darren briskly. 'Didn't realise you were here Tay. Not saving lives tonight?'

'I think I just saved yours,' he grins.

'Yep,' says Darren pointing a finger towards the drinks. 'Another beer I think.'

I laugh as he wanders off.

'Thank you for rescuing me,' I say, accepting a plate of cheese from him.

He smiles.

'You don't need rescuing. Let's get a drink.'

An hour later we're dancing cheek to cheek, and it feels lovely. Of course I've drunk another glass of wine or two since then and removed my coat. My body feels on fire and his hand on the small of my back makes me heady.

'Thanks for coming,' he says quietly. 'I know it's not what you're used to.'

'The sausages were a challenge,' I joke.

The music changes and John Legend's *All of Me* begins to play.

'I can't offer diamonds but a sausage on a stick, always.'

'Promises, promises,' I say boldly, feeling the wine relax me.

'I'm sorry about your ex-fiancé.'

Just the mention of Roddy makes the rash itch. I fight the urge to scratch.

'I wish you'd let me give you something for that.'

'I don't take drugs,' I say firmly. 'I know the papers have me down as a lush and raging drug addict but it's not true. I've never even puffed a joint. So, I'm not going to be taking ecstasy anytime soon.'

Good that's that out in the open.

'Right,' he says, twirling me around. 'I was thinking more of an antihistamine,' he smiles.

'I'm sure once everything gets sorted with Daddy it will go,' I say, impressed at my own positivity.

He leads me to a couch where a guy strumming a guitar moves over for us.

'Hey Tay,' he says. 'You must be on uppers. I heard you had a long one last night.'

He *is* a drug dealer, I knew it. I give him a sideways glance. He seems amazingly relaxed for someone on uppers. He introduces the man as Matt and accepts a couple of cans from him.

'Do you work with all these people?' I ask.

He laughs.

'Not all of them. Talking of work, how did it go with Blundell?'

'Apart from the fact he thinks I'm a size 14 and calls me *Poppet*, it went great.'

'Have a beer to ease the pain,' says Taylor.

'I'm going to be making sandwiches in a size 14 overall. Can you imagine what a comedown that is? I always had people making sandwiches for me,' I say.

He cracks open his can and takes a swig. I wait for someone to offer me a glass. Either they're in short supply or no one bothers with them as everyone seems to be swigging from cans or bottles. I pull back the ring pull, take a swig and shudder.

'You're not needed tonight then?' says Matt.

'No, it's my first night off in nine months.'

Well that clinches it. That's why he's home so late. God knows where he peddles drugs but he's obviously well known. They all seem very upmarket for dealers. Probably high-class ones, supplying celebs and the like. The press will be all over me if I'm seen with him.

'Is there a back way out of here?' I ask.

'I expect so,' laughs Matt. 'Ashamed of us are you?'

'I just don't think it will be good for me to be seen leaving with Taylor.'

'I know I'm a bit of a comedown for you but isn't that a bit extreme?' smiles Taylor.

In fact I don't think it will be good for me to be seen leaving here, period. It's most likely known for its high-class drug parties. What if Roddy sees the story? It's enough the papers are assuming I'm a drug addict but if I'm seen leaving with a well-known drugs dealer that will be the end.

'You can leave on my arm if you like,' says Matt.

'It doesn't make much difference does it? You're the same aren't you?' I say.

'Same in what way?' asks Matt.

'You both deal in drugs.'

'I do,' says Matt, 'I'm not so sure Taylor is as qualified.'

Qualified? They take it very seriously don't they?

'The press will have a field day with me,' I say. 'They already have me down as a druggie.'

'As a pharmacist its part of the job description,' laughs Matt.

I stare at him. Hang on a minute. Geoff said he was an anaesthetist, Matt is a pharmacist. Oh God, that means ...

'You're not a drug baron?' I ask Taylor.

'No, sorry to disappoint.'

'He's a surgical registrar,' says Matt, 'specialising in A&E.'

Peas and rice. Who would have thought it?

Chapter Twenty-One

It's a beautiful sunny December day. Colder than the Arctic mind you, and what am I doing? I'm walking my shit to what feels like the other end of the world. Snow-frosted trees and carol singers remind me it will soon be Christmas. I'm down to my last thousand pounds. I don't know where the money goes and, apart from the gifts for the Landales' party, I haven't bought a single Christmas present yet. Mind you, there isn't anyone apart from Chelsea to buy for, although I'm thinking I should buy a little something for Ruby, and perhaps Taylor. My heart quickens at the thought of Taylor and I push his image from my mind. What am I doing with these people? Chelsea is forever going home armed with cheap booze and perfume and I've a fridge full of sausage meat. Yes, you heard me, *sausage meat*. Geoff gets it cheap. I don't have a clue what to do with it and have taken to feeding the stray cat with it. Of course, the stray cat now strays to the outside of my boat more than anyone else's.

I push the wheelbarrow over a bump and Ruby gasps.

'Arseholes,' she says. 'A bit of shit just flew out of your cassette.'

This is so gross.

'Are you sure it was mine?'

'Do you see anyone else with a wheelbarrow of shit? Yeah I'm sure.'

This is totally mortifying. We stop and Ruby studies the cassette.

'It's got a crack in it,' she says.

'Crap in it?'

'Yes, well no, a crack in the cassette.'

How can it have a crack in it? I've not been passing billiard balls have I? Okay I've been a bit constipated with all the upset but hell I've got to go to town to crack the thing. Honestly this could only happen to me couldn't it? Only I could have a crack in my loo cassette.

'Watch the bumps or you'll be spilling it everywhere,' says Ruby, her dangly earrings swinging beneath her bow cloche hat. It occurs to me I could give her one of my designer hats for Christmas. Thinking of hats reminds me of clothes and I realise I have nothing to wear for the new job. I don't think Stella McCartney is quite the thing is it? I'll be the best dressed sandwich maker in town.

'I need clothes for Blundell's,' I say.

'I'll take you to Primark,' she says excitedly. 'You'll love it. We can go when I finish today.'

Now I know I've reached the pits. The rich bitch has finally succumbed to the deprivation of Primark. There surely can be no turning back. Then I look up and see the ultimate shame coming towards me. I blink. Well, you never know it might be a mirage. But no such luck. In just a few seconds I'll be bumping into my ex-fiancé's new fiancée while pushing a wheelbarrow carrying a leaky cassette full of my shit. This is best to be avoided. Bumping into Pug-face is best avoided at any time, never mind while pushing a wheelbarrow of your own ... Well yes, the less said the better. If only the ground would open up and swallow me. I close my fists so my cracked and broken nails can't be seen.

'Bollocks,' I mumble.

To make matters worse she has that satisfied look of someone who is getting a good shagging. If I didn't know better I'd swear that is a post-orgasmic flush on her face. But I know Pandora is priggish about sex. She'd never do it during the day. I lower my head and pray she doesn't recognise me.

'Poppy Wellesley,' she shrieks. 'Is that really you?'

There's no justice is there?

She's wearing a beautiful pashmina over one shoulder of her cashmere coat. I feel a pang of envy. How dare she steal Roddy from me and under my nose too? I try not to look at the ring on her finger but the bling is so big it's impossible not to see it. I can't believe the size of it. If I threw her in the river she would sink straight to the bottom. Now, there's a thought.

'Hello Pug ... Erm Pandora,' I stutter. 'Fancy seeing you here.'

She looks at the wheelbarrow curiously.

'Poppy, you're looking ... different. I never knew you liked gardening,' she says sweetly.

That's because I don't. Ruby stifles a giggle.

'This is Ruby,' I say.

'Ruby,' echoes Pandora raising her eyebrows. 'That's an unusual name isn't it?'

'Is it?' says Ruby. 'So is Pandora isn't it? I've only ever heard of Pandora's Box. You know, open it and there's trouble.'

I move the wheelbarrow and it tips to the side. I watch horrified as a small amount of shit seeps out. I wince and Ruby quickly points at Pandora's pashmina.

'That's a lovely scarf,' she says.

'It's Dior, and it's a pashmina actually,' says Pandora primly.

She looks into the wheelbarrow, sniffs and pulls back.

'What is that?' she asks.

'Manure,' says Ruby who's sharper than a penknife. 'We're on our way to my allotment.'

'Good God, you are actually gardening Poppy. Isn't it the wrong time of year though?' asks Pandora, who is suddenly an expert on all things naturalist. It's all that sex she's having.

I look at Ruby.

'I'm preparing the soil,' she says.

'How quaint,' smiles Pandora, glancing at my fingernails.

I push them into my pockets.

'Lovely ring,' says Ruby.

She'll run out of things to compliment Pandora on soon and then what will we do?

'I bet that cost a bit. You want to be careful around here. There's some that'll chop your hand off for that.'

Pandora doesn't seem in the least intimidated and holds her finger out to me and in that moment I feel totally justified in chopping off her hand myself.

'I told Roddy I didn't want a similar ring to yours but he assured me yours was much smaller.'

Bitch. I hate her.

'I saw in the papers that you have a new boyfriend, *Troy* or something. He's very handsome.'

'Taylor,' I correct. 'And he's just a friend.'

How can you get Troy and Taylor mixed up. Honestly, she could at least get my friends' names right.

'That's not what the papers said.'

'Yes well, the papers said you were twenty-five,' I say bitchily, gripping the wheelbarrow.

Ruby pulls a face.

'I think a bird has just pooed on your scarf,' says Ruby. 'That's good luck isn't it? We must get on Poppy. We've got a shit load to get through.'

I close my eyes and sigh. Oh no, it didn't splash onto her pashmina did it?

'Oh no, it's ruined,' cries Pandora rubbing at the pashmina like a woman demented.

'We must go,' I say, feeling guilty.

'Give Roddy our love,' says Ruby, marching forward with the wheelbarrow.

'Bye,' I call.

'Stuck up cow, that'll teach her,' laughs Ruby.

'I can't believe she saw my nails. She'll tell everyone. I've never felt so ashamed in my whole life.'

'They're only nails,' reprimands Ruby. 'I know a great place in the market. We'll get them done after Primark.'

'The market?' I stutter.

No way. I'm Poppy Wellesley. I don't have my nails done in the market. I just don't. They probably use metal nail files. I don't even want to think about it.

'It's only a fiver.'

'Where do they get their polish from, Homebase?' I say sarcastically.

'You can mock,' says Ruby. 'But it's all you can afford now isn't it?'

She's not wrong. I so miss those days of being rich, spoilt and pampered. There and then I decide to get Roddy back no matter what it takes. Although I think wearing Primark clothes is not what it takes.

'Let's get Primark over with first. I may not be in a fit state to go to the market after that.'

'You'll love Primark,' she says, brimming over with excitement while I'm brimming over with dread. 'You won't believe it when you see it.'

I think she's right on that one.

Browsing clothes in Primark is like having teeth pulled without anaesthetic. I'm amazed at the number of people who actually do seem to enjoy it. I've never seen so many tattooed women together in one place. It's like a tattoo convention. I'm shoved to the side by a woman swinging her saggy breasts and resist the temptation to point her in the direction of the underwear department. I don't imagine they do bra fittings here and if they do I dread to think what they're like. A case of grab and guess I imagine. Another woman knocks me sideways while grabbing the last black halter top. She needn't have bothered. I'd happily have stepped out of her way. I wouldn't be seen dead in this stuff. Ruby on the other hand is piling her basket high with it.

'You need a few tops and jeans. That's all I wear round the offices,' she says, holding the most grotesque blouse I've ever seen against me.

'Offices?' I gasp. 'You never mentioned offices. I thought we just made sandwiches.'

'We have to deliver as well,' she says, trying on a scarf.

I look around despondently and when I turn back Ruby's gone. It's all I can do not to scream her name at the top of my voice. She can't leave me here alone, she just can't.

'Ruby,' I say calmly. 'Where are you?'

I feel my head spin. She could be anywhere. This place is huge. I watch in shocked horror as the woman with the saggy breasts stuffs two halter tops down the front of her jumper. From the size of those breasts it wouldn't surprise me if she had several dresses and a handbag down there as well. She's probably supplying the whole of Walthamstow. I'm still staring when her eyes lock onto mine. Bollocking shit. I'm pushed along the aisles and come face to face with a terrified looking woman. At least I'm not the only one scared to death. That's a relief. Then I realise I'm looking at my own reflection. God, is that what I look like? I'm like the heroine out of a horror movie; you know permanent fear on my face. Is this what Pandora saw? I need to get out of here.

'Ruby,' I cry, 'where are you?'

I look around and feel myself grow dizzy. My arm is grabbed and I scream.

'I found you this,' says Ruby.

My heart is hammering so loudly that I barely hear her. She holds a long flowery skirt in one hand and a cropped green jumper in the other.

'I'll take them,' I say in a high-pitched voice.

'You all right doll,' says wobbly breasts.

'Yes I'm fine,' I say, pulling Ruby to the tills.

'Don't you want to try them first?' asks Ruby.

No, most certainly not. It's probably an open changing room. Oh, too unbearable for words. I'll have nightmares about wobbly breasts for the rest of my life. Finally we are out of the store and it takes me ten minutes to stop scratching my arms.

'Let's get a coffee and then we'll go to the market,' says Ruby and I begin to think I'm on an endurance course. My mobile trills and I pull it from my bag. It's Roddy. My heart somersaults as I answer it.

'Hello,' I say, my voice shaking.

'Is it true Poppy? Are you seeing someone else? I don't think I can bear it. Pandora said she saw you and ...'

He can't bear it? He's marrying someone else isn't he? I'm having to bear that.

'Pandy said you told her some boat wanker called Tyler was your boyfriend. You can't be serious?'

Can't anyone get Taylor's name right? And I never told Andy Pandy any such thing.

'Why didn't you tell me you were engaged to Pandora?' I ask angrily.

'I tried to. It's not what I want Poppy. Do you think I'm happy?'

Ruby leads me into a Starbucks and pulls her mobile from her beaded shoulder bag.

'You know I only want you. P'pa's making a fuss that's all. I'm hoping everything gets sorted with your father and this wedding to Pandy won't happen and ... Damn, I've got to dash Pop, can I come to your boat again soon? We'll have a little jaunt and a chat. The thing is I'm in a bit of a fix.'

'Roddy ...'

The line goes dead and I sigh. The only little jaunt my boat does is to the bank on the other side. Didn't he notice how small my boat was? Most likely he was too busy looking at my bum.

'Geoff is getting a delivery of Chanel perfume tonight, do you want some?' Ruby asks.

'Oh,' I say. 'Real Chanel?'

'Of course,' she laughs.

'How much is it?'

'Ten quid for 50ml.'

'Ooh yes, and the wine if he's getting any.'

This is awful isn't it? I'll be shoving tops down my blouse next. It was so much easier pulling out my black American Express card.

'Do you want a skinny latte?'

'If he's getting them,' I say absently, checking my reflection in my handbag mirror. I look like a mad woman. My eyes are bright and my hair is wild. Another year of this and I'll be sectioned.

'Not from Geoff you dope. Do you want a coffee *now*?' she asks, clicking her fingers in my face.

I doubt if I'll last another week, let alone a year. Bing Crosby singing *Winter Wonderland* blares from the coffee shop's speakers and from the window I see a sign to Santa's Grotto. This is going to be the worst Christmas of my life. There'll be no parties, no family gathering and no turkey unless Geoff can get me a cheap one of course. I shall take great pleasure stuffing that while thinking of Roddy and his bollocking p'pa.

Chapter Twenty-Two

After Primark the last thing I need is the market but Ruby is insistent. Snow is falling and the smell of rotting sweet cauliflower mixed with the pungent odour of fried onions is playing havoc with my stomach and to make matters worse the place is full of those smug happy couples who barge into you because they only have eyes for each other. I swear one couple would have trampled me to death rather than unlink hands and go round me. I had to duck under their arms. They even have a little cuddle when buying fish and a little congratulatory kiss when it's handed to them. You'd think Mr Alpha Male caught it himself. I know, I'm just jealous.

'A lovely pair of melons for a pound,' hollers a market stallholder while winking suggestively at me. Another trader bangs on about a pound of bananas.

'I want some tomatoes,' says Ruby. 'Do you want a bowl?'

I shake my head. No one in their right mind buys food from a market stall do they? I'm certainly not going to start now. You get what you pay for if you want my opinion. My eyes land on the Christmas stall and I approach it hesitantly. I do need decorations for the tree though and these are very reasonable. I feel a pang at the thought of Christmas. This time last year I was placing my Christmas order at Harrods. Now look at me, I couldn't be further from Harrods if I tried.

'Alright there darling?' asks the stallholder. 'Do you want some balls?'

'I could do with some balls,' I say without thinking.

Oh no, did I really say that? Here of all places.

'Two boxes for a quid. You want large or small?'

I stupidly blush and can't find it in me to say large so opt for two boxes of small balls.

'Can I have some tinsel too please?'

'Course yer can darling.'

I might as well brighten the boat up for Christmas. I take the carrier bag and then see the stall next door is selling two boxes of mince pies for a pound. Mince pies will be okay won't they? They're in a box and everything. I'm not likely to catch anything from those. I buy two boxes and pop them into the carrier bag.

'Oh, you're buying things,' says Ruby, peeking into the bag.

'Not much,' I say, letting her lead me to a stall overflowing with cheap handbags and shoes. I wrinkle my nose in disgust. Don't you just hate fake handbags? Who seriously buys a fake Dior or Hermes when the real thing is so much better? God, I so detest being poor.

'Oh look at these Poppy,' she says, pointing to a pair of bright red boots. I struggle to hide my horror. They're seriously redder than Rudolph's nose and have a frightening resemblance to the ones Miss Tits and Tease wore for our spanking workshop.

'Aren't they just fabulous?' says Ruby, trying one on.

I certainly wouldn't be seen dead in them but then I wouldn't normally be seen dead in this market either. Oh, what has become of me? A few weeks ago I was preparing for a wedding shoot in *HELLO!* magazine and now I'm studying dominatrix boots and buying cheap mince pies. Mummy would die of shame if she knew.

'A fiver,' says the stallholder.

Ruby parades up and down in the boots. All she needs is a whip and suspenders and she's there. I clap my hands together to keep them warm as Ruby does her cat walk.

'You need a decent pair of turtle doves,' says the stallholder looking at me, 'not those bleedin' flimsy little things.'

'Turtle doves?' I repeat

He points to my gloves.

'Oh, these are Vivienne Westwood's,' I explain.

He hands me a pair of woollen mittens.

'They look bleedin' useless. I'd give 'em back to your mate Vivienne if I were you and get yourself a decent pair of turtle doves. 'Ere, try these. Usually one fifty but to you, a quid. Can't be fairer than that can I?'

I must admit the gloves are a lot warmer than Vivienne Westwood's. I hand over a pound and sit beside Ruby as she takes off the boots. I glance over at the fruit stall as I wait.

'Two punnets of cherries for a pound.'

I've never seen food so cheap. I peek shyly at the cherries. Two punnets for a pound, that's ridiculous. If I wash them properly it will be okay won't it?

'Don't be suspicious, these cherries are delicious,' says a blond guy behind the stall who is giving me a wide grin. Do all these people compose atrocious poetry?

'I'll have two,' I say, feeling bold.

'You want a cucumber?' he asks. 'Going at 20p. I don't wanna take 'em back with me.'

20p. I'd be stupid not to buy a cucumber for 20p wouldn't I? I can always throw it away if it's rubbish.

'I wouldn't mind a cucumber,' I say and blush again. Honestly you'd never think I was a woman of the world would you? Well, I'm not a woman of this world that's for sure.

'I'll throw in some mush for you,' he says.

I look at Ruby and frown.

'Mushrooms,' she smiles.

'Thank you very much. Mushrooms would be very nice.'

Have I gone mad? Ten minutes ago I'd vowed not to buy anything and now I'm overloaded with cherries, cucumbers and *mush*.

'What do you think?' asks Ruby, parading in front of me in her bright red boots. She looks like a walking postbox.

'They're lovely.'

'Fab. Let's buy some chestnuts and then we'll get a hot dog or something. Do you fancy one?'

I gag at the thought. I'll have furred arteries by the time Christmas arrives if I carry on like this.

'I could do with a cuppa,' she says.

We stroll across to the chestnut stall where I find myself buying not only chestnuts but a bag of mixed nuts and a box of Milk Tray. Well, it was only a pound.

'We can decorate your tree when we get back and then maybe go to the chippy,' says Ruby.

Never mind decorating the tree what about my thighs? I'll have thighs like tree trunks if I carry on eating like this. We traipse through the market to Jackie's café where Ruby gets us a hot dog each and two mugs of very grey-looking tea.

'There you go,' says Ruby, clearly happy to be showing me around her territory. We sit opposite a man who is filling in a betting slip. Roddy would be at home here. They could exchange racing tips. I so wish Roddy wouldn't bet on the horses. We wouldn't be in this mess if he left the gee-gees alone. I sniff the hot dog dubiously and take a small bite. I look for somewhere to dispose of it but all I have is my Hermes handbag and it really doesn't deserve that. Maybe I should buy a fake Hermes for disposal of cheap food. I've got a sinking feeling that this may not be the last time. I take another nibble and sip my murky grey tea.

'We'll pop to Chloe's and get our nails done. I might get my eyebrows tinted. Do you want a tint?'

God forbid. If Roddy and I get back together I would prefer he recognises me. Ruby will be getting me a beehive and a tattoo if I'm not careful.

'I think I'll just stick to nails,' I say, nibbling the hot dog.

Ruby drains her mug and I follow suit. We continue on, stopping every so often for Ruby to peruse a bargain. Finally we reach Chloe's beauty salon, that's if you can call a small open space in the middle of the market a salon.

'Where do you usually go?'

'Martine's in Belgravia,' I say proudly.

'Ooh cool,' says Chloe. 'I bet it's bloody nice there.'

Well, it's certainly warmer and I would have been offered a drinks menu by now and a complimentary Harrods mince pie.

'Do yer want a cuppa? I've just boiled the kettle. I don't have that posh perfumed tea though, just good old builders' tea. Is that okay?'

'Well …'

'I'll just give the mugs a rinse.'

'No it's fine really,' I say quickly.

It's enough I'm going to get furred arteries without listeria on top.

'I saw you on the telly didn't I?' says Chloe.

'She's been in *HELLO!* magazine too,' says Ruby with evident pride in her voice.

'Ooh, that's amazing,' coos Chloe, plonking a mug in front of me with *I'm a great shag* printed on it. This is certainly the wrong mug for me isn't it? I've not had a shag since I turned thirty-two. I'll probably never have a shag again and I've certainly never been called a great shag. What am I thinking? I've never used the word *shag* in my life. Ruby twists around to face me.

'I can't believe you're here,' she says.

Frankly neither can I. Chloe begins filing my nails while I sit nervously watching. Fifteen minutes later I feel fairly confident that she actually does know what she's doing and allow myself to relax.

'I'll give you that cheque before you go, Ruby,' she says, applying a cover coat.

'Great, Taylor will be thrilled. How much did you raise?'

'Nearly a thousand,' says Chloe, beaming.

I pretend not to be interested and drink from my *great shag* mug. Well, Mummy certainly can't say I'm not getting back to normal now can she?

Chapter Twenty-Three

I stare at myself in the mirror and rub my eyes. God, I've got wrinkles. I've aged four years in the space of four weeks. I'll need Botox if this continues. I wonder if Chloe does that at the market. I need to get myself back in shape. I'm getting all out of proportion. I'm certainly living up to my title as truffle queen. I've totally overlooked how many of them I've actually been eating. I don't have a team of umpa lumpas and someone has got to check them now that Bill is selling them. This can't go on, not the selling of the truffles I don't mean, but me eating them. I'll never win Roddy back if I'm fat and wrinkled. I make a firm decision to cut back on junk food and get into a beauty regime. Falling into my sardine bed with a large glass of red in one hand and a mince pie in the other is not a regime, and hanging off the helm is not exercise, and a fruit bun does not constitute a healthy lunch. This has got to stop. I check my depleted bank balance online and sigh. I can't believe I have so little. I've been working my arse off selling sandwiches and traipsing around offices, and that's all I have and that's with my little truffle business. It's unbelievable. I slap a small amount of La Prairie onto my face and massage it in. I need more money if I'm to survive on this boat. After all, I have a cat to support now. Although I rather think the cat adopted me rather than the other way around. I glance at the box of Milk Tray. One won't hurt will it? I need a sugar lift to help me think. I study the selection and then pop a caramel before checking my reflection in the mirror again to see if the cream has removed the wrinkles. No, they're still there. I'm falling apart. My father is a crook, my mother throws back cocks like no tomorrow, my fiancé, or I should say ex-fiancé, only wants my engagement ring, and Balls hasn't made contact since his mother came for Christmas. I'm struggling to come to terms with the fact that Roddy is engaged to Pug-face. I can't believe he did it so quickly. Anyone would think she was ... My hand freezes over an Exotic Delight and I feel my heart palpitate. Oh my God, Pug-face isn't pregnant is she? Surely not. I shove the Exotic Delight into my mouth and follow it up with a Caramel Softy. No, if she was we'd all have known about it by now. I whack on more La Prairie and slap a good amount of coconut oil on top and then apply some eye cream for good measure. That must do it surely. I stand to put the kettle on when the Christmas tree lights flicker and then all the lights go off. Now what? This stupid boat is going to be the death of me. I fumble with my phone and switch on the torch. The hot water light is out. There's nothing for it but to go next door to Taylor. I feel a small surge of excitement at the thought. It's been several days since his mistletoe kiss, and the party, and I'm beginning to think he may be avoiding me. Mind you, the way I'm looking these days, I can't really blame him. I fumble in my bag for my lip pencil and swipe it across my lips before dragging a comb through my hair. I pop my head through the hatch and shiver. My heart beats a little faster when I see his lights on. I climb carefully from the boat and edge towards his, the cat following me. I tap hesitantly on the door and listen; the faint strains of classical music reach my ears. The hatch is opened and his smiling face pops through.

'Hello,' I say nervously.

I don't want him to think I'm chasing him do I? He looks at me oddly for a moment.

'Hi, how are you?' he says, opening the hatch further.

'I was just wondering if you had power, mine seems to have gone off.'

'Ah,' he says knowingly. 'Let me get my jacket. I'll come and have a look.'

A few minutes later I learn that I need a new card for the electric meter.

'I'll walk with you to get one,' he offers. 'The shop on the corner is open till six.'

He smells gorgeous and looks it too.

'Aren't you working?' I say. Mostly because I can't think of anything else to say.

'I'm on nights.'

'Oh.'

I wish he would say something. He's probably thinking of ways to get away from me. Let's face it, what man wants a fat thirty-two year old with no money, wrinkles and a mother who throws back cocks like no tomorrow and ... Oh my God, and a face covered in oil. I must look like a basted chicken. How could I have been so stupid? What must I look like? I rummage in my bag for a tissue.

'Here we are,' he says entering a café. 'I thought we could have a coffee and croissant, unless of course you want to get back.'

'No,' I say hurriedly.

I just want to get this bollocking oil off my face. I rush to the loo and wince at my reflection in the mirror. My face is shinier than the cue ball on a billiard table and oh, Jesus, I've got black lips. I look like a shiny vampire. Oh no, I must have grabbed my eye liner pencil instead of my lip pencil. This is dead embarrassing. I scrub viciously at my face and then tie my hair back neatly into a bun before heading out. He smiles wickedly at me.

'I wish you'd said something,' I say.

'For all I know you may like the Goth look when going out for coffee.'

'Very funny.'

The waitress places the croissants and coffee on the table. Just when I'd made a decision to eat healthier, still I suppose one won't hurt will it?

'Do people like you go to the cinema?' he asks, stirring sugar into his coffee.

'People like me?' I question.

'You may be used to your own private cinema.'

As it happens ... Ooh is he going to ask me to go with him by any chance?

'I love the cinema,' I say.

'It's not a premier or anything,' he smiles. 'It's a little fundraiser. But if you'd like to come, unless of course you're busy doing something else.'

'No,' I say before he has even said when. That smacks of being a lonely bored spinster doesn't it?

'Great. It's Wednesday. I'm finishing at three and planned to do some Christmas shopping if you wanted to join me for that first.'

'Mmm,' I say thoughtfully. 'I suppose I could. I still need to get a few things,' I say nonchalantly so as not to appear too eager.

'Great,' he grins.

'Great,' I agree.

'Let's get you charged up shall we,' he says with a wink.

If only. Roll on Wednesday.

Chapter Twenty-Four

'Logs for a lovely lady,' calls a voice.

I open the hatch to see Dusty.

Dusty is here
To bring you warmth and cheer
With your logs and coal
Merry Christmas ho ho ho

'Here are the logs you ordered and some kindling. Shall I check that cooker of yours?' he says handing me a large sack.

'Your poetry is getting worse,' I say.

He nods.

'I think you're right,' he laughs.

He lugs another sack onto the boat and then glances at my cooker. I wait while he fiddles with a pipe at the back.

'You should get this fixed,' he says calmly. 'Nothing serious but I would see to it in the New Year if I were you.'

'Okay,' I say relieved.

I stir chocolate I'd been melting. Dusty looks at the fresh truffles I'd put on a tray.

'They look tasty,' he says, licking his lips.

'I'll give you some when they've chilled,' I say, as the cat weaves around my legs.

I go to open the hatch to let Dusty out and come face to face with Roddy.

'Roddy,' I say surprised.

'All right mate,' says Dusty.

'Who the hell are you?' Roddy asks rudely.

'This is Dusty,' I say. 'He supplies things for the boats.'

'God help us. Sounds like a bollocking cowboy.'

Dusty gives him a mean stare and climbs from the boat.

I rush back to the chocolate, tripping over the cat in the process.

'You've got a cat? How did you get that?'

'I didn't give birth if that's what you're wondering,' I say. 'Do you want some soup? I've got some on the stove.'

He looks at the cooker warily.

'Has the cat been near it?' he shudders.

'Of course not.'

'What soup is it?'

'The Savoy's soup of the day. They'll be delivering the main course soon,' I say irritably. 'It's Heinz thick pea soup.'

He wrinkles his nose as he looks around. I take the carrier bag he offers and see champagne and caviar inside. Ooh lovely. It's seems like forever since I had caviar.

'I still can't believe you're slumming it like this,' he says, a vein in his forehead pulsating.

He thumps the kitchen counter and shouts *damn your father.*

I'm not sure my father is altogether to blame. Okay, he started the ball rolling but Roddy and his father haven't exactly helped.

'I could kill him,' he finishes, loosening his tie and kicking the cat away.

'You leave him alone, he's all I've got to speak of,' I snap.

'He's brought nothing but trouble on you.'

I pick up the cat and hug him tightly.

'He's company.'

'Not the bollocking cat, I'm talking about your wretched father.'

I nod.

'Oh right. Yes, I could kill Daddy too.'

He grabs me and pulls me down onto the cushions. The familiar smell of his aftershave comforts me and I surrender to his embrace.

'Tell me you're not seeing that ghastly Tyrone chappie from the boats?'

'I'm not,' I say.

'It's bad enough Chelsea has got involved. She's telling everyone that you have a modern day Jack Sparrow on the canal selling cheap wine and perfume to help those who don't have much. You should hear her. She makes him sound like bollocking Robin Hood. You do realise that kind of thing is against the law don't you?'

'I'm not doing it.'

He struggles to get upright and reaches for the champagne.

'How's Balls doing these days? Filling in his time with duels is he?' he says sarcastically.

'His mother is staying and ...'

'That's women out of the picture then.'

Oh why did Daddy have to get frozen just before my wedding? We should be choosing menus and sending out wedding invites at this time. I am sure Roddy still loves me but I feel so confused.

'Let's have some caviar and champers and then ...' he stops on spotting the wine in the corner. He picks up a bottle and studies it.

'I thought you had no money Pop. How can you afford this?' he asks suspiciously.

I don't believe it. Is he trying to make me feel guilty because I'm not living on bread and water?

'The Jack Sparrow guy ...' I begin.

He slams the kitchen counter making the cat dart into the bedroom. I wish he'd stop doing that; this boat is barely staying together as it is.

'It's that Tyrone isn't it? The one you were half-naked with on the deck? It's frightful Poppy. Can you blame my parents reacting the way they do? You were plastered all over the tabloids.'

I catch the glasses as they slide across the little table.

'Why are you here Roddy? You're marrying Pandora aren't you?'

He runs his hand through his hair and groans.

'Yah, what's new?'

'Roddy ...'

'I want a good filly. Is she a good one do you think?'

'Roddy,' I say shocked.

How can he ask me that? Is that all women are to him, breeding machines?

'I need to put her out to stud.'

I can't listen to any more of this. I jump up and walk to the hatch.

'Roddy, please ...'

'Great, thanks Bruce,' he finishes.

I sigh. He's been talking on the bloody phone again. I fight the urge to rip it off his ear.

'I don't know how it happened. One minute you were gone and then I'm engaged to Pandy. I'm in a catch-22. P'pa is threatening to stop my allowance, credit cards, the lot if I don't marry well.'

His eyes widen.

'I say Pop, do you still have your ring? The thing is I'm in a rotten fix. I'm just about holding these chaps off.'

He surely isn't still after my ring? I'm saved from replying by a knock on the hatch. I open it and the lady who owns the dogs looks tearfully at me. I struggle to remember her name.

'I'm so sorry to bother you dear,' she says, her voice trembling. 'Can you help us, poor Jim's cat is stuck and ...'

'For God's sake,' groans Roddy. 'You don't want to get involved in this.'

I grab my coat and scarf and climb onto the deck.

'Just a minute, erm ...'

'Rose,' she says helpfully.

'What are you doing?' Roddy asks suspiciously. 'What are you, bloody Catwoman now?'

'That cat is Jim's life,' says a tearful Rose.

'Jesus Christ,' mutters Roddy.

'You could help,' I say.

'Now I know you've gone insane,' grumbles Roddy.

'Ignore him,' I say while wondering how I can possibly rescue a trapped cat. 'He's more used to shooting animals than saving them.'

'That's a bit unfair,' protests Roddy. 'I don't shoot bollocking cats.'

Rose grabs my hand and pulls me along the walkway to where Jim is sitting looking desolate on his boat.

'Jack is trying but he can't get his hand down there,' he says. 'We can't leave him in this weather.'

Jack is bent over the boat with a torch.

'He's stuck down here,' he says pointing the torch.

'I don't know 'ow the little bugger got there.'

The cat is stuck between boats. This is all I need.

'He hates the water,' sighs Jim.

I know how he feels. I jump back as a rat runs across the deck. Holy shit.

'You all right love?' Jim asks.

I nod and peek between the boats and see a shivering cat looking wide-eyed at me. There's a warning look in his eyes and I visualise lots of spitting and scratching, from the cat that is, not me. I turn to Rose.

'I don't think ...'

'You've got tiny hands and slim arms,' says Jim.

Not to mention newly manicured nails.

'A slim one like you should be able to get him.'

Flattery will get you everywhere that's for sure. I look up to see Roddy approaching us in his Armani overcoat, his signet ring glinting under the boat lights.

'I can't have this,' he says assertively. 'It's bloody stupid. It'll scratch your coat. Dash it Pop, that's your Donna Karan isn't it? It's only a bloody cat. There's bollocking hundreds around here. If one drowns it won't be the end of the world. They can get another.'

Oh dear.

'Who are you?' asks Jim.

Roddy ignores him and grabs me by the arm.

'Pop, I can't stay that long. If you're going to waste time on a cat what does it say about us?'

'You're wasting time on a bitch,' I say, and feel very proud of myself. 'What does that say about you?'

I look back at the cat.

'Do you think you can reach 'im?' asks Jim anxiously.

Roddy whistles through his teeth.

'Are these your friends, along with that other one that nicks booze?' he demands. 'This can't be good for you.'

'I never said he stole the wine, Roddy.'

'Yeah, who are you calling a thief?' asks Rose. 'I hope you ain't talking about Geoff. He helps the boat people a great deal. We're not rich like you lot.'

Oh dear, I do believe the 'lot' includes me. I step onto Jim's boat and look to Roddy for help but he turns away in disgust.

'No wonder you make the papers,' he snaps.

'His name's Coco,' says Jim. 'It might calm him if he thinks you know him.'

I sigh.

'Here, Coco, come on boy.'

Roddy huffs and marches along the walkway.

'Text me when you're acting normal,' he calls. 'I really want to spend time with you.'

How about getting engaged to me instead of Pandora aka Pug-face? I try to grab Coco and feel myself slip forward. Rose pulls me back by my coat and I take a deep breath before trying again. God, it's freezing.

'Come on Coco,' I say softly, reaching my hand down into the space and grabbing the cat. I grasp him tightly and then lower my other hand to lift him up. I have him in both hands now and am about to lift him when I lose my balance. Rose cries out and grasps my coat, but she is too late. I'm hanging onto the cat for dear life and feel sure we're both going to end up in the river. The cat meows loudly and struggles in my arms.

'I've got you,' says a familiar voice and strong arms set me upright. Taylor gently takes Coco from me and before I have a chance to thank him I'm being hugged by Jim.

'Thank you, thank you so much,' he cries.

'We're so grateful,' says Rose.

I look to see if Roddy is still here and my heart sinks when I realise he has gone. I couldn't let the cat drown could I?

'Let's get you in the warm,' says Jim.

'I'm fine, I really should get back,' I say, and then realise Jim is talking to Coco.

If I hurry I should be able to text Roddy and get him to come back. He can't have got far. I make him sound like an escaped criminal.

'No, you must have fish and chips with us. The van comes tonight,' says Rose gleefully, fish and chips evidently being the highlight of her week. I don't recall ever having fish and chips from a van. Can you even imagine fish and chips cooked in a van? I've had fish and chips at the top restaurants in London but never from a van. Right now I just want to get Roddy back so we can talk.

'I've already eaten today,' I say, thinking of my thighs.

'You're allowed to eat more than once a day,' laughs Rose.

Only if I want to be the new face of Michelin Tyres.

'On us,' says Jack.

'No, on me,' says Jim.

'You'll 'ave some, won't you Taylor?' says Jim as he hugs Coco.

'Sure, we'll have a gherkin too, won't we Poppy.'

I glare at him. Do I look like a gherkin kind of woman?

'Okay,' I say reluctantly. 'I just need to fetch my phone.'

I rush back to the boat and grab my phone to see there is a text message from Camilla.

Desperate, can you meet for tea at Claridge's tomorrow. I've got an emergency meeting with shrink tonight. Hugo is such a bastard.

Never mind Hugo, what about Roddy? All men are bastards if you ask me. I phone Roddy and get his voicemail. I'm just about to leave a message when Taylor knocks on the hatch.

'Rose is off to get the fish, do you know what you'd like?' he asks.

'Aside from the gherkin,' I say, 'not a clue.'

He laughs.

'I'll tell her to get cod.'

He spots my cat sitting by the log burner and smiles.

'She's made herself at home hasn't she? Have you given her a name?'

'How do you know it's a girl?' I ask stupidly.

'There are little giveaways. You've got them too,' he smiles, his eyes glancing at my breasts.

I blush.

'No I haven't.'

'You could have fooled me,' he laughs exposing his white even teeth. He really is lovely. If only he was rich. I know doctors aren't poor but he isn't rich like Roddy or Camilla or me, or at least as rich as I used to be. Although, I suppose right now he is richer than me. Come to think of it, everyone is richer than me aren't they?

'I meant I haven't named the cat.'

'Ah,' he says rubbing his hands together. He looks at the caviar and champagne.

'You're not completely adverse to fish then I see?'

'My fiancé brought it,' I say.

'Your fiancé?' he queries.

'Okay,' I say irritably. 'My ex-fiancé.'

He nods at the caviar.

'I've got some crackers that would go nice with that caviar.'

Will it indeed. I suppose he'll want my champagne next.

'Jim would like to try it I reckon,' he smiles.

I sigh. Oh well why not? I'm not going to eat my way through the whole lot am I? I hand him the Harrods carrier bag and manage to climb elegantly from my boat. I feel I'm getting the hang of it now. I reach the deck and straighten up only to get my heel caught in the planks of the walkway again. I fly forward and he turns in time to catch me. I land in his arms laughing.

'You're always rescuing me,' I say.

'It's becoming a pleasurable pastime,' he smiles, his face close to mine.

'What the buggery do you think you're doing? Unhand my fiancé.'

It's then I see Roddy and groan. He is storming along the walkway.

Chapter Twenty-Five

Taylor releases me and turns to Roddy who promptly smacks his fist into Taylors jaw. I gasp and watch as Taylor falls to the ground.

'Oh my God, Roddy, what are you doing?' I cry.

'Stay out of this Pop,' says Roddy sounding all masterful. What a pity he can't lay his p'pa out like that.

He puts his fists up and begins bouncing on his feet. It's like something out of *Rocky*, although I can assure you Roddy does not have Sylvester Stallone's physique. Taylor is nearer to it, not that I'm noticing or anything. Taylor gets up and rubs his jaw. I see his lip is cut. This is awful, although it is rather nice to think they are fighting over me, although I suppose at the moment it's only Roddy that is fighting over me. All the same it's exciting. I wonder if there's time to send a quick picture text to Chelsea and Camilla and maybe Sophie. You know, just a quick one, saying *men fighting over me.* No of course not, what am I thinking? I've got to stop the fight not text the whole world that it's happening with a picture. All the same, shame to miss such a great opportunity isn't it? It would look great on Twitter with *ItsRainingMen* as a hashtag. It wouldn't be so bad to trend then would it?

'I'm so sorry ...' I begin but Taylor ignores me.

'She's your ex-fiancée actually,' he says crossly. 'Didn't you dump her after she lost all her money?'

Quite right too.

'And as such I can do what I like as long as Poppy doesn't object.'

Ooh, I'm not objecting. He wipes his lip on the back of his hand and removes his glasses.

'Hang onto these will you?' he says, handing them to me.

'You know nothing about our kind,' snarls Roddy, aiming another punch which Taylor avoids by smartly sidestepping.

Our kind? What does that mean? He's watched *Divergence* too many times.

'I don't want to know your kind if that's how you carry on, and I'd advise you not to hit me again,' warns Taylor.

Taylor looks rather gorgeous with a split lip or maybe I'm just kinky. I really shouldn't attend spanking sessions, they get me all worked up.

'Listen old chap, you keep away from her, do you hear?' snarls Roddy, bouncing on his toes and sticking out his fists. I've never seen Roddy so excited.

'I think that's more for Poppy to say,' says Taylor brusquely.

A small crowd has gathered and all we need are the paparazzi to join us. Wait till Mummy sees this on the front page of the papers. Rose's dogs start barking and snow begins to fall making it look like a nativity scene gone wrong. All we need is someone to start off Good King Wenceslas and we will be well away.

'Poppy is not interested in you,' says Roddy.

Hang on a minute.

Taylor turns to me and as he does so, Roddy dashes forward and aims a punch to Taylor's chin. I wince as Taylor goes down on the wet walkway.

'Ooh that was out of order,' yells Rose.

'Lay him out,' shouts Jim.

Taylor gets up and wobbles slightly. I can barely look. He walks angrily towards Roddy.

'I advised you not to hit me again,' he says through gritted teeth.

I hold my breath as Taylor launches himself at Roddy and they land on the snow covered walkway.

'Can't you stop them?' I ask Jim.

'You don't break up a fight love, unless you're the police.'

Right, that's it then. I fumble in my bag for my phone, not to take the picture of course, although while I've got it in my hand ... I see Geoff running towards us and breathe a sigh of relief. I look down at the writhing bodies. Geoff skids to a halt at my side.

'Who's Taylor fighting with?' he asks.

'Roddy, my fiancé, I mean ex-fiancé.'

'Taylor, what are you doing? Watch your hands mate.'

Chelsea joins us and stares wide-eyed at the bodies writhing on the ground.

'Oh my God, is that Roddy?' she cries, stating the obvious as only Chelsea can. 'What is he doing here?'

The two men clamber to their feet with Roddy still flailing around. He has a cut eye. I run to him before he can throw another punch.

'Roddy, that's enough. You're not a fighter,' I hiss. 'You'll come off worse in the end. Come back to the boat and I'll look at your eye.'

He brushes my hand away.

'I'm going to finish this,' he says firmly.

'I wouldn't recommend that,' warns Taylor.

'You're out of order. You're just taking advantage,' growls Roddy, launching himself at Taylor again.

'Call the police Geoff,' I plead.

Roddy is throwing punches left right and centre and Taylor is nimbly avoiding all of them.

'Roddy, will you please stop,' I scream.

Taylor then gets Roddy in an arm lock.

'I'm escorting you off the canal,' he says.

Roddy lifts his knee and smashes it into Taylor's groin.

'Ooh fudge berries,' groans Chelsea.

Taylor doubles over and Roddy goes to aim another punch when Taylor rams his head into Roddy's stomach and they both roll backwards.

'Oh no,' squeals Chelsea.

We watch in horror as they roll back, off the walkway and into the canal.

'This is bloody exciting,' says Jack, rushing forward and reaching out to help Taylor. 'Fetch blankets Rose, the canal is freezing.'

Chelsea and I rush forward to pull Roddy up. He sits panting and shivering on the boardwalk.

'Roddy, this is stupid.'

He lifts himself to his feet and pushes me away.

'I'm going home to where people are civilised. How could you do this to us Poppy? We had a good future together and you threw it all away.'

Tears prick my eyelids. That's so unfair. I didn't do anything. He called off the engagement, not me.

'Pandora's parents just don't cut it. It's a filthy business, the whole thing. I won't have the same lifestyle with her. It should have been us, *The socialite couple,'* he says through chattering teeth.

I try to take his arm but he brushes my hand away.

'I'm sorry Roddy.'

'She can't help me, not like you. We helped each other didn't we?'

'Roddy, I hate all this too. But ...'

'As for you,' he adds, pointing to Chelsea. 'You're an embarrassment to your family, buying cheap goods from peasants.'

'Okay, that's enough,' says Geoff.

Roddy grabs me by the arm and leans towards me.

'Can I have the engagement ring? I promise to pay you back. I'm in over my head. It's your fault after all. It wouldn't have been a problem if you hadn't ...'

'Roddy, I didn't break it off, you did.'

'What choice did I have?' he yells, before letting out an enormous sneeze.

'I think it might be best if you left the canal,' says Taylor stepping forward. He throws a blanket around Roddy's shoulders.

Roddy moves back.

'I'll text you,' he says without taking his eyes off Taylor.

I'm almost wishing he won't. He glares at the crowd.

'It's illegal what you do. Robin Hood my arse. I pay my taxes, I bet that's more than you lot. I'm not letting you make a mockery of me. I'll bloody report you. Arseholes.'

'Roddy,' I gasp.

Jim steps forward angrily.

'Just a minute you pompous git ...'

'Leave it Jim, he's not worth it,' says Taylor.

'I wouldn't give him the ring,' says Geoff. 'You need it more than he does.'

He's upset. Maybe he is more devastated about our break up than I thought. Or is he a rat by nature as well as by name? I shiver at the memory of the rat from earlier.

'You'll all ....' he wrinkles his nose and we all wait for him to sneeze. 'Be sorry,' he finishes before marching off. The crowd disperses and those that are left look at me sorrowfully.

'I never knew you were engaged,' says Rose.

'Best off without 'im if you ask me,' says Jim.

'You okay?' asks Geoff.

I'm feeling far from okay. I look down the boardwalk and see Balls striding-towards us, his long coat flapping in the wind behind him. He lifts his ivory-tipped walking cane and waves it. I'm in a living nightmare.

'Truffles, it's me, Balls.'

'Balls,' I say in a shocked voice.

There is hushed silence. I really don't think I can take any more excitement.

'No beating around the bush, what?' he says on reaching me and falls dramatically to one knee only to groan as he does so.

'That's my bad one,' he says.

Balls has a bad knee? He alternates them and looks up at me. This can't be happening. Please don't let this be what I think it is.

'Frogs' knickers,' gasps Chelsea.

'This is better than the pictures,' remarks Jim.

'You can't pay for this kind of entertainment,' says Jack.

The soft strains of Frank Sinatra singing *Silent Night Holy Night* drift out from one of the boats and I feel like I'm back in the nativity scene minus the baby Jesus of course, although right now I wouldn't be at all surprised if he popped up too. This is worse than the *Rocky* scene with Roddy earlier.

'It's freezing Balls,' I say.

'Too right,' says Jim. 'And not only my balls, my toes feel like blocks of ice too.'

'There's only been one other woman in my life,' Ball says emotionally.

'Really, I hadn't realised,' I say in a strained voice. 'Who's that?'

'My mother, but now it's time …' he pauses dramatically and reaches into his pocket and produces a huge solitaire.

'Oh no,' I gasp.

'Oh trollops,' says Chelsea.

This would look amazing on Facebook wouldn't it? One minute I can't get a man to marry me and now they're queuing up. Well, not queuing up but you know what I mean?

'Pops old girl, will you marry me?'

Peas and rice. Only I could get proposed to outside in the snow where it's minus degrees. I blink snowflakes out of my eyes and wipe my runny nose.

'Balls, I'm really flattered but the thing is …'

Before I have even finished my sentence Balls springs up and looks angrily at Taylor. Not again. This is like a bad dream.

'Is it because of him?' he bellows. 'I saw the papers.'

Oh what? Taylor raises his eyebrows and his lip curls into a half smile. He removes his glasses again. He is still wrapped in the blanket but I swear he's enjoying this.

'I'm not having this,' growls Balls. 'I need you to step down old chap, Pops is already spoken for.'

I am? I watch horrified as Balls whips off his coat. Taylor rolls his eyes before Balls hurls himself at him. I watch as they wrestle on the walkway.

'This has made my day,' says Jack.

'I don't think it has made Taylor's,' laughs Geoff.

Taylor and Balls roll around for a few seconds and then thankfully Balls jumps up.

'I'm not a violent man,' he says shakily.

Oh good. He isn't about to pull out a pistol then. Honestly, nothing would surprise me tonight. Taylor wipes his lip.

'Sorry old chap,' says Balls.

'No worries,' smiles Taylor. 'I'm getting used to it,' he says as he picks up the blanket.

'Balls, the thing is, I'm really not over Roddy. I need more time,' I say.

Like the next ten years.

He nods and pulls on his overcoat.

'Right, got it,' he says. 'A month okay?'

I speechlessly nod.

'I'll be in touch then,' he says and all we all watch as he strides back down the boardwalk swinging his stick.

'Toodle pip,' he calls over his shoulder.

'Surreal,' says Geoff.

'You getting that fish then Jim?' asks Taylor as if nothing has happened. 'We've got some champagne and caviar courtesy of Poppy.'

'Blimey, can't be bad,' laughs Jim.

'I really should get back,' I say, not wanting to go back at all.

'I've just fought off two men for you so you've got to try our fish and chips and a pickled gherkin, you can't possibly go back.' says Taylor taking my arm.

A gherkin is not something I get every day. In fact it's becoming a night of firsts isn't it?

'Ain't you had fish and chips before?' questions Rose.

I shake my head.

'Not from a van,' I say.

'You're in for a feast,' she laughs.

'Fish and chips is lovely from the van,' says Chelsea.

Oh dear, at this rate I'll be living off kebabs and greasy burgers. They disappear to fetch the gastronomical delight and Taylor leads me to his boat.

'Make yourself at home. I'll just get out of these wet clothes and take a shower.'

'I'm so sorry,' I call above the running water. 'I don't know what came over Roddy.'

I'm trying hard not to visualise his gorgeous body under that water.

'You're very popular,' he says.

'I assure you my life is not normally like this. I feel so bad about this evening. It felt like everyone was ganging up on you. I'm so sorry.'

'I'm not sorry. It means I'm seen as a threat.'

My mouth turns dry. I click on the CD player and *All of Me* begins to play. This song is following me around. I lean back onto the couch and let the gentle movement of the boat relax me.

The water is turned off and he appears in the doorway wearing a towel. I come over all hot and I quickly remove my eyes from his delicious body.

'Am I a threat?' he asks looking into my eyes so I have no choice but to meet his. He lifts his hand to my neck and I shudder with anticipation.

'Let me give you something for that rash. It's anxiety. I promise I'm not going to give you an A class drug,' he smiles.

His smile gives me butterflies in my stomach. He returns wearing jeans and a white shirt and produces a tube of cream. He holds my hair away from my neck and gently rubs the cream onto the rash. I'm getting so aroused it's ridiculous. I've not had sex for so long, that's what it is.

'This should help,' he says. 'I don't get what you see in Roddy.'

'He always felt like the right one,' I say.

It's the truth. Roddy always felt like the right partner. Okay, maybe he's not that manly, but you can't have everything can you? We have the same background, we know the same people, we holiday in the same places, and we have the same interests apart from the gambling of course.

'Even now? Now you know real people?'

'Roddy is a real person,' I say. 'I know he can be pompous but we all have our imperfections, including me. I'm a snob, I know I am.'

'Roddy doesn't seem to tolerate your imperfections. Personally I like them. Poppy with her perfect imperfections.'

I smile shyly.

'I'll take some beers to Jim's,' he says as he opens the fridge.

I see the hypodermics sitting on the shelf and wince.

'They're for a diabetic on the canal. I get his medication from the pharmacy as he can't get around that easily. We're a little community here.'

That's something of a relief.

'Why are you living on a boat?' I ask, accepting a beer from him. I'm getting used to this now and snap the lid off easily with a bottle opener

'What's wrong with living on a houseboat?

I blush.

'It's just as a registrar you must make enough to buy a house ...'

'I had a house. Quite a nice one actually. One day I came home early and found my wife in bed with another man.'

'That's terrible,' I gasp.

'Yep,' he says, taking a swig from his bottle.

'I don't have money like you. A lot of my money goes to a small hospital I set up in Africa.'

'Oh,' I say surprised.

'It's nothing much,' he says, looking embarrassed.

I remember the cheque that Chloe had given Ruby and wonder if that was for the hospital.

'A boat seemed like fun and everyone on the canal was so nice. Geoff recommended it. He's lived on boats most of his life. He's quite a sailor.'

'Yes I know,' I say rolling my eyes.

'Ah, the stuff he sells ... It's not that bad. Mostly end of line stock and cheap imports.'

'From off the back of a lorry?'

'No, nothing stolen, mostly smuggled in. The authorities get uptight about not paying the import duty but nobody suffers. Geoff just boats out once a month and buys the stuff dirt cheap and sells it on. The boat people have never had it so good,' he laughs.

'I hope Roddy doesn't do anything stupid,' I say worriedly. 'He was pretty angry when he left.'

Roddy is such a creature of impulse.

'It must be difficult for you losing everything and then getting lumbered with us lot,' he smiles.

I'm beginning to enjoy the lumbering actually. There is a bustle of activity outside the boat.

'We're here,' shouts Rose.

Even the fish and chips is starting to appeal. Maybe Christmas won't be so bad after all.

Chapter Twenty-Six

'Oh Camilla,' I say, taking her hand across the table.

'Apparently it's not his fault. His parents have decided I'm not the right match.'

'But you've been going out for yonks.'

She rummages in her Mulberry and pulls out a handful of tissues. Mascara streaks down her cheek and I diplomatically point it out. We're in Claridge's and I'm so relieved to get a sit down in such luxurious surroundings. I feel like I've come home. I'd been traipsing around offices all morning and I feel I deserve a good cup of Earl Grey in a bone china teacup. Mind you, I can't say I'm impressed with the sandwiches. They're nicely cut and all that but a bit sparing on the egg mayo. They're not like the sandwiches Ruby and I make where the egg mayonnaise runs out when you take a bite. Still, it's all about class and presentation at Claridge's isn't it? And I can't deny their chocolate éclairs are to die for. Except that I'm not comfortable eating them while Camilla is having a meltdown and, let's be honest, Claridge's is just not where you have a meltdown is it? But that is exactly what Camilla is having over a salmon and cucumber sandwich. I'm so delighted to be out and having tea somewhere decent that I really don't mind if she has a full blown breakdown so long as I can drink in the luxury. Fish and chips from a van are all very well, and turned out to be very nice as it happens, but this is more what I'm used to.

'Why doesn't Hugo stand up to them?' I say.

'Maybe he doesn't want to marry me either. I'm starting to think I was just a bit of fun. I bloody hate money. It shouldn't be like this when you fall in love.'

She pops sugar cubes into her cup and wipes her eyes.

'It's not like we're living in the eighteenth century is it?' she sobs, tears splashing into the Earl Grey. 'They want him to marry a woman from a titled family. What difference does it make Poppy? My parents have money. What does it matter if they don't have a title?'

I gaze longingly at the chocolate éclair. Personally I never understood what she saw in Hugo. He was always a bit of a plonker, a definite *Four Weddings and a Funeral* Charlie.

'You know Hetty, the bitch with the long nose?' she spits.

I discreetly move the éclair.

'No way,' I say. 'You're kidding.'

Her look assures me she isn't.

'Yes, she's been after him for yonks and ...'

A waitress approaches and refills our teacups. She seems oblivious to Camilla's meltdown.

'Is everything okay?' she asks with a smile.

Does it look like it?

'Lovely, thank you,' I say.

'Could I have a glass of champagne please?' asks Camilla. 'Second thoughts make that a bottle.'

'Do you think you should?' I ask worriedly. 'Sometimes alcohol can make things worse.'

She scoffs.

'Hetty?' I ask. 'Are you sure?'

'Yes, I hate the bitch. Did you know she was multi-orgasmic?'

'She is?'

'Yep, three times a day apparently if the rumours are true'

Bollocking arse. I'm three times a year if I'm lucky. I blame Roddy. Three times a day though, who's got the time for that?

'Unbloodybelievable,' I say, grabbing the éclair. I certainly need it after hearing that.

'She's only got to see a vibrator and her hips are bucking,' Camilla says viciously.

Well, I suppose mine might too if my vibrator had any batteries, but three times a day ... Is that normal? This really is not the kind of conversation you have in Claridge's and most certainly not over their afternoon tea.

'I really love him, Poppy,' she sobs and I put the éclair back on the plate. Just as well I suppose. I really can't afford to gain any more weight.

'He's got no backbone, you're better off without him.'

'Is that what you think about Roddy?'

I picture Roddy and feel a little pang in my stomach. I so need that éclair.

'Still, you've got titled parents and look what's happened to you,' she says biting into a mini cherry tart. Oh well, if she's going to. I grab the éclair and take a large bite. As soon as the sugar hits my bloodstream I feel a million times better.

'At least you don't have to worry about getting into your Valentino wedding dress now,' Camilla says heartlessly, like I need reminding.

I swallow the last of the éclair and grab a slice of fruit cake. Camilla throws back the contents of her glass before refilling it. She hiccups before stuffing a sandwich in her mouth.

'I mean what's the point of money?' she says through a mouthful of smoked salmon and horseradish. 'Seriously what is the point?'

'You can drown your sorrows in Claridge's,' I say helpfully, and you don't have to traipse around London with a basket of sandwiches and wheelbarrow a box of your shit. You just simply flush it away like the rest of the world. Who'd have thought the thing I crave most is to be able to flush away my shit? And of course you can live in a nice warm flat instead of a freezing cold barge and you don't have to wear a size 14 overall. Mind you, if I eat much more I'll be moving up to a size 16. I groan inwardly at the thought. I've never ever been a size 16. Before I know it I will become that wobbly breasted woman I saw in Primark. Camilla throws back the champagne and downs some pills.

'What are they?' I ask alarmed.

'I suppose you're right. I could be in your shoes, drowning my sorrows in that godawful Wetherspoons and making sandwiches for the working classes.'

I've never been to Wetherspoons but I don't bother to correct her.

'Should you be taking pills with champagne?' I ask anxiously.

'I can't face life any more,' she says miserably.

Christ, bollocking Hugo isn't worth dying for. She calls the waiter over and orders another bottle of champagne.

'Maybe we should get pissed,' she says.

'Maybe we should get the bill,' I say sensibly.

She ignores me and holds her glass out for the waiter to fill it. I sigh and allow him to refill mine too. If you can't beat them join them.

An hour later and we have consumed the selection of cakes, one and a half bottles of champagne, and a substantial number of sandwiches. Camilla has gone to the loo and I'm swallowing coffee like no tomorrow in an effort to sober up. The waiter brings the bill and asks if I'd like another coffee. I look towards the door of the loos and check the time on my mobile. I hope she's not throwing up. Not in Claridge's. It just isn't where you throw up is it? Wetherspoons maybe but most certainly not Claridge's.

'I'm waiting for my friend,' I say.

He winks at me.

'Of course,' he smiles.

He *thinks* I can't pay the bill. I *know* I can't pay the bill. Where the hell is Camilla? I look at the doors again and fidget.

'I think she went to the bar,' says the waiter, clearing the table.

Oh no. She'll be on the floor if she drinks any more and who's going to pay the bill then? I pick up my handbag and make my way to the bar. Camilla isn't there. I head to the toilets where I have nightmare visions of her throwing up all over her Jasper Conran suit. Lying on the sink is her Mulberry.

'Camilla,' I say to a closed cubicle door.

No reply. Panic begins to engulf me. I push open the doors one by one until I reach a locked one.

'Camilla, are you in there?'

I don't want to kick the door open like a rampant Charlie's Angel, only to find some strange woman sitting in her smalls. Trust me, it just isn't what you do in Claridge's. I tap on the door again.

'Is anyone in there?'

My face feels flushed from the champagne and my whole body is now growing hot to match it. There is a groan from the other side of the door.

'Camilla, is that you?'

God, this is a disaster. Someone has got to pay the bill and the only thing in my handbag is a spent scratch card. I don't think it will be a fair exchange for a luxury afternoon tea at Claridge's. I pull my mind back to the matter in hand which is finding the person who can pay the bill.

'Camilla,' I say again before crouching on the floor. Please God, don't let someone walk in. The last thing I need right now is to get arrested for lewd behaviour in a public loo. I peek under the door and spy Camilla's Jimmy Choos and the hem of her Jasper Conran skirt. Oh God, she's on the floor.

'Camilla, you drunken bitch, open the door. You have to pay the bill.'

I stare at her delicate ankles and feel sick. There's a buzzing in my head and the faint sound of Frank Sinatra singing *Let it Snow* reaches my fuzzy brain. My body seems to be vibrating and I realise it is my phone buzzing in my handbag. I pull it out. It's Roddy. God, he chooses his moments doesn't he? A loud sneeze resonates down the phone.

'Hello Roddy.'

'Pop, I'm in a bit of a fix.'

Never mind your fix, what about the fix I'm in? He should be in this loo with Camilla's prostrate body on the other side of the door.

'Roddy I can't talk. I'm in Claridge's and Camilla's collapsed.'

'I really need the ring Truffles. It's not like you're wearing it is it?'

What? Didn't he hear me?

'Look Roddy ...'

'The thing is Pop, these chaps are known for cutting off body parts,' he says shakily.

What is he talking about?

'You don't want them to cut off mine do you,' he whimpers. 'Isn't it enough I have bloody pneumonia from defending your honour.'

Defending my honour? God, don't I have enough with Camilla's comatose body. I can't be thinking about Roddy's body parts right now.

'Roddy, Camilla has ...'

'If I don't give Diamond his money, I'll lose an ear or something. I don't want something chopped off. Oh God, what if they chop off my ...'

It's like a scene out of *Goodfellas*.

'Roddy, can I call you back? It's just that Camilla is ...'

'Hold that thought. I need to take another call.'

I don't believe this.

'Roddy, go fuck your Bluetooth.'

I click off the phone and bang on the loo door.

'Camilla, come on. We have to leave.'

Jack Diamond

Roddy steps away from the roulette table. What do they mean he can't have any more credit?

'Do you know who I am?' he asks.

'I'm sorry sir.'

'Get me the manager,' he says angrily.

A few moments later a well-dressed man approaches him.

'Is there a problem Mr Tarleton?'

'They won't give me credit at the table.'

'That's right sir.'

'What do you mean *that's right sir*?' mimics Roddy.

The casino quietens as heads turn to see what the commotion is about and Roddy lowers his head. Bugger it. It's not right making a spectacle of a chap like this.

'Your father has requested we do not give you credit Mr Tarleton.'

'What the hell has my father got to do with it?'

'He does pay off your debts sir.'

'Damn you,' Roddy snarls marching to the bar and ordering a whisky. He throws it back and is about to order another when the waiter places a glass in front of him.

'Compliments of Mr Diamond,' he says nodding to the other side of the bar.

Roddy feels like his insides are falling out. Jesus, how could he have not seen him? He throws back the whisky and turns to see Mad Jack sitting next to him. He puts a restraining hand on Roddy's shoulders. He's wearing a Bluetooth headset and in Roddy's opinion looks a right wanker.

'Ello Rodders. You're not leaving already are yer? Yer ain't seen me dad yet,' he smiles, pulling a knife from his pocket.

'Oh God,' groans Roddy.

Mad Jack slowly peels an orange and Roddy feels some zest spray into his eye.

'Gambling in the afternoon Rodders. I 'ope you ain't gambling away the money you owes me?' says Diamond from behind him.

'No, it's credit,' says Roddy, spinning around on his chair and winking at Diamond.

'Are you mocking me?' says Diamond.

'Yeah, you mocking us,' repeats Mad Jack Junior.

'No, I got orange in my eye,' explains Roddy.

Diamond sits beside him and unbuttons his jacket.

'Another whisky me ole mate? Yer look like yer need yer nerves calming.'

'I'm getting the ring,' Roddy says hurriedly.

'Yeah, you keep saying that me ole mate. The thing is your fiancée, the new one that is, I 'ave to say Roddy I'm envious of your way with women. I wish Jack Junior had your knack.'

'I get slappers easy enough,' says Mad Jack, looking hurt.

'Not like ole Rodders 'ere you don't.'

'*Say a command*,' says a robotic voice.

Diamond snaps his head up.

'For Christ's sake,' he mumbles

'It's this thing, it ain't working,' moans Jack Junior fiddling with the Bluetooth.

'As I was saying,' continues Diamond. 'Your new bird 'as a flashy ring. Now I don't wanna be cutting that off 'er finger do I? Know what I mean?'

Roddy blanches.

'Don't touch Pandora,' he says hoarsely.

'Ave a drink Roddy, you're a bag of nerves. You don't look well.'

'I think I've got pneumonia,' says Roddy in an attempt to elicit some sympathy.

'That's what 'appens when you go on the piss Rodders,' laughs Diamond.

'*Say a command*,' repeats the robotic voice.

'For fuck's sake,' Diamond bellows, grabbing Jack Junior's phone. 'I'll ram this down your bleedin' throat in a minute.'

Roddy wonders if there is a chance to escape but Jack Junior meets his eyes and Roddy knows there isn't. Mad Jack Junior slowly runs his finger along the blade of the knife.

'I got a problem Rodders. I don't like being taken for a fool. It 'urts me feelings, know what I mean? You keep telling me I'll get me money but I don't see it. Do you think maybe old Jack Diamond needs glasses?'

'Ha ha, you wearing glasses, now that's funny,' laughs Mad Jack Junior.

Diamond whacks him across the head.

'Keep your bleedin' thoughts to yourself.'

'I'll get it, I will,' says Roddy.

Jack Diamond makes a clicking sound with his tongue.

'I'm easy going, Roddy. But me son, well 'e gets upset for me don't you Jack Junior?'

'Do I?'

Diamond sighs.

'Oh yeah,' says Jack Junior lifting the knife and studying it. 'I get really upset, yer know. And if you don't get the money prick, I'm gonna have to cut something off your pretty body, know what I mean?'

Roddy fights back a whimper.

'I'll get it, I will, but please don't cut something off my pretty ... my body.'

He doesn't even want to think what the something might be.

'That's a good chap,' says Diamond. 'Oh, I got your Christmas card.'

He hands a red envelope to Roddy.

'Merry Crimbo.'

'I didn't ...' begins Roddy.

'Don't worry about a card for me Roddy. All I want for Christmas is a sparkler.'

'I'll have it by ...'

'I tell yer when to 'ave it by Rodders.'

Roddy nods. He's got to get the ring off Poppy before those bloody boat people nick it. Christ, these people are maniacs.

'Why don't you give the little slapper a bell,' says Mad Jack Junior. 'Tell 'er 'ow it is.'

'Yeah, we'll give you some privacy,' says Diamond.

Roddy walks to the other end of the bar and taps in Poppy's number.

Chapter Twenty-Seven

Right, must not panic. The last thing we need is a scene. Shit and bollocks. I turn on my heel and rush to reception. This is just not what you do in Claridge's. An over made-up receptionist greets me.

'Good afternoon madam, did you enjoy your afternoon tea?' she asks pleasantly, her eyes moving past me and onto a waiter hovering behind. Jesus, they think I'm going to do a bunk. Mind you, the way things are going I may well have to consider it.

'My friend, she's unwell. She's locked in your toilet.'

They look at me blankly.

'She's paying the bill,' I add earnestly.

That should galvanise them into action.

'Oh,' says the receptionist, biting her coral pink lip.

'Can you open the door?' I ask.

'I'll get security,' says the waiter.

An overweight security man wanders towards us carrying a bag of what I presume are door-opening tools. I lead the receptionist, the waiter and the security man to the loo like a modern day pied piper. They look at the door. I'm not sure what they expect. Camilla is not going to emerge as a werewolf wielding a chainsaw is she? At least I hope not.

'Hello, are you okay in there?' shouts the security guard.

'She's not deaf.'

'She may be unconscious,' he says.

In that case she won't hear him will she? It would have been easier if I'd just kicked the door down myself.

'Can you just open it?' I say worriedly.

'I wouldn't want to interrupt anything,' he says sharply.

Exactly what does he think he's going to interrupt?

'She's been in there like forever. There isn't anything left for you to interrupt,' I say angrily.

The receptionist coughs nervously and glances at Camilla's handbag on the sink. I remember the pills she was popping earlier and feel my stomach lurch. The security man fiddles with the hinges and lifts the door off. Camilla is lifeless on the floor her Jasper Conran suit crumpled. I'll castrate Hugo.

'Camilla,' I yell in her ear, 'can you hear me?'

She mumbles and I could cry with relief.

'We need to pay the bill,' I say, and get a scathing look from the over made-up receptionist.

She can give me the look but I bet she wouldn't be happy with my scratch card.

'We need to get her out of here,' says the security guard.

'Yes of course,' I say, helping him to lift her.

'Get your hands off my arse,' mumbles Camilla. 'I'm still compost menace you know.'

I smile.

'I think she means compos mentis,' I say.

I throw her arm across my shoulder.

'I have your Mulberry,' I whisper. 'Do you have cash?'

The over made-up receptionist coughs and exchanges a look with the waiter.

'Are you sure she's okay?' asks the security guy. 'Do you want us to phone a friend?'

'I'll ask the audience,' I quip, but from their deadpan expressions I guess that they don't get it.

'A cab would be great.'

'Sorry for upsetting the apple tart,' mumbles Camilla.

'Don't worry dear, you've drunk too much,' says the security guard.

'More money than sense,' whispers the receptionist.

I so wish that were true, in my case anyway.

'You'll feel as right as rain after you've slept it off,' says the waiter.

Camilla sighs.

'Don't look at me in that tone of voice,' she grumbles.

I drag her down the hallway, struggling to carry our handbags.

'Let's get a drink,' she says pulling away from me.

'No more drinks Camilla,' I say, pushing her against a wall and handing over the cash from her purse. Finally I lead her through the doors into the cold December air.

'Whoa, had one too many 'ave we?' asks the cab driver. 'I don't know if I can take you with 'er in that state.'

Camilla's eyes close and it's all I can do to keep her upright.

'Camilla,' I shout, 'you can't go to sleep.'

As I pack Camilla into the cab her handbag slips from my shoulder and the contents scatter onto the pavement. It's then I see the empty pill bottles and my heart sinks. Oh no, she's only gone and done something stupid. If this is what money does to you I'm better off without it.

'Take us to the nearest hospital please?' I say anxiously.

He looks at Camilla and quickly helps me collect the contents of the bag.

'Jump in,' he says.

'Bloody rich kids,' he mumbles as he starts the engine. 'Got bloody everything.'

We sure have.

Chapter Twenty-Eight

The Salvation Army are singing carols outside the gates of the hospital and as we approach, the singers part like the waters of the Red Sea to Moses. The cab driver helps get Camilla out of the cab. It's all I can do not to burst into tears. Oh God, don't let Cammy die, not at Christmas, not that I would want her to die any other time you understand but Christmas is so much worse somehow isn't it? I grab the arm of a passing nurse.

'My friend has taken pills and she's been drinking,' I gabble.

She follows me to the doors where the cab driver is dragging Camilla from the taxi. She calls to another nurse and they take Camilla off him.

'Thank you so much,' I ask the driver. 'How much is it?'

He waves a hand and disappears through the doors. Camilla is wheeled along the corridor with me following. They crash into a cubicle and I stand helplessly dangling two handbags with my head spinning from the champagne. I hear running feet and pray it is a doctor. The curtains are swished back and I turn to see Taylor. He looks different in his doctor's outfit and a stethoscope around his neck.

'It's Camilla,' I say, bursting into tears. 'I think she's taken an overdose.'

He says something to a nurse and checks Camilla's pulse.

'How long ago did she take the pills and do you know what they were?' he asks calmly.

I hand him Camilla's bag.

'All the bottles are empty and she's drunk loads,' I say, feeling panic overwhelm me.

'What did she drink, and how long ago?' he asks tipping the bag upside down and spilling its contents onto a table.

I look at him pleadingly.

'Please do something,' I beg.

'We will, what has she been drinking?'

'Champagne.'

'Have a cup of tea in the waiting area. I'll be back,' he says.

He disappears down the corridor. I drop my head in my hands and wait, listening to the ticks from the waiting room clock. I phone Chelsea and tell her what has happened. She weeps down the phone and says she will call Cammy's parents and Hugo. I get a text from Roddy saying, *I must have the ring or I'll be mincemeat.* I'm not sure if he means I'll be mincemeat or he will. He really exaggerates sometimes. He should be in my Dolce & Gabbanas. I've got no money and an unconscious friend. A whole hour passes before Taylor enters the room. I try to gauge from his expression whether Cammy is okay but he gives nothing away. He sits beside me and rubs his eyes.

'She'll be fine,' he says.

I could kiss him but resist the urge and burst into tears instead. I feel his arm around my shoulders.

'She's been pretty sick. We had to pump her stomach I'm afraid. She'd mixed so much stuff. Do you know why she did it?'

'Her boyfriend Hugo dumped her.'

He raises his eyebrows.

'Do you want to call her parents or ...?'

'Chelsea is doing that. They should be here soon.'

'You can see her if you wish.'

I could hug him but a hospital is not quite the place is it?

'I understand if you want to leave our shopping trip tonight,' he says, but I hear the disappointment in his voice.

'Oh no,' I say. 'If Camilla is okay then I'd really like to go. It's been a crap afternoon.'

His face lights up.

'Great. I'll show you where she is and then when you're ready we can go from here if you like? I finish in ten minutes. Are you sure you're up to it?'

'I'm fine really. I've been looking forward to it.'

'I hope you don't mind if we swing by the music shop? I'm thinking of getting Geoff a new guitar. The one he has is so useless. Ruby is donating a few quid, you can too if you want?'

'I'd love to,' I say.

I feel so relieved that I would say yes to anything right now. Okay, maybe not anything, but you know what I mean. I am led along the corridor and into a room where Camilla looks washed out and miserable.

'I'm so sorry,' she sobs.

'He's not worth it,' I whisper.

'I know,' she says grasping my hand.

Taylor leaves us together and I stay until her parents and Hugo arrive. I can hardly look at him and mumble *arse* as I pass. It's a relief to walk outside. I take a deep breath of the cold evening air and see Taylor waiting for me. Life on a boat is really not so bad and I'm making true friends, and friends who actually care about me rather than my money. We walk slowly and huddle close together as we weave through the crowds. The Christmas lights above us and the bright decorations in the shop windows are magical.

'Thank you for what you did for Camilla,' I say.

We pass a roast chestnut stall and share a bag of hot chestnuts on our walk to the music shop. Lights twinkle around us and snippets of Christmas carols tease as we pass shop doorways. Finally we reach the music store and Taylor heads to the guitar section. I'm drawn to the piano and while Taylor discusses guitars with the assistant I tinker with it. Piano lessons were forced on me as a child and now for some reason I'm missing it. I think of the grand piano at Daddy's Oxfordshire home and decide to make more use of it when this is all over, if this is ever over of course. I'm getting quite into it and am playing *Silent Night* when Taylor joins me and begins singing, sounding so much like Michael Bublé that I widen my eyes in astonishment. Another customer joins in on the drums and I find myself thinking how Roddy would die from embarrassment if he were here. We become a jazzy threesome for a few minutes until I realise that Taylor has stopped singing. I look up to see him staring at a woman. She's gorgeous and I find myself looking at her enviously. Her skin glows and her thick wavy chestnut hair hangs around her shoulders in soft waves. She looks like a model. She's most certainly a size 10 and doesn't have breasts that slap you in the face when running. In fact they are perfect. I look at Taylor who is mesmerised by her and I feel a stab of jealousy. I close the piano softly and stand beside him.

'Hello Taylor, fancy seeing you in here,' she says in a clear crisp voice. She completely disregards me. 'How are you?'

'Hi Lisa,' Taylor says without taking his eyes off her.

I cough in the hope he may remember me. He turns and takes my arm.

'This is Poppy,' he says, introducing me.

'Poppy,' she repeats.

Is she deaf?

'Hello,' I say.

'That's an unusual name isn't it?'

'I'm afraid it's the only one I've got,' I say, forcing a smile.

It's better than a plain name like *Lisa* isn't it?

'Did you get my card?' she asks, making eye contact with Taylor.

I swear if I fell convulsing to the floor they wouldn't notice. I sigh but notice that Taylor's hand is still on my arm.

'Yes thanks. So how are things?' he says and I detect a tremble in his voice.

'Good, we should catch up,' she says fluttering her long lashes.

Taylor opens his mouth to speak when the assistant calls him over.

'Do you want to collect when you've finished your other shopping sir?'

'I should let you get on,' she says. 'Get in touch Tay. The ball's in your court,' she adds flirtatiously. We watch her walk out of the shop.

'Are you hungry?' Taylor asks.

I nod. It seems like forever since my afternoon tea from hell.

'Fancy some sushi?'

'Sounds great,' I say.

Twenty minutes later I am surrounded by colourful dishes with names I am unable to pronounce.

'Sorry about earlier,' he says quietly.

'It's okay,' I say, accepting a glass of rice wine.

'That was my ex-wife. I haven't seen her in a year.'

'Oh,' I mumble.

God, his ex-wife, I don't believe it. She takes a lot of competing with.

'Seeing her brought back bad memories,' he says, handing me a bowl.

'I'm sorry,' I say.

He shrugs.

'You play a mean piano,' he says brushing my hand.

'You've got a mean singing voice.'

He laughs.

'Some would disagree.'

His knee touches mine and that wonderful warm feeling courses through my veins.

'I'm really pleased you came tonight, especially after all that's happened.'

He is? Even after seeing Miss Perfect Lisa?

'I'm pleased to be here,' I say sipping my wine and feeling happier than I have felt in a long time.

'What happened with Camilla?' he asks.

I swallow a rice roll and sigh.

'I think she thought an engagement was on the cards. It seems his parents prefer multi-orgasmic Hetty with the titled parents,' I say, rolling my eyes.

'Multi-orgasmic?' he questions, smiling at me over his glass.

'Yes, it seems she's only got to think about it and you know ... Three times a day apparently,' I break off and blush.

What am I saying?

'Of course, it's not the same for all women,' I say stupidly. 'Your average woman doesn't, you know, three times a day.'

I wish I could shut up. It seems whenever I am with him the subject of sex always seems to rear its head.

'Is that right?' he says looking into my eyes.

Although with Taylor I imagine I could be bucking my hips pretty quickly. I blush profusely at the thought and almost choke on my wine.

'Managed to get engaged since I last saw you?' he asks with a wink.

'No, I'm having a break from that,' I laugh.

I never realised sushi could be so much fun. Taylor enjoys telling me about the names and origins of the dishes and persuades me to try each one, and laughs as my eyes stream from tasting the wasabi. We hardly notice as the restaurant slowly empties and I realise we are the only table left. Taylor apologises to the waiter as he pays. Once outside in the crisp cold air we continue perusing the shops until one by one their lights are switched off. Finally, we hail a cab and make our way to the Embankment. A special screening of a Laurel and Hardy silent movie is showing in a tiny cinema.

'Proceeds are going to my little hospital in Africa,' he says modestly as we enter.

During the evening I meet more of his work colleagues and friends. I learn a little about the hospital which I discover is in Zimbabwe and is called 'Havers Hospital for Children'.

'It sounds amazing,' I tell him while thinking he looks more gorgeous tonight than at any other time.

'It's not at all glamorous, but it's important to me.'

We sit in a corner, sipping hot chocolate and laughing with his friends until it is time to go home. As he walks me back to the canal I put my arm in his. At one magical moment fine snowflakes begin to fall.

'I thought I'd make truffles as Christmas presents for people on the boats,' I say feeling the Christmas spirit overpower me. It's all these fairy lights twinkling on the canal and the dusting of snow on the boats.

The truth is I hadn't considered it until now but it seems like a good idea.

'Sounds like the perfect present,' he smiles and my heart flutters.

He gently dusts snowflakes from my hat. 'I'd invite you back to mine for a coffee but I rather think I wouldn't be able to resist the mistletoe, or rather, you under it.'

I shiver. It sounds like a good reason to go back to his if ever there was one.

'You could come to mine for coffee,' I say.

'You've got mistletoe too haven't you?'

Damn it.

We reach *Amelia* and stand under the light from the moon. My stomach flutters and my heart pounds.

'Thank you for a wonderful evening,' I say gratefully.

'My pleasure.'

I pull my coat sleeve over my hand to hide the rash eruption that flared up from Camilla's overdose. He places his hand over mine.

'It's fine, just one of Poppy's perfect imperfections.'

He leans forward and I swear my lips purse in readiness.

'You've got snow on your lashes,' he says reaching his hand out. My eyes close just as his lips brush mine. Who needs mistletoe? A pleasurable sigh passes through my open lips and I hear him groan before pulling away.

'Goodnight Poppy. Thanks for coming.'

Then he's gone and I'm left standing like a spare part at a wedding.

Chapter Twenty-Nine

'Is this right?' Chelsea asks, rolling my handmade truffles in flaked almonds.

'It's not rocket science,' says Camilla, nursing the cat and sipping a rose tea.

'I don't want to do it wrong. Not now Poppy's selling them.'

'I'm not selling many,' I say.

Chelsea looks like a 1950's housewife in her frilly apron. She gyrates her hips to Michael Bublé's *Jingle Bells* and throws back half a glass of mulled wine.

'I love this,' she says pouring more into her glass. 'Do you want some Cammy? I'll open the mince pies soon.'

Camilla rummages through the box by the Christmas tree.

'Seriously, you only paid ten pounds for this Miss Dior perfume,' she asks, holding up a bottle.

'Yes and the mulled wine is only one fifty a bottle and you get nicely tipsy on it,' she giggles.

'Yes, we've noticed,' I say, moving the bottle. 'It's three in the afternoon Chelsea.'

'It's Christmas week,' she says petulantly.

'Roddy says it's scandalous. It puts people out of work he says,' pouts Camilla.

'Mulled wine?' asks an amazed Chelsea. 'I never knew that.'

'No silly, all this smuggling of cheap stuff,' says Camilla sharply.

Chelsea sips from her glass and sighs dreamily.

'Well I think it's lovely,' she enthuses. 'I don't care what Roddy says. I love Christmas.'

'What does Roddy know?' I say, feeling my anger rise.

I take the truffles and place them in my tiny fridge which is stuffed with truffles, beer and wine.

The hatch opens and Dusty pops his head in.

'I've got your coal,' he says climbing into the boat. 'This should do you for over the holiday.'

'I've got something in return,' I say, pulling out a box of truffles.

'What are you doing?' asks Camilla. 'He's a pedlar.'

I shoot her a dirty look before handing the truffles to Dusty.

'Merry Christmas Dusty,' I say cheerfully.

For a moment he looks quite overcome.

'It's not much,' I say quickly.

'That's really nice of you. I'll save them for Christmas Day.'

Camilla scoffs. Honestly, what is wrong with her these days? Dusty turns to her and before I can stop him he grabs the mistletoe from the hook and holds it above her head before plonking a huge kiss on her lips. I gasp and Chelsea claps a hand to her mouth. Camilla tries to leap from the scatter cushion but the swaying of the boat throws her back down. Her face turns as red as a beetroot.

'Oh, oh ...' she stammers.

'Fudge berries,' says Chelsea.

'Merry Christmas,' smiles Dusty before climbing out of the cabin. I bite back my smile and offer Camilla some mulled wine.

'How dare he?' she blurts.

'What's wrong with you these days? This past week you've been unbearable?'

'It's that Hetty and her multi-thingy's,' declares Chelsea, holding out her glass for more.

My mobile rings and loses signal as soon as I answer it. I grab my coat and climb onto the deck. It rings again just as I drape myself across the helm. I could be a calendar girl.

'Pop I'm really in a fix.'

Is this all Roddy can talk about these days? He's in a fix? He should be draped across the helm of a boat. I'm starting to feel like Marilyn Monroe.

'Hello darling,' calls a man from a passing barge.

'Do you think ...?' continues Roddy.

To hell with it all, I mean do I really need the bollocking ring. I've got a little bit in the bank and I'm earning my own money now and frankly I'm beginning to think that money isn't all it's cracked up to be. Just look at Camilla.

'You can have the bollocking ring,' I say, only to hear my phone cut out. Just as well, it was a rather rash decision. The boat rocks from the wake of the barge and I hang onto the helm for dear life.

'Miss Wellesley?' says a stern voice.

I jump down onto the deck and come face to face with a policeman, or should I say a schoolboy masquerading as a policeman. Honestly, can they get any younger? I feel a surge of excitement. Have they released Daddy? What am I thinking? Daddy is in the Bahamas or at least he was the last time I heard. He's probably defected to Cuba by now or wherever it is you go when you are on the run. I hesitate for a second and wonder if I should admit to being Poppy Wellesley when Chelsea jumps on deck waving mince pies.

'Poppy, these are so nice. Did you really buy them from Lidl?'

Right, a bit hard to deny I'm Miss Wellesley now isn't it?

'Yes that's me, Poppy Wellesley,' I say to the policeman. 'How can I help you?'

'Oh hello,' says Chelsea. 'Would you like a mince pie?'

'Not while on duty, thank you.'

'I thought it was alcohol you couldn't have on duty,' I say.

'No, we don't accept anything that could be considered a bribe.'

Mince pies a bribe? He surely isn't serious.

'Oh I wasn't bribing you,' says Chelsea. 'They're from Lidl'.

Like being from Lidl makes all the difference.

'And who would you be?' he asks.

That will teach her.

'What are you two doing?' calls Camilla climbing from the boat.

'I'm Chelsea and this is Camilla,' says Chelsea.

The constable nods to Camilla and turns back to me.

'We're investigating a claim that someone on the canal is smuggling in goods from abroad. Your name was mentioned and ...'

Chelsea chokes on her mince pie.

'My name was mentioned?' I squeal.

Can things get any worse?

'Who mentioned my name?' I say, my voice raising an octave. I couldn't sound more guilty if I tried.

'Fudge berries,' groans Chelsea.

Please God, don't let her say anything incriminating. In fact it's best if Chelsea doesn't say anything at all.

'We had an anonymous phone call and they said you knew of this so-called smuggling.'

I glare at Camilla.

'We don't know anything about anything,' mumbles Chelsea offering around the mince pies. Thank God Geoff didn't get those.

'Has anyone sold you cheap perfume?' he asks.

I scoff, much too loudly actually, but he doesn't seem to notice.

'Cheap perfume?' says Chelsea in a high-pitched voice with her face turning red.

'Cheap perfume?' I repeat. 'Do I look like the kind of woman who would wear cheap perfume? My father is Sir Rupert Wellesley.'

Although on reflection that's not a great commendation being as my father has been done for fraud. I so wish I could take it back.

'You're *the* Poppy Wellesley?' he says his eyes widening.

He makes me sound infamous.

'Yes that's her,' says Chelsea.

'You're living *here*?' he asks.

No, I'm here on my holidays. Honestly the stupid questions some people ask.

'Pandora calls it her septic tank,' smiles Chelsea.

At that moment I am saved by the bell or more precisely, the ringing of my mobile. I give the policeman an apologetic look and click it on.

'Pop, you must listen. I'm really in a fix ...'

He's in a fix. He should be here facing this policeman. Never mind his fix. I'm about to be arrested for wearing smuggled perfume.

'I have to go Roddy. I'll call you back.'

'So no one has offered you cheap perfume. You're absolutely sure about that?'

'I wouldn't buy cheap perfume,' I say, 'or ...'

'Cheap mulled wine?' adds Chelsea.

'Mulled wine?' he asks.

'Yes, we have some,' smiles Chelsea.

'Very expensive mulled wine,' I say, 'from Lidl.'

Lidl, what am I saying?

'Actually ...' begins Camilla.

At that moment a message comes through on his radio.

'If you say a word Cammy I swear I'll chuck you in the river,' I hiss.

'You never would,' she challenges.

'I would,' whispers Chelsea. 'I like Geoff.'

'So,' he says, clipping his radio back. 'You ladies don't know anything about cheap goods being flogged around the canal'

We all shake our heads dumbly, although Camilla's wavers between a nod and a shake.

'Can I check the boat?' he asks. 'It's just routine.'

'It's a mess,' I say, remembering the box of wine, perfume and truffles sitting in the corner.

'That's not a problem,' he says.

'I'll lead the way,' says Camilla.

'Fudge berries,' says Chelsea.

'Sorry?' says the policeman.

'I just said we should cook the fudge berries for the fudge berry cake. It's tradition at Christmas.'

What is she on?

He allows us to go first and I give Camilla a little shove.

'Here it is,' I say. 'Not much to see.'

He looks around and admires the Christmas tree.

'Very festive,' he comments.

His eyes wander to the box on the floor.

'That's ...' begins Camilla.

'Are my Christmas presents,' I say, pushing it back.

He nods and picks up a bottle of mulled wine.

'Where did you buy this?' he asks.

Shit, shit.

'Harrods,' says Chelsea in a heartbeat. 'Every year we buy it from Harrods. Where else would you get a decent Mulberry wine?'

'Mulled,' I correct.

'I thought you said you bought it from Lidl.'

Peas and rice!

'Lidl and Harrods,' I say quickly. 'We buy from both. We like a variety.'

'Yes that's right,' nods Chelsea.

She pours half a glass and knocks it back.

'Yes, mulled wine. It's lovely,' she says and coughs. 'Would you like some?'

'Not while on duty,' he says firmly.

'So, why do you think our anonymous caller mentioned you?' he asks, turning to me and meeting my eyes. I try hard not to turn away.

'I don't know. It's very strange.'

'Very strange indeed,' echoes Chelsea who is really getting into this now.

He nods and looks around the boat.

'Have you got a leak?' he asks.

'You do it in here,' says Chelsea opening the loo door.

'He said do I *have* a leak, not that he wants one,' I say, snatching the bottle of mulled wine from her hand. 'Stop drinking.'

'It's the cooker,' I say.

'You need to watch that,' he says studying the gas rings before turning to the steps. 'Right, here's my card should you get offered anything suspicious and ...'

I snatch it from his hand as Camilla rushes forward.

'Have a good Christmas,' he says disappearing through the hatch.

'Frogs' knickers,' sighs Chelsea.

'I don't know what I'm doing with you,' groans Camilla.

I shove a bottle of Dior perfume at her.

'Here, you can have it for a fiver.'

'Really?'

'What a fab Christmas. Cheap booze and perfume, isn't it fun Camilla, breaking all the rules,' says Chelsea gleefully.

Camilla dabs her wrist with perfume.

'Well I suppose so,' she says helping herself to a mince pie. 'But I so wish I was spending it with Hugo.'

'I so wish I was spending it in a house,' I say miserably.

'I so wish I was ...' says Chelsea thoughtfully.

Camilla and I look at her and let out a collective sigh. Roll on Christmas.

Chapter Thirty

It's Christmas Eve and I'm beginning to realise that the good thing about being filthy rich at Christmas is that you don't have the stress of full car parks or the battering of your credit card. You get your chauffeur to drop you outside the stores and everything is put on your personal account. The goods are nicely gift wrapped and delivered to your apartment the same day. Christmas is so easy when you're super filthy rich. But now I'm super filthy poor and struggling around Asda while Noddy Holder's *Merry Christmas Everybody* grates on my shattered nerves. People are shopping as if a nuclear war has just broken out and they have to stockpile food for the next hundred years. The past few days the boat people have been making fairy lanterns and preparing an outside feast for their Christmas lights ceremony. I'd had my invitation of course, and Ruby is dragging me to it.

'Whether you want to or not,' she'd said. 'You will love it. Bill is donating pork pies and Christmas cake and Geoff gets the mulled wine. I thought you could donate some truffles.'

I felt I had to contribute something more than truffles so I've popped to Asda to buy a hundred sausage rolls, or should I say fight for a hundred sausage rolls. I lean towards the freezer and am practically knocked in to it by the horde of shoppers. I know I've been frozen but this is taking things a bit too literally. I nearly get lynched when another woman sees I have taken the last box of sausage rolls.

'Hey, you can't take all those.'

Unless sausage roll rationing is in force I really don't see why I can't. I'm amazed I get out alive. Personally I hate sausage rolls but I think the boat people will like them. I push my way through the throng and am almost at the till when a man jumps out in front of me.

'Good afternoon madam, and how are you on this lovely festive day?'

'In a rush actually,' I say, looking for a way past him. I really don't want to end up in a Christmas brawl in the middle of Asda. That will finish Mummy off.

'I can't let you go without giving you a taste of my banger,' he says nudging me.

You don't get this in Harrods.

'Excuse me?' I say, watching a little rivulet of sweat form on his forehead.

He produces a huge sausage and holds it in front of me.

'Have a bite of that.'

No wonder this country is going to the dogs.

'I'd rather not,' I say, turning my head away.

'Go on. A bit of this with your turkey and you won't know what's hit you.'

He won't know what's hit him if he doesn't remove that offending thing from my face.

'I'm a vegetarian,' I lie.

'Oh,' he says, taking a step back as if I had just told him I was a vampire out on a lunch break.

I push past and head for the tills. I wonder what Mummy is doing. I suppose she and Daddy are on a beach somewhere, drinking martinis. Not together of course. I try not to think of Marcus's fancy dress party which will be happening in a few hours. Everyone is going. I had hoped Balls would phone and ask if I wanted to go with him but he's obviously decided his mother is better company. After all, I did say I needed some time didn't I? I so wish people wouldn't take everything I say literally. I'd not heard from Roddy since his last *I'm in a fix* phone call. It's party season so I suppose he is busy living it up with Pug-face. I'm sure he'll phone again when he gets into another fix. I wander back to the canal, passing buskers and street artists and realise that I'm not missing Roddy at all. I find myself skipping along the boardwalk to see the boat people preparing for the Christmas lights party. Paper lanterns are being hung along with fairy lights. A small stage is being erected close to Ruby's boat and tables are being covered with festive tablecloths. I hurry onto *Amelia* and begin heating my sausage rolls. It's going to take a while as I can only get a tray of ten in at any one time. I force myself not to think of tomorrow. It's the first time I've been alone over Christmas and I have no idea what I'll do with myself.

Ruby knocks at six and takes a plate of sausage rolls and a box of truffles, and I follow her with another. The boardwalk is packed with people, some in fancy dress while others are trussed up warmly. Music is playing and the smell of roasting chestnuts and fried burgers reaches our nostrils.

'Mmm, I love the Christmas lights ceremony,' Ruby smiles.

We hand the plates to Bill.

'Evening girls, all right Poppet? I got another order for them truffles.'

I'll be a truffle entrepreneur before I know it. I smile and look around for Taylor but there is no sign of him or Geoff.

'Is Chelsea coming?' asks Ruby.

'They're all going to a friend's fancy dress party,' I say, trying not to show my disappointment.

'Aren't you going?' she asks, surprised.

'I ...'

'They didn't invite you did they?' she says crossly.

'No,' I say accepting a burger from Bill.

'Arses, still you'll have more fun here. Let's get some mulled wine.'

We push through the crowd to the bar and Ruby takes two glasses. I sip my mulled wine and feel the warm liquid run through me.

'There's Pete,' she says and waves.

Oh no, not Mr Crotch. He strides towards us with a swagger and attempts to swipe a bottle of beer as he passes. I think it's supposed to look cool except he swipes a bowl of crisps at the same time, sending them flying over someone's dog.

'Hey girls,' he says, stepping over the crisp covered dog.

'Hi Pete, it's all looking good isn't it?'

'It sure is,' he says drunkenly, his eyes travelling to my breasts.

'How are you?' he asks, his eyes not moving.

'We're fine,' I reply and Ruby stifles a giggle.

The music stops. Ruby links her arm in mine.

'We're starting,' she says excitedly, handing me a programme.

The beer-fumed breath from Mr Crotch wafts across as we sing carols. By the time we finish my ears are ringing from his booming voice. The DJ spins a drum roll as the lights are turned on. The canal is lit up and really does look like Blackpool pier.

'Hurrah,' cries Ruby, plonking a kiss on my cheek.

'Hurrah,' repeats Mr Crotch, also leaning forward to kiss me.

Ruby drags me to the buffet table and Mr Crotch follows.

'I'm starving,' says Mr Crotch.

'He's like a lost dog,' I whisper.

'He's a leech. None of the women like him.'

Bill hands out Christmas cake and I remember the truffles I had made especially for him. I nip back to *Amelia* and take Bill's truffles from the fridge. I've made him rum and raisin, which I know he will like, and in the shape of button mushrooms. I think he will get the joke. I have written on the box *'Ain't no call for posh mushrooms around here.'*

'Need a hand,' says a voice behind me and I turn to see Mr Crotch.

'No thanks I'm fine,' I say.

'Nice boat,' he says, peeking inside.

Yes, it may well be but that's as much as you're seeing.

'Hello Pete.'

I smile with relief at Taylor.

'Okay to come on board,' he asks.

'The more the merrier.'

Pete backs away.

'Hi Taylor,' he says, looking slightly flustered. 'I was just off to get some food.'

Taylor simply smiles and steps into the boat.

'I came to give you this. I saw it on my way home.'

He hands me an evening paper and I read the headline even before he gives it to me.

MP arrested for fraud casting doubt over Sir Rupert Wellesley charge.

I scan the article and feel my heart leap.

'It doesn't say your father is scot-free but it hints he could have been a scapegoat,' he says looking at me intently.

I grab my phone and wave it around like a mad woman.

'Shall we get some chestnuts?' he asks. 'You'll get better signal on deck.'

He's right of course but all I can think of is that I may be rich again. I'll get my life back. I'll get off this dump of a boat. I'll actually wear my Valentino wedding dress and become Mrs Roddy Tarleton. I look at Taylor and realise that right now that is the last thing I want. Life's a bugger isn't it? I throw my phone back into my bag and take his arm.

'I'll do it later,' I say, enjoying the feel of his body close to mine.

We stroll back to the party. Taylor hands the newspaper to Ruby and a few of the boat people huddle around to read it.

'Have you got your money back then?' asks Dusty, who looks completely different out of his dungarees and anorak.

'I don't really know,' I say truthfully.

Geoff lumbers along the walkway with two large crates and Dusty rushes to help him.

'I've got more in the car. We got it all last night. Aftershave, perfume, mulled wine, lots of booze and the silk purses you asked for, Ruby.'

'Ooh fab,' she cries.

'Will you leave the boat?' Dusty asks.

'I don't know,' I say.

The truth is I don't know anything any more. A week ago I would have done anything to get my life back. Now, I'm not sure it's actually worth getting back. I'm hugged by Rose, and Jim's cat purrs around my ankles.

'I'm so pleased for you. I saw the news about your father.'

I lean down and stroke Coco and struggle to hold back my tears.

'What news is that then?' asks Geoff.

'Poppy's getting her money back,' says Ruby.

'I don't know for sure,' I say.

'Let's go for a walk shall we?' says Taylor. 'Enjoy these lights.'

I nod. We walk silently for a while. He stops and unwraps his scarf and gently ties it around my neck.

'How's the rash?'

'Better,' I say.

In fact it has almost gone. Just his presence seems to make it disappear. Where's the bloody mistletoe when you need it?

'You don't seem very happy about the news,' he says.

'It's unexpected.'

'Do you think you'll go back to Roddy?' he asks.

He looks into my eyes. I can't think of anything with his lips so close to mine.

'He's engaged to Pandora.'

He runs his hand through my hair.

'Where's the mistletoe when you need it?' he smiles.

'My sentiments exactly,' I say, hearing my voice quiver.

'We could just pretend.'

'Yes,' I say softly.

Then his lips are on mine. The sky is suddenly lit up with an explosion of colourful fireworks. I hug closer to him and feel I could melt into his body as his lips devour mine.

The kiss deepens and I feel like my lips are bruised. I press against his body, not able to get enough of him. The fireworks pop and crash above us coupled with the distant chorus from the boat people singing Christmas carols. My hands press against Taylor's chest and I can feel his beating heart. There is a vibrating between us and for a second I try to work out what is happening when he curses and pulls a pager from his pocket.

'Damn,' he groans, releasing me. 'I'm sorry, I should have said. I'm on call and have to go back to the hospital.'

I ask you, who has my kind of luck?

'Taylor, Poppy,' shouts Ruby. 'Come and join the fun.'

'Ruby to the rescue,' smiles Taylor.

'Yes,' I say.

'Merry Christmas Poppy.'

'Merry Christmas Taylor.'

I don't believe my luck. I really don't.

Chapter Thirty-One

Waking up alone on Christmas morning is no fun at all. After stoking up the log burner I make myself a coffee and scoff two mince pies before throwing on a warm jumper, jeans and my fur. I climb onto the deck and check my phone. There is a Merry Christmas text from Chelsea.

I'll try and pop over later. And a rather miserable one from Jeremy which reads, *Don't get too excited. The bank accounts are still frozen.*

Jeremy sure knows how to keep my feet on the ground. I trundle back inside and huddle by the log burner with the cat on my lap and a copy of *House and Home* magazine. I consume another mince pie with Radio 4's Christmas service blaring from my iPhone. I stare at the glorious pictures of a country home similar to the one I had hoped for Roddy and me. It's stunning and the gardens are spectacular. I give the magazine one last angry glare before ripping it into pieces and chucking it in the fire. A quick glance in the fridge reminds me I have nothing for Christmas dinner. I was hoping someone would invite me over if I'm honest. Not that my friends are spontaneous. The canal is so quiet you could hear a pin drop. There's no sound of music or people chatting. No chugging of passing barges. Just the ringing of distant church bells, which would be lovely and festive if only I weren't alone. I polish off another mince pie, sing along with the carols and finally decide to walk to the little corner shop which I remember is open today, to buy myself a chicken breast. I ask you how sad is that? Maybe I'll get a Christmas pudding for one and make the whole day even more miserable. I wrap myself up and climb onto deck where my phone rings.

'Merry Crimbo darling. It's me Mummy,' she shouts.

My mother seems to think that you have to shout when calling from abroad.

'Have you sunk yet?'

'It's a narrowboat not a cruise ship.'

'Are you dangling over the side?'

I'm so glad no one else can hear our conversation. Although the way she is shouting I imagine half of Long Island can.

'Should I be?'

'To get signal. Don't fall in though, not on Christmas Day,' she laughs.

'Signal seems to be fine today,' I say, aware of a stray Alsatian on the boardwalk that is growling viciously at me.

'Where are you spending the day?' she asks.

'I'm home alone,' I say gloomily.

'Christ on a bike, why are you alone? It's Christmas Day, surely someone will have you.'

She makes me sound like a lost orphan who needs taking in.

'I prefer to be alone,' I lie, feeling the dog's eyes on me. I wish he'd stop baring his teeth. I have visions of him pouncing any minute and I'm not geared up to do my Katniss Everdeen impression.

'Well, soon you'll be back in Belgravia where you belong and not a day too soon. I think Roddy should pull his socks up and get rid of Pope Paul's daughter and put that ring back on your finger ...'

'Mummy ...'

'I'll be in touch. I always knew your father wasn't a crook.'

I don't believe I'm hearing this.

'Time for cocktails, or should I say *cocks*,' she laughs.

With that she hangs up and I'm alone again, aside from the snarling Alsatian. I switch off the phone. After all no one else is going to call me now are they? I pop back inside to get my gloves and spot Taylor's present under the tree. I pop it into a carrier bag so I can put it outside his hatch. When I climb back on deck the dog has gone. I sigh with relief and walk to the shop. There's a light snowfall but the sun is shining and it's a pleasant walk even if I am alone. I turn out of the canal entrance and walk straight into Taylor.

'Hi,' he says surprise evident on his face.

I'm so happy to see him, I'm sure the pleasure shows.

'Merry Christmas,' I say.

He's wearing a new jumper. His hair is slightly tousled from his shower and he smells and looks gorgeous.

'I felt sure you would be with your friends today,' he says apologetically.

I shake my head.

'No, I'm just about to buy a chicken breast for one.'

Why did I have to say breast? There are thighs and drumsticks aren't there? Trust me to sound like a sex-starved woman yet again.

'How about you?' I ask. 'Are you off anywhere?'

'Only the soup kitchen at lunchtime,' he smiles.

'Oh God, you don't have to do that. I can get two breasts,' I say hurriedly.

He grins. Me and my mouth, there's no controlling it is there?

'I'm not going for my lunch. I'm actually going to help.'

I pull a face. What an idiot.

'Of course,' I say, stepping past him towards the shop.

'You're welcome to come, that's if you're not doing anything else.'

It's all I can do to stop myself jumping up and down with excitement.

'I'd love to,' I say.

'We can get lunch after. There has to be a pub open somewhere.'

It's getting better and better. I hand him the carrier bag shyly.

'I bought you a present. I was going to leave it on deck but ...'

'Why don't we go back to my boat, have a coffee and mince pie.'

Another mince pie? This is no good for my cellulite but I nod all the same.

'I've got a little something for you.'

This is turning into the best Christmas Day ever. I follow him back to his boat with church bells ringing in the distance.

Chapter Thirty-Two

I watch eagerly as he unwraps the gift. He smiles at the box.

'It's a whisky glass. I had it inscribed,' I say cheerfully.

'I didn't expect anything. Thanks very much.'

He kisses me on the cheek before handing me a small prettily wrapped box. I open it with trembling hands to find a delicate silver-beaded bracelet with a disc that has been engraved one side with *Amelia* and on the other *Truffle Queen*.

'I thought it fitting,' he laughs.

'It's absolutely gorgeous,' I say.

'It's not a Tiffany or anything.'

'It's perfect.'

He clips it onto my wrist and looks at it admiringly.

'It looks good,' he says before draining his glass of mulled wine. 'Right, let's get to that soup kitchen shall we?'

I nod happily

I've never helped in a soup kitchen and feel a little apprehensive but it turns out to be one of the best experiences of my life. Everyone is so friendly and extremely grateful. I find myself chatting to people as if I've known them for years. Taylor, however, really does seem to know many of the homeless who come in for their dinner. He's friendly, happy and relaxed and I can't take my eyes off him. His face is animated and my heart quickens when he smiles at me. Christmas carols play in the background and it feels like the best place to be on Christmas Day. Several hours later, after helping with the washing up, we leave and stroll along the Embankment and look for a pub to have lunch.

'It's been a lovely day,' I say, feeling the cold wind on my face.

'You're easy to please,' he says, pointing out a pub. 'How about there?'

I nod. I'm quite happy to go anywhere as long as I'm with him. We enjoy a turkey and cranberry sandwich with trimmings, which I have to admit is as good as a Blundell Christmas special.

'That's a nice jumper,' I say, curious to who had bought it for him.

'My mother sent it. She lives in Jersey and every year I get sent a new jumper whether I need it or not. How about you?'

'No I didn't get a jumper,' I laugh. 'I'm the woman with everything, remember.'

'This is true.'

We finish lunch and play a game of dominoes which he wins easily. He points to the dartboard.

'Are you game?'

'I've never played darts in my life,' I admit.

'We'd best all stand back,' laughs the landlord.

My attempts at darts turn out to be rather hairy, especially with a second glass of cider in me.

'At least you know you'll be safe when she throws the dinner at you,' says the landlord.

We leave an hour later, warmed and slightly tipsy.

'A walk along the Embankment,' he suggests.

The snow is falling heavily now and we crunch it beneath our feet. We walk in silence for a while taking in the sights and smells. I feel his hand touch mine and I enfold it in his.

'What's happening about your father?' he asks.

'I don't know.'

I feel nicely relaxed from the cider and a warm sense of anticipation envelopes me. There's a whole evening ahead of us. We stop at a crepe stall and buy two chocolate banana crepes and sit on a bench overlooking the Thames to eat them.

'What will you do with the boat?' he asks, handing me a serviette.

The truth is I don't really want to think about getting my old life back. Not on such a perfect day as this. I shrug.

'So much has changed,' I say reflecting on the past.

He puts an arm around my shoulder and pulls me closer. His body feels warm and safe, and I rest my head on his shoulder. I could stay that way forever. The Christmas lights reflect across the Embankment. He points out something on the river and as I turn my head to look, he leans towards me and his lips touch mine. I fold into his arms and surrender to his warm sensual kiss. My body arches towards his and I'm overcome by a passion I've never experienced before. I never want to leave his arms. It feels so right to be there. His fingers entwine within mine and his lips travel to my neck making me shiver.

'Shall we walk back to the boat?' he whispers. 'It's getting dark and cold.'

I can barely speak so I just nod.

He pulls me up and hugs me tightly before wrapping his scarf around my neck.

'Let's go,' he says.

I meekly allow myself to be led back along the Embankment, the cosy feeling wrapping itself around me like a warm blanket.

Chapter Thirty-Three

Roddy asks the cab driver to wait. Damn Poppy. The journey had not only cost him a bollocking fortune but taken him nearly two hours. These thieving cab drivers sure make the most of Christmas. He pulls up the collar of his coat and puts on a pair of gloves. He tries Poppy's mobile again only to have it click into voicemail. The canal is quieter than the last time he was here. Everyone slumped in front of their TVs watching pointless Christmas shows, he thinks. For a moment he finds himself wondering how Poppy spent the day. It wasn't the same without her at Dunbarton Hall. Pandora is so damn clingy and what's worse she runs to P'pa every time she thinks he is having a little flutter. Well damn her too. Damn all women. Poppy has been bloody difficult about the ring. She could have handed it over days ago. He bought it after all. Surely he's entitled to have it back. It's not his fault Wellesley turned out to be a crook. Although things are looking up on that front if yesterday's news was anything to go by. Still, he can't bank on that, it could all backfire and they'd be back where they started, and he really needs to get those bloody Jack's off his back. The boardwalk is slippery and he walks slowly. The canal is lit with Christmas lights and he's grateful. What a hell hole. How Pops can stick it he'll never know. He checks the time. Seven o'clock, she surely won't be in bed yet.

He passes boat after boat and becomes disorientated. Has he passed *Amelia*? He steps around a cat and struggles to remember if it is Poppy's. Then he sees her little barge bopping on the water. Christ, how does she cope living here? He climbs onto the deck and taps on the hatch. There are no lights on and his heart sinks.

'Poppy are you there?' he calls.

Where the hell can she be? He thought she had nowhere to go over Christmas. She'd better not be with that wanker Tyrone. He waits a few seconds before trying the hatch. Damn, it's locked. He bangs his fist angrily against it.

'Damn you Poppy,' he hisses.

He grits his teeth, before clicking on his Bluetooth. Two minutes later he is talking to a locksmith.

'I'll pay you triple,' he says desperately. 'I need to get into my boat. It's freezing out here.'

'It'll cost you I'm afraid,' says the locksmith.

'I'll pay whatever,' says Roddy recklessly.

'Okay. I'll be there in a minute,' says the locksmith, realising he is onto a good thing.

Twenty minutes later and a hundred and fifty quid poorer, Roddy is in the boat. He locks the hatch behind him and begins to methodically search the barge. The bollocking ring has got to be somewhere. He pulls bag after bag out of the wardrobe, rummages through the bedside cabinet and even empties the fridge in his desperation. He falls against the cooker and bangs his fist upon it. Where in hell is the bollocking thing? If he doesn't give the ring to Diamond tomorrow he'll be well and truly in Shit Street. He takes a beer from the fridge and downs it before pulling out another. He throws saucepans from the cupboards and looks in them. Where the fuck do women keep their jewellery? It's then he spots the small pot on the kitchen counter. He holds his breath and pulls the lid off. There glittering in front of him is the ring. He sighs and reaches out for it.

'Come to Papa,' he says, his mind so focused on the ring that he doesn't notice the smell of gas.

Chapter Thirty-Four

'I'll just freshen up and change,' I say, while not really wanting to part from Taylor for even a few minutes.

'You smell fresh enough to me,' he says, sniffing my neck.

'I'll be five minutes,' I say, fingering my new bracelet.

'I'll come and get you if you go a minute over,' he says kissing me on the cheek.

I part from him reluctantly and walk to *Amelia*. I want to look and feel gorgeous for him. My loins throb at the thought of it. I slip my key into the lock and go to turn it but nothing happens. It doesn't move. I take it out and try again but still nothing happens. I step back to make sure it is *Amelia*, after all I have drunk a bit. I push the key in again and am trying to turn it when the hatch opens and I come face to face with Roddy. What is he doing on my boat, and on Christmas Day? Isn't he supposed to be at Dunbarton Hall with Pug-face?

'Roddy,' I say, hardly able to believe my eyes.

My muddled brain tries to work out how Roddy can have got onto my boat.

'You're back at last,' he says, roughly helping me down.

'How long have you been here?'

'Long enough,' he says sharply.

'How did you get in?' I ask puzzled.

'I broke in, that is I got a locksmith to break in for me.'

'What do you mean you broke ...?' I stop when I see the mess behind him. Oh my God, I've been burgled. Who would be so desperate as to burgle me? I sigh at the sight of the broken truffles on the floor.

'What happened, who did this? Have you called the police?'

'I needed the ring Poppy,' he says, his eyes darting. 'You've been teasing me with the bloody thing for days.'

I gape at him.

'What are you talking about? Are you saying you did this? Roddy have you gone insane?'

One look at his face tells me he may well have done. He looks possessed.

'Why didn't you just ask me?' I say, realising that he had several times.

'Diamond is going to cut bits off me. He's threated one piece a day after Christmas Day if I don't get his money but I haven't got any bollocking money Pop, have I?'

He grabs a beer from the fridge and downs it. By the smell of him it isn't the first either.

'They're known for cutting off ears Poppy.'

'And you'd be lost without yours,' I say pointing to the Bluetooth.

I see the ring has gone from the pot and shake my head.

'It's not yours to take Roddy, you gave it to me.'

'Do you want to see me end up in little pieces?' he yells.

'I'm sure they are just threats, who would do that kind of thing? Anyway it's your own fault for borrowing money. You shouldn't have got into debt in the first place.'

He scoffs.

'What's that you're wearing?' His eyes feast on my bracelet.

'How much have you had to drink?' I ask nervously.

'I don't know, whatever was in your fridge,' he says, throwing keys at me. 'These are the new keys to your dingy dirty boat.'

Tears sting my eyes and I push past him.

'You can leave my dingy dirty boat and take your stupid ring with you. I'm going to change. Taylor's waiting for me.'

I head for the bedroom but am pulled back roughly.

'Oh no, you're not going to that scoundrel,' he hisses. 'You're making a fool out of me with your antics on this boat. You can't even keep yourself out of the papers can you? Don't you have any respect?'

This is becoming more like a *Titanic* re-enactment by the minute. I struggle to get out of his arms but he holds me tightly.

'What happened to us Pop? We were good together. We could have had it all, money, status, the lot. Your fucking father did for us. But it could get better couldn't it. You still want me don't you? You're not really interested in that loser Taylor are you?'

He pushes me against the cooker.

'Roddy,' I say breathlessly.

His lips crush against mine until they feel numb and his hand slides up my thigh.

'God, I've missed you Poppy,' he groans, pushing against me and ripping at the buttons on my dress.

'Roddy, you're drunk,' I say, struggling to get out of his embrace.

I'm wedged against the cooker and can't even lift my knee. I look up and my eyes meet Taylor's through the window.

Taylor places a box of Harrods truffles onto the coffee table and then changes into a clean shirt. He checks his watch and smiles. She's five minutes late and no doubt playing hard to get. After a last check he leaves his boat and walks slowly to *Amelia*. The boat is moving a lot and he wonders what on earth she can be doing. He taps on the hatch but she doesn't seem to hear him. For a moment he thinks he hears voices. He peeks through the window and stares at the scene in front of him and is transported back to a year ago. He sees Lisa and Simon all over again. Poppy meets his eyes and he turns away. He should have known. Someone with her background wouldn't take someone like him seriously. He pushes the memory of Lisa away and jumps off the deck and back to his boat. He's been hurt once by a woman, he's not a fool. He won't let it happen again, not for some rich bitch that's for sure. If it's that wanker Roddy she wants then she is welcome to him.

Why doesn't Taylor help me? I feel nauseous pinned against the cooker by Roddy. I lean behind and fumble for something to help get Roddy off me but there's nothing. My hand grasps a pipe at the back of the cooker. It feels loose but I pull on it and kick my legs out. Roddy tries to grab my hand but grasps the pipe instead. It comes away and gas hisses out into the boat.

'Roddy, get off me,' I scream.

'We can still be together Pop. It looks like your father will get his money back and I can chuck Pandora and ...'

The ring falls from his pocket in the struggle and I grab it before he can. I dive for the hatch banging my head as I do so. I've got to get away from Roddy.

'Give me that Poppy. I need that ring. For God's sake what's wrong with you? Do you want Diamond to finish me off?'

I rush up the steps and fall onto the deck with Roddy reaching out for my ankles. I stand panting and look at Taylor's boat. The lights are off and Taylor is nowhere.

'You've gone mad Roddy.'

'Give it to me Poppy,' Roddy snarls, reaching towards me.

I jump off the boat and slip on the boardwalk. He follows and grabs the hem of my coat. I turn to slap him when a strange noise from the boat makes us both turn.

'Oh God, the boat,' I cry. 'What have you done?'

Roddy tries to free the ring from my clenched hand. I kick his shins and make a run for it, only to fall on the slippery boardwalk. He grabs my arm and wrenches it. I kick out and hear him groan as my foot connects with his groin. I lift my hand in the air before throwing the ring.

'No,' he cries, his eyes following it.

I watch as the ring flies through the air. It hovers for a second and then lands with a plop in the river.

'Have you lost your mind?' groans Roddy. 'Do you know what that ring is worth?'

At that moment I really couldn't care. I've lost everything else so a little thing like a ring isn't going to make much difference now is it? There is a strange sizzling sound from the boat. Roddy widens his eyes and then everything seems to move in slow motion. The sizzling sound stops and I hold my breath. There is an enormous bang and a flash, and the windows of my boat fall like hail around us. Roddy shields his face as the hatch is sent spinning through the air before splashing into the water. Mistletoe berries land on the boardwalk in front of me. I stare in horror as my boat tips to the side and then there is only blackness.

Chapter Thirty-Five

'I don't need an ambulance,' I argue, clutching the cat tightly. My Louboutin shoes and Gucci clutch float past followed by my Oscar de la Renta pumps and Marc Jacobs handbag. My whole life is drifting past my eyes and I'm finding it hard not to dive into the icy river to rescue it. A little flotilla of Christmas baubles pass before me and I feel my eyes mist with tears. How could Roddy do this?

'You must have frogmen or whatever you call them. I demand you drag that river,' bellows Roddy.

I can't believe he is still ranting on about the ring.

'It's not procedure sir, not for personal belongings,' the police officer says patiently.

I can't take my eyes off the Louboutin shoes. This can't be happening. I now no longer have a home or shoes. I paid ten thousand pounds for that boat and now it's at the bottom of the canal, along with just about everything else I own. Roddy gives me a filthy glare.

'I hope you're happy,' he snaps.

'You must have insurance sir.' says the police officer.

Roddy's face lights up. No doubt he'll try to get a refund on the lock he just had fitted too. I'm surrounded by flashing lights. Firemen pull up what remains of *Amelia* and the police cordon off the area so the paparazzi can't get in. Taylor wraps something around my arm and I turn to him.

'Taylor ...'

'Stay still. I'm taking your blood pressure.'

'I need to explain ...'

'I'd rather you didn't. The truth is we're worlds apart Poppy. Everyone knows who you are. I'm just one doctor amongst many. I've never been to The Ivy. I don't even want to go there. That's your life, it's not mine and let's face it, Roddy is more your kind of bloke than I am.'

I shake my head emphatically and feel it throb.

'It wasn't how it looked ...' I begin.

'You should get to hospital,' he says softly.

'But ...'

'Poppy, Poppy,' screams a voice.

I look up to see Chelsea barging through the cordon.

'It's okay,' says Taylor. 'Poppy knows her.'

'Fudge berries,' she cries on reaching me. 'What happened?'

I nod towards Roddy, who is being checked over by a paramedic, and begin to cry.

'The boat is gone,' I say, between hiccups. 'A gas leak.'

I wipe my eyes and see that Taylor has gone.

'I threw the ring into the river.'

'Good on you Poppy,' she smiles.

'Where am I going to live?'

She places a hand on mine.

'Haven't you seen the news? I've been texting you all evening.'

'I turned my phone off after speaking to Mummy.'

'Your father is coming home. He was set up. That MP that was arrested has admitted to making him the scapegoat. You're getting your old life back Poppy. You'll be back in your Belgravia flat before you can say *trollops*.'

I look at her.

'What did you say?'

'*Trollops.*'

They're thawing out Daddy?

'All right miss. Let's get you checked over,' says the paramedic.

I'm getting my old life back? Why do I not feel happy?

Chapter Thirty-Six

'Are you absolutely sure?'

'Yes, I saw them in Miranda's with your truffles.'

'Taylor and Miss Perfect Breasts were selling my truffles?'

'Who's *Miss Perfect Breasts*?' asks Sophie.

'Miranda's were selling your truffles. I suppose they got them from Bill Blundell,' explains Chelsea.

'Who's Bill Blundell?' asks Sophie.

I so wish people would keep up.

'I worked for him,' I explain.

'I didn't know you had a job,' says Sophie. 'What did you do?'

'I made sandwiches,' I reply.

'Golly, how awful.'

'It wasn't that bad. In fact I quite enjoyed it.'

'And she sold her truffles,' says Chelsea.

'Bill Blundell makes them now. I gave him the recipe,' I say.

'No way,' says Sophie.

'How do you know he's seeing her?' I ask. 'Maybe they just bumped into each other.'

'They were ... You know, they were ...'

Camilla sighs.

'Spit it out Chelsea,' she snaps.

'Yes, they were what?' I ask.

'You know, they were like cosy together.'

I don't believe this. One minute he was coming on to me and the next he's back with his perfect breasted wife.

'Did you speak to him?' I ask.

She shakes her head.

'He didn't see me. I miss the boat Poppy, don't you?'

I miss Taylor. It's New Year's Eve, six days after *Amelia* went down. I can confirm that Poppy Wellesley is rich again. I'm back in my Belgravia apartment. Daddy has returned to helping those on death row and Mummy spends her days giving interviews on what it was like to be poor. Thankfully this does not include an account of who changed my nappies or her throwing back cocks like no tomorrow. Roddy is claiming a nice figure on the insurance for the ring. I've not seen him since *Amelia* sunk but I'm presuming he's okay and that all his body parts are intact. He's tried to call me so presumably he still has at least one ear. I have ignored all his messages. I've not heard from Taylor and as I don't have his number I can't contact him.

We're all at Sophie's club, having pre-party drinks before going on to Marcus's to celebrate New Year, and I really can't get into it. I'm having trouble concentrating on just about everything. I just keep having these sex-fuelled fantasies about Taylor. Well, let's face it I was cut off in my prime wasn't I? There I was all geared up for it and what happens? I get my old life back. I'm not complaining, at least I don't think I am, but I do miss having a boyfriend. And although being rich again makes life much easier, I can't help missing that simple life I had when I was poor. I can't believe Taylor is back with Lisa.

'You need to put it all behind you,' says Sophie primly. 'After all, you can't mix with those people now can you? It was bad enough when you had to, but now ... Well it would be abslootly ridiculous and you most certainly can't make sandwiches, that's what staff are for.'

'Everything isn't about money you know,' says Camilla.

Sophie shrugs.

'Whatever. You're still upset over Hugo. I think we all need a holiday. I wish the summer would hurry and come and then we can all go to Capri.'

'You've only just got back from Verbier,' I point out.

Sophie glares at me and then beckons to a waitress.

'Who wants a pink gin?'

I brush down my new Dior dress and grab Chelsea's arm.

'I need the loo, come on.'

'Oh okay,' says Chelsea.

'Me too,' says Camilla.

Sophie rolls her eyes and nurses her pink gin.

'She's driving me mad,' I say as we all surge into the ladies.

'Me too,' says Camilla rummaging in her Dolce and Gabbana clutch.

I pull my spanx out of the crack in my arse and sigh with relief. I really should try not to drink too much. Getting out of this bollocking thing is a nightmare. I look at my reflection in the mirror and sigh. I don't understand why these things are happening. Just as I meet a nice, sane, normal man who isn't married, or in debt, or worrying about his bits being chopped off, everything goes wrong again. I know getting my money back isn't wrong, but you know what I mean. It was quite a shock to lose the boat. I fiddle with my bracelet and feel tears prick my eyelids. This is no good is it? I can't cry my way into the New Year can I? I'm thirty-two years old. I'll be thirty-three soon. God, I'm truly on the shelf. I really am one of those sex-starved spinsters who's likely to shag senseless the first man who steps forward. Then again maybe not, seeing as that first man is likely to be Balls. I don't imagine Balls has ever been shagged senseless. Oh, what I wouldn't do to shag Taylor Havers senseless. Actually, what I wouldn't do to stop thinking about shagging someone senseless. In fact, I've never used the word *shag* so much in my life. I'm acting like a raging nymphomaniac these days.

'We should get going,' says Chelsea.

'I need a few more drinks in me,' says Camilla. 'Hugo is bound to be there with multi-orgasmic Hetty.'

'And Roddy is bound to be there with Pug-face Pandora,' I say.

'And ...' begins Chelsea.

We look at her.

'I'm bound to do something stupid if I'm sober,' says Camilla.

'I thought it was the other way around.'

'Do you think Geoff is on Facebook?' asks Chelsea.

'I don't think you should go there,' I say.

'Why not? Facebook is okay isn't it?'

I sigh.

'I mean, I don't think you should think about Geoff. It's doomed.'

'Are you lot coming?' calls Sophie. 'It's going to be an absloot divine evening. We don't want to miss anything.'

'Right, ready girls?' asks Camilla.

'Let's do it,' I say.

'Let's paint the town red,' says Camilla.

'Bring it on,' says Sophie.

'Let's party,' I say.

'Lock up your daughters,' says Chelsea.

Oh dear, it really does get worse.

Chapter Thirty-Seven

The place is heaving when we arrive. A live band is playing *Blame it on the Boogie* and the champagne is flowing. Hugo is indeed here with multi-orgasmic Hetty and her curly extensions and fake nails. What does he see in her? I find myself waiting for her to break into one, an orgasm that is. I'm not quite sure what I will do if she does mind you. Roddy is also here with Pug-face Pandora. He seems in possession of all his ears, well, the two of them anyway. He's walking well too which is a good sign that nothing else has been chopped off. The place is full of couples. That's all you need to see when you're on the shelf isn't it?

'I feel so bloody out of it,' says Camilla, grabbing a tray of drinks from a passing waitress. 'We'll take those thank you.'

'Is that a good idea?' I ask.

'It's a brilliant idea,' she smiles.

God, we've got hours to go yet. I spot Balls out of the corner of my eye and quickly turn around. Not fast enough it seems. He rushes over and grabs me in an embrace.

'Pops, I heard about the whole bang shoot on the boat. Bloody tragic. A bomb was it?'

A bomb. Is he mad?

'Bloody pirates. Roddy told us all about them. Lock them up and throw away the key if you ask me.'

'They're not pirates,' says Chelsea hotly.

'What does Roddy know?' says Camilla, throwing back another glass of champagne. I need to get that tray off her. 'He only knows what horse to bet on and he can't even get that right.'

'Yes, right Camilla ...' I say nudging her.

'Ooh talking of the wanker ...'

I see Roddy heading towards us.

'I thought you would only do something stupid if you were sober,' I snap.

'She's obviously not drunk enough,' says Chelsea.

Pug-face gives me a piercing glare and I swear I get a twinge in my buttocks. She's probably stabbing a Poppy voodoo doll.

'Poppy,' says Roddy, hovering uncomfortably in front of me. He fidgets and then hurriedly kisses me on the cheek. God, is that another monogrammed shirt he's wearing?

'Nice shirt, it suits you,' says Camilla. 'A RAT original is it?' she snorts, collapsing in a fit of giggles.

'Hello Rat ... Roddy,' says Chelsea.

'Evening Tarleton,' says Balls. 'We were talking about the old boat blowing up, shocking business what. Bloody pirates.'

'They're not pirates,' says Chelsea angrily.

'Bloody thieves though,' says Roddy.

'They are not thieves or pirates,' says Chelsea more loudly than she should.

'It's not Pirates of the bollocking Caribbean Chelsea and that guy is not Robin Hood. He's nothing but your common or garden thief. It's my taxes that pay ...'

'Do shut up Roddy,' I snap.

'How dare you,' says Pug-face, pushing herself between Camilla and Chelsea and knocking a glass from Camilla's tray to the floor.

'Shit, now look what you've done you silly bitch,' curses Camilla.

'How dare you,' repeats Pug-face, turning red.

'What on earth is the matter with you these days Poppy?' says Roddy.

'Stop calling them thieves,' cries Chelsea.

I somehow don't think we'll still be here at midnight. Chelsea takes the two glasses that are left on the tray and empties them over Roddy's head. I can't believe it, Chelsea of all people.

'Oh my God, way to go Chelsea,' laughs Camilla.

'You bitch,' snarls Pug-face throwing herself at Chelsea.

Camilla puts the tray down and heads for Orgasmic Hetty. This can't be happening. I don't know who to restrain first. Pug-face is yanking Chelsea's shiny streaked hair and pulling her along the ballroom towards the main door.

'Out, out,' she screams.

'What the bollocks is going on?' demands Marcus.

'I'm so sorry Marcus, things got a bit heated,' I apologise.

'If you want my opinion wherever you go there is trouble Poppy.'

Hang on a minute, I'm not the one dragging Chelsea around the ballroom by her hair or throwing champagne over Roddy. There is a scream as Chelsea lashes out at Pug-face.

'Pug-face Pandora started it,' I say.

'What did you call me?' she squeals.

Oh shit. Meanwhile Camilla is being restrained by two guests while Orgasmic Hetty quakes in a corner. I think she's quaking anyway. She could be having one of her orgasms I suppose.

'What did you call me bitch?' yells Pug-face, shoving me so I fall against Marcus.

Her hair is hanging wildly around her face and the front of her Prada dress is torn. Chelsea limps after her, carrying her Jimmy Choo slingbacks.

'Pug-face,' I say.

'For fuck's sake,' groans Roddy. 'I don't know you Poppy. I really don't. Those boat bastards have got a lot to answer for.'

Orgasmic Hetty makes a run for it and there is a growl from Camilla as she gives chase. The room is silent and all eyes look on as Camilla and Hetty crash onto the stage scattering drums and cymbals.

'Someone do something for Christ's sake,' barks Marcus.

Hugo stands frozen and looks on horrified as Hetty fights off Camilla with a tambourine. I've seen nothing like it. I take Chelsea by the arm and between us, with Balls' help, we drag Camilla back.

'Don't worry, we're leaving,' I say, lifting my head proudly.

'Go back to your silly boat people. That's all you're fit for Poppy Wellesley,' says Pug-face stiffly, pushing her chin out.

God, she's ugly.

'I'm really sorry Poppy but I think it is for the best,' says Marcus.

Camilla adjusts her dress and I try to yank down my spanx. I'm dying for a pee but I really don't want to stay here a minute longer and it is certainly going to take longer than a minute to get this spanx off.

'I never thought you'd prefer thieves and wankers to us,' says Roddy nastily.

'Well I do,' I throw back as I take Chelsea's hand.

'If you're lucky you may get there in time to get thrown inside with the lot of them and then see how you like that,' chimes in Pug-face.

'What?' cries Chelsea.

'They're all history. The police are doing a raid tonight and they'll catch them red handed with their stolen goods. They'll be behind bars by the morning. You're lucky they didn't break into your boat Poppy,' says Roddy with a smirk.

'I leave burglary to you Roddy,' I say as I turn to the door with Chelsea, Camilla and Balls following me.

Chelsea slaps him across the face and it is all I can do not to join her.

'How could you?' she asks.

'My taxes ...' he begins.

'Do shut up Roddy. You've never paid tax in your whole life,' Camilla snaps.

'By Jove this is jolly good fun,' says Balls, catching his coat and stick as they are thrown into the street.

'Now what?' asks Camilla, pinning a pashmina over her torn dress.

If I don't have a pee soon ...

'The canal,' says Chelsea excitedly.

'I'm not sure that's a good idea,' I say, feeling a little tremor of excitement at the thought of seeing Taylor again.

'Why not?'

'What if Roddy is right and there is a raid?'

'We don't want to make the papers,' says Camilla. 'Not so soon after Poppy getting her money back.'

'Surely we should warn them,' says Chelsea.

'By Jove, she's quite right you know,' says Balls waving to his chauffeur.

'Let's go,' says Camilla running towards the Rolls.

I guess my pee will have to wait.

Chapter Thirty-Eight

Taylor weaves through the crowd, careful not to spill the drinks and looks for Lisa. His head is aching and he really could do with being somewhere a little quieter but everywhere they had tried had been packed. He places the tray onto the table and sits opposite her.

'Sorry it took so long.'

She flicks back her hair and smiles.

'The busiest night of the year,' she says, clinking her glass against his.

'Here's to the New Year, Tay.'

He takes a swig of beer and says,

'I'm selling the boat. I've got a buyer.'

Her eyes widen.

'Oh. You never said anything before.'

'I didn't want to bring it up while you were coping with your mum's illness.'

Her eyes well up with tears and she smiles weakly.

'I can't thank you enough Tay for your support the past few days.'

'What are ex-husbands for?' he smiles.

She places her hand on his.

'I'm so glad we're friends again Tay. I really want you to be happy. I'm so sorry it didn't work out with that rich girl ...'

He slides his hand from under hers.

'It's for the best. It's given me that push I needed.'

'What will you do?'

'Devote more time to Zimbabwe. It's long overdue.'

'What about Poppy?'

Just hearing Poppy's name gives him butterflies in his stomach. He pictures her pretty face with her smile that lights up the world, and the innocence that shows in her beautiful eyes. He isn't likely to forget her is he? Everywhere he looks there are reminders of her. He'd given up reading a newspaper because even if she wasn't in it, her father might be and then she would be mentioned and then he'd remember her with Roddy all over again. The last thing he wants is to be around for the wedding. The photos will be plastered all over the dailies no doubt. He'd made the right decision, he was sure of that. He'd been stupid to think he could have a relationship with someone like her and he'd been even more stupid to let himself fall in love with her.

'Don't you think you should tell her how you feel?' says Lisa.

'I imagine she's completely forgotten about me,' he says sharply, 'and I'd really prefer not to talk about her.'

He only wishes he could not think about her but she occupies his mind from the minute he wakes to the moment he falls asleep. Lisa nods. She'd known Taylor long enough to know that his mind was made up. She also knew him well enough to know that her own relationship with him was never going to get past friendship now. He might forgive but Taylor never forgot.

'Let's hope the New Year holds good things for both of us,' she says now lifting her glass in a toast.

He lifts his and nods.

'Here's to new beginnings.'

Chapter Thirty-Nine

My stomach churns as we arrive at the canal. We climb from the Rolls and make our way down the walkway. It is freezing cold and we're dressed in our party clothes. This has got to be the worst idea Chelsea has ever had. My bare shoulders prickle with the cold and my feet are already numb. It really isn't the weather for evening dresses and Jimmy Choos. The canal shimmers under the Christmas lights which wink merrily at us.

'I don't imagine the police will come out on New Year's Eve,' says Chelsea through chattering teeth.

'They don't have the day off Chelsea, just because it's New Year's Eve.'

'Of course they'll come,' says Camilla. 'This is their busiest night.'

'It's the police, Cammy, not the Harrods New Year sale.'

'You know what I mean,' she says, pulling a half bottle of champagne from her tote bag. I swipe the bottle from her. If I'm going to do this then the only way is drunk. I try to ignore the unease in my stomach and my bursting bladder.

'I'm not so sure this is a good idea,' I say, wishing I was back in the warm cocoon of the Rolls.

'Come on Pops, let's have a little fracas,' bellows Balls, yanking the bottle off me and taking a long swig.

'I'm dying for a pee,' I grumble.

Of course it doesn't help that during the ride in the Rolls the spanx had ridden up my arse. One look at the river under the shimmering lights and I'm walking like a constipated duck. One false move and I've had it. I only need to sneeze and I really won't be responsible for the actions of my bladder.

The canal is peaceful but we can hear distant music. As we get nearer I see Geoff's boat is lit up. There seems to be a party on the boat and the music is clearly emanating from there.

'Maybe I should wait here,' I say.

'In this weather?' exclaims Camilla. 'You'll be a block of ice by the time we get back.'

I'm about to answer but am silenced by the wailing of sirens.

'That must be the police,' says Chelsea.

Never mind the police what about my bladder?

'They might not be coming here,' says Camilla.

'By Jove let's have a look,' says Balls excitedly.

He pulls a pair of opera glasses from his jacket pocket.

'They're coming here,' he says calmly.

'Fudge berries,' cries Chelsea. 'What do we do?'

'We need to warn them,' says Camilla. 'Come on let's go.'

I stand rigid and make a useless attempt to move my right leg. No, I can't do it. I can't even walk cross-legged at the moment. It's reached that critical stage. You know the one I mean. The 'I'm stuck where I am' stage.

'I can't move,' I say.

'But they're coming,' squeals Chelsea.

'What's wrong with your legs?' asks Camilla.

'There's nothing wrong with my legs.'

'Come on then.'

'I can't, because there is an awful lot wrong with my bladder.'

'You're kidding.'

I wish I was.

'Stop drinking the champagne then,' orders Chelsea.

Great idea except it's a bit late now isn't it?

'Do a splash in the river old girl,' says Balls.

He surely isn't serious. How the hell am I supposed to do that? It's different for men isn't it? Does he think I can somehow hover over the water and pee? Men say ridiculous things don't they?

The sound of the sirens stop and the blue police lights reflect on the boardwalk. This is really not helping in the least.

'They're here,' announces Balls.

'We have to go,' panics Chelsea.

Why me, why do these things happen to me?

'I'm sure once you start walking it will pass over,' says Chelsea unhelpfully.

I fear that once I start walking it will do more than pass over.

'Take one step at a time,' says Camilla.

'Take a piss in the river, that's the best thing,' adds Balls, swigging from the champagne bottle.

I wish he would stop talking about having a splash and taking a piss, It really isn't helping. I wait a few more seconds and then gingerly take a step forward. As it happens Chelsea is right and the urge has passed over.

'Let's go,' yells Chelsea, running ahead.

We reach Geoff's boat where people are milling around outside. The music is so loud that they never heard the sirens. I feel a pang of sadness as I realise how much I miss this life. I miss my friends.

'Geoff, Geoff,' yells Chelsea as she clambers onto his boat.

Camilla jumps on after her and I follow. I'm so nervous now that I can barely breathe.

'Hello there,' says a guy, offering me a can of beer.

'You must be freezing in that dress,' says another.

'Poppy, is that you?' says a familiar voice and I turn to see Rose.

'Rose, the police are coming. They know about Geoff smuggling stuff.'

'Here they come. Man your boats,' shouts Balls.

'You told the police?' asks Rose, widening her eyes.

'No no, I didn't ...'

'Thanks a bunch,' says Geoff coming to the hatch.

'We didn't,' insists Chelsea, looking at him doe-eyed.

'Well no one here did, that's for sure,' he says angrily.

'Never mind who told them old chap,' pipes up Balls. 'The thing is what are you going to do?'

'Chuck it in the canal,' cries Jim, giving me a filthy look.

I don't believe this. I've come to help them and they're all blaming me for putting them in it. They surely know I wouldn't. Suddenly everything goes crazy and people are running around like headless chickens throwing things into the water. I step into the boat and hurry to the loo. Just seeing the inside of a boat again makes me miss *Amelia*. Who'd have thought it, me craving for the boat life? I climb back onto the deck and look for Taylor, but there is no sign of him.

'Poppy, you're going to freeze to death.'

I turn around to see Ruby with a blanket and then see the police officers charge towards the boats. I take the blanket and look at Taylor's boat but there are no lights on. Surely he isn't working tonight? It is then I see a For Sale sign and my breath catches in my throat. How can it be for sale? Taylor loves it on the canal. He must be serious about Lisa. They're moving in together. I don't believe it. He's a bloody fast worker isn't he?

'Did you tell the police?' Ruby asks.

I'm about to answer when several officers surge onto the boat.

'Stand to one side ladies please. We have a warrant to search these boats.'

'We've done nothing wrong,' protests Ruby, standing in front of the hatch.

'That's not what we've heard. Now move aside.'

'You're going to have to make me,' she says, splaying her arms so she is covering the hatch.

The policeman grins and roughly grabs both her hands.

'Right, you were warned. I'm arresting you for obstructing the police.'

I watch helplessly as they lead her away in handcuffs.

'Hey, just a minute old man, what are you doing?' roars Balls, running to Ruby's aid. 'By Jove, this is a bit much, what? Manhandling women, that's not fair game.'

'What did he say?' says another policeman.

'Sounded like he was taking the piss and insulting us,' says the other.

Oh dear, this doesn't bode well does it?

'Right come on you.'

They handcuff Balls and I sigh. Lord Wyndham-Price arrested. If we don't make the news now, we never will. I step to one side as two officers barge into the boat.

'This is bloody good fun Pops,' calls Balls.

He has a strange idea of fun.

'I'll get you both out,' I shout.

Ruby is dragged away kicking and shouting *fucking pigs.* The officer's rifle through the cupboards and drawers, throwing stuff everywhere. They finally leave and climb onto Jim's boat. I look for Chelsea and Camilla and spot them trying to stop the police getting onto Rose and Jack's barge. I stare horrified as one of the officer's slips on the deck and falls over the side into the canal. This is not good. I so wish we'd stayed at the party.

I watch as a policeman handcuffs Chelsea. God almighty, it's going to cost me a fortune to bail this lot out of prison. Just as well I've got my money back.

'They can't take Rose and Jack. What about the dogs?' she cries as they drag her away.

Camilla looks at me helplessly and I run to her aid.

'They've done nothing,' I protest, standing firm next to Camilla.

'Get out of our way,' an officer yells.

'You'll have to make us,' I say, sounding bolder than I feel.

'Bloody hell,' says Camilla.

'Right that's it,' shouts another police officer, hurling himself towards me. 'You're really in trouble.'

Camilla throws her pashmina at me.

'Tie me up,' she cries.

'Have you gone crazy?'

'Tie me across the hatch. It will stop them getting in, at least for a time.'

'Well, I ...'

'Do it,' she shouts.

I begin tying her up. I was never much good as a Brownie with knots and stuff. Perhaps I should have paid more attention to Miss Tits and Tease and picked up a few tips. I grab a piece of rope from the deck and then step back to observe my handiwork. I hear a scuffle behind me and turn to see more policemen heading towards us, waving batons. God, it's turning nasty. I watch helplessly as Geoff is knocked to the ground. Several other boat people are beaten back by the police and panic begins to overwhelm me. Two jump onto the deck pushing me to one side.

'Move away,' they shout.

Camilla kicks out as the policemen approach her.

'I'm not giving in without a fight,' she cries, kicking out crazily from beneath her Ralph Lauren evening dress A policeman grabs my arm and I feel my dress rip. That's just great isn't it?

Rose pops her head out of the hatch and with a wink says,

'It's okay girlies, we've got nothing to hide.'

Camilla nods to me and I'm about to untie her when a policeman pushes me away roughly before pulling her arm out of the tied pashmina.

'Get off me you bully,' she shouts.

More police rush towards us and I see following behind them are the paparazzi, flashing their cameras as only the paparazzi can. I've never been so happy to see them in my life. At the sight of the photographers, the police back off Camilla and the boat people.

'What's happening then Poppy?' A photographer shouts as I'm arrested.

I've never been arrested before. It's not something you do is it? First Daddy and now me, we're becoming the crime family of the year. They'll be writing a book about us next. This does not bode well for my marriage prospects does it? Thirty-two and not a wedding in sight, in fact not even a man in sight. I smile at Balls who is looking at me admiringly.

'I like a woman with spunk,' he says, licking his lips. 'I find it incredibly sexy.'

Okay so there is one man in sight. Someone please kill me. I really couldn't face becoming Lady Balls Wyndham and having lots of little Balls. Before I can give it much more thought, I'm thrown roughly into the back of a police van.

Chapter Forty

'Where's my daughter? I hope you have her in a decent cell.'

The door to the outside world slams behind my mother.

'Do you have any idea who I am?'

I can smell Mummy's White Gardenia perfume from the other side of the clink.

'Is that your mother, Truffles? Please say it is,' says Chelsea.

Unfortunately it is.

'Mother, there is no such thing as a first-class cell,' I shout.

'Well there certainly should be. I'm Lady Wellesley. You do realise that you are holding the daughter of Sir Rupert Wellesley, Minister for family, don't you?'

That's not a great recommendation is it? They'll probably keep me here longer now. She storms through the door and strolls past the cells, trailing White Gardenia in her wake.

'Where are you? Have they treated you well? I brought Liam, Daddy's solicitor. Has there been ill treatment?'

'I'm over here,' I call, 'and it's not Guantanamo Bay Mummy'.

Chelsea's lips quiver.

'We're so glad to see you,' she says, welling up.

We've only been here an hour and Chelsea is already cracking.

'This is what they do,' she says. 'Show you a window to the outside world and then close it again so you'll be begging to tell them what they need to know.'

'Chelsea, we have nothing to tell them,' I say.

'They'll force it out of us.'

'It's the police, not the bloody Taliban,' snaps Camilla.

'My God, look at the state of you. How did that happen? Look at your dress and the state of your hair,' says Mummy, covering her mouth with her hand.

'Tell me the truth, did they?'

'Did they what?' I ask.

'You know?'

'No I don't.'

'Not yet but they will,' whimpers Chelsea.

I wish I knew what they were talking about. If Chelsea carries on like this I shall have no choice but to slap her round the face myself.

'Tally-ho there old girl,' waves Balls from the opposite cell.

'Less of the old from you Balls and what on earth are you doing here. Do you want to see your reputation in tatters? If you hang around my daughter long enough, trust me, that is what will happen.'

'She's a feisty little filly, worth hanging around for,' he grins.

Oh dear.

'Mummy, can you arrange bail for everyone?' I ask.

'Everyone?' she says, looking at Ruby and Geoff. 'Are you sure we should get involved?'

'We are involved. I'm sitting in a cell or hadn't you noticed.'

She sighs.

'Of course I've noticed. How could I not. Look at the state of you. I've brought you clean clothes and some make-up. You can't leave looking like that. The paparazzi are outside. You have a strange way of celebrating New Year, that's all I can say.'

'We don't want your sodding money do we Rube,' says Geoff nastily. 'We'll pay our own way, thank you very much.'

'You see. They don't want our sod ... money.'

'I don't know why you bothered to help them Poppy, they're an ungrateful bunch,' says Camilla.

'We wouldn't be here in the first place if it wasn't for you lot,' snarls Geoff.

I wish they wouldn't keep calling us *you lot.*

'I'm not so sure it was Poppy's fault,' says Ruby.

'She told her poncey boyfriend though didn't she?'

'No, it was ...' begins Chelsea.

I shake my head. It's bad enough Taylor wants nothing to do with me. The least I can do is minimise the damage for Chelsea.

'Open the doors please and release my daughter and her associates. I will see to the bail,' says Mummy clicking her fingers at a policeman. If she's not careful she'll be thrown in with us. 'Come along, hurry up.'

She sure pushes her luck.

'Do you have a brief?' asks the policeman.

'What on earth have her briefs got to do with it, young man? I would advise you not to discuss my daughter's underwear. But if you must know I have brought clean ones.'

I close my eyes in despair.

'He means, do you have a solicitor,' I say.

'Why didn't he say that then? I have a first-class one with me as it happens and Camilla do something with your breasts, it's disgraceful the way they are almost hanging out of that dress. I never thought I'd see this day Poppy. I really didn't.'

The door slams again and Taylor stands looking around. He looks so gorgeous I could have him right here, right now, in the cell. Ooh that would be kinky wouldn't it? I finger the bracelet he gave me. He glances my way and then walks towards Geoff. I fiddle with my hair and pull at the spanx which has now somehow rolled itself into a nice little lump at my midriff. This is just great isn't it? When I finally get to see him again not only am I behind bars but I look like something the cat's thrown up. I open my mouth to speak and then I see Lisa.

'Tay mate, thanks for coming,' says Geoff, giving me a piercing look.

Why won't he believe I had nothing to do with this?

'Right, you lot can go,' says the policeman. 'Your brief has sorted everything. Try to keep out of trouble.'

He unlocks our cell doors and Chelsea falls into my mother's arms.

'Frogs' knickers,' she cries. 'I thought we were going to be locked up for ever.'

I walk to the door tugging at the spanx as I do so. I'm never wearing a spanx again. I look like I'm wearing a spare tyre. I go to pass Taylor when he turns and faces me.

'Hello Poppy,' he says softly. I melt on the spot.

'Hello,' I say.

I grab Mummy's shawl and attempt to cover the spare tyre. At that moment Balls flings an arm around me.

'Come on Pops, let's get a hot toddy inside you.'

I try to shrug his arm off.

'Happy New Year,' Taylor says.

'And you,' I say miserably.

'How's Roddy?' he asks a hint of coldness in his voice. 'Blown up any more boats?

'He's very well thank you,' interrupts Mummy. 'Now if you'll excuse me I'd like to get my daughter out of here. Her days of slumming are well and truly over.'

'Not that I know of,' I say. 'I've not seen much of him. I saw your boat is up for sale.'

'That's right,' he says brusquely.

'Come on Pops,' says Balls. 'There's still time to party.'

'Don't let me hold you up,' says Taylor.

I'd do anything for him to hold me up. If only Lisa weren't with him. I could tell Mummy and Balls to sling their hook and tell Taylor how I feel about him, but I'm swept out of the building by Mummy and Balls, and don't even manage a backward glance.

Chapter Forty-One

'I'm really not sure,' I say hesitantly.

That's an understatement. I'm actually very sure I'm not doing it.

'You've got to do something,' insists Camilla.

'Why don't you do it?' I ask. 'If you're that keen.'

'There's no urgency is there? I'm not over thirty like you, and I don't have a scandalous history, like you, and besides, I am seeing Charlie. You're not seeing anyone.'

And a right Charlie he is too, but I don't say anything. Scandalous history ... that's a bit harsh isn't it? You'd think I was an axe-wielding psychopathic serial killer.

'Of course, there is always Balls,' says Chelsea. 'He likes you ...'

My expression stops her in her tracks.

'It's not like you can have Taylor is it?' chips in Camilla, popping a Harrods champagne truffle. 'At least Balls is available and you won't do better than him for financial security.'

'And you'll be a Lady,' adds Chelsea.

'You two are worse than my mother, and being a Lady isn't enticing me to marry Balls. You've got to do better than that.'

But they're quite right of course. I need to do something or I'll be thirty-three before I know where I am. I reach for a truffle but Camilla moves them out of my way.

'You've had four. You've got to watch your weight if you're husband hunting.'

Bugger this. If I can't have truffles I might as well commit hara-kiri. Besides, I don't want to be husband hunting; it's everyone else who thinks I should be.

'What do they do there exactly?' I ask.

'You just sit there for a couple of hours while men chat to you. After two minutes the buzzer goes and the next one comes,' says Camilla, seemingly the fount of all knowledge where speed dating is concerned.

'Sounds nice doesn't it Poppy?' says Chelsea.

I glare at her.

'You really think speed dating sounds nice do you Chelsea?'

'Well ...' she mumbles.

'Sounds like a cattle market,' I say, grabbing a truffle while Camilla isn't looking.

Maybe Balls isn't such a bad choice. Let's face it I don't have any other choice do I? And he has been wooing me the past week, or should I say wooing Mummy. It seems our credibility as socialites is in serious danger after my behaviour on New Year's Eve. Mummy has tried to convince me that marrying Balls is my only option.

'Who else is going to have you?' she'd asked. 'Half of society has turned its back on us.'

She's quite right of course. I'm a 32-year-old spinster tainted with scandal. It couldn't get any worse. But marrying Balls and having lots of little Balls just makes me shudder. So with that thought in mind I totter off to The Bell Hotel for a speed dating evening. This is not my idea of fun. To make matters worse I'm early. I'm offered a Sea Breeze on the house. Oh well, I suppose it's better than nothing. As the men start trundling in I order another. This is most certainly something you can only do half pissed. Twenty minutes later and we're directed into the dating area, and I'm given another Sea Breeze. It seems you can't have enough of these. I'm directed to a table and by now my stomach is churning with too much vodka. I think about snacking on a packet of crisps but decide it's not quite the thing when dating is it? I'm starting to think I can't go through with this when my first date plonks himself opposite me.

'Hey, I'm Rupert but you can call me Rupes.'

Oh God, really?

'I'm Poppy,' I say.

'What shall I call you?' he asks.

How about Poppy? After all, it is my name.

'I know, I'll call you Popsie.'

Not unless you want a knee in your groin you won't. I take a gulp of Sea Breeze.

'So, what do you do Popsie? I'm in advertising.'

'Well I ...'

'I'm planning on branching out,' he continues.

'That's ...'

'Everyone says I should. "You're too good for this place," they say ...' he laughs loudly leaning his chair back.

I drain the last of my Sea Breeze. God, this is more dire than I imagined it would be.

'I'll get you another,' he says, jumping up.

Good, maybe he'll just make it back in time before the buzzer. It's like a TV game show. He rushes back with the Sea Breeze.

'What did you say your job was?' he asks.

'I'm a pole dancer,' I reply, taking a swig from the bottle.

'Wow, way to go.'

Talking of going, where's that bollocking buzzer?

'Tell you what Popsie ...'

The buzzer goes. Thank God.

Rupes is followed by Lucca, who I can't understand at all. I'm not sure if it's him or because I'm now pissed. It doesn't help that Lucca buys me another Sea Breeze. By the time Finley takes the chair I'm well gone. Just as well because all Finley can talk about it is Downton Abbey and how he worked on the set.

'I really want to work on films,' he says. 'Do you like films?'

'Oh yes.'

'Do you have a favourite?'

'Psycho, I can relate to it,' I grin.

I don't think I've yawned so much in my entire life. My bum is sore from the chair, which is more uncomfortable than a church pew. I try to take the weight off my backside by pushing down with my arms and lifting my arse up. I look like I'm levitating when Doug appears. I have to say of all of them Doug is the nicest but I'm now slurring my words and I see Doug is far from impressed. Oh well, I really can't see myself going out with a Doug, but then again I suppose anything is better than a Balls. What has become of me? Only a few months ago I was the socialite of the year with a fabulous wedding looming. The truth is, all I want is Taylor. Finally Mike plonks himself down and I sigh.

'All right babe?'

My final contestant has a shaved head and a ring through his eyebrow, not that I have anything against that, you understand, but with this particular guy it just doesn't work somehow. He winks.

'Three minutes ain't long is it? So cut to the chase I'm looking for fun, know what I mean? I don't want any ties. If it's serious you want then I ain't the guy.'

'I'm looking for marriage,' I say.

He rocks on the chair and then stands up.

'Right, see yer around,' he says before walking off.

The final buzzer goes and I sigh with relief. I'm beginning to think Balls is not a bad choice after all.

'A drink before you leave,' says Rupes as he dives in front of me.

'I'd love to,' I lie. 'But I've got a pole session this evening.'

With that, I make a quick exit and wave down a black cab, if you can call throwing myself in front of it waving it down.

Chapter Forty-Two

I look at Camilla and raise my eyebrows.

'Is she serious?' I ask.

'Yup.'

'I don't get it,' says Chelsea.

'You can't say Roddy's name,' I explain. 'It's a game.'

'It sounds stupid,' she mumbles taking a plastic wedding ring.

That's the smartest thing Chelsea has said in a long time.

'You mustn't say my future husband's name,' says Pandora smugly. 'Whoever catches you out gets your ring and the person with the most rings at the end of the shower wins.'

'Ooh yey, sounds great,' mocks Camilla.

'I don't get it,' whispers Chelsea.

'Ooh these are fabulous,' Pandora gushes as she opens my gift and tosses the wrapping paper to one side. 'You really shouldn't have.'

She's quite right, I really shouldn't have.

'It was my second choice,' I say.

'Oh really, what was the first choice?'

A hit man.

'It wouldn't be fair to say, would it?'

Camilla fights back a snigger. It's Pandora's bridal shower and we're all gathered around her like flies around a cowpat. Pandora is in her element when she's the centre of attention. She pushes my Harrods cruet set to one side and rips open another gift. Camilla reaches for a bottle of wine and I shove my glass at her.

'A set of knives, oh Chelsea, how thoughtful.'

All the better to stab you with.

'Ro ...' she begins and we all look at her. 'Whoops nearly,' she laughs.

The girls chorus *well done*. Bloody hell, it's not that hard not to say Roddy is it?

'I'm glad you like it, I didn't know what to get,' says Chelsea.

'Why are we at a bridal shower?' whispers Camilla. 'I thought that's what they had in the States not in England.'

'It's all the rage,' snaps Pandora who's got ears like an elephant.

'Yes, it is,' says a red-headed woman.

'You must be so excited,' says Sophie.

'It's not every day you get married,' says Chelsea.

The room goes silent and all eyes are on me. Here's one who won't be getting married, they're thinking.

'Are you okay Truffles?' asks Pandora in a sloppy voice.

'Of course,' I say airily. I never ever said she could call me Truffles.

'It's just we all know that you're still crazy about that boat chap.'

'Have you seen him since?' asks Sophie.

'He's back with his ex-wife,' says Pandora, ripping open yet another present.

'Anyway, you're marrying Balls aren't you?' says Pandora before gushing over a set of towels.

I could wrap her body in those couldn't I, after I've stabbed her with the knives?

'No, I'm not.'

'Everyone thinks you are,' she says. 'Even Ro ...'

Whoops nearly.

'Everyone is wrong then aren't they?'

'Anyone for a top-up?' asks Camilla. 'That's the only way to get someone to say Ro ... whoops.'

I hold out my glass.

'Anyone but you,' she hisses. 'I don't trust you when you're pissed. I've seen you looking at those knives.'

Camilla is such a spoilsport.

'Aren't you going out with anyone?' asks Sophie.

'No she isn't,' says Chelsea.

'Nor are you?' I say defensively.

'She isn't thirty-two though is she?' says Pandora.

What's so bad about thirty-two? It's not like I'll self-destruct when I hit thirty-three is it?

'Balls is a good catch,' someone adds.

'Ooh yes,' says the redhead.

Perhaps *she'd* like him then.

'You can have him honey,' I say. 'Because I really don't want to marry Balls,' I reach for the wine bottle.

'*OK!* magazine said you'd hit rock bottom,' says Pandora's sister and bites her lip.

There is silence.

'I'm in *OK!* magazine?' I say hoarsely. 'Why didn't you tell me?'

Chelsea looks sheepish.

'We didn't want to upset you.'

'It's not the best piece about you,' says Camilla.

'Here it is,' says Pandora, who obviously couldn't care if I'm upset.

I tear back the pages until I find the article. *The socialite who has everything can't find a man to take her on.* Oh that's just great isn't it, what if Taylor reads it?

'It isn't true anyway,' says Chelsea. 'Balls will take you on won't he and Ro ...'

This is such a stupid game.

'You nearly said it,' giggles Pandora. Has Roddy gone totally insane marrying her?

'I'd rather be dead than on the shelf,' says Pandora.

'Careful what you wish for,' Camilla mumbles as she moves the knives.

What I wouldn't do to go back to the boat. I could kill Roddy for blowing the thing up. Whoops, good job no one can read my mind. And thanks to him the boat people hate me. I'll never see Taylor again. He'll go on to re-marry Lisa and probably be miserable. I sip my wine and close my eyes. I can see Taylor so clearly, it is as if he is sitting in front of me. At that moment Sophie changes the music and *All of Me* blares from the speakers. I don't believe it. It has to be a sign doesn't it?

'That's our song,' I say.

'What?' says Camilla.

'Taylor and me, this is our song.'

'That's lovely, isn't that lovely Camilla?' says Chelsea as my phone starts to ring. I grab it, I am sure it's him.

'Hello,' I say breathlessly.

'It's me, your mother.'

I sigh.

'Yes I know. I haven't forgotten your voice.'

'Lord Balthazar Wyndham-Price has just asked your father for your hand in marriage. You should accept.'

'What? How can he ask Daddy when he hasn't asked me?' That's a bit arse about face isn't it?'

'You never used language like this until you got involved with those boat people.'

I squeeze past everyone and head for the hallway.

'I'm not saying yes,' I say.

'Your father has agreed wholeheartedly. Don't be a fool and turn him down. You're not getting any younger you know.'

I scratch my neck nervously. Chelsea pops her head around the door.

'Poppy do you want ...?' she breaks off and claps a hand over her mouth.

'Fudge berries Poppy. You're only breaking out again.'

I dash to the hall mirror and stare at my neck. God, it's worse than ever. I need Taylor, this is clearly obvious.

'Do you think you need a doctor?' asks Chelsea anxiously.

A thought occurs to me and I nod eagerly.

'Yes, I do.'

'You do what?' asks Camilla.

'I need a doctor,' I say. 'I should go to A&E.'

Chelsea looks confused.

'I can take you to Harley Street. You don't want to go to A&E, you'll be forever in there,' she offers.

'Sounds good to me,' I say. 'The longer I'm with an A&E doctor the better.'

'I get it,' says Camilla, grabbing our coats.

Chelsea shakes her head.

'I don't.'

'Here,' says Camilla, shoving Chelsea's faux fur at her. 'Trust us.'

'Oh frogs' knickers, I hate hospitals,' she groans.

'They're not that bad,' I say, waving to Pandora.

'And they have dishy doctors,' adds Camilla.

'Oh,' says Chelsea. 'I get it now.'

After all, Taylor is the only doctor who is able to heal my rash simply by being there.

'Thanks for a fab evening,' says Camilla.

'You're not going are you? We haven't done the recipe for love game yet,' says Pandora.

'Have to miss it I'm afraid. What a bugger.'
Chelsea and I nod in agreement and waltz out into the cold.
'Right,' says Camilla. 'A&E here we come.'

Chapter Forty-Three

'This is a bit grim,' moans Camilla. 'That guy over there has his arm hanging off. I don't think you're going to be priority.'

We wander to reception and I show the receptionist my rash.

'There is a five hour wait. Would you prefer to see your own GP?'

'Five hours?' gasps Camilla.

'Even then I can't guarantee you'll be seen. It may be longer.'

'Christ, these poor buggers will be dead before then.'

I shake my head and we mosey to the waiting area.

'God, it's like *World War Z* in here,' says Chelsea, grimacing.

Someone throws up next to Chelsea's Chanel handbag.

'There must be an easier way of seeing Taylor,' says Camilla, moving two rows back. 'God knows what we'll leave with but I feel sure it will be more than we came in with.'

I watch as doctors in white coats come out of cubicles but not one of them is Taylor. Don't tell me of all the nights this is his night off. That's typical isn't it? The man with the arm groans.

'That will get gangrene in it,' says Camilla, all knowledgeable. 'They ought to see to him.'

'Are you a nurse?' asks the man. 'How serious is it?'

'Well, I ...' begins Camilla.

'I've been here six hours,' says another man. 'I think I've got a bladder infection.'

Camilla shrugs nervously.

'I don't want gangrene,' says the other. 'Nurse, where's the doctor? I don't want bloody gangrene.'

'Now look what you've done,' I say, nudging Camilla.

'You *probably* won't get gangrene,' says Camilla, trying to calm him down.

'You're trying not to alarm me now aren't you?'

Trust Camilla. We'll have a riot on our hands next and all because I want to see Taylor. I'm not sure what I'll say to him when I do see him of course.

'Can't you fake a fainting spell?' whispers Chelsea.

'Yes, A-S-A-P please,' agrees Camilla.

'I can't jump the queue,' I say. 'It wouldn't be fair.'

'You think it's fair putting us through this? We're the only ones here in designer clothes.'

The consulting room door swings open and a doctor strides out. Chelsea rushes towards him. What is she doing?

'Is Doctor Taylor Havers on this evening?' she asks. 'Only it is urgent that we speak with him.'

A silence descends over the waiting room and all of the patients look at us. Oh dear, I think they will all turn on us like an angry mob and throw us out of the waiting room.

'Dr Havers isn't here this evening I'm afraid.'

Bugger.

'When will he be here again?' I ask.

'He won't be. Now, if you'll excuse me. Richard May,' he calls.

'About time,' says the man with the dangling arm. 'She said I've got gangrene.'

'Are you medical staff?' he asks, turning to Chelsea.

Does knowing an anaesthetist, a registrar and a pharmacist count?

'Sort of,' I say. 'We know Dr Havers.'

'Dr Havers has left so I'm afraid we can't help you.'

Left? What does he mean *left*? Why would he leave? Even if he was re-marrying Lisa he wouldn't leave his job would he?

'Why would he leave?' I say.

'I don't know,' says Camilla, 'but can we leave too please before we catch bird flu or something.'

I let them lead me from the antiseptic-smelling waiting room, past the smoking area outside, and towards Camilla's Range Rover. All I can think about is Taylor. His boat is for sale and he's left his job. Are he and Lisa moving away? This is terrible. I need to tell him I love him ... I stop in my tracks. The realisation of how I feel hits me like a sledgehammer. I never realised it until now but I love him, I love him more than I ever loved Roddy and I certainly love him more than I could ever love Balls. Whatever happens I need to tell him, even if he does love Lisa, and even if I spend my life alone, I need him to know that I love him.

'There's that guy,' says Chelsea pointing to the man with the dangling arm. 'They've sent him home already. They're quicker than at Harley Street aren't they?'

'I have to tell him I love him,' I say passionately.

Camilla and Chelsea look at me.

'Is that wise?' Camilla says.

'Of course, no matter what happens I need to tell him.'

'But you don't know him,' says Chelsea.

'I know I've not known him long but it feels like all my life,' I say, opening the door of the Range Rover.

'But you barely spoke to him,' says Camilla, nodding towards the dangling arm man.

I sigh.

'Not him, I'm talking about Taylor.'

Camilla exhales.

'Thank God. For a minute I thought you'd totally lost it.'

'But we don't know where he is,' says Chelsea.

'We have to find him,' I say.

'How do you suggest we do that?'

'I don't know. A private detective maybe?'

'A private detective?' repeats Chelsea.

'Well, what would you suggest?' I ask.

'But a private detective?' says Chelsea. 'I mean, fudge berries.'

'I've got to do something before Balls proposes haven't I?'

'There's one in Soho,' says Camilla, her face lighting up.

'Soho?' repeats Chelsea.

'Will you stop repeating everything we say,' I snap.

My phone vibrates in my bag. It is Balls. I haven't got long to find Taylor. Balls will propose and I'll have no choice but to say yes. After all, who else will marry me? Mummy is quite right. I'm in no position to be choosy.

'Let's go,' I say, turning my phone off.

'What now?' says Chelsea. 'But it's nearly nine o clock.'

'He'll be there,' says Camilla.

Chelsea and I look at her suspiciously.

'Okay,' she says, 'I hired him once.'

I widen my eyes.

'Hugo was acting a bit strange so I had him followed.'

'Fudge berries,' Chelsea gasps.

'He's still acting strange,' I laugh.

'I'm not sure about Soho,' says Chelsea, nervously fiddling with her Chanel handbag.

'It'll do you good,' says Camilla, pushing her into the car.

A tremor of excitement runs through me. I'm going to find Taylor. The question is what will I say to him when I do?

Chapter Forty-Four

We stand outside the seedy building and try to ignore the woman in the leather jumpsuit standing in the doorway.

'Are you sure this is it?' I ask, averting my eyes from the woman's white thighs.

'I think so,' says Camilla uncertainly. 'Although, *she* wasn't there the last time I came, or at least I never noticed her.'

'She's a bit difficult to miss,' whispers Chelsea.

'Hey darlings, you coming in?' the woman says in a well-practised husky voice. She winks at Chelsea.

'Fudge berries,' squeals Chelsea, clutching at her faux fur.

'She must be freezing her tits off,' says Camilla.

'Don't say it so loudly,' hisses Chelsea. 'Otherwise she'll think we're interested.'

'What do you want to do?' asks Camilla. 'We can't stand here all night.'

'I'll do whatever you want me to do,' says the woman in an over-the-top sexy voice.

'I wasn't talking to you,' says Camilla.

I shiver. This is ridiculous. What am I doing? I'm Poppy Wellesley, once poor but back again, daughter of Sir Rupert Wellesley, multimillionaire and MP for Belgravia, admittedly with a bit of scandal behind him but if I continue like this I'm going to have an even bigger scandal behind me. I'm rich, in fact I'm very rich. I live in a penthouse in Belgravia. We have a country estate in Oxfordshire. We're the privileged. I'm soon to be engaged to one of the richest men in the country, yet again. Now I'm standing outside a sleazy building in the red light district of Soho. The smell of Chinese food wafts over us and Chelsea sniffs appreciatively. I take a deep breath and walk towards the entrance.

'Oh frogs' knickers,' utters Chelsea. 'We're going in.'

She makes us sound like the 2nd battalion 8th marines. Anyone would think we were storming the building.

'Private investigator Henley,' I say primly to the scantily clad woman and then realise I sound like I'm introducing myself.

She straightens up immediately.

'I ain't doing nothing wrong,' she says defensively.

'Where can we find him?' I ask, trying to stop my teeth chattering. How she can stand there half-undressed and not turn blue is beyond me.

'I think it's the next floor,' says Camilla switching on the light.

We climb the dingy staircase and all I can hear is Chelsea repeating frogs' knickers like it's a mantra. It's colder in here than it is outside.

'I don't think we should be doing this,' she mumbles.

'We're only walking up the stairs,' I argue.

'All the same I don't think we should be doing it. I've got a bad feeling about this.'

The stairs creak as we climb them. We're halfway up the second flight when the light clicks off. I scream and Chelsea cries her usual *fudge berries* and Camilla squeals *Holy shitballs what's happening*? I swear we all expect some ghostly figure to jump out of the darkness. I fumble for a light switch and knock into Chelsea

'Oh my God, who's that?' she squeals.

'It's me,' I say.

'Who's me?'

'What do you mean, who's me. It's me, me.'

I rummage through my bag for my phone and turn on the torch.

'There's the switch,' says Camilla.

'I don't like this,' mumbles Chelsea. 'I hope he can tell you where Taylor is. I don't want to come here ever again.'

'He's a private eye,' I say, 'not a psychic. He isn't going to be able to tell me tonight is he?'

Camilla points to a plaque on a door while Chelsea keeps hitting the timer switch.

'This is it,' says Camilla, knocking on the door.

'Yeah,' calls a voice.

'Not very welcoming,' I whisper.

Camilla opens the door and we all peek inside.

'Hi, we've come to see private investigator Henley,' she says politely.

'That's me, come in, take a pew.'

A half-eaten, curled up sandwich sits on his desk. I wrinkle my nose at the sight of it. It's definitely not up to the standard of a Blundell sandwich. A small two-bar electric heater glows in the corner but the room is still cold.

'What can I do you for?' he asks.

'I need to find someone,' I say, leaning forward and squashing a doughnut with my elbow. Jam oozes onto his desk.

'God, I'm sorry. I didn't see it.'

He pulls a tissue from his trouser pocket and wipes his desk before removing the offending doughnut.

'Missing persons is it?' he asks casually, as if all his clients elbow the said doughnut at their first visit.

'Not exactly,' says Chelsea, 'although he has gone missing in a way.'

I give her a sidelong glance.

'He's not missing as in mysterious circumstances,' says Camilla.

'A moonlight flit was it then?'

'Not exactly,' I say.

'How has this person gone missing then?'

'I don't know if he is actually missing ...' I begin.

'It's just that she can't find him,' says Chelsea.

He sighs, and fiddles with the ham sandwich as if deciding whether to finish it or not. I'm praying he decides the latter as I don't think I could stomach watching him eat it. He turns and throws it into the wastepaper basket where it joins the doughnut.

'Does he want to be found is the question,' he says, opening a drawer and pulling out a toothpick. For a moment I thought he was going for his gun. This just gets worse.

'He doesn't know I'm looking for him,' I say.

'She's not that scary,' adds Camilla. 'I don't think he'd sell his home and leave his job to avoid her.'

Oh God, I never thought of that.

'He wouldn't would he?' says Chelsea.

'Have you got a photo of him?' he asks.

I shake my head.

'What's his name?'

I'm beginning to wish I hadn't started this. Maybe I should marry Balls; after all it would be a whole lot easier wouldn't it?

'Taylor Havers,' I say.

'Doctor,' says Chelsea.

'Last seen on Regent's Canal …' adds Camilla.

'No, he was last seen at the police station near Regent's Canal,' corrects Chelsea.

'Does it matter where he was last seen?' I ask. 'He has a boat on Regent's Canal that is up for sale; can't you find him from that?'

He widens his eyes.

'He's selling a boat?'

'Is that a lead?' I ask hopefully.

'Not really. It's just my mate is looking for a boat.'

Never mind his mate, what about Taylor?

'We're not here to discuss your mate are we?' says Camilla firmly.

He pulls a pad from his jacket pocket.

'Does he want to be found is the first question we have to ask ourselves?'

'Why wouldn't he?' I ask.

'Maybe he owes money. Perhaps people are after him, that kind of thing.'

'He's a doctor,' scoffs Camilla.

'Often the worst.'

I fidget in my chair.

'Look, I need to find him soon. Balls is going to propose to me and I will have to say yes. I have too much pressure on me you see. I need to find Taylor so that …'

'Balls?' he interrupts.

'Can you focus on Taylor Havers,' says Camilla. I can imagine her thumping the table like the bad cop in a cheesy movie.

'Where do you think he might be?' asks Chelsea.

I look at her and sigh. I despair of her, I really do.

'I'll need more information. Where is he working and …'

'I don't know,' I say.

'Girlfriends?'

'Lisa,' says Chelsea.

His face lights up.

'Great, a lead. Lisa who?'

'Havers,' I say.

'His wife?'

'Ex-wife,' I answer.

He sighs.

'So we have an address which is a boat that's for sale and one he doesn't live on any more presumably. A job that he has now left and an ex-wife called Lisa. Have I got that right?'

We all nod.

'And you expect me to find him?' he says picking at his teeth with the tooth pick.

'Sounds like plenty to go on,' says Camilla, standing up.

'It'll cost yer,' he says, writing down figures.

'I'll pay whatever.'

'Love has no price huh?' he smiles.

'He has a friend named Geoff, he's an anaesthetist,' says Chelsea dreamily.

'Oh and a friend in Chelsea Walk,' I say, remembering.

'You never told me that,' says Camilla.

'And a hospital in Africa,' I add.

'I'm not going to Africa,' he says quickly. 'I'd need danger money for that.'

'Why don't you start in good old England? Regent's Canal for a start,' says an irritated Camilla, grabbing my arm. 'Let's go. We've given him all the intel we have.'

Camilla sounds like she's briefing Jack Bauer at CTU headquarters. Investigator Henley pushes a dog-eared business card across the table.

'Take me card and give me a bell if you think of anything else. Who should I contact when I have some news?'

'Poppy Wellesley,' I say, writing my number on his notepad. I take his card reluctantly and slip it into my Hermes.

'Have you reported it to the police?' he asks as we walk to the door.

'Reported what?'

'That he's missing.'

'But he's not ...' Why do I bother? 'No I haven't.'

'You should.'

'We'll get right on it,' says Camilla, pulling me out of the room and mumbling wanker under her breath.

'You recommended him,' I say.

'He was better than this when I used him.'

Let's just hope he finds Taylor before Balls gets a chance to propose. I can only stall him for so long.

Chapter Forty-Five

'I don't know what she sees in him,' says Geoff, passing the magazine to Ruby.

'Probably his money,' says Ruby, studying the photo of Balls and Poppy. 'After all, that's what she's used to ain't it?'

Taylor downs the remains of his pint.

'Another?' asks Geoff.

'Rose and Jack will be here soon,' says Ruby, passing the magazine back to Taylor.

'Okay, one more,' says Taylor, studying the photo again. He thought Roddy was bad enough but what she sees in this guy is beyond him. It's a whole other world, this aristocratic one of hers.

'She was really down to earth at the end though weren't she?' says Ruby.

'It was most likely a front. I found her with that idiot Roddy don't forget.'

'I still don't get it,' says Ruby frowning. 'She seemed right off him if I remember.'

'Well, I saw them,' he says with finality in his voice.

Taylor looks past her to a man sitting at the bar. The guy is holding the evening paper but seems to spend more time looking at them than the paper. He tries to place him but there doesn't seem to be anything familiar about him at all.

'I wish you would change your mind,' Ruby says.

'What? Sorry Rube, I wasn't listening.'

'I wish you wouldn't sell the boat, we're all going to miss you like crazy.'

They wave as Rose and Jack enter the pub and Taylor meets the eyes of the man at the bar. He lifts his paper so the contact is broken.

'It's for the best Rube.'

Rose plonks herself next to Ruby and pulls the magazine from Taylor.

'The rumours are she is going to marry this one,' says Rose.

'She'll be bloody mad if she does. I remember him, barmy bloke if you ask me,' says Jack.

'Money turns their heads I suppose,' says Rose. 'But Poppy was alright, weren't she Jack? She got Jim's cat that time didn't she?'

'She told the old bill about our little arrangement though didn't she?' says Geoff angrily. 'That weren't the actions of a friend, at least not in my book they weren't. Got me in trouble at work that did.'

Private investigator Henley pricks up his ears.

'She may have been under pressure from that Roderick bloke.'

'Roddy,' corrects Taylor.

'I think it was him that told the police,' says Rose.

'It's behind us now anyway,' says Taylor, scrunching up the magazine.

He hates these reminders of Poppy. It won't end here either. It will soon be everywhere he looks.

'How is the fundraising going?' asks Rose, sensing that Taylor wants to change the subject.

'We're a fair bit short but I'm hoping to raise something at the talk.'

'I can't believe it,' says Geoff. 'Things won't be the same without you.'

'Who's that bloke?' says Jack, nodding at Henley. 'He keeps looking at us.'

'No idea, but it's not the first time I've seen him.'

'Perhaps you've got an admirer Ruby,' laughs Geoff.

'Yeah right, he's not my type,' she smiles.

'More like Taylor,' says Jack. 'That's who he's been looking at.'

'Not my type either,' laughs Taylor.

He glances at Henley and wonders if he should approach him.

'Do you think you'll see Poppy before you leave?'

'I've got no plans too,' Taylor says firmly. 'I think it's best that way.'

'I agree,' says Geoff.

'Well I don't,' says Ruby. 'You should give her a chance to explain.'

'I know what I saw.'

'If he doesn't want to see her then he doesn't want to see her,' says Rose. 'Let's face it, she hasn't come to the canal since New Year has she?'

'She probably knows the boat has been sold.'

'Can we drop the subject? I don't want to see her and that's that,' says Taylor draining his glass.

Private investigator Henley stands up and dons his jacket. He's heard enough. No point harassing the poor bloke. Bloody women. They can be pushy bitches at times. He finishes his drink and leaves the pub. He texts Poppy Wellesley as soon as he is in his car.

I've some news. Can you come by the office at your earliest convenience?

Taylor watches the guy leave and tries to remember if he has met him before.

'I disagree with you Rose for once. I think you should see her before you go Taylor. There is nothing worse than regrets,' says Jack.

Taylor looks into his beer before saying,

'It won't change anything.'

'It's better than leaving things open-ended,' insists Jack.

'I agree,' says Ruby.

'I don't know where she lives,' he says, 'so I can't.'

'She's always at that restaurant isn't she?' says Ruby excitedly. 'I'll find out when she's going to be there and let you know.'

'How do you plan to do that?' asks Geoff. 'You'll be arrested for stalking.'

Taylor looks at her warily.

'I don't know Ruby.'

'Leave it to me. I'll find out.'

Taylor sighs.

'Sorted,' smiles Ruby.

Taylor is not at all sure it will be sorted but part of him would very much like to see Poppy again even though he isn't admitting it.

Chapter Forty-Six

I burst into tears.

'Fudge berries,' says Chelsea.

'You could have broken the news a bit gentler than that,' says Camilla, handing me a tissue. 'Don't you have a heart?'

'I'm a private dick, not a Sunday school teacher,' says Henley.

'He actually used those words?' I hiccup. 'He doesn't want to see me.'

'I don't want to see her and that's that,' repeats private investigator Henley. 'Those were his exact words.'

He folds his notebook and shoves it back into his jacket pocket.

'We heard you the first time,' snaps Camilla. 'Do you have anything to drink around here?'

'I've got some cooking sherry.'

'Cooking sherry?' repeats Chelsea.

'What are we supposed to do with that? Make her a bloody trifle,' says Camilla angrily.

'Sorry I haven't got champagne on ice. We're not all rich you know,' he says, plonking a half bottle of sherry onto the table and handing me a mug. I throw back the sherry and shudder.

'I don't believe it,' I say, pouring more into the mug.

'I don't believe you're drinking it either,' says Chelsea.

'I mean, I don't believe Taylor said that. What have I done for him to feel that way?'

'You actually spoke to him did you?' questions Camilla, sniffing the sherry bottle and pulling a face.

'Jesus, don't drink too much of that stuff,' she warns. 'I reckon it's been here longer than the building.'

'Not exactly,' says Henley. 'I listened in on their conversation and he made it very clear he doesn't want to see you and if you don't want that ...'

He puts a hand out to take the sherry bottle but I pull it towards me.

'Their conversation?' queries Camilla, while I knock back another glass. 'Where was this?'

'In a pub by the canal. Here's my bill.'

He pushes a piece of paper across the table to me. I look at it. I've now got to pay him for the bad news? Things really do get worse don't they?

'This means he must still be on the boat,' says Camilla, shaking me by the shoulders. 'You should go and see him.'

'He doesn't want to see her,' says Henley.

'Shut up,' snaps Camilla.

I drain the mug and feel my head spin.

'I'm going to marry Balls,' I say miserably. 'I'm not going back to the canal, everyone hates me there.'

'Of course they don't. Pull yourself together,' says Camilla.

'I think they do hate her,' agrees Chelsea.

'Thanks a lot Chelsea,' I say fumbling in my bag for a Valium. 'You always manage to make a person feel worse.'

'I hope you're happy,' says Camilla to Henley.

'You asked me to find him,' he shrugs and pushes the bill a little closer. I wipe my eyes and fish out my chequebook. God, I don't believe this. Six hundred pounds to be told someone hates me. Okay, maybe he doesn't hate me but he doesn't want to see me again, ever. I don't understand it. That's that then. I can't put Balls off any longer.

'I need a beer,' I say.

Chelsea and Camilla let out a collective sigh.

'This has got to stop, especially if you're going to marry Balls. You really can't behave like this when you're Lady Balls Wyndham.'

'Behave like what?'

'Drinking beer from the bottle. Drinking beer period,' says Camilla. 'Telling your staff they can leave early because you'll fill the dishwasher.'

'That's terrible,' says Henley sarcastically. 'You'll be washing up next.'

'Shut up,' says Camilla.

'We know you make your own bed,' says Chelsea.

'Shameful,' quips Henley. 'You'll be ...'

He stops after receiving a piercing glare from Camilla.

'And you've been serving yourself at functions. I've seen you,' scolds Camilla. 'You can't do that when you're Lady Balls.'

'And now you're drinking cooking sherry,' says Chelsea. 'You certainly can't do that when you're Lady Balls.'

Life as Lady Balls is beginning to sound very dull.

'Yes, where will it end?' says Henley with a snigger.

He's quite right of course. It has to end somewhere doesn't it? I'm turning into someone my own mother doesn't recognise.

'Okay,' I say. 'You're right. I've got to stop this.'

I push the sherry bottle away.

'Thank goodness,' sighs Camilla.

'I'm going to Taylor's boat to tell him that I love him and even though he hates me I don't care.'

'Good for you,' says Camilla. 'That's the spirit.'

'That's so romantic,' says Chelsea, colour flooding into her cheeks.

'Sorted,' says Camilla.

I'm not at all sure it will be sorted but it will be nice to see Taylor again.

I pick up my Hermes and make for the door.

'There's not a minute to lose,' I say dramatically.

Well that's true isn't it? Balls won't wait much longer.

Chapter Forty-Seven

I step out of the bedroom for the sixth time and parade in front of Chelsea and Camilla.

'Not sure. What do you think, too formal maybe?' Camilla asks Chelsea.

Chelsea pulls a face.

'You don't want to seem out of his league,' says Camilla.

'I agree,' says Chelsea, popping open a bag of cashews.

I trudge back to the bedroom and throw more clothes from the wardrobe onto the bed. I pull on a pair of jeans and a Dior tunic and parade again.

'You look fat in that,' says Camilla.

'What?' I gasp. 'Are you sure?'

I never used to. I must stop eating truffles.

'Yes,' says Chelsea.

'Would you rather we lied to you?' asks Camilla.

'Actually, yes I would. You're doing nothing for my confidence.'

Camilla holds up my Boden tunic.

'How about this, it's perfect.'

'You don't think it's too casual?'

'You're going to see Taylor on his boat, not attend a film premiere.'

I change again and parade one more time.

'Fab,' says Camilla. 'You can wear that lovely Dior jacket of yours. Put your hair up.'

'Yes, men like to see the neck,' says Chelsea, crunching a mouthful of nuts.

'How do you know?'

'I read it somewhere.'

'Wear nice earrings and the bracelet he gave you,' instructs Camilla.

'I'm so nervous,' I say. 'I'm not sure I can do this.'

'Of course you can,' snaps Camilla.

'I'll come with you,' offers Chelsea.

'I think I should do this alone,' I say.

Anyone would think I was on an assassination mission.

'Are you sure?' asks Chelsea.

'She's going to Regent's Canal, not darkest Peru.'

'Just trying to help,' says Chelsea sourly.

'And don't wear too much make-up,' advises Camilla.

'In fact, don't wear any,' says Chelsea.

I'm really not sure about their advice.

'She ought to cover those circles under her eyes,' says Camilla.

What circles?

Perhaps you can get a facial before you go, shall I phone Bonita?' asks Chelsea.

'I'm going *now*. You'll be suggesting I get liposuction and Botox next.'

'Only trying to help,' repeats Chelsea.

'I'm going to put some make-up on and then I'm going. Can I take your Porsche?'

She gives me an anxious look.

'Why don't you get your own car? You've already buggered up my satnav,' she whines.

That's so untrue. Her satnav has always been a bit temperamental.

'I don't want to go in the Bentley do I? I don't want to make him uncomfortable.'

'She's quite right,' says Camilla, pulling my tunic over my hips.

After applying the make-up and dragging my hair into a bun I pop out for inspection.

'Great,' says Camilla. 'Go knock him dead.'

Chelsea throws me her keys and I head nervously out of the flat. It's now or never.

I leave the Porsche at the entrance and slowly walk along the boardwalk. I pull my scarf over my mouth and my hat low so my eyes can't be seen. This makes it pretty hard to see where I'm going, especially as the Christmas lights have now gone. How can Christmas seem so far away? I finger my bracelet and walk cautiously towards Taylor's boat. Memories rush at me and I feel quite dizzy from them. What if Lisa is with him? Oh no, I never thought of that. I scramble around in my brain to think of a reason why I would be knocking on his hatch, aside from the real reason of course. I can't very well declare my love in front of Lisa can I? I'll just say I'm visiting everyone for old times' sake. No, I can't say that, can I? Taylor's boat is getting nearer and oh God, the lights are on. I hear the faint sounds of music. He's home. My heart races and my throat turns dry. I take a deep breath and climb on deck. I finger the bracelet like a rosary and then with held breath I rap on the hatch. I wait but there is nothing. I cock my head and strain to hear voices but all I can hear is the music. I tap a little bit harder this time and straighten my clothes.

'Yes,' he calls.

He's home. I push my hands into my coat pockets.

'It's me Poppy, can I come in?'

I try the hatch. It's locked.

'Can I come in? I really need to talk to you.'

There is no response. Oh God is he still angry with me?

'The thing is I can't marry Balls without telling you how I feel.'

The music stops. I take a deep breath, pull back my shoulders and say loudly.

'I know you're angry with me but I need to tell you that I love you. I can't marry Balls without you knowing that. I can't stop thinking about you.'

There I've said it. Amazingly it is much easier saying it to a closed door. I'm only hoping on the other side of the closed hatch, Lisa isn't fuming. The hatch is flung open and I stare open-mouthed at an old man with a white beard and a captain's hat. He could pass as a stunt double for Captain Birdseye. Oh dear, this most certainly is not Taylor.

'Oh,' I utter.

'Do I know you?' he asks, squinting at me.

I certainly don't know you. How embarrassing is this? I've just declared my love to a complete stranger and not the most appealing one at that.

'I'm so sorry I thought you were Taylor.'

'Who?' asks Captain Birdseye.

'Taylor,' I repeat. 'I thought I was talking to him so obviously when I said that I loved you I didn't mean that I loved *you.* What I meant was that I loved Taylor.'

I watch as his nose reddens from the cold.

'Ah,' he says thoughtfully. 'So the *I can't stop thinking about* you bit wasn't for me either then?'

I shake my head.

'No, it wasn't. I actually don't love you at all. I'm really sorry about that.'

I don't believe I'm having this conversation. Did I just apologise for not loving him?

'Probably just as well,' he says after giving me the once over.

Bloody cheek. He swipes a hand under his nose.

'It's Taylor that I love and can't stop thinking about. He used to live on this boat.'

'I live here now.'

'I can see that,' I say with a sigh. 'I don't suppose you know where Taylor has moved to?'

'I never met the guy. If you don't mind me saying, shouldn't you know where he lives if you love him and shit?'

He's absolutely right of course.

'We argued,' I say and realise how petty that sounds.

'Have you thought of asking some of the other boat owners where he moved to?'

'I'll do that,' I say, knowing damn well that I won't.

'Sorry I'm not him but you can come in for a drink if you want,' he says, patting his hair down with his hand.

'I need to get back,' I say, 'but thank you.'

I give a little wave and climb off the boat, slipping as I go. Nothing changes there. That's it then. I gave it my best shot. There's nothing for it now but to marry Balls, and Taylor will marry Lisa. All I can do is pray for serendipity to step in and let's face it, the chance of that happening are a million to one. I'm doomed.

Chapter Forty-Eight

'It's difficult to see inside,' Ruby says as she peeks through the window of The Ivy.

'I thought your source was reliable,' says Rose.

'It's best to check though,' says Ruby.

'Isn't that Tom Cruise?' says Jack. 'Would it be okay to ask for his autograph?'

Everyone turns to look as Tom Cruise walks towards the entrance.

'We don't want to embarrass Poppy,' says Ruby.

'There isn't time for that Jack,' says Rose.

'Are you sure she is in there?' asks Taylor.

'The text said she arrived ten minutes ago, so they are probably still looking at the menu,' says Ruby, pushing her nose against the window. 'It's now or never.'

'I think this is a bad idea,' says Taylor. 'I don't know why I'm doing it.'

He checks his watch and sighs.

'I don't have long Ruby.'

'We won't let you miss your train, I promise. It's meant to be, I'm sure it is.'

He really isn't comfortable with this. High-class restaurants aren't his thing. He's not altogether sure about talking to Poppy either. It seems to him she is getting on very well without him. Seeing her is just going to stir everything up again. He really doesn't need unsettling a few hours before his flight.

'I can see her,' Ruby squeals.

Taylor straightens his tie and tucks his shirt into his trousers. What he wouldn't do to throw his comfortable jeans on. Jack slaps him on the back.

'Go on mate, give it your best.'

'Good luck darling,' says Rose, kissing him on the cheek.

'Fingers crossed,' smiles Ruby.

He pushes open the entrance door and looks around. A waiter approaches.

'Good evening sir, can I take your coat?'

'I'd like a table for one please.'

'Have you booked sir?'

Taylor shakes his head.

'No, I haven't. I only want the table for a few minutes. I need to speak to one of your patrons, Poppy Wellesley.'

'Are you dining with Lord Wyndham-Price and Miss Wellesley?'

He knew this wouldn't work. He should never let Ruby talk him into things.

'No I'm not but if I could have a table for one that would be great.'

'I'm afraid that won't be possible sir, not without a booking. May I offer you a drink at the bar?'

The door to the restaurant swings open and Taylor sees Poppy. He's overcome with longing and has to fight the urge to walk to her. She looks stunning. He'd almost forgotten how amazing she was. Lord Wyndham-Price leans towards her; he has a hand on her knee. A couple from another table approach and Poppy looks up happily. Taylor realises that he is out of place here. He can't compete with Lord Wyndham-Price and the truth is he doesn't want to. He shakes his head angrily. He shouldn't have come. They belong in different worlds. He would never eat in a place like this, not with the kids in Africa struggling on a bowl of rice. What was he thinking of? This is not the kind of woman for him. He's too easily swayed by Ruby. This is not the kind of life he wants and Poppy would never be comfortable with his way of living. He reaches for his overcoat.

'Excuse me sir,' calls the waiter. 'We've just had a cancellation. I can give you that table. If you'd ...'

'No thanks,' says Taylor, 'I've got to be somewhere.'

The waiter watches him walk out and shrugs. He picks up the phone to call the lady who had come in earlier.

'Lisa Havers please,' he says. 'It's The Ivy.'

Chapter Forty-Nine

I play with my Roasted Devonshire Chicken. My stomach is churning so much I feel nauseous. I know Balls is going to propose and aside from throwing up, I have no idea how to stop him. He's fidgety and edgy. Every time he opens his mouth I jump in with a silly comment.

'Poppy,' he says, looking at me earnestly.

'This chicken is delicious isn't it?' I say, almost gagging on it.

'Shall we get some champers?' he asks. 'I've something special to ask you.'

Help, here it comes.

'Isn't that Major Wallace and his wife,' I say nodding my head towards the table by the window. Oh good, this should stall things a little but I know I've got to let Balls propose at some point. Mummy has assured me that if I say no she will turn her back on me for good.

'You'll be forty before you know it,' she'd said harshly.

'Not for a few years yet,' I'd argued.

'Your womb isn't what it once was, you know. Things tighten and dry up. It's like the desert. Before you know it yours will be declared an historical landmark.'

A bit extreme but I get her point. Balls waves to Major Wallace and I let out a relieved sigh. I've bought a little more time. Time for what I'm not quite sure.

'Poppy, how lovely to see you,' says Mary Wallace. 'Mwah, mwah,' she air kisses me. 'You look beautiful as always.'

Balls rests his hand on my knee.

'She does, doesn't she?' he says admiringly.

'Won't you join us?' I ask.

That should buy me a bit more time.

'We'd love to but we're off to the theatre.'

'I love the bloody theatre,' bellows Balls. 'You can't beat old Willy Shakespeare can you?'

'Absolutely old chap,' agrees the Major. 'Ooh I say isn't that Tom Cruise?'

We discreetly glance over at the group that have arrived.

'I bloody love Tom Cruise,' says Balls.

I sip my wine and attempt a little more of the Devonshire Chicken. Hopefully Tom Cruise will sidetrack Balls for a while. Put yourself in my Louboutins. What would you do? My original beau, the rat, aka Roddy Tarleton dumped me for another woman. I have to admit to being quite relieved about that now. Roddy is a rat in designer clothing. Then Balls bounces along and I've another potential husband. Not many women are that lucky are they? The only problemo is that I'm not in love with Balls and I realise now that I have never been in love with Roddy. The only man I can think about is Taylor and God knows where he is. Probably all loved up with Lisa somewhere. And at that precise moment, almost as though I'd conjured her up, she walks through the door and as though on cue the music changes and would you believe *All of Me* begins to play. It's surely a sign isn't it? Is this serendipity? I'm a great believer in signs and Lisa walking in and then *All of Me* playing, well it's too difficult to ignore isn't it? Our eyes meet and I quickly turn away.

'I need the loo,' I say, jumping up.

A waiter rushes to pull back my chair.

'Could I have a beer,' I ask, heading for the ladies.

'A beer?' echoes Balls.

'Of course,' says the waiter.

I dive into a cubicle and pull out my mobile. I need advice but why I phone Chelsea is beyond me. I'm not thinking straight that's the problem.

'Lisa is here,' I say, flopping onto the toilet seat. 'What do I do?'

'Did she see you?'

'Yes, our eyes kind of met before I focused on her perfect breasts.'

'Frogs' knickers Poppy, why were you looking at her breasts?'

'I don't know, but that's not the point ...'

'Has Balls proposed?' she asks.

'No not yet. He's been sidetracked by Tom Cruise.'

She gasps.

'Fudge berries, you're having dinner with Tom Cruise, you never mentioned ...'

'That's because I'm not.'

'But you just said ...'

'He's in the restaurant, that's all. Forget about Tom Cruise.'

'Oh,' she says, disappointed.

'Lisa just walked in and she's not with Taylor. What shall I do?'

There is silence at the other end of the phone.

'Chelsea, are you still there?'

'I'm thinking.'

That's a first.

'The thing is, as she walked in guess what music they played?'

'Music?' she echoes.

This is so frustrating.

'*All of Me*, they played *All of Me*. Do you think someone is trying to tell me something?'

'Who do you think that someone is?' she asks.

Why do I bother?

'Fate, serendipity, you know. It's like I'm being told to look for Taylor. What do you think?'

She sighs.

'I don't know Poppy. Your mother said you should get back to normal and marry Balls.'

My mother also said spanking my best friend with a hairbrush was getting back to normal so what does she know?

'I'm going to ask her,' I say, standing up.

'Ask her what?'

'Where Taylor is living,' I say, straightening my clothes.

'But I don't think your mother knows.'

I roll my eyes. I swear I'd have got more sense talking to the loo roll.

'Not Mummy, I'm going to ask Lisa.'

'But ...'

I click off the phone and march out of the loo and back into the restaurant only to find Lisa has gone.

Chapter Fifty

I look around but there is no sign of Lisa. Balls waves anxiously and I head back to the table. The waiter places a glass on the table and is about to pour my beer.

'I'll take that,' I say, relieving him of the bottle.

'Pops, why are you drinking beer? I've just asked for some champers. I really don't think you should drink from the bottle.'

I take a large swig and fight back a belch.

'What happened to the lady who just came in?' I ask the waiter.

'What lady?' asks Balls, looking baffled.

'Her name is Lisa,' I say, looking at the waiter hopefully.

He shrugs apologetically.

'I'm sorry madam I'm not sure who you mean. I'll see if I can find out for you.'

Another waiter appears and I realise my luck has run out. He pops open the champagne and Balls reaches his hand across the table. His other places a small pink box between us. I gulp and feel myself break into a cold sweat. My neck itches and that makes me think of Taylor which in turn makes it itch even more. Balls takes my sweaty hand in his.

'Pops ...'

I hold my breath. I feel sure I must be turning blue.

'By Jove, old girl, what's going on with your neck?'

I lift a hand to cover the rash and then see it is on my fingers too. This is very déjà vu.

'Is it excitement?' he asks.

He surely isn't serious.

'Yes probably,' I lie.

He pushes the pink box towards me.

'Pops, will you do me the honour of ...'

'Excuse me madam,' says the waiter.

I lift my head and give him a grateful look.

'The lady you asked about left a note for you. She booked the table for friends so she wasn't actually dining here herself.'

He hands me an envelope. I take it nervously and feel the rash go manic. I rip it open and pull out a note

I think you should know that Taylor is leaving for Africa tonight after a talk at Hilldene festival hall. He has no intention of returning. We are not together, it is you he loves.

It's me he loves. A warm sensation travels through my body. Taylor loves me and he's leaving for Africa tonight. What? Africa? He can't go to Africa. If he loves me why is he going to Africa? Where the hell is Hilldene? More importantly where is Hilldene festival hall? A leaflet drops out of the envelope. It's an invitation to a talk by Dr Havers on his hospital in Zimbabwe. It starts at eight, lasting one hour with time for questions afterwards.

'What's the time?' I ask.

'The time?' repeats Balls.

I pull my mobile from my bag. It's a quarter to seven. I've got an hour before it starts and another hour for the talk.

'I've got to go,' I say jumping up.

'Go where?'

'Hilldene festival hall,' I say, grabbing my bag and the beer bottle.

'Where is that?' he asks, looking at me like I've gone mad.

'I've no idea,' I say rushing towards the entrance with Balls on my heels. I'm just hoping it's not too far away.

'But Pops, what about ...?'

I wave to Eddie and dive into the Bentley.

'I'm so sorry Balls,' I say, blowing him a kiss. 'But I'm going to Africa.'

He stares at me open-mouthed.

'Africa, by Jove old girl, why on earth would you want to go to there? It's full of Zulus and God knows what. I thought you were going to Hilldene.'

'I'm so sorry Balls, I'll explain everything later.'

He stands on the kerb the pink box in his hand. I watch him through the back window until the car turns a corner and I can't see him any longer.

'Take me to Chelsea's,' I tell Eddie.

I pull my phone from my bag and call her. I can't turn up at Hilldene festival hall in a chauffeur-driven Bentley can I?

'I need your Porsche,' I say before she can speak.
'What?'
'I'm going to Hilldene.'
'Where's that?'
'I've no idea.'
But I'm determined to find out.

Chapter Fifty-One

It takes forever to get to Chelsea's. It's like the whole world is out in their cars.

'It's rush hour,' says Eddie calmly.

'I've got to drive to Hilldene,' I say, on the verge of tears.

'Where on earth is that?' Eddie asks.

Does anyone know where Hilldene is? It will be just my luck that it's one of those villages where strangers are not welcome. I'll drive through it in the Porsche and disappear in a layer of mist, never to be seen again.

'I've no idea,' I say, tears pricking my eyelids.

We reach Chelsea's and I dash up the carpeted stairway to her flat. We quickly google *Hilldene* on her laptop and stare at the screen.

'I can't see it. Can you?' Chelsea asks.

I check my phone. Time is passing really quickly. A cold shudder passes over me.

'What if it is miles away?'

We lean closer to the screen and nearly headbutt each other.

'I see it,' she squeals.

'It's in Buckinghamshire,' I groan. 'That will take forever.'

'Peas and rice, why is he giving a talk there?'

'I need to print out a map,' I say hitting the keyboard like a maniac.

'But you'll have the satnav.'

'The satnav that doesn't work properly,' I remind her.

'You broke it.'

That's debatable but I don't have time to argue.

'Taylor loves me,' I say, pushing Lisa's note into her hand.

'Frogs' knickers,' she gasps.

'He's leaving for Africa after the talk. I've got two hours to get there.'

'It will take longer than two hours to get to Africa.'

I exhale.

'Chelsea, I'm going to Hilldene, remember?'

'I'm getting confused.'

What's new?

'I can navigate,' she says.

Navigate us into a ditch, no doubt.

'I'll be fine,' I say.

'Two eyes are better than one,' says Chelsea.

'I've got two eyes. Don't you mean four eyes are better than two?'

'Only trying to help,' she says sullenly.

I consider her offer. I suppose driving into the unknown would feel more comfortable if I had company, but Chelsea, I mean, put yourself in my Diors?

'Okay,' I say.

Her face brightens.

'Oh cool.'

Chelsea helps me set up the satnav and it lights up immediately. I'm feeling quietly confident. I hand her the map in the hope that we won't be needing it.

'Let's hit the road,' says Chelsea, just a touch overexcitedly.

I'm going to find Taylor who loves me. My spine tingles with pleasure.

'There is a breakdown card in the glove compartment,' she says cheerfully.

'Breakdown card?' I query.

'Just in case,' she says.

'The Porsche is okay isn't it?' I ask nervously.

She nods but it's one of those unconvincing nods. You know the kind I mean? I give the satnav a *don't mess with me* glare and start the Porsche. I feel like we're on an expedition to the Antarctic. I move off and a high-pitched voice screams at me making me jump out of my skin.

Hello Yves Flamboyant here. Whether you're urban beauty, metrosexual, or just fashion conscious, this stylist shows you the way to arrive and make an entrance. If the shoes and belt don't match go back and change. Fabulous begins before you even turn the key, baby.

What the ...?

Now take the third right, I said right, you know the hand that the Queen waves with.

I'm so gobsmacked by Flamboyant that I almost miss the turning. How am I going to find Hilldene with Yves whatsisface prattling away?

'Ah yes, I forgot about him,' says Chelsea on seeing my expression.

'You forgot about him?'

'I was trying him out and he got kind of stuck,'

Only Chelsea could have a stuck satnav voice. I make it onto the motorway and thankfully, apart from keeping the interior well lit, Yves stays quiet. It takes us just under an hour to reach Buckinghamshire. I glance at the clock on the dashboard. It's now eight. The talk will have started. My stomach churns at the thought of seeing Taylor. I've no idea what I'll say. He did say he never wanted to see me again didn't he? He may still mean that. I only have Lisa's note saying he loves me. What if she was playing some kind of cruel joke on me? What if he really does think our worlds are too far apart? Oh God, what if he's right?

Sharp left in five hundred yards, don't miss it, squeals Flamboyant. *Take a sharp left baby.*

'Next left,' repeats Chelsea.

'Not for five hundred yards,' I argue.

Take the turning baby, says Flamboyant.

It hasn't been five hundred yards has it?

'He always tells you too late,' says Chelsea anxiously. 'Take the next exit or we may never get off the motorway.'

What kind of useless satnav is it that tells you to take a turning too late? I take the next left and find myself driving along a country lane and through a village. There are no street lights and I look to see if this is Hilldene. Rain patters gently on the windscreen and I groan. I take a bend and Flamboyant tells me to keep left. I reach the end of the village and go to take another bend in the road.

Turn left, you know left, the one the Queen uses to wave with and then ...

Flamboyant loses his voice and the car is plunged into darkness as the satnav dies.

Chapter Fifty-Two

I come over all hot. This can't be happening. *We've Only Just Begun* by The Carpenters plays on the car radio and I shudder. It's like the bloody satnav is threatening me.

'Shall I check the map?' asks Chelsea.

There's a lay-by ahead and I pull into it. Bloody Flamboyant. The car most likely got sick of his camp voice. Right now I'd do anything to hear it again. I struggle to revive him and fiddle with the connection until finally he comes back on. I try to punch in the postcode.

'Why are the buttons sticking?' I ask.

Chelsea fidgets.

'It does that. I don't know why. It went funny after you broke it.'

'I didn't break it,' I snap.

I feel her shrug.

'Well, that's why I put Yves Flamboyant on. I thought a different voice might fix it.'

What was I thinking of, bringing Chelsea to help? My heart is racing as I see time is running away. At this rate I won't do it. With shaking fingers I punch in the postcode and we are off again, but I have a nagging doubt that the postcode is right. I don't want to end up in bloody Glasgow. A dimly lit pub sign catches my eye and a sharp left into the car park sends the map flying to the floor. A man lounging outside the pub gives us an odd look.

'Fudge berries,' whispers Chelsea. 'Do you think we should lock the doors?'

I lean down and fumble for the map before discreetly locking us in. We study it for a few seconds but nothing seems to match up with where we are. My neck is tense and there is a mild thumping in my head. We reset Flamboyant, even though he's as useless as shit, and reverse out to continue our journey, careful to avoid any bumps in the road that may upset Flamboyant and disturb the connection. Oncoming headlights blind me and my head throbs. The light pitter-patter of rain turns into hailstones.

'Oh no, it's hailstoning,' says Chelsea, stating the obvious as only Chelsea can.

This can't be happening. Flamboyant directs me back onto the motorway. I turn the windscreen wipers on full but I can't see a thing and my head is banging away like a jungle drum. We're going to die on the way to telling the man I love how I feel.

Exit ahead baby, shouts Flamboyant.

Oh no, I'm in the wrong lane and can't see the car in front let alone the next exit. I'm bound to miss it. Then of course, it could be miles before I'm able to get off this stupid motorway. I fight back tears and strain to see through the mist. This is terrible and Flamboyant isn't being much help. He yells, *take the exit* echoed by Chelsea, and I swerve across to hoots from the car behind. I zoom along a country lane and before I know it I'm zooming through a puddle sending a tsunami to the surrounding countryside. The car gives an uneasy shudder. We must be almost on top of the sodding festival hall by now, but ten minutes later we find ourselves still travelling down the country lane. Chelsea struggles to read the map but it's too dark in the car. I take a bend and realise we are back in the same village. Flamboyant is silent and I'm nervous.

'This is like the other village we went through,' says Chelsea.

I sigh.

'That's because it's the same one Chelsea.'

'Fudge berries,' she gasps.

'Why are we going through the same village?' she asks after a moment's reflection.

'Because, Dorothy lose-the-dress-but-keep-the-shoes Flamboyant here told me to,' I say angrily, aware that time is against me.

We go past the hall and the pub and then Flamboyant springs into life with the immortal words, '*Take the motorway*.'

All we've done is go around in a circle. It's twenty past eight and I haven't got a clue where we are. Let's face it, going round in circles is all I've ever done where men are concerned. The windscreen wipers swish back and forth like crazy and Flamboyant shouts *exit ahead*. Please let this be the right exit. The talk will be over soon. I can only hope the audience has plenty of questions or I'm totally buggered.

Continue for ... begins Flamboyant.

The car is thrown into darkness and Yves Flamboyant dies. Why can't the bugger die when I want him to? Believe me, that time will come but it's not now. Not at eight fifty in the middle of nowhere. There are no street lights, no people and now no Yves Flamboyant. It's pissing down with rain and the wind is howling around us. I'm beginning to wish we'd bought a panic alarm.

'This isn't good is it?' says Chelsea as she turns the map around.

'And the map's wrong. It's got nothing familiar on it.'

I fiddle with the satnav power lead and by some freak of nature the thing lights up. I don't want to push my luck and risk Flamboyant going into a sulk so take the risk and assume it is still set to the destination. We continue on. It's then I realise that we are passing the same hall, the same church and the same bloody pub and it's not even Groundhog Day. I slam my foot on the brake and catapult Chelsea forward so she bangs her head on the dashboard.

'Have we arrived?' she asks, rubbing her head.

'It's the same village, Chelsea.'

She shudders.

'It's a bit creepy this,' she groans. 'Why do we keep coming back here?'

I slap my hand on the dashboard.

'Flambloodyboyant, that's why,' I say angrily.

I climb from the Porsche and step into a puddle. Muddy water splashes onto my faux fur and my boots. I could cry. Why is it whenever I see Taylor I look like I've been dragged through a bush backwards? I stomp angrily back to the village hall with Chelsea running behind me. I fling open the door and stare in surprise.

'Frogs' knickers,' mumbles Chelsea.

We gaze at what appears to be Zumba for the over seventies. Somewhat wrinkly women are jumping up and down to Beyonce's *Crazy in Love*. It's a horrendous sight and I can't possibly describe it.

'You're a little late,' says a breathless woman with blue hair.

Do what? I know all this business with Daddy losing his money has aged me but blimey, it's not that bad is it? Good job I've got the money back. It sounds like I need a complete overhaul.

'Oh no,' says Chelsea, 'We're not pensioners.'

I close my eyes in exasperation.

'What I mean is ...'

'How can we help you?' the woman asks, her face hardening.

A Valium and a darkened room would be nice, I want to say, but instead show her my map.

'Do you know where this is?' I ask, pointing at Hilldene.

'Ah, did you pass the pub on your way in?

Oh yes, several times. I'm getting to know it very well.

'Go back to the pub and then onto the motorway.'

Not again.

'The second exit is the one you need. You can't miss it.'

Want to bet? She's not met Flamboyant. Its nine o'clock when we get back into the car. They will be starting the questions and if there aren't many Taylor will up and leave before I even arrive. If this is serendipity then you can shove it.

'It will be okay,' says Chelsea, reassuringly.

Except now the bloody car won't start and aside from kicking the hell out of it I have no idea what to do. I drop my head onto the dashboard. Water in the electrics Chelsea assures me.

'That's it then,' I groan. 'It's not meant to be.'

'Wait,' cries Chelsea, pointing ahead.

I follow her finger to a mobility scooter.

'It's only past the pub,' she says stupidly.

'I can't go in that,' I protest. 'And it's a long way past the pub.'

'We can both squeeze on it. Come on there isn't a minute to lose. We'll bring it back afterwards.'

I shake my head.

'He's going to Africa,' she says, 'this is your last chance.'

Shit and double shit. I reach the scooter with Chelsea hurrying behind me. Chelsea climbs on and gestures for me to do the same.

'Are you licensed to drive a scooter,' I ask.

'What?'

'Are you licensed to ...?'

'No are you?'

'Well no but ...'

She sighs.

'We'll never make it if we walk will we?'

The thought of being wedged onto the mobility scooter with Chelsea is one very scary thought indeed.

'It's not like it's a real scooter,' says Chelsea turning the key.

We're squashed so tight on the thing that I can barely breathe. Chelsea starts it up and we're off. Zooming along the country lane, if you can call doing ten miles an hour zooming. Ten miles an hour or not, it's still pretty hairy. I freeze at the sight of the motorway but Chelsea notches the thing up to maximum power before I can say anything. We are drenched with spray from each car that whizzes past us and even though we are on the hard shoulder we're almost knocked over by the buffeting we get. Rain lashes our faces. My heart is in my mouth as well as just about everything else that could fly into it. I point ahead as the exit comes into view and Chelsea steers into it, driving straight through a puddle as she does so. We are drenched but, hallelujah, the signs say Hilldene and the village is much bigger than the last one and it is easy to spot the festival hall. We shudder to a halt. I don't have time to beautify myself. My fur is soaked and Chelsea tries to flick specks of mud from my face as we walk to the door. My heart is pounding. I can hear it banging in my ears. I'm not sure if it is because I'm nervous or from the scooter journey. What if he won't talk to me? The rash starts to itch and I fight the urge to scratch.

'Come on,' says Chelsea, pulling me through the door.

We enter a deserted foyer. A poster with photos of African children stands at the entrance to another door. It is announcing Doctor Havers' talk.

'You're too late,' says a man at the door.

Chapter Fifty-Three

'He's left already?' I say, struggling to hold back my tears.

'No, he's still here but you've missed the talk I'm afraid.'

'We only want to ask a question,' says Chelsea, pulling me through the doors and into the hall. There is a hushed crowd with all eyes on the stage. I look where Taylor is sitting. My breath catches in my throat at the sight of him. He looks more delicious than I remembered. I wish I could say the same for me. Chelsea ushers me to a spare seat at the back. I fall into the chair and stare at Taylor like a lovesick teenager.

'Next question?' says a man sitting next to Taylor. He points to a woman in a blue polka-dot dress.

'You look awful, take this off,' Chelsea hisses, pulling at my coat.

'Will you miss England?' asks the woman. 'It's a big commitment to travel all the way to Africa but to actually live there. There must be something you'll miss. It will be a whole different life.'

I hold my breath. Taylor lifts a glass of water to his lips before answering.

'It will be a whole different life, you're quite right, but there's nothing to keep me in England,' he says. 'I feel I can offer a lot more to the kids in the hospital than I can to anyone here.'

My heart sinks. He doesn't want to stay. Surely if he loved me he would have some doubts wouldn't he? Am I doing the wrong thing? The last thing I need is to embarrass myself. God knows I've embarrassed myself enough the last few weeks.

'No woman to keep you here?' asks the man seated beside him with a laugh.

I wait with bated breath.

'It would take a special woman,' heckles someone from the audience.

'The children are all I care about,' Taylor smiles.

That's it then. He's more or less saying there is no woman who will match up to his hospital in Africa.

'The excesses of the rich in England disturb me, especially after seeing what happens in third world countries.'

I go to stand up but Chelsea pulls me back.

'What are you doing?' she whispers.

'Leaving, because he doesn't want me or any woman by the sound of things,' I say fighting back tears.

'You can't come all this way and not tell him how you feel, and you certainly can't go back and marry Balls if you haven't told Taylor the truth, besides which, I didn't risk my life on a pensioner's scooter just so you could change your mind.'

'We're the rich remember? Didn't you hear what he said?'

I wonder if I can sneak out before Taylor sees me.

'Any more questions before we wind things up?' asks the man.

Chelsea's hand shoots up and I hide my face so he can't see me.

'Would you accept a donation?' she asks.

'Of course,' says the man. 'If you'd like to ...'

'Of half a million,' she interrupts.

There are gasps from the audience. What? I think she must be having a breakdown. Taylor sits up as a hush falls over the audience.

'Half a million?' echoes the man.

Chelsea nudges me.

'You want to help him don't you?' she whispers.

What the hell. In for a penny in for a pound and let's face it, I've got plenty of pounds haven't I? I stand up and step into the aisle so Taylor can see me and give a little wave.

'Hi,' I say timidly. 'I did actually dress up for the occasion but everything got ruined after our journey turned into something out of *The Bourne Supremacy*.'

He stares at me as I try to dust off the dried mud.

'I was wondering, do you think half a million would cover my ticket to Africa. I'd like to help. It's either that or marry Balls you see.'

The audience turn to look at me and then back to Taylor. It must feel like Wimbledon for them. Taylor is silent and I find myself rambling on.

'The thing is I really don't love Balls and ...'

I can't believe I'm sharing my life with all these people much less allowing them to see me looking like I've just crawled out of a sewer.

'Being rich is all very well but the truth is I much preferred it when I was poor ...'

'She's rich,' I hear someone gasp.

Yes, well I don't always look like this do I?

'So did I,' adds Chelsea, not that Chelsea was ever poor.

I wish Taylor would say something if it's only to tell me to bog off.

'Yes, the lady over there in the pink hat,' says the man next to Taylor.

'I think the rich giving to the poor is great.'

I look towards the familiar voice and see Ruby smiling at me.

'And what you saw on Christmas Day wasn't what you saw at all,' I say turning back to Taylor.

'What did he see then?' shouts Geoff.

'Well ...' I begin.

'Because it all seems suspicious to me,' he finishes.

'Let her talk,' shouts someone from the audience.

'Roddy made a pass at me. I was fighting him off. He ransacked my boat, looking for the engagement ring and ...'

The door is flung open and two elderly women rush in followed by a policeman. They point at me and Chelsea.

'That's them. They just jumped on Marge's scooter and took off.'

I shrug apologetically at Taylor.

'I'm so sorry,' says Chelsea. 'Our car broke down and we had to get here before Taylor Havers finished his talk.'

'No reason to steal someone else's property,' says the policeman approaching us.

All I need is to be arrested before I get to tell Taylor how I feel.

'You drove here on a mobility scooter?' he queries.

'Not the whole way,' I say, 'just part of it, and Chelsea drove.'

He smiles and I feel my shoulders relax.

'You drove that scooter,' Geoff calls to Chelsea, looking at her admiringly.

She nods and blushes.

'Way to go Chels,' he says winking.

Excuse me? Trust Chelsea to muscle in.

'The thing is I have this rash and you're the only doctor that can shift it,' I say, my eyes fixed on Taylor.

'Is that right?' he grins.

I nod.

'And I have all this money and I haven't a clue what to do with it. I thought I could bring it to Africa.'

The policeman looks baffled.

'Sorry sir, but I'm afraid they will need to come with us.'

'Just a minute,' says the man sitting with Taylor. 'I think it was all a charity stunt, isn't that right?' he asks nodding at me.

I nod back. Taylor steps down from the platform and walks towards me.

'You'd really give up your money and come to Africa?' he asks.

I pull a face.

'Not give it up exactly. We might as well have a nice African house if we're going to live in Africa.'

He grins.

'You'd leave England and everything behind?'

I nod.

'It's just that all of me loves all of you,' I say. 'And I prefer being poor if I am with you.'

Well, a little bit poor. I can keep some of my money can't I? No point roughing it. He pulls me into his arms and Chelsea whoops.

'I've missed you,' he whispers.

I cling onto him. This time I'm not letting go, no matter what happens.

'I've missed you too,' I reply.

'I can't offer much Poppy.'

'That's fine with me,' I smile.

The policeman steps forward but is pulled back by one of the old ladies.

'It was in the name of love,' she says.

'Lovely it is too,' says her friend.

Someone in the audience starts to clap. I feel sure it must be Ruby. It's followed by a low hum of applause at first and when Taylor kisses me the applause erupts and the whole crowd are on their feet clapping and cheering. I melt into Taylor's arms and return his kiss. I know in that moment that nothing matters as long as I am with him and that being with him is all I will ever want.